PUNCTURED HEART

by Sheridan Lee

ISBN: 978-1-956654-11-0

Content Disclaimer: This book deals with domestic
violence and other mature themes. While the author has
endeavoured to address these sensitive matters in a
compassionate and respectful manner, the issues covered
may trouble some readers. Discretion is advised.

For Joy

SHERIDAN LEE

ACKNOWLEDGEMENTS

Punctured Heart would not be the story it is without the tireless force of Jeanette Cameron. Thank you for everything you've done to teach, guide and support me. I still struggle to understand how you saw potential in my horrendous first draft, and am staggered by what we created together during the editing process. Thank you for tenderly carrying and sculpting my vision, dear friend.

A huge thank you to Cynthia Hickey and the team at Winged Publications for taking a chance on me. When I finished third in the *2021 Taking Flight* contest, I never imagined I would stay on your radar.

A shout out to Michelle (and Paul!) for being my first BETA reader before I knew what that even meant! Your insight and encouragement fuelled me. Thanks to nurse extraordinaire Karen for helping me with the medical related sections, and to Jay-Maree for cheering me on and demanding the next book. I promise you'll have it soon!

Thanks, Dad and Mum, for your practical support with my writing endeavours, and big hugs to the ever-patient Mr Wonderful and our five awesome girls. Life would be rather boring without you six.

And my Heavenly Father. Thank You for loving me. I'm eternally grateful.

GLOSSARY OF AUSTRALIAN WORDS

Dag – an eccentric but entertaining person, a character
Milo – A malted chocolate beverage
Schmick – Smart or stylish
Serviette – paper or cloth table napkin (paper, in this story)
Sloshed, Sozzled – Intoxicated with alcohol
Woolies – Slang for *Woolworths* supermarket (not sheep!)
Woop Woop – An imaginary remote town/place far from anywhere

CHAPTER ONE
To Come Undone

My eyelids fluttered open. Had I heard a message notification *bleep*? I blinked and focused on the ambient sounds around me. Was that the shower? Yawning, I rolled on my side and peeked at the glowing clock next to the bed.

Three past four in the morning. I glanced toward my ensuite, where a crack of light shone under the door. Why was Jude in the shower?

I fell back against the satin pillowcase, no idea when my husband had come home from work. I had collapsed into bed at midnight after a long day of work and parenting. Alone. Again.

I reached for my mobile phone and pressed the side button. A blinding image of my swimsuit-clad children filled the screen. I squinted from the sudden glare and smiled at my children's bright eyes and wide grins. Hair in shades of brown glinted in the sun from our beach swim yesterday afternoon. A pleasant memory to compensate for another cancelled night out with Jude. We still had not celebrated our thirteenth wedding anniversary two weeks earlier. I sighed at the innocent faces of my babies.

No messages. Had I imagined the sound?

I returned my phone to the bedside table and rolled into a comfortable sleep position. Flashes of light lit the white ceiling.

Jude's phone. He never left it unattended.

I sat up. The shower still rained on my naked husband, a sight

I had not seen in weeks. I imagined rivulets of water cascading over his short-cropped light-brown hair, down his thick, tanned neck and broad, sculpted chest. He prioritised time for the gym in his busy schedule and looked spectacular at thirty-six.

My heart kicked up a beat, and I bit my bottom lip. Perhaps I should sneak a peek? A familiar heat warmed my belly but was soon quashed by an ever-present tight ball in my stomach.

Only he initiated advances now, and they had been few and far between in the last six months. I would not dare join him in the shower, no matter how much I ached to stare into his deep-blue eyes and run my thumb along his plump, kissable lips.

Not anymore.

The light from Jude's phone brought me back to the present. Why had someone messaged him so early? Did he have another legal client in prison? Was it something to do with the huge case he had worked on for four weeks?

I crept over to Jude's side of the bed. The cool doona chilled my legs. I pressed the side button with caution, and the screen came to life. His passcode had changed months ago, but I could read messages on the locked screen. A photo of Jude's Maserati decorated the background behind a message from his secretary.

"What does she want?" I whispered.

Paula: I HOPE YOU MADE IT HOME SAFELY, JD. YOU DESERVE SOME REST AFTER ALL YOUR HARD WORK. SLEEP WELL.

Since when did she call him JD? His nickname, short for Jude David, was reserved for his closest mates.

My pulse throbbed, and my heartbeat accelerated. Why had Paula worked so late? She was his personal assistant, not a law clerk or legal assistant. A person could only do so much photocopying.

The seed of a thought pricked my mind. My hands trembled, and I lowered them to my lap. I inhaled a slow, deep breath and shook my head. It could not mean *that*.

"No. That's ridiculous." I slipped back across the bed where the edge of warmth still clung to the sheets.

But what if it was ... *that*? A thin sheen of sweat coated my hands and armpits. I scrunched my nose and closed my eyes. "Please, give me wisdom, God."

Christine. My sister would help me. I grabbed my mobile handset, unplugged the charger cable, and scooted back across the bed.

My skin too clammy for fingerprint recognition, I fumbled with the screen and typed in my four-digit passcode. I opened the camera application and aligned our phones.

A bathroom cupboard door thudded. My heart thundered in my chest, and a whoosh of blood rushed to my ears. When had Jude finished in the shower?

I illuminated the message on his phone and snapped a photo. With a push across the silky bedlinen, I slid under the sheets and plunked my phone next to the bed.

The click of a light switch was soon followed by a soft squeak of a door hinge and the pad of large feet across the bedroom floor. Jude climbed into bed with a rustle of material. Our king-sized bed was too large to sense any dips in the mattress when we both slept on our respective edges.

I lay still, my back to the middle of the bed, and willed my heart to slow.

The room brightened with a beam of light from Jude's phone.

I breathed slower, deeper breaths and waited. What difference did it make if he knew I was awake? He would still ignore me. I sucked in a quiet breath and blinked back tears. Darkness soon followed, and moments later Jude's muted snores sounded in the space between us.

"Mummy, where's my Avengers unnies?"

Ryan, my six-year-old son, popped his angelic face and mop of light ash-brown curls around the wall of my walk-in-robe, where I buttoned my shirt.

"Hmm?"

He puffed out a harsh breath. "Avengers unnies, Mah-mee! I gotta wear Cappen 'Merica today, or Joel'll be the winner!" His blue eyes darkened. He resembled his father when upset.

"What're you talking about?" I had not slept well after Paula's message, spending the next hour in prayer followed by a one-sided conversation where I scolded my impetuous brain for doubting my husband's faithfulness. My backup alarm had woken me, and now I had to rush everyone out the door in time for school and work.

I pushed past Ryan into my ensuite and grabbed my hair comb. "I washed all the undies you left in your washing basket." I rammed the comb through my shoulder-length waves and winced. "Why're you and Joel flashing your underwear to each other at school?"

He shook his head. "It's boys' stuff, Mummy. You won't unnastan."

I pressed my lips together to stop a laugh. "Well, please stop it. You could get in trouble."

Ryan placed his small hand on my elbow. "S'okay, Mummy, we do it when we have peeing races in the toilet. Andre checks for teachers."

Urination competitions and posted lookouts in Prep? I blew out a breath before I tied my hair into a ponytail. Ryan was so different to his older sisters. "I wish you wouldn't participate in peeing contests. What if someone missed their aim and wet you?"

Ryan's eyes sparkled. "Daddy says it makes it more a-citing."

My smile vanished. "Exciting." I kneeled at the bathroom cupboard and groped for my makeup bag at the back of the top shelf.

Was I jealous of my son's relationship with Jude? Whenever my husband slunk home next—which had been to sleep in recent weeks—we would discuss the situation. Jude's encouragement needed to stop. Otherwise, urine sword fights were the next step.

Disgusting.

I puffed pale translucent powder over my pasty skin with a

flourish. "Please don't tell me Daddy's given you tips?" I adhered a single layer of brown-black mascara on each set of eyelashes. Makeup was overrated.

Ryan shrugged. "He showed me the best tekic."

I scrunched up my face while I applied a dab of cherry lip gloss. "The best tekic?"

"Tekic, Mah-mee! Tekic!" His voice ratcheted up in pitch. "The best way."

"Oh! Technique!"

He executed an exaggerated eye-roll. That child.

"Well, enough toilet talk." I scrutinised my appearance in the mirror and grunted at the passable face staring back. "Please put your school shoes on and get your bag. We need to get in the car."

Ryan dawdled out of the bathroom while I neatened the benchtop. Fuelling another one of Jude's rants nit-picking at my inability to keep the house in order was not on today's agenda. Not that he was home long enough to fault-find.

I threw my jacket over the crook of my elbow, grabbed my handbag, and darted out my bedroom door. "Jessica! Samantha! Five-minute warning!"

I raced across the hall and down the stairs. Striding into the kitchen, I dumped my belongings on the circular glass table in the breakfast nook. Why the children always ate at the kitchen bench, I would never understand.

I gathered dirty breakfast dishes from the marble island bench before bundling the crockery and cutlery into the dishwasher located in the spacious butler's pantry. Without a doubt the children would clean up after themselves one day, like I insisted.

I glanced at the clock on the microwave. No time for coffee. I pulled my ready-made sandwich from the fridge and rummaged through the open boxes of muesli bars for a crunchy apricot bar to scoff while I drove.

The drive to work would be different next year when Jessica started Year Seven. She had a place confirmed at Haileybury

College, where I worked. I grinned, excited by the prospect of teaching her English if I was able to pick up a junior class.

The doorbell rang.

Ducking out of the butler's pantry, I popped my breakfast and lunch on the kitchen table. I glided along the front entryway to open up for Jessica's friend who needed a lift to school while her mother was sick.

Instead, I stared into the bright-green eyes of a middle-aged gentleman with a box in his hand.

"Delivery for Jude Burke."

I eyeballed the small brown package.

"Your name?"

"Victoria Burke."

He offered the screen of his smartphone. "Sign here, please."

"Sure." I scribbled with my finger and accepted the parcel. "Have a wonderful day."

The delivery man tucked his mobile phone into the back pocket of his trousers and broadcast the most glorious smile I had seen on a man in months. A dimple peeked from his stubbled cheek and removed years from his face. "You too, Mrs. Burke." He winked and walked back to his van.

My cheeks warmed.

A clatter of footsteps reverberated along the driveway. "Hello, Mrs. Burke! Sorry I'm late!" Meghan said in a rush of air. Her customary kempt updo had slid into a crooked side ponytail which matched her uneven socks and upturned collar. Flushed cheeks enhanced her olive complexion.

"No worries, sweetheart. I'm a little behind schedule too."

She burst through the doorway and scampered to the internal garage access.

I placed the box on the front buffet and locked the house. "It's time to go! Meghan's here!" I called up the stairwell.

Jessica clomped down the polished merbau staircase and kissed my cheek. "Morning, Mum! You look cute today. Blue suits you."

Jessica was my eldest daughter and a light in my life. Tall for her age, she had medium-brown hair similar to my own and hazel eyes like my sister's. Almost twelve going on sixteen, fashion had become a big interest to her in recent months, along with making sure I looked nice for her father. She thought my appearance could lure him home more often and it weighed on me.

"Thanks, darling. Did you sleep well?"

"Yup!" With a smile, she dashed off to the garage.

I verged on another shout to the dawdlers when Samantha and Ryan galloped down the steps.

"Yo yo, Ma," Samantha said with the smirk of a cheeky nine-and-a-half-year-old. So much for learning anything useful in her music class at school.

I laughed and pulled her into a tight hug.

Samantha squirmed to escape my arms, her tolerance for physical affection set to a hug a week.

My daily hugs bugged her, but my Bing Crosby impersonation annoyed her more. "I looooove yooooou, Samaaaanthaaaaa—"

"Not that song again, Mum!" Her brows puckered over her blue-green eyes. "Please!" Other than her golden-brown hair, Samantha was my double.

I kissed her forehead and released her.

Ryan pouted on the bottom stair. "What about me? Is there a Ryan song?"

"Not in *High Society*, sweetheart, but I can make up another song for you if you like?"

His lips extended, and his eyebrows buckled under the weight of his wrinkled forehead. "Okay. A song where I meet Iron Man and Thor eats tacos with me."

"Ah. Okay ..." I peered at Ryan's feet. "But first, where's your shoe?"

He shrugged. "Dunno."

I thrust my arms out. "If you spent more time looking for shoes and less time searching for undies, we could be in the car by now."

I huffed a breath and searched for the missing black school lace-up. I jogged to the family room—not an easy feat in the heels I wore today—and explored under the couch. After a growl and quick scan of the lounge and rumpus rooms, I ascended the stairs to Ryan's room and found the offending shoe under his bed. With an internal scream, I picked myself up off the carpet and trotted down the stairs.

"In the car!" I thrust the shoe at Ryan, collected my things from the kitchen, and dragged my son to the garage. "In!"

I opened the driver's door of my black BMW X1, rolled my bag and lunch into my jacket, and tossed it onto Jessica's lap next to me before I buckled my seatbelt.

"Is Dad home for dinner tonight?" Jessica asked.

I reversed down the driveway and locked the remote gates.

Was Jude home for dinner tonight? That was the question of the year. Along with the question "Are you sleeping with Paula?" which I shook from my mind. "I'm not sure yet." I focused on the road.

She growled and crossed her arms. "We haven't had dinner as a family for weeks, you know."

Yes. I knew. My heart cracked a little each day from Jude's absence. "I know, sweetheart. He's busy at work." With Paula. I narrowed my eyes and blew out a breath.

"Work, shmirk. Aren't we important to him?"

I shot a glance at Jessica before I planted my foot on the brake pedal. "Of course, you're important to Daddy. He's been focused on a big case and needs to work longer hours." At his office desk. With Paula sprawled across it. I gritted my teeth and shoved the concept of infidelity from my mind. Now was not the time or place.

I blew out a sigh and wriggled in the seat. Just another day in the Burke household.

♥ ♥ ♥ ♥ ♥ ♥ ♥

I grabbed my sandwich and phone and hustled to a secluded garden near the staff offices at work. I needed to settle my mind once and for all.

Christine answered after two rings. "Hey, sis."

"Hey," I said. "Do you have a minute?"

"Sure. It's my day off."

I exhaled.

"What's up, Vicki?"

I stared at the sandwich in my lap. "Jude received a text message at four this morning from his secretary."

"What! What did she want?"

"Let me find it. I captured a photo of his phone while he showered."

"That's an early start."

"He wasn't getting up for work." I scrolled through my phone. "He climbed into bed after his shower."

"Oh."

"Yeah. I need you to tell me I'm being paranoid." I pulled the handset away from my ear and spoke louder. "The message said, I hope you made it home safely, JD. You deserve some rest after all your hard work. Sleep well." I tucked the phone between my shoulder and my ear. "Sounds professional enough, but I didn't feel comfortable with her calling him JD. It's too—"

"Familiar." Christine harrumphed. "It should be Mr. Burke or Jude, not JD. Why's she working so late?"

"I've no idea. She has no law qualifications, so she can't help with the case. It's not like she can call people at two in the morning to set up meetings. Chrissy? You there?"

"Her message is too personal. I mean, the late hour is one thing. Caring about his well-being and hoping he sleeps well crosses the professional line, I think."

"You do?"

"Yes. If Patrick received a similar message from one of the women at work, I'd be annoyed."

I blcw out a long breath.

"Even the wording could mean something else."

I froze. "What do you mean?"

"You deserve some rest after all your hard work? Really? Jude may've legitimately worked late, but he might also have been hard at work on some*one*, Vicki."

My stomach dropped. Tears pricked my eyes, and a lump caught in my throat. "Y-you think?"

"It's possible. Can't you call someone at the firm and find out how late they worked on the case last night?"

"I could call Derek. He's Jude's right-hand man."

"Contact him and go from there." Christine sighed.

I shifted on the wooden bench, my throat thick.

"Can I pray for you?"

A tear slipped down my cheek. "Please. I need all the wisdom I can get."

Christine poured out a faith-filled prayer to God.

I murmured in agreement, and my heart lightened a fraction. With a quick farewell, I ended the call and dialled Derek's mobile number.

"Victoria! How are you, gorgeous?"

I wished Jude still spoke to me with similar exuberance. "Hey, Derek, I wanted to check if you managed some sleep last night after such a late one. I assume you worked on the case with Jude?"

"Yeah," he said with a chuckle. "I look like sh—ah, terrible, but I'm here."

"Thanks for sparing me from your colourful vocabulary."

"Sorry, gorgeous, I forgot I'm speaking to the queen herself." He laughed. "Must be the lack of sleep. Tumbling into bed at two a.m. is a hard slog after a six a.m. start."

My breath hitched, and my chest tightened. "You got to bed at two o'clock?"

"Yep. Left the office with everyone else at one-thirty. We were all knackered."

A brewing storm in my midsection zapped away my hunger. "I bet. Well, I won't hold you up any longer. Making sure Jude was treating you right." Unlike me.

"You're the sweetest. If you ever get sick of the boss, call me. He's one lucky devil."

I gulped. Lucky devil, indeed. "Thanks, Derek. All the best."

"You too."

Where had Jude been between one-thirty and four? The ball in my abdomen tripled in size, the weight a burden I struggled to contain.

I messaged Christine with unsteady fingers.

Me: DEREK SAID EVERYONE LEFT AT 1:30 A.M.

Christine: YOU'VE GOT TO BE KIDDING ME! WHAT WAS HE DOING FOR 2+ HOURS?!

Christine: I KNOW YOU HATE CONFRONTATION, BUT YOU NEED TO CONFRONT JUDE.

I slumped.

Me: I KNOW. I'LL MESSAGE HIM AND FIND OUT WHEN HE'S HOME.

Christine: CALL ME IF YOU NEED ANYTHING ELSE. DON'T FORGET YOU HAVE THE MIND OF CHRIST. YOU GOT THIS. XX

Me: THANKS. LOVE YOU. XX

Christine: LOVE YOU TOO.

I opened my thread of text messages with Jude and scanned the one- and two-word replies he had sent over the past month. My heart sank.

I eyed the time. Twenty minutes until I needed to be back inside. A phone call would be better than a message he could ignore.

"Thanks for being with me, God, no matter what happens." I dialled Jude's number.

"Sable Burke Lawyers, Felicia speaking." At least his phone diverted to reception. I could not speak to Paula right now.

I cleared my throat. "Felicia, it's Victoria Burke. Is Jude around?"

"Mrs. Burke!" Felicia's sweet, cheerful voice greeted me. "Could you hold for a moment? I think I saw him walk into the kitchen.”

"Of course." I unwrapped my ham-and-cheese sandwich and nibbled at my lunch. My appetite had vanished, but no sane teacher wanted to be known for their tummy grumbles.

The line crackled, and I swallowed my mouthful.

"Victoria."

The hairs on the back of my neck stood on end to the low rumble of Jude's voice. His deep timbre still affected me. "Jude. Do you have a moment?"

"What do you need?"

Nerves attacked my chest, and my mouth dried. "I, ah, needed to talk to you a-about, ah, something. When will you be home tonight?"

He sighed. I could imagine him running his fingers through his hair. "It's going to be another late night."

"Please, Jude. The children haven't seen you in weeks, and what I have to say is ... important. Can't you stop by for even an hour? Tuck the children into bed and talk to your wife?" A sting pricked my eyes. "Please?"

Another blustered puff greeted my ear. "Is it that important? I'm swamped."

I narrowed my eyes and dropped my voice. "Is your marriage and family important?"

A third sigh. "Yeah. Okay. I'll be home around eight o'clock."

"Okay. Thanks. See you th—"

"Bye."

I forced down the rest of my lunch.

The afternoon and dinner rush flew by. Before I knew it, Jude's footsteps trod through the door from the garage, and the squeals began.

My hands shook as I washed dishes, preoccupied with the difficult conversation ahead. The children's laughter floated from the lounge room, where they giggled with their dad.

I popped my head into the room twenty minutes later. Jude crawled along the floor with Ryan and Samantha on his back. All three laughed. Jessica lounged on the couch in a fit of giggles.

My heart flipped. "Okay, it's time to pray." I gazed at my three little rays of sunshine. "I'm so impressed with you all for getting ready for bed by eight."

"Of course we did," Samantha said. "We wanted as much Daddy time as possible."

My gaze drifted to Jude. I arched a brow at his remorseful face before clapping twice. "Okay, on the couch."

Everyone sprawled on the modular cream-leather lounge suite and I prayed. After a rowdy chorus of *amen*s, the children smothered my face in kisses which I returned in similar fervour. "Goodnight, my darlings. Daddy will tuck you in."

Ryan whooped and jumped on his father's back. "Let's go, Daddy 'orse!"

I gasped when Ryan's small hand brushed the shelf containing my antique crystal vases. "Be careful, Ryan!" My unsentimental sister had left our precious family heirlooms in my care.

Jude beamed, the kind of smile to reach his dazzling blue eyes, and my heart fluttered when he turned to me and winked.

I watched my family depart from the room with renewed peace in my heart. I must have taken Paula's message out of context. How could Jude gaze at me like he had moments ago without love in his heart?

Jude reappeared five minutes later and settled on the couch next to me. "You wanted to talk about something?" He searched my eyes, and the telltale warmth swirled in my tummy.

"Yes. I. Ah—"

"Yes?" He shifted close and extended a hand. His fingers brushed mine, and my heart stopped.

I cleared my throat. "Where were you last night?"

His fingers stilled, and he blinked. "At work. Why?"

"I woke to a text message on your phone while you were in the shower. You forgot to set your phone to silent."

He heaved a deep breath, and the corner of his mouth curved up. "Is that all?" He stroked my knuckles. "Sorry, baby. I didn't mean to wake you."

He had not called me "baby" in a long time.

My resolve faltered until Christine's face came to mind. I straightened. "It's not that. The message itself concerned me."

His shoulders stiffened. "What do you mean?" He released my hand. "Did you read my message?"

"Yes."

Jude swore under his breath.

"Why was Paula working so late with you? She's not a lawyer."

He cleared his throat. "She photocopies documents, makes coffee. I dictate emails and letters for her to send the following morning."

"She needs to be there until three-thirty in the morning?"

His eyes darkened and jaw clenched. "She works when I say she works."

I pressed my lips together and stared straight into his eyes. "Right. So, when everyone left at one-thirty, you, what? Unlocked the building and dictated messages to her for another two hours?"

He stood and crossed his muscular arms. His piercing gaze unnerved me. "Who said everyone left at one-thirty?"

I rose to my feet with my spine straight and head raised. "Derek."

"That son of a—"

"Stop it, Jude! Did you go back to her place and work on her for two hours?" My stomach soured.

"Come on, Vicki, you're being crazy now."

I stared at him.

He shook his head. "How cliché. You think I'd sleep with my personal assistant?"

I laughed. "Well, you're not sleeping with me, so it makes sense—"

"Don't be ridiculous! We have sex!"

I gawped. "We do? When, Jude?" I spread my arms. "When I'm asleep? After I take a memory-wiping pill? We haven't made love in two months!"

His derisive laugh fuelled my anger. "You keep count, huh?"

My hands vibrated, desperate to strike his beautiful face. "Of course I do! You're the only man I sleep with ... the only man I've ever slept with! I gave you everything on our wedding night."

The smirk slipped from his face.

Strength siphoned away from my body and tears brimmed in my eyes. "But you don't want what I have to give, so stop lying and answer my question," I said, my voice weak. "Are you sleeping with Paula? Yes or no?"

Every nanosecond of eerie silence dragged my nerves through a metaphorical paper shredder. My hope drained with each passing moment, and my heart wailed a silent cry of helplessness.

He shoved his hands into his pockets and stared over my head. "Yes."

CHAPTER TWO
Blood and Glass

"Th-thanks for your honesty. You can go to work now." A tear fell down my cheek. I stepped toward the lounge room doorway, and Jude grabbed my wrist.

"That's it?"

I turned and shrugged. "What's there to talk about? I lost you years ago, Jude. This"—I waved an arm in the air—"is now a marriage I can't pretend to want. You broke your vows and have no respect for me, our thirteen years of marriage, or the children." I slouched, and my chest heaved. "I'm going to bed."

I yanked my arm clear of his grasp and hauled myself up the stairs to cradle my broken heart.

The next few days dragged in a blur of work and child-rearing. How could I function knowing Jude had betrayed me with the one thing I desired? He knew the importance of intimacy. Why was I not enough?

I batted away tears and checked my mirrors before merging into the morning traffic.

"Mummy?"

I caught sight of Ryan in the rear-view mirror. "Yes, darling?"

"Thanks for washing The Hulk."

A tiny smile nudged my lips. "My pleasure." I could count on my babies to cheer me up.

Jessica shifted in the seat next to me. "You and your undies, Ry. You're so weird."

"Daddy says it's boy stuff. I like it when we do boy stuff." He giggled. "Joel's brother in Grade Four showed him how to aim and pee, but Daddy showed me."

Jessica squealed. "That's gross, Ry!"

I pinched my lips together and tried to block from my mind the impressive image of Jude leading by example.

"If I were a boy, I'd want to know things like that," Samantha said.

Meghan tittered in the seat behind me. "My dad freaks out when we walk in on him in the bathroom. It's hilarious."

Jessica turned in her seat. "Have you seen his—"

"Jessica! That's enough talk about ... all that." Was every conversation a direct reminder of the one thing denied to me? An assault of vivid images whirled in my cerebrum, and my pulse spiked. I wanted to scream at the mental-image of Jude to get dressed. What a time for a brain insurrection. I would lose my mind without a respite from the torment. I stared out the windscreen.

She snickered. "Please, Mum. I know what you and Dad do when your bedroom door's closed."

I raised my eyebrows and widened my eyes. If only what she imagined were real. "Jessica. Please."

"What do you and Daddy do?" Ryan asked.

I glanced over to my eldest daughter, who wore a smirk. My cheeks burned. "Can we please not have this discussion today?"

"Just saying."

"What? What!" Ryan said.

"They play adult games, Ry," Samantha said. "Gross stuff I'll never do."

"Thank you, Samantha." My tone was gruffer than I intended.

Poor Samantha had walked in on the birds-and-bees discussion I had with Jessica earlier in the year. The questions of my eleven-year-old had shocked me. My cluelessness embarrassed me and destroyed any conceptions I had of the good job I performed in my parental role. Children were exposed to so much more at younger ages than I had been as a child.

"Are you doing anything over the holidays, Meghan?"

"Not sure, Mrs. Burke. I'm excited for Year Seven, though. I can't believe this is the last day of Grade Six, Jess!"

I tuned out of the conversation and decided to forgo the stress of work today. Haileybury had finished classes a week ago, but today was our staff break up. I lacked energy for pretence this year.

We reached the school drop-off zone, and the children bundled out of the car. After an exchange of farewells and words of sentiment, I drove home.

I parked inside the garage and grabbed my mobile phone from the cupholder. After a brief conversation with the receptionist at Haileybury, I leaned back in my seat, staring at nothing.

Tears stung my eyes, and my chest burned. Why had Jude and I married in the first place? Because we assumed we loved each other? Or because I thought him the sweetest guy to ever grace my world? Maybe because he was breathtaking. Exquisite. Beautiful.

And I was not.

Average in every way except for my ample cleavage, I still possessed hang-ups about my appearance.

When Jude and I had met, I had been an awkward, plain-faced sixteen-year-old girl with short brown wavy hair, metal braces trailing my teeth, and a frame skinnier than a rake. Hollywood could have cast me in one of those cliché high school movies as the bullied smart girl no one except the science geeks wanted to know. I had lived the part. A few boys at school had sniggered when I found out their nickname for me: Ugly Barbie.

I spent puberty in tears and prayer, in hope my body would even out in its proportions and my face improve the way wine did with age. Insecure and shy, I was shocked when an almost nineteen-year-old Jude drew me into conversation on the first day of a Christian summer youth camp. A shock I soon grew accustomed to when the days and weeks melted into the months and years we were together. My physical transformation was not akin to an ugly duckling changing into swan form, but I became a little more comfortable in my skin. I gained a few curves following Jessica's birth and became content with a face closer to pretty on the scale of looks.

I moved indoors from the garage and flopped on the couch. I had not seen Jude in three days. No indents in his pillow or wrinkles on his side of the bed. No text messages or phone calls. Nothing since our argument.

He had changed after he attained his law degree, distancing himself from church and immersing himself in the cutthroat, competitive work environment of law practice. He abandoned godly friendships and invested time in the company of men with questionable moral standards to follow his pride on a path destined for riches and glory. I could almost pinpoint the downward trajectory of our marriage to the day he saw himself as the boss. He had climbed the corporate ladder with long work hours, grappled each rung, and crushed all opposition at the law firm he now led. Like a wolf on the hunt, Jude had focused on the next kill, the next deal, until it paid off and he became partner.

Moisture dampened my cheeks. I cried for my children. For me. My heart was splintered, my mind lost in the stalemate of my existence. I mourned the hope now extinguished from my marriage.

I pulled my smartphone from my pocket and opened Jude's contact information. His exquisite face and perfect smile stared back from the screen. How could this be the end? I needed to hear his voice.

He answered the call after five rings.

"Jude?" I prayed for guidance and strength. "Please talk to me. I ... miss you."

A sigh murmured on the other end of the line. "You said you don't want me."

Air gushed from my lungs. "I never said that." My dry throat was in desperate need of water. "I said the marriage we have right now is undesirable. Not you." I clutched my phone closer. "I've always been faithful to you in every sense of the word. B-but the man I married left me a long time before he slept with ... *her*."

The silence consumed any final fragments of peace I possessed and laid waste to my future. I choked back a sob.

"Are you in a back office? It's quieter than normal."

"I'm at home. I-I felt ill." Pointing a finger at him for my lack of sleep would not help. "I dropped the children at school and came home." My lip quivered. "Please come home, Jude."

"Maybe later."

"I'll be here. I—"

The phone line disconnected.

"I love you," I whispered. "I think."

I retrieved the huge pile of unfolded, clean clothes and dropped the basket on a dining chair. We planned to spend Christmas with Christine and Patrick in Wagga Wagga next week. I had overworked the washing machine the last few days.

I spent an hour folding garments and another hour ironing Jude's shirts. He had five left in his wardrobe, so I initiated a pre-emptive strike against any future yelling related to my laziness in case he came home.

I had relaxed a moment with a cup of tea on the lounge room couch when the internal garage door squeaked open. "Jude?"

"Glad to know you weren't expecting a lover."

I stared at the crumpled state of my husband.

He zoned onto my face with bloodshot eyes, and his mouth pulled in an unattractive grimace. His whitened fingertips gripped the door frame. "Cos you'd never sleep with another man, hey, virtuous wife of mine?"

I huffed out a breath. "Have you been drinking again?"

He laughed. "What's it to you?"

I pinched the leather arm of the couch. Jude drank to excess most of the time.

One of his superiors had introduced him to the wonderful world of whisky to celebrate Ryan's birth. Jude kept an ample stash at the office because I disliked his drinking at home. The moment he caught a whiff of smoky scotch in his glass, he could not stop at one shot. Often three or four, sometimes five, were downed. I never knew if Mr. Moody would be my companion or a dark, depressed character.

"Let's not be juvenile."

He squinted and bounded several heavy steps toward me.

I scrambled off the couch away from him.

"Juvenile. Really." He glanced at the bookshelf near the doorway. "You know what's *juvenile*, oh perfect one? Storing all this heirloom crap from your dead grandparents."

I shook my head and darted closer to the shelves. "Jude. Please."

He pushed past me, and I fell on my hands and knees with a yelp.

I shrilled "No!" as his powerful arm swept my keepsakes onto the floor in one swift motion.

The contents of the shelf crashed to the floor in an ear-splitting boom.

Tears coursed down my cheeks. I gaped at the carnage before I glared back at the stranger surrounded by his destruction. What just happened? I shivered, and my heart hammered in my chest. My gaze darted from the mess on the floor to the doorway, then back to Jude. A wave of queasiness swept over me. I rose to my feet and stared. "I shouldn't have asked you to come home."

His jaw twitched. His eyes flashed, and his face hardened. Jude seized two quick steps and pushed a flat hand against my chest.

With a squeal I fell hard into a low bench near the couch and struggled to breathe.

He grabbed me by the front of my T-shirt and yanked me up.

I cried out. The heavy stench of alcohol on his breath overwhelmed my senses.

"Are you kicking me out of my own home?" His bloodshot eyes

pierced me, and I imagined the darkness pumping through his veins. His teeth clenched. I had never witnessed him on a razor edge like this before.

My limbs shook, my legs weak. "No. I ..." I pushed back against his fist and fought the compulsion to dry wretch. Sound had reduced to a constant thud.

His fist vibrated against my chest.

I almost wet myself.

"Look what you forced me to do!" Belligerence thrummed in his voice.

I trembled but steeled myself in a silent prayer. "I didn't do anything. You have ... no control." The words fell from my mouth before I could stop them.

His face turned a fiery crimson, and his eyes bulged. "I'll show you no control, you self-righteous, cavilling parasite!"

In a grit of teeth, his fist worked hard and fast. The first punch burned a trail of fire along my jaw, splitting my lip mid-scream and loosening a tooth.

By the second sickening crunch of skin and bone, stars filled my vision and air ceased to exist. My neck seemed to snap out of joint, while blood splattered onto the floor and over my T-shirt.

His chest heaved, and he dumped me onto the carpet.

I landed hard on my left hip. Deep sobs convulsed my upper body while sharp pain shot down my sciatic nerve and travelled the length of my left leg. Swivelling onto my bottom, the side of my shoe crunched shards of irreplaceable history. I cowered on the floor with my legs curled close around me. Warm liquid dribbled through my knickers and jeans. My face screamed, in more pain than I ever recalled in my life, which included three long labours and difficult births.

Every molecule in my body registered agony.

Jude yanked hard on my hair—the pain of which seared my skull—and lifted my face.

I screamed.

"Shut up!" He lifted his palm to strike my uninjured cheek.

I swallowed my screams and nodded, sobs shaking my body. Pain ripped through the roots of my hair, and I stifled a moan.

He smirked.

I wanted to bite the smirk off his face.

He knelt in front of me and patted my cheek.

I flinched.

"Oh, baby," he cooed. "Don't be afraid of me. I love you." His hands roved my body and cupped my wet backside, pulling me toward him until I fell against his chest. He groaned. "If I didn't need to get back to work, I'd do you on the floor right here. I can tell you want some, my little nympho."

My stomach curdled, and bile rose to my mouth. Would he break more of my face if I vomited on him? I choked down the lump in my throat and prayed a silent, desperate prayer.

Jude squeezed my bottom and kissed the top of my head.

My toes curled. I clenched my fists and strained every muscle to keep from pushing away and riling the beast.

"I'll be home late, so wait up for me. We both know you need a rough ride tonight. A belated anniversary celebration." He stood and stumbled out of the room.

I collapsed onto shards of crystal the moment the garage door closed. My legs scrunched against my chest, and I clasped my hands around my ankles in a vain attempt to stop my limbs from shaking. A deep sob bellowed out of my mouth, and tears streamed down my face.

CHAPTER THREE
Pick Up the Pieces

I am blessed and highly favoured. The words seeped from my anguished heart and shuddered in my chest.

Tired from crying, I scrubbed at the bloodstains in the cream-coloured carpet, scouring in vigorous circles. My arms ached. Tears clouded my vision. Mucus trailed from my nose and mingled with the pool of tears and blood on my top lip. Three became one and dripped onto the bloodied cloth I rubbed hard against the lounge room floor.

I stood and surveyed the scene. Small red splotches of blood speckled the hallway carpet to the bathroom. The empty shelf on the bookcase reflected the condition of my own heart.

Where had I gone wrong?

I bent with a sigh and picked up broken shards of crystal. I needed to vacuum the floor to snatch away all the fine dust-like pieces before I collected the children from school. My future here might be uncertain, but leaving the house in disarray grated against me.

The children. What would I tell them?

My heart lurched for my three cheeky monkeys, and the tears spilled over my cheeks once more. I wiped my face with a shaky hand, reminded of the painful swelling where Jude had hit me.

Thank God he had left the house in the aftermath. How could I shield myself from his uncontrollable anger in the future?

I kneeled in the hallway and rubbed at spots of blood with focused attention. Each stubborn mark faded but failed to disappear. I leaned back and sighed.

I stumbled to the kitchen for a fresh cloth and some rubber gloves. The *Seinfeld* theme song blasted from my mobile phone. I absorbed a deep breath before swiping the screen.

"Hey, babe!" the upbeat voice of my best friend, Amber Jones, greeted me. "You on lunch break?"

I blinked back tears. "Hey." My busted lip hurt when I spoke.

"Vic, are you okay?"

A sob ripped out of my throat.

"What's wrong? Did Jude cancel date night again? Talk to me."

I sniffed and wiped the sleeve of my T-shirt across my eyes and nose. My throat tightened, choking me. "No. He didn't." I tried to slow my breaths.

Amber cleared her throat. "Then what happened?"

A long sigh blustered from my lips. "He hit me."

An eerie calm before the storm I knew would come.

"Excuse me?" Steel juddered in Amber's vocal cords. "It sounded like you said he hit you."

I rasped a response.

"What! What do you mean he hit you? When? Where? Are you okay?" Her voice rose in pitch and amplified with each question. "Oh, my goodness! Where are you?" Shuffling sounds were followed by a thud and a curse.

"Ah you okay?" I whispered.

Amber grumbled before her voice echoed, "I tripped over the stupid skateboard getting to the car. You're on speakerphone. You haven't answered any of my questions, Vic, so get to it."

A hint of a tiny laugh flitted in my chest at the brusque love of my friend. "I'm at home, cleaning." I screwed up my face and hissed at the painful movement. "Yoush the key, and I'll tell you e-vwee-fing."

Amber sighed. "I don't want to hang up on you. Can you put

your phone on speaker so I know you're okay until I get there?"

Hot tears clouded my eyes. "Okay."

"Thanks, babe."

An offensive odour permeated the bathroom. Earlier, startled by seeing myself in the mirror, bruised and broken, with blood dripping from my lips, down my chin, and onto my new white T-shirt, my stomach had refused to keep itself together. I placed my phone on the bench, pulled on a pair of gloves, and unclogged and cleaned the sink.

"Traffic's pretty bad today. Melbourne sucks sometimes."

I rinsed the cloth and wrung out the water. "Ah huh." Removing the gloves, I trundled down the hallway to the storage cupboard and dragged the vacuum cleaner to the lounge room.

"Jush haf to facuum."

"Okay, babe."

Any other day of the week a session with the vacuum cleaner relaxed me. But not today. Today my chaotic mind whirred, and my heart bled from the puncture wound inflicted by the man I once adored.

Jude. My love. What happened to you? To us? Thirteen years of shared life reduced to a punch in the face. The kind soul I had once stood tall and proud beside with his bold prayers and practical help for those in need had vanished.

I stared at the vacuum handle in my hands. The loud suction droned, unsuccessful at blocking out the never-ending cycle of thoughts while I pulled the machine backwards and forwards.

I needed everything tidy before packing clothes for our impromptu holiday and collecting the children. My plans to visit Christine next week had changed half an hour earlier while I crawled along the floor amongst blood and glass. The last thing I needed was Christine and the boys exposed to Jude and his recent aggression. I had to keep them and my children safe. I prayed for the courage needed to make that particular phone call to Christine. And my parents. I could put it off for another day or two.

I switched the vacuum cleaner off and indulged in the momentary quiet.

"Just a few minutes away, hun," Amber said.

"No woh-wees." I shoved the vacuum cleaner back inside the storage cupboard and trudged up the stairs toward my bedroom. "I'm going to haf a quick shower."

"Okay. I'm going to hang up now."

"I'll shee you shoon."

I tossed my phone on the bed and stepped into the shower.

The watery massage soothed my back while I probed my face with gentle strokes, using a soft facecloth to remove the final traces of blood, mucus, and perspiration. My mouth and gums ached under my broken lip, but I was too afraid to touch inside my mouth in case it resulted in subsequent damage. After a quick hair wash, I dried off, dressed, and staggered downstairs.

The kettle's whistle drew me to the kitchen. Amber's eyes popped when she spotted me. She pulled me into a bear hug. "You look terrible, Vic."

I stepped back. "Fanksh for da compwehment."

"Have you iced your mouth?" Her jawline hardened.

Tears pricked my eyes. "Wash the firsh fing I did."

"You can't stay here." Amber poured the tea and set our steaming mugs at the island bench.

"I know. I'm going to book shum countwy accommodation for the week and pack shoot-caysh-esh for the childwen and me."

"You're welcome to stay with us." Amber arched an eyebrow.

"Fanksh, but a change of shee-nuh-wy will be gweat for all of ush."

"Have you told your parents? Or Chrissy?"

I shook my head, wide-eyed. "Pweesh don't tell them. I need time to ... fink."

Her lips thinned. "Hmm. Okay."

I sipped my tea, and pain shot through my gums. "Fink you could get a head shtart on the packing for me, pweesh? I fink he wooshened a toof, and I need to shee if Dean can fix it."

Amber's words escaped in a string of yeses.

After I called my dentist friend, who assured me of an emergency appointment slot, I located some suitcases for Amber and headed out the door. What would I tell Dean? I grappled with a valid excuse while I drove to the dental surgery. The truth was not an option, but perhaps a story not too far from reality could work.

"Are we there yet?"

I held in a sigh and answered for what seemed like the fiftieth time. "No, Samantha, we still have another hour to go."

A succession of cries and moans filled the rear seat of my SUV.

Our trip had taken much longer than I had anticipated. Anyone who lived in or around Melbourne knew our great city experienced non-stop growth with continuous roadworks and major congestion.

The trip from Black Rock to the country regions of Victoria was always a pleasant drive. I avoided going home after collecting the children from school and headed east through the suburbs. We travelled along the scenic route of winding roads through the Yarra Valley and Dandenong Ranges. The forested roadways with lush green fronds, tall towering eucalypts, and peaceful views could still the heart and mind of the most restless soul. Although this route happened to be less direct than if we travelled along the main freeway or highway, I wanted to offer my own treasured childhood memories to my children.

I recalled many trips along these same roads when my family visited my grandparents in north-east Victoria. My favourite memory was the rare occasion Mum would prepare an early dinner, and Christine and I would travel in our pyjamas at night. Those car rides were fun, even when Christine teased about scary monsters lurking in the forest outside our car windows. No matter what she said, my confidence never wavered when Dad guided our vehicle through the darkened forest to the light of Nan's front verandah. I had always been content and secure with Dad.

My stomach knotted, and a new reality shattered the peaceful scenery which whizzed by: my children may never be safe with their father again.

I held back threatening tears. The children speculated where we were going, what it would be like, and if it had essentials like an Xbox and Netflix. A smile touched my lips at the animated exchange.

How blessed I was with such beautiful children. Hearts of gold even in the midst of trials.

I had struggled to watch the mix of emotions cross Ryan's face when he noticed my bruised cheek and chin this afternoon. Jessica and Samantha had stared at me, wide-eyed with raised eyebrows. No amount of makeup could hide the fist-sized marks or the fear and uncertainty I knew was etched in my eyes. Thank God Dean bonded my loose tooth to its neighbour so talking, eating and drinking was easier. I had brushed off their concerns, dodged their questions, and led the children to believe I had fallen. Which I had, before and after Jude broke my heirlooms. They had been quick to pray for me before they resumed their enthusiastic conversations.

"Ryan! Stop poking me, or I won't let you play the new Lego Xbox game Uncle Steve promised to get me for my birthday." With two weeks until Jessica turned twelve, her excitement bubbled.

When had my baby girl grown? I concentrated on the road while she gushed about the gifts she hoped to receive and the people she would like to invite to her family birthday dinner.

"I'm sorry, Jess-ca. I won't do it again." I smiled at the promise Ryan was certain to break. "Mah-mee!"

"Yes, sweetie?"

"Will Daddy be staying in the country with us?"

"Not this time, Ryan." I sighed and assessed my children in the rear-view mirror. I would do everything possible to protect their precious hearts.

Daddy dearest indeed.

I needed to stop thinking about him. The dimple in his cheeks. The flash of his smile. The thrill up my spine when he gazed at me with those familiar blue eyes. Was it possible to change my well-formed habits as a long-time wife and lover? A despondent breath shuddered through my chest and heaved up the pain within me. For a rejected woman, I dreamed too often of his touch and recalled the memories of our intimacy in the early years with increased frequency.

The first and last man I ever pursued, my husband, had soon become an all-encompassing passion of mine. A passion which overshadowed all others. Before I met Jude, basketball had consumed my every waking moment. Fantasies of dominating the court while I skidded along shiny wooden floors, my adept hands strong and grip firm mid-dribble before launching a ball with skilful thrust, were constant thoughts. I imagined myself on the Under-Eighteen State team and had laboured toward reaching my goal within a few months.

Then Jude came along, and my dreams started to shift, subtle changes after I discovered his aversion to sport. I contemplated a future with him where I could still play basketball. The shift started with small compromises. "Why don't you focus on a career which will last your lifetime, not a decade," Jude would say. "You're smart, why not education? Teach the next generation." His suggestions were logical although my family had questioned my change of heart. Jude insisted Dad projected his dreams onto me. My parents assured me they had my best interests at heart, and Christine often said I appeared happiest with a basketball in my hands. But a ball could never love me like a man would.

I followed Jude's suggestions and applied for Secondary School teaching once I graduated Year Twelve, majoring in English and humanities because Jude said physical education was pointless. He moulded my thoughts with each word, smile and touch. Basketball disappeared into the mist of my youth while memories of his warm hands wrapped around my waist, pulling me close to kiss my lips with inimitable perfection, possessed my every thought.

It wounded me to admit all that had remained of our relationship before this afternoon had been our physical connection. We had not touched in two months. I had thought the drought in our bedroom was a simple hiatus and not the telltale sign of a disintegrated relationship.

All because of her. Paula's face flickered to my memory, and I growled. She had worked at Sable Burke Lawyers for a little over a year but had succeeded in digging her talons into my husband in such a short amount of time.

I stared out the windscreen and forced my brain away from Jude's affair. *Oh, Jude.* On cue, images pounded my mind, and I struggled to breathe under the weight of my memories. The way he used gentle hands to sweep aside my hair and brush my neck with his mouth. His hot breath on my cheek while he nibbled my ear. Long, lingering kisses which intensified with heat and pressure. The undeniable ache in my belly, the need for more. So much more.

The agony of my cheek and jaw where he punched me twice and split the lip he once caressed with tenderness.

I had to get him out of my head. The rocky steps of grief were now familiar and smooth underfoot. Years had passed since I enjoyed his tenderness, and my heart mourned the loss.

Would I ever share a bond of intimacy with another man like I had shared with Jude? Would I want to?

Shame heated my cheeks when my desire for him refused to die. Perhaps Jude hit me harder than I thought and knocked sense out of me. I blinked back tears. I had become that foolish woman one reads about in gossip magazines who pines after her abusive husband.

I overtook a slow vehicle, my focus back to my thoughts once I re-entered the correct side of the road.

Why had this happened to me when I remained faithful to God all these years? I knew He loved me, but I missed my husband. I missed his soft-spoken words from our youth, and sitting next to him in church. I missed the sensations of being a contented married woman surrounded by the strong arms of her husband in sleep. And I missed his tenderness. Only a broken individual would dream of the warmth of her husband on her lips despite the sting of injury hours earlier. I needed help.

I stared out the windscreen, and the velvety voice of Brian McKnight on the car stereo assaulted my heart with one of my all-time favourite tracks. 'Still' rang out through the Harmon Kardon speakers and stabbed my shattered heart with ruthless strokes. Yes, I still wanted him, but never again. We were over the moment he struck me.

"Mum! Stop! Mum!" Jessica's screams yanked me out of my dangerous daydream when the car skidded.

A set of large headlights and the huge grill of a truck spun out of view, followed by a ball of white. My ears exploded with the unimaginable sounds of metal grinding metal, shattering glass, splintering wood, and the sudden silence of my children's cries.

CHAPTER FOUR

Despair Comes to Call

Deep throbs in my temples pulsated down my face. My head vibrated and buzzed with similar ferocity to my lower leg. Bright light filled my vision. I breathed in a whiff of antiseptic, and pain surged through my skull. Tinny music droned from a nearby radio.

I blinked and stared into the face of a green-eyed stranger who hovered above me. Her strawberry-blonde hair was tied back, and wisps of curls splayed about her face like hand-pulled fairy floss.

"W-wherrre ... amm I?" I laboured against a delay between thought and speech.

"It's good to see your beautiful eyes at last, Victoria. My name's Patricia, and I'm taking care of you here at The Alfred ED."

My head verged on the edge of explosion. The light above my face pierced my eyes like a dagger while a collar clamped around my neck stilled my movements. I imagined myself akin to a wooden toy soldier, my limbs stiff and supine along the hospital bed and my right leg stinging with a war wound. Nausea billowed, and I pressed my dry lips together so my stomach contents would stay put.

"Can you tell me your full name and date of birth?" Patricia checked my pulse.

"Vvv ... Vic-toria ... J-Jade ... Burke." Sandpaper rasped in my throat. "De ... Decemm ... bber ... tw-wenty-th ... three."

"Do you remember what happened to bring you here to the hospital?"

I squeezed my eyes shut and searched the recesses of my mind. "Nnn-no." I opened my eyes and blinked from the glare.

"You'll adjust to the light soon." Authority resonated in Patricia's gentle tone. "You were in a car accident a few hours ago and have a significant leg wound and a mild head injury. We're keeping you in a C-spine collar as a precaution. Someone will be here soon to escort you to X-ray so we can rule out fractures. I've sent your bloods to Pathology. Why don't you rest a little?"

A car accident? The Alfred ED?

My head buzzed with questions, but the more I tried to focus, the foggier things seemed. I closed my eyes. Two voices whispered behind a curtain to my right.

Patricia tapped on a keyboard at a small computer kiosk to my left. "Oh, your husband's been contacted as well as your—"

My eyelids flew open, and I croaked, "N-noo." My heartbeat kicked up several notches.

Patricia gaped before she typed at the computer with a tight smile. "Your parents have also been notified."

I slowed my breathing and tried to nod.

The background radio chimed the beginning of a news bulletin.

The agony in my leg throbbed without end. I tried to move and ease the discomfort, but the pain prevailed. Straining my eyes, I watched fluid drop at a slow and steady rate in a nearby intravenous drip. Why was I here? I blinked and stared at the stark-white ceiling, my brain on a hunt to call to mind the events which led me to this bed.

Phrases floated on the airwaves from the radio news broadcast: "Worst road trauma since ... eight dead, three hospitalised ... serious injuries ... eye-witnesses feared for their lives ... alleged alcohol or substance abuse ..."

I strained to recall my movements earlier in the day. Vague thoughts about a holiday floated to the surface of my memory.

Holiday! I was driving the children to—

"M-my ... ba-bies!" my voice cracked, and Patricia jolted. A lifetime seemed to pass by before I formed the next plea. "Wwwwhere ... are my ... chhhil-dren?"

Her pensive green eyes answered me before she spoke. "I ... I'm so sorry to inform ..."

A sudden ringing drowned out all sound, and my heart smashed into a thousand pieces. I wheezed hard, gasping from shallow breaths. Images of their sweet faces darted through my mind before dizziness filled my head and everything went black.

I blinked against the brightness.

A profusion of equipment filled the small hospital room. Machinery ticked, beeped, and buzzed all around me. A cool puff of oxygen pumped into my nostrils before exhaustion forced my eyelids closed again. My body ached all over.

This was not a nightmare. This was real.

The pressure of loss and grief constrained my chest, and my lungs burned. A cardiac monitor beeped in loud bursts before a petite, blonde nurse rushed into the room.

I opened my eyes and struggled to breathe.

"You're okay, Victoria. You're okay," she said. "My name's Jennifer, and you're in ICU at The Alfred. How're you feeling, darl?"

"Not ... guh-ood," I rasped. The ache of loss compressed my chest more than the pulsations in my right leg.

"Can you tell me or point to where it hurts?"

No drug existed to stem the intangible bleed to my heart, so I lifted a finger at my leg.

Jennifer fiddled with a drip which I assumed delivered my pain medication.

Everything about the room was foreign to me. So many tubes, wires, and unfamiliar technology filled the small footprint of space. Buds of anxiety pricked my brain. I focused on a blank section of the wall and counted slow breaths.

"I know this all looks scary, darl. But we're taking good care of you. We had to perform surgery after the accident. There were signs of rhabdomyolysis precipitated by the muscle injury in your leg." She pointed to a tall, rectangular contraption with several bags of fluid attached. "This machine helps your kidneys. It's still early days, but a few markers have come up in your bloods which look promising." Jennifer held my wrist in her fingers and checked my pulse. "I expect your stay in ICU will be brief, perhaps a few more days. If you're ever in pain or need anything else, please let me know." She checked a few screens, pressed several buttons, and busied herself with work.

My arm hurt from the pinch of an automated blood pressure cuff. A similar squeeze crushed my heart, and I mourned my losses. Life without my babies, without a semblance of normal. Patricia's face when I asked about the children came to mind, and I fought back tears.

My children. My flesh and blood, my beloved sweethearts, were gone.

Gone.

I shut my eyelids to block memories of faces I would never gaze at again. They were now safe in the arms of my Father in heaven, but my head and heart hurt so much. How would this knowledge ever comfort me? I remained behind, left to mourn their loss. The loss of their growth and emerging personalities. The demise of their youth, their adult years. The grandchildren I would never have.

Was there any point to my life now? If I refused this treatment, could I check out permanently too?

Tears slipped onto my pillow. I mourned a future torn away from me in the blink of an eye. No more bedtime stories and warm hugs. Or awkward conversations about undies, peeing contests, and childish jokes. No more yelling to brush teeth, exasperation over empty milk cartons in the fridge, or hearing endless whining about homework.

Waves of guilt, pain, and anguish hit me like a crashing breaker. Again. And again. My consciousness was afloat at sea. I hyperventilated. The pain in my chest matched the incessant beeps from a nearby monitor.

If only I had focused more on the road. If only I had seen the truck sooner.

If only.

If only.

I wept with a profound, inescapable, soul-crushing cry. The endless abyss of grief struck me harder than I ever imagined. And in that moment, I knew I would drown in my own tears, and I was content in that knowledge.

A gentle hand touched my arm, my soul soothed by the warm strokes of soft fingers above my elbow. I searched through tears to witness Jennifer's softened expression.

"You're allowed to cry. The world you knew will never be the same, but you'll get through this." She adjusted the fluid dosage rate in a nearby IV drip before she turned her attention back to my face with a soft smile. "That truck ploughed through four vehicles, darl. It wasn't your fault, so don't carry the burden of guilt."

I was not at fault?

"You need to focus on getting better so you can look after your son."

My heart stuttered, and my chest tensed. My son? Ryan had survived? "H-he's ... a-li-vve?"

A fresh wave of tears trickled into my pillow. My lungs heaved, but the vice which had clamped on my heart released its death grip. My distraction was not to blame, and my son was alive. Alive!

Jennifer leaned closer. "You didn't know?"

I shook my head, thankful to be free of the restrictive collar.

"Oh darl! I'm so sorry! I read a note on your chart which said you asked about your children. You thought they were all gone?"

I nodded while tears tickled my ears and neck. My girls were gone, shattering my heart beyond recognition. But Ryan was still here. I would continue dragging myself along this journey called life for Ryan's sake. "Hhhow ... is h-he?"

The smile I wanted to curl on Jennifer's face never surfaced. "The only information I have is he's in a coma. Beyond that, you'll need to speak to his doctor. I can arrange for someone to visit you soon, although you won't be fit enough to visit him for at least another week."

A coma.

I pressed my lips together in an unsuccessful effort to stop more tears from trailing onto my pillow.

♥ ♥ ♥ ♥ ♥ ♥ ♥

"It's been three days without any change."

My stomach churned. I stared at the short, dark-haired neurosurgeon who stood next to my hospital bed. I could not recall our initial meeting several days ago when I was under heavy sedation. "W-what ... does th-that ... m-mean?"

Dr. Singh clasped his hands together. "It means Ryan has not come out of the induced coma, so we will continue to monitor his brain for swelling and treat him for possible infection." He pushed the side of his spectacles with an index finger. "After we drained fluid from the brain, he suffered a postoperative seizure, and we induced a coma to give him time to heal. His brain activity appeared promising, so we reduced sedation three days after surgery over a course of two days, but he has not woken yet."

I initiated several deep breaths to calm my frantic pulse. My lungs spasmed on each inhale. "Ssssso ... w-what now?" I brushed a finger under my wet eyes.

He gazed out the window. "We wait." He turned his head, and his piercing black eyes drilled into my face. "I spoke with Dr. Gleeson. He believes you will be transferred from ICU today. Once you are settled in a ward and can travel safely in a wheelchair, we will arrange for you to visit your son once a day. Hearing your voice may help him wake."

I offered a small, lopsided smile. My chest tightened. I needed to see my son.

Dr. Singh's prediction came true, and my transfer from ICU occurred three hours later, to the delight of my parents. Now they could visit with me much longer each day. Dad and Mum had taken turns with Christine and Amber and kept vigil at my bedside when hospital protocol permitted. My vague recollections in ICU included shadows of visitors.

"It's nice to see you awake for longer, darling." Silver markings discoloured the area under Mum's eyes. "Amber dropped off a replacement phone Mike set up for you when she visited. Christine sends her love." Mum sniffed and brushed away a tear. "She apologised she couldn't extend her stay but will be back soon." She pointed to a large bouquet of flowers near the window. "Your friends at Haileybury sent this over a few days ago. So lovely."

I had wondered about the flowers, which brightened my room.

Her gaze darted from Dad's sombre face to mine. "Jude popped in to visit. He thought it best to stay with Ryan so we could stay with you, which was considerate."

I bit my lip. Amber must have stayed true to her word and not told my family about my run-in with Jude. Otherwise, Dad would be plotting his murder. Once I was alone, I would message Christine and update her using my new mobile phone. God bless Mike and Amber.

"Oh! You slept through your birthday and Christmas, so we thought we'd celebrate once you're well?" Mum's hands fiddled in her lap. "Soon we'll have you walking around."

Dad squeezed my hand with a watery smile. "Don't overwhelm her, love. She's barely been awake the past eight days. Victoria will get about when she's ready."

I smiled at Dad because talking still frustrated me. An MRI had confirmed no serious head injuries other than a mild case of contrecoup, a diagnosis which gave me great relief. It explained the speech issues I endured. Not verbose by nature, I had been frightened by the loss of free communication.

"You doing okay, baby girl?"

I croaked a "yes" to Dad.

He tightened his grip on my fingers and grabbed Mum's hand with his free one. A tear tracked down his cheek, and a guttural yelp wrenched from his lips. "Our p-princesses."

Mum slipped her arms around Dad's waist, and her head bobbed against his chest, which muffled her cries.

My tears spilled over.

Three days later, a middle-aged orderly with tree-trunk legs and a round face entered my hospital room with a wheelchair. "Ready to see your son?"

I nodded.

The orderly detached the drip bag from over my bed and hooked it on a pole at the back of the wheelchair before she positioned me into the seat. She turned to my parents. "We'll be back in twenty to thirty minutes if you'd like to have a cup of tea at the café?"

"Of course. Victoria, we'll be back soon." Mum kissed my forehead and turned to Dad. "Come, dear."

Dad kissed the top of my head before he guided Mum from the room.

The orderly pushed my wheelchair through several corridors, into a lift, and down another passageway, scanning her access pass at the ICU entry. Once the heavy doors closed, she leaned in front of me. "I know you're fresh out of ICU and can guess what it might be like to visit your son, but he's on a ventilator and has much more equipment in his room." She touched my hand and offered a small smile. "Will you be okay alone? Or would you like me to stay?"

I gulped a rush of saliva. "A-aalo-ne."

The orderly nodded and pushed the wheelchair to a partitioned area.

My breath came in short bursts, and I squeezed my eyes shut. I could do this. I opened my eyes as a nurse lowered the bed.

"Now you can see him better, Mrs. Burke," she said.

I gazed at the sleeping boy in front of me. I covered my mouth with a shaky hand to stop the cry which burgeoned in my chest. My heart thundered against my ribcage. This could not be the same vivacious boy I once chased down from our backyard lemon tree.

Ryan looked frail. My stomach dropped at his pallor. He lacked the usual redness in his cheeks, along with his silky hair. Tears stung my eyes at the missing mop of curls. His chest rose and fell with the help of a ventilator. A small tube balanced underneath his nose connected to a larger tube attached to his throat.

I placed my hand over his small one below a plaster cast which clung to his arm from elbow to wrist. "Ba-by." Pain enfolded my chest and squashed my lungs.

Ryan seemed peaceful, which comforted me, but the large bed dwarfed his small body. He appeared small and helpless.

My heart broke to see him, bald and broken, but the selfish part of me treasured the time I had. I clutched his warm hand, willing my son to wake from his comatose state, and stared at his sweet face, studying each contour and freckle.

Such a beautiful boy. His thick, long eyelashes were identical to Jude's, but his soft and pliable heart contrasted his father's.

I blew out a breath and lowered my chin to my chest. Ryan needed to wake up. I whispered a broken prayer for Ryan's well-being, for his strength to live, and strength for myself. I raised my free hand to wipe away my tears.

Ryan had never experienced a hairless day in his life, and I scrunched my nose at the horrible look. I would remind him of this moment if he ever threatened to shave his head in the future. Not on my watch, mister. A strangled laugh escaped my lips.

The ICU nurse entered the room and attended to the equipment.

I leaned forward and kissed Ryan's frangible hand. I longed to kiss his cheeks, but his head was too far away. "I ... lo-ve yyy-you, R-ryan."

A sob rippled through my torso, the staccato of my heart in time with one of the monitors in the room. My vision blurred, and I lingered in silence, my fingers connected to Ryan's while a cacophony of sounds resonated around me like an electronic symphony humming a melody straight to my soul. *Be strong and courageous. Do not be afraid.* I brushed my fingers across my eyes and rested in the words of comfort.

Ryan was a brave little boy with a tenacious spirit. He would fight to regain consciousness, I was certain. Dr. Singh had said Ryan may respond to my voice, so I croaked out a few words while I studied his face. Happy memories filled my mind.

I peeked at the clock on the wall. The orderly would return soon.

Ten minutes later she escorted me back to my room and helped me into bed. My injured leg throbbed, so a ward nurse administered some oral painkillers. The staff were weaning me from the heavier, more addictive analgesics. In no time my hand would be free from the drip.

No sooner had the nurse left the room than Dad entered red-faced and heaving. His fists were clamped at his sides. Mum scurried in behind him.

My breath hitched. "W-wwhat's ... wr-rrong?"

Mum pursed her lips. "We bumped into Jude at the café."

Uh oh. Two days ago, Christine had been my voice and shared the news with our parents over speakerphone after I had messaged her the previous night. Dad received the news of Jude's affair and subsequent face-smashing like a shot of arsenic. Mum burst into tears and hugged me while Dad's features hardened and his eyes burned. Mum and Christine had talked him off the figurative ledge.

Dad's eyes bulged, and his hands mimicked strangling someone. "That arrogant, self-centred ... weasel!" Dad glanced at Mum. "You and Christine shouldn't have stopped me from barging into ICU and beating him to a bloody pulp the other night. He's sitting smug a floor away while my baby girl suffers."

Mum rubbed his back. "Calm down, Pete. It's not good for your blood pressure. You don't want to be banned from the hospital, do you?" She pinched the bridge of her nose and turned to me with a sigh. "Jude expressed an uncomplimentary comment about your driving ability while we waited for our coffees, insinuating the accident was your fault. Your father aimed a fist at him, but Jude ducked and hurried away."

I cringed. "I'm s-sso ... sssorry."

Dad closed his eyes and sucked in several breaths. The pulse in his neck slowed, and his gaze locked with mine. "Victoria. Darling." He reached for my hand. His grip was gentle. "Never apologise for that ... poor excuse of a man. Ever." He lowered his head and kissed my temple. "Understood?"

With a sniff, I squeezed his hand.

A knock sounded at the door, ushering in a team of allied-health professionals who shared a plan for my rehabilitation. The day continued to drag in-between conversation with my parents and nurse health checks.

Dad and Mum said their farewells after an orderly delivered my dinner meal, and I picked at the food until it became a stodgy lump. I reached for a book Mum had left next to my bed and had read three chapters when a shadow filled the doorway.

"Happy New Year, Victoria."

My heart raced, and the hair on my arms stood to attention. The book fell from my hands. I shook my head when Jude drew near. "N-no ... clossser." I reached for the button to contact the nurse, and his body stilled.

"Victoria, I won't hurt you. Don't press the button. Please."

I shut my eyes. "W-why?"

"Baby, I'm sorry. I got stuck in my head when you said I shouldn't have come home, as though you wanted to terminate our marriage." Jude pulled a seat next to my bed.

I could smell his overpowering, expensive Clive Christian cologne and opened my eyes. He was close but too far away to slap. At least he had the decency to appear forlorn.

"Can you forgive me?"

I stared at his perfect face, those full lips I loved to nibble on, eyelashes longer than my own, and deep-blue eyes I had often lost myself in. Now my insides crawled. "O-one ... ddday."

He narrowed his eyes. "What's wrong with you? Why can't you speak properly? I sacrificed time to have a conversation."

I clenched my jaw and assessed my fingernails. Long enough to inflict damage if he came close enough. I blew out a breath. "Car ... acc-cid-dent."

Jude sneered. "I know that. I was so freaking angry with you when I found out. You ran away? With the children?" He shook his head, his face sombre and eyes distant. "The worst plan in history, Vicki. Look what you did to the kids."

My eyes stung, and I blinked back tears. This *was* my fault. If I had stayed at Amber's, my girls would be alive and Ryan would be conscious.

"Thank God Ryan's still with us. Have you seen him?"

I wiped my eyes with a tissue from the bedside table. "Y-yes."

Jude rolled his broad shoulders. "When he's conscious and healthy, I intend to pursue full custody if you leave me."

What! My vision blurred, and blood rushed in my ears. Over my dead body would he parent my son.

Jude quirked his lips. "Unless you intend to forgive me. Then we can return to life as usual."

Life as usual. What would be worse: to live the life of a single mother drained from a constant legal battle over custody or to return to that house where I could be used, lied to, injured or worse. I clenched my hands together.

He cleared his throat. "Our daughters' funeral will be held on Friday at two o'clock."

My heart stopped, and I stared at him. "W-what?" Friday was Jessica's twelfth birthday.

He inspected the drip attached to my hand. "I can't leave the girls in storage indefinitely. It's been eleven days. They charged extra fees to house them over the Christmas period. Like we could choose the time our children died!" He shook his head. "The cost is exorbitant, and this whole"—he waved a hand at me—"thing needs to be put to bed. Our girls are dead, and we can't do a thing about it." He rubbed a hand over his face. "They need to rest in peace, not rest on ice. I had to make a decision."

The hospital staff would not grant my release by Friday. Unbidden tears fell down my cheeks. "B-but ... I'mmm he-ere?"

Jude shrugged. "Get someone to live stream it. I'm not investing more finances into a dead-end project."

Dead-end project? Was he serious?

Jude rose from the chair. "Friday. Two p.m." He swaggered to the door. "Think hard about the kind of life you want for our son too."

Our gazes locked and I shuddered.

His deep voice lowered a note, and I fought the desire his words created. "I know what I want, baby." He walked out.

His footsteps echoed in the hall, and I burst into tears.

CHAPTER FIVE
The End of the Beginning

I shoved a handful of tissues against my face. What could I do? I prayed before I reached for my phone. My fingers trembled with each button press, and I erased several errors in the jumble of my words.

Me: I WISH I COULD SPEAK IN SENTENCES, THEN I'D TELL YOU JUDE VISITED AND INVITED ME TO A FUNERAL FOR THE GIRLS I CAN'T POSSIBLY ATTEND AND LEFT ME WITH AN ULTIMATUM: FORGIVE AND FORGET OR LOSE CUSTODY OF RYAN.

As I touched my book, messages pinged on my phone.

Christine: I'M SO ANGRY RIGHT NOW, I COULD EXPLODE! PATRICK'S MASSAGING MY SHOULDERS, BUT I THINK HE'S STRENGTHENING HIS HANDS SO HE CAN THROTTLE JUDE.

I huffed a wry laugh. What else was a brother-in-law for?

Christine: WHEN'S THE FUNERAL?

Me: FRIDAY AFTERNOON. I'LL MESSAGE MUM TO CONTACT MR. NASTY.

Me: I NEED ADVICE. AND PRAYER. PLEASE KEEP US ALL IN PRAYER.

Me: I MISS YOU SO MUCH. XX

Christine: PATRICK HAD SOME ANNUAL LEAVE APPROVED. WE'RE THINKING A ROAD TRIP FOR THE ELLISONS IS IN ORDER. SEE YOU FRIDAY?

I cracked the biggest smile my lips had formed in months. The unfamiliar stretch hurt my cheeks.

Me: YES! PLEASE. THANK YOU SO MUCH. HUGS TO PATRICK. PASS ON LOTS OF APPROPRIATE SISTERLY HUGS. ;)

Christine: HUG HIM YOURSELF ON FRIDAY. NOTHING APPROPRIATE WILL HAPPEN HERE TONIGHT!

I laughed out loud. Memories of playful times which led to steamy moments with Jude flooded my mind. My smile faded, and a sigh shuddered in my chest.

Me: AS MY STUDENTS SAY, TMI. (ENJOY YOUR MAN. HE'S A ONE-OF-A-KIND.) LOVE YOU. XX

Christine: LOVE YOU TOO. SEE YOU FRIDAY. XX

I grabbed my book. Excitement overshadowed my grief and anger for a split second, and I urged Friday to rush into existence.

"What a beautiful ceremony." Mum held my hand through our tears. She patted my hand and wiped her eyes. "Amber said she'll visit tomorrow."

Patrick Skyped me from the funeral, and I had watched the ceremony with my hand clasped around Ryan's.

Dad's chin wobbled. "I kept my promise and avoided ... him." He pulled his phone from his pants pocket and stared at the screen. "Christine messaged. They're here." He stepped outside the room.

I wiped my face with another clump of tissues. I had messaged Christine and asked her to leave the boys outside my room in case seeing their auntie with a multicoloured face traumatised them. Now in a low-tech room free of my IV, my face was still a mess of colour, my hand still had a cannula attached, and my bandaged leg still throbbed. Two weeks had passed since the accident.

Mum disappeared from the room and I lay in bed and sniffled.

A few minutes later, Christine and Patrick walked through the door. My sister burst into tears and barrelled her way through the room to the side of my bed. She clung to me as our sobs bounced off each other.

"Oh, Vicki."

Several tissues materialised in front of us, and we both laughed. "Th-thhanks, Ppat-trick," I said.

"How're you feeling, sis?" Patrick rubbed Christine's back.

I ripped my gaze from his affectionate touch and peered at his face. "To be ... eex-pected." I kissed Christine's cheek, and she stepped back into Patrick's arms. Oh, to be loved like that. "Yyyyou re-cccord-ed th-the ce ... cere-mmony?"

He dipped his head. "I've emailed it to you."

A fresh sheen of tears glazed my eyes. "Thhha-nks."

Christine's face contorted into a scowl. "Patrick had to hold me back from scratching his eyes out." She shook her head. "I can't believe he couldn't wait another week for you to be discharged into the rehab centre. They're your daughters too!"

Patrick held his wife close and whispered in her ear.

I nodded. What could I say?

Dad re-entered the room. "The boys want to know if they can see Auntie Victoria. Blair said to ask you, Christine, whether she's too scary to look at or not."

Christine sighed and stared at me. "You're not too scary looking." She turned to face Dad. "I think a short visit will be okay."

I spent the next twenty minutes surrounded by my three nephews, Blair, Grant, and James, and listened to all the fun games they had played on the car trip from Wagga Wagga. They lounged on the bed after strict instructions from their mother not to touch my legs. Even fourteen-year-old Blair lay in the huddle and shared favourite memories of Jessica and Samantha.

James patted my shoulder with a hand similar in size to Ryan's. "Is Ryan still sick?"

"Yes, bubba," Christine said. "Auntie Victoria has trouble talking, remember?"

"Yeah, I 'member the chat in the car, Mummy."

Patrick tilted his head toward the door. "How about you boys say goodbye to your auntie. She needs some rest."

Blair slid off the bed and kissed my cheek. "We're praying for you and Ry. My youth group are too."

Tears burned at the back of my eyes. "Th-anksss ... Bb-lair."

I hugged each young man before Dad, Mum and Patrick whisked them to the café downstairs.

Christine cozied up next to me on the bed and leaned her back against my pillow. "So, what now? Have you thought about Mr. Nasty's ultimatum?"

I sighed. I had thought long and hard for the past three days and still had not found a definitive answer. I struggled to reconcile in my mind—and in my heart—his apparent remorse against the picture of his violent arm destroying my cherished crystal vases. The image of his fist impacting my face. I needed to forgive Jude for the emotional pain he had inflicted on me for years and physical pain on that terrible day. But I also did not have to live with him because we were bound by marriage. "I ... think I ... shhhh-ould—"

"Mrs. Burke?"

Christine and I both gazed up.

"Y-yyesss?"

Dr. Singh had entered the room. "I apologise for the interruption, but I need to speak to you. I was in a meeting when you visited Ryan earlier."

I pointed to Christine. "Sss-sisss-ter." I pointed to Dr. Singh, moved my fingers in a talking motion, and gave him a thumbs up.

Christine snorted. "I think that's her way of saying you can speak, doctor."

I bobbed my head, and Dr. Singh grinned. "Okay." His face sobered. "A concerning development has occurred with Ryan's brain activity." He cleared his throat. "I spoke to your husband on the phone and need to make you aware of the situation." He pushed his glasses up on his nose. "The ICP has shown—"

"Sorry, doctor, but what's ICP?" Christine asked.

"ICP is Intracranial Pressure monitoring. We use it with our brain-trauma patients in ICU to monitor cerebrospinal fluid pressure in the head."

Christine and I nodded.

"ICP necessitated the initial surgery and now shows slight changes, but we cannot pinpoint the cause. Our staff will keep you updated."

I puffed out a long sigh and gave Dr. Singh a firm nod.

He turned on his heel and left the room.

What would I do if I lost Ryan too?

I blinked back tears which threatened to spill over. I *would not* think like this. Ryan would recover, and I would face the next difficult situation with my son by my side.

Jude: TIME'S TICKING. MAKE YOUR CHOICE.

My arms thrummed to smash my fist through something hard. I closed my eyes and blocked out my smartphone screen. Deep, slow breaths infiltrated my chest and expelled the heat which zinged inside me.

A week had passed since Jude gave me the ultimatum, and my transfer to a private rehabilitation centre closer to home would take place in a few days' time. Black Rock was still my home, even with all my reservations, but knowing Jude could visit me at any time put me on edge.

Footsteps approached my room. "You all set?" an orderly asked, his hands clasped over the handles of a wheelchair.

I pulled myself into a seated position on my bed and shifted my legs over the edge. The large bandages on my right leg were now replaced with a light layer of gauze and a compression-sock cover.

"Won't be long, and you'll be walking again."

I settled myself into the wheelchair with little assistance. My strength had increased along with my determination to recover from my wounds.

My vanity, which was deficient at best, had taken another blow when the fasciotomy surgery left behind an elongated scar from knee to ankle in a conspicuous line on the outside of my leg. A less noticeable scar on my left thigh, where the nurse accessed my femoral vein for my kidney treatment in ICU, was also added to the canvas of my skin. The specialist promised the scarring would lessen over time, but I knew it would always be unattractive.

We travelled along the familiar path from my ward to the ICU.

Ryan was still unconscious, but we had had a small win yesterday afternoon. He had squeezed my hand when I croaked his name. A positive amongst compounding negatives. His brain activity continued to fluctuate, the cause still unknown, and I continued to pray and believe Ryan would pass this hurdle and awake.

"H-hi, Ffflo," I said to Ryan's daytime shift nurse.

"Hello, beautiful mamma. Are you still on track to be discharged in a few days?"

I smiled and nodded.

"Good. Dr. Singh said he wanted to speak with you, so I'll see if he's free."

I reached out and touched Ryan's pale cheek.

Prickles of brown sprouted from his scalp. In another month or so, his hair would be long enough to hide the scars on his head.

I drank in all of his features, from his button nose similar to Jude's to the curvature of his soft ears. Ryan had generous earlobes like me, and his chin favoured my side of the family. His hairline resembled his grandfather's before Dad's hair thinned on top.

"Mrs. Burke."

I turned to face Dr. Singh.

"I wish I had better news."

My throat constricted.

"I am concerned about your son's lack of response to the tests we have performed."

My breath hitched. "W-what ... sort of t-tests?"

Dr. Singh removed his spectacles and pinched the bridge of his nose before he hooked the frames back over his ears. "Testing his brain activity.”

My chest crushed my lungs, and white spots danced in my vision. I moaned a soft sob. “B-but ... his hhhand m-moved.”

“I saw the note on his chart. Although encouraging, it’s not indicative of recovery.”

I clenched my jaw. Tears pooled in my eyes, and I blinked them back.

“We will perform some cranial nerve tests later today and an MRI and EEG tomorrow.”

My hands shook. “To de-deterrrrmine?”

“Whether he is brain dead.”

My chin quivered, and my body shook.

“I am sorry, Mrs. Burke. I will let you know the outcome of the tests, and we can discuss the situation further.”

I burst into tears.

“Come, darling, let’s get you settled in bed.”

I nodded to Mum after my arduous trek from the bathroom. Exhaustion blanketed me after a night of troubled sleep. Dr. Singh’s distressing words had played on a horrible, endless loop.

After the orderly had escorted me back to my room yesterday, I had messaged Christine and Mum. We had spent the afternoon in tears, prayer, and conversation. Everyone had returned to my hospital room in the morning. Patrick extended his leave so he could stay in Melbourne with his wife and children.

A nurse informed us of our meeting with Dr. Singh in his office at four o’clock. Patrick volunteered to stay with the boys while Dad, Mum, Christine and I attended. My chest tightened at the reality of Jude being present.

The next two hours were torturous for my nerves and heart.

Before long, Christine pushed my wheelchair into a small office with several chairs in front of a large glass-and-metal desk.

Dr. Singh waited at the modern workstation with his gaze glued to a computer screen. He tapped at a small keyboard. "Come in and sit."

Someone stood at the back of the room. I clenched my jaw, turned, and nodded to Jude in his custom-made suit and tie. How did he look so good when my life had unravelled at my feet?

Everyone occupied a chair. Dr. Singh scanned each face in the room before settling on mine. "Ryan suffered a brain haemorrhage overnight. We believe it began with an undetectable slow bleed to the brain." He lifted his shoulders. "After extensive testing, I regret to inform you that your son is brain dead."

A strangled sob rose to my throat. This could not be happening. Not my baby boy!

Tears coursed down my face, my vision a blur of saltwater. My chest burned, my lungs unable to perform under the weight of the news. Arms wrapped around my shoulders, a mass of shuddering limbs and broken people. I bawled, my body limp and listless. Life was unfair!

A surge of heat rose inside, and I screamed. The web of arms pressed tighter against me, and I soaked in their strength. Their kindness. Their love.

Today ended any plans I might have hoped for the future. My life was stripped bare, my pain exposed, and my heart bled.

Dr. Singh's lips continued to move. Who cared what he said? Life was over, my hope once again trodden under the feet of death. My heart gaped with the latest puncture wound inflicted in a cruel twist of my imperfect existence.

"Victoria?"

I blinked.

Christine's face appeared in front of me. "What do you think?"

"Huh?"

Her eyes softened. "Organ donation. Ryan could save lives."

I shuddered and wrapped my arms around my waist. I had entered the twilight zone. Turning my head, I found Jude's tear-filled face.

He ran a hand across his eyes, and his shoulders slumped. His head bobbed.

I turned back to Christine, blew out a breath, and sighed. "Y-yes."

I tried to listen to everything Dr. Singh had to say, but I zoned out when he communicated about scans to test organ-transplant viability.

What did it matter? My son would never wake up. Whether his entire body lay in a box in the ground or parts of him remained made no difference to me.

Ryan was not coming back.

Jude and I signed a stack of release documents so the hospital could move forward with their tests and potential surgeries. All I wanted was to hug my son one last time.

The opportunity to say goodbye approached later in the evening. After numerous tests, Ryan's heart, liver, both kidneys and pancreas were deemed fit for transplant surgery. Five people would be given a second chance at life because of Ryan's gifts.

My family helped me sit on Ryan's bed and surrounded me while I embraced my son. Warm to the touch and linked to a plethora of machines with cables, tubes and cords, he still appeared alive. His chest lifted on each ventilated breath, but he was far too still for sleep. I mourned the once familiar warmth of his body snuggled against mine, a habit formed as a toddler when he climbed into my bed at night.

Ryan was gone.

I kissed his soft cheeks with my tear-stained lips and touched the spikes of hair on his head. I ached to run my fingers through his baby-soft curls one last time.

Patrick snapped final photos of my baby and me while my nephews leaned against the bed and said their final, tearful goodbyes to their little cousin.

Jude entered the room with a bowed head.

A swell of juxtaposed emotions filled my chest, but grief won over my anger, and I reached out an arm for him. He deserved the right to this final moment with his son.

Jude stepped close, his body shuddering on each breath. We cried with our arms around our son, our three heads pressed together.

The end of the journey had come. Our family of five had been whittled to three. Now we were severed again, and I could not imagine my life here anymore.

Discharged from the hospital the day after I hugged Ryan for the final time, I transferred to the rehabilitation centre along with my broken dreams. I relied on a wheelchair the afternoon of his funeral, relieved to attend the service with fellow mourners. Ryan was buried beside his sisters at the local cemetery, where my family gave me privacy to visit Jessica and Samantha's graves.

The tiresome days of retraining my body to walk and my mouth to talk—a process filled with physical, mental and soul-stabbing pain—turned into weeks. My patient physiotherapist encouraged me, but he also pushed my body. Hard. My speech therapist suspected my speech issues resulted from expressive aphasia and was overjoyed when my prayers and conversations erupted into sentences longer than three words seven weeks after the accident.

My new home was simple but functional. An adjustable single bed filled the centre of the room accompanied by a small wooden bedside table and metal desk lamp. A low coffee table nestled near a grey two-seater couch which hunkered under a large window with a view to the car park. Tucked into a corner beside a storage cupboard balanced a small, wheeled table, which I used to eat my meals in bed.

My parents were at my bedside most afternoons to lift my spirits, like they had at the hospital, although some days I wished everyone would leave me alone. Amber popped in for visits around work shifts and school duties. She smuggled in decadent pastries every Saturday morning for a sneaky brunch.

Christine drove down a few times to sit by my bedside. She updated me on the latest family news and helped me with the prescribed physiotherapy routine. She sacrificed her time to be with me, and I loved her all the more for it.

I wanted her to stay longer and visit more often, but I understood all too well the responsibility of raising a family, running a home, and paying the bills on time. My chest constricted, and I rasped shallow breaths. I ignored the sting of tears and pressed my hands against my thighs. All that remained was my job, not the important people who had infused my life with joy.

"Hey, cuz." Christine thrust her arms out toward our cousin, Sergeant Steve Morgan, who walked into my private room at the centre. A respected Victoria Police Officer, he had been granted permission to be our case liaison regarding the fatal collision.

"Hey, gorgeous. How's the family?"

I winced and discharged a deep, calming breath. Life still rolled along for everyone else.

Christine relayed the latest antics of her sons while Dad and Mum embraced him.

A memory flashed through my mind, and I clenched my hands. Ryan grinned, dressed in Jessica's black dance tights with his Spiderman T-shirt and undies, and charged down the hallway to Jessica's bedroom with Samantha cackling behind him.

I lowered my head and brushed away an errant tear.

Steve dropped his bag on the floor, settled on the edge of my bed, and pulled me into a warm embrace. "Hey, beautiful."

"Hey, Stevie." I pressed a gentle kiss to his scruffy cheek.

"You ready for this?"

I nodded.

Steve stepped back to his bag and emptied its contents onto the small, wheeled table.

He had telephoned the day before to say he had sensitive information to share. The promise of closure the police report offered was cold comfort but better than nothing since my memory of the accident was hazy.

I glanced at the few chosen photographs of the accident site and almost vomited.

"Oh, Vicki," Christine breathed out.

Dad, Mum, Christine, and I cried silent tears, our gazes drawn to the photos.

They depicted a scene worse than any action film or horror movie I had ever seen. Fractured shells of vehicles were melded together in three connected piles of twisted metal with mountain ash and stringy gum shrapnel splintered all over the site. Large sections of these felled trees impaled vehicles and their unfortunate inhabitants; the finer details obscured by an edited blur of the sensitive images.

The remnants of my vehicle came into view, triggering a new stream of tears down my face. The crushed driver's side door of my X1 was the sole visible panel of my car. The weighted sections of a 4-axle semi-trailer, the source of the collision, compressed the rear of my vehicle.

I shook my head, my mouth open. How had Ryan survived the initial crash?

Steve cleared his throat. "The truck driver's blood alcohol concentration more than doubled the legal limit."

"Such a waste," Mum said. "We have laws for a reason."

Steve regarded my face with downturned lips. "Forensics confirm Jessica and Samantha died on impact." He cleared his throat a second time. "Their suffering would've been very brief, if at all."

I had no desire to dwell on how Ryan might have suffered and was grateful for Steve's restraint. "Thanks for coming," I whispered.

My will to live was at an all-time low during the gruelling weeks of rehabilitation. I spent much of my free time immersed in Scripture or playing a podcast or sermon in the background to assuage my depression. I slept between therapy sessions and cried an ocean of tears. No one begrudged me time to mourn, but I knew my spirit needed to surpass the pain I endured. I prayed and exercised, and my faith stretched like my limbs.

Jude visited several times over the next eight-week period. I humoured his hints for reconciliation in the early weeks while my speech was still hindered and my thoughts laborious to verbalise. But I soon grew tired of how sorry he was for everything. Sorry for how he had treated me. Sorry for being unfaithful. Sorry for leaving me that afternoon to clean the mess alone.

Yet in the next breath he would accuse me of ruining our life together, denying him forgiveness. His complaints would fill the majority of his visits. How my selfishness living in a rehabilitation centre affected him when I could relearn to walk at home or the unnecessary cost of a housekeeper to perform my duties. Jude even accused me of sabotaging our marriage because my lack of interest had pushed him back into his secretary's arms. The more I saw him, the more I wanted to get far away from his toxicity.

One evening in mid-March, Jude announced he had slept with our babysitter. Alexa was our long-legged, vivacious young neighbour. She had supervised the children on the rare nights Jude and I would go out or on evenings I had work commitments. The last time she had watched the children was a week before the accident when I had to attend the Secondary Presentation Night at Haileybury.

I imagined Alexa's long legs wrapped around Jude's body, her pouty lips on his. Had they slept in my bed? My heart pounded, and heat flushed through my body.

"Can't you keep your pants on for a second? You're unbelievable, Jude!"

He narrowed his eyes. "What do you expect me to do when

you're here twenty-four hours a day without a hint of affection. I have needs, Victoria."

I gaped. "Are you being serious? You have needs?" I spat a sardonic laugh. "So, it's fine for me to stay chaste for months when you weren't interested, but you're allowed to have women on the side?" Chills shivered down my spine. My gaze bore into his face. "You make me sick."

His eyes darkened, and his voice quavered low. "How dare you speak to me like this." He stepped close to where I occupied the bed. "My life flushed down the proverbial toilet because of your selfish, stupid decisions." He straightened and eyed me with a cold stare. "You ran away and murdered my children," he said, his voice gruff. "You're a selfish, unfeeling cow and brought this on us. This is all your fault."

My hands shook. I wanted to scream, rip out his hair, claw at his beautiful face, and slap him senseless, but I knew I would regret my actions the moment I stooped to his level. I pressed the assistance button next to my bed before Jude could stop me.

A male staff member entered my room. "Do you need anything, Victoria?"

Jude stared me down. "No, everything's fine."

"Are you sure, Victoria?"

I released a deep breath and murmured a silent prayer for wisdom. "Please remove my husband from this room."

To my great relief, the centre staff asked Jude to cease his visits.

Our final interaction kicked me into gear. I arranged for Steve to accompany my parents to collect the children's and my personal belongings from what used to be our home. Now homeless but more at peace than I had been in months, I farewelled my past life and reached toward the new and unknown.

CHAPTER SIX
Moving Forward

"Hey, beautiful." Steve arrived for his usual Tuesday afternoon visit.

I turned and grinned at the face in front of me. "Hey, Stevie! Thank you so much for helping Mum and Dad sort out my things. I hope Jude didn't cause you any issues when you grabbed my stuff?"

Steve bent and kissed my forehead before he reclined on the seat next to my bed. "Nah, he wasn't there."

Now three weeks after my altercation with Jude, I idled on my bed, Bible in hand, my mind filled with the endless possibilities ahead of me.

"I ensured Uncle Pete and Aunt Jacki were safe and sound, and I carried your heavy suitcases down those awful stairs. You need to find a better place next time."

A laugh died in my throat. A better place. I lived in Black Rock, a suburb many Melburnians dreamed of living in, but I doubted a better place existed without my babies.

My heart hurt again, and my vision clouded. "Hmm, yeah. Thanks for the tip."

Steve winked. "Anytime. Now. How's the patient? Stacy wanted to visit, but Toby has a cold. My little man needed extra hugs on the couch."

"The little man." I blinked back the wetness in my eyes and fought against the rising heat in my chest. No mummy hugs on the couch for me. "Send my love to Stacy and give Toby a big hug from me."

Stacy had been a close friend in secondary school. We were snobbish English literature and history comrades. Steve and Stacy finally met at my twenty-first birthday after I had sprouted the virtues of my cousin to Stacy for years, and they had tied the knot seven years ago. Stacy was a successful barrister and had put a lot of her life on hold until recent years.

Steve reached into his jacket pocket, unfolded a thin document, and handed it to me. He shrugged. "It's better than nothing."

I skimmed through the car insurance papers until I spotted the all-important payout cheque. I swallowed a sob. So little money? I should have insisted Jude pay the higher premium for agreed value instead of market value. I sighed and refolded the papers. "Please thank Stacy for arranging this. I know it's far beneath the likes of her usual work, and I'm thankful she offered."

Steve's eyes sparkled. "I'll pass your message on. Stace was so relieved you owned the vehicle and not ... him. It would've been much more complicated to access the funds if you'd smashed his car. Like I'd love to do to his pretty face."

Happiness eclipsed my heart when I thought of Jude at the mercy of my saint of a cousin. A nervous laugh bubbled in my chest. I brushed aside my guilty conscience, placed the papers on my nightstand, and turned back to Steve.

"Vicki?" A frown creased the angular features of his face.

"Yeah?"

He cleared his throat. "If you need anything ... absolutely anything when you're discharged in a few weeks, I want you to know Stacy and I will do everything in our power to help. Stacy's already started building your legal case for divorce, so you'll get the best outcome possible when the time comes. We have a guest room always available to you. Or even one of the investment properties up north you could use?"

I reached out to squeeze his hand. "I appreciate your kindness.

But ..."

"But what?" If Steve could gather me up and pack me in cotton wool to keep me safe for the rest of my life, I knew he would not hesitate to do so.

I sighed. "I need a change. A real change. If my life has ever qualified for midlife crisis status, it's now. I need to find a quiet town to lay low and heal." I gave a half-hearted shrug. "Or something like that."

He stared at me with pensive eyes and leaned across to kiss my forehead. "Okay. Make sure there's a nice BnB in the area so Stacy and I can visit."

"I promise."

Steve said goodbye and left the room the moment my vision blurred with tears. How could I tell my family I wanted to escape catching glimpses of their happy lives? Steve still had a wife and son to dote on. Christine still had the privilege of packing lunches for her boys, and Amber still chaired the school parent committee for her kids. But me? I had nothing. No one.

I snatched the insurance papers and threw them on the floor. A sob wrenched in my rib cage as I imagined Stacy cradling Toby on the couch, ensconced in a blanket and toddler-approved television. A flashback to Patrick holding Christine firm against his chest stabbed into my heart and unleashed another waterfall of tears.

♥ ♥ ♥ ♥ ♥ ♥

"Jude called me last night." I reclined on the floor of my room in a tracksuit with my leg stretched like the physiotherapist had shown me while Amber lounged on my bed. I pretended the words I uttered had not twisted my gut and bombarded my mind with anxious thoughts.

Amber rolled her eyes. "Why?"

I leaned forward and extended my arms toward my toes. "He apologised for what happened the last time he visited. He wants to see me." A shudder coursed through my body.

Her eyes widened. "What did you say?"

I relaxed from the stretch and shrugged. "I told him not to call again, hung up, and blocked his number. Finally." I shook my head.

"What does he want?"

I pursed my lips and stretched forward again. "He sounded annoyed, angry. Said I owed him for destroying his happiness. I cut him off mid-sentence." I blew out a breath. "I'm contemplating a move away from Melbourne. Away from the memories, but mainly to be away from him." *And your marital bliss.* I gritted my teeth and stretched.

Amber nodded. "I figured as much from the cryptic message you sent me a few days ago. So, what's the plan? Are you starting with a location or looking for a job role to fill?"

I eyed Amber, shrugged, then turned and continued to stretch my right leg. My calf muscle twitched with the beginnings of a cramp, and I grimaced.

Amber helped me stand and rest on my bed.

She had been my closest friend since attending my church one Sunday morning almost eighteen years ago. A twinge stung my heart as I contemplated a life far away from her. It would be the first time in seventeen years we lived farther than twenty kilometres apart. The most thoughtful woman I had ever known, Amber understood a sea change was the best decision I had determined in years. I trusted her judgment better than my own.

"I say start with the location, then find the best-fitting job in the area."

"Hmm. I was thinking along those lines." I hugged my friend and enjoyed the embrace.

Not the tight hugs I once shared with Ryan when I tucked him into bed at night, or an awkward but loving side hug with my tweenager, Jessica. I thought of Samantha and her dislike of physical affection. I had relished any time she had climbed onto my lap for a movie night, with popcorn overflowing from our bowls and a favourite movie on the television like *Despicable Me* or *Princess Diaries*.

I smiled at the memories and promised myself to write them down before they faded with time—if it were in the realm of possibility to forget shared moments with my children.

Amber squeezed my shoulder. "Mike and I wanted to give you a little something to help with your move." She presented a crisp pink envelope, her face aglow.

"Thank you." Tears welled in my eyes. I smiled at the swirled handwriting on the front.

"You haven't even opened it. How do you know you want it?"

I giggled and turned the envelope over in my hand. Breathlessness rose in my chest. I ripped across the top of the vanilla-scented package to reveal a small white piece of folded paper. A voucher for a day spa? Makeover? Manicure and pedicure?

I unfolded the paper and gasped at a bank cheque in my name. "T-two thousand dollars? I ... I'm ... speechless." Tears gushed down my cheeks and onto my tracksuit pants.

Amber drew me into a warm hug. "So long as you don't break out in song like a Disney Princess, I can live with your speechlessness. I'm sorry it's not more, but it's what Mike and I can give right now. We love you. You deserve to start afresh, babe. You do have your own bank account, yeah?"

"That much I do have ... if nothing else."

Amber cupped my shoulder. "Chin up, Vic. You'll get through this stronger than before. Who knows? Perhaps when the time's right, you may end up with a joint bank account again"—she waggled her eyebrows—"amongst other things."

A bellow of laughter erupted from deep inside me when, for the first time in months, I imagined life with someone else.

The moment passed in a breath, and the reality of my situation sunk in. My laughter died, and insurmountable despair gripped my insides.

Life would never be the same without my little butterballs.

♥ ♥ ♥ ♥ ♥ ♥ ♥

"What's all this?" I counted eleven additional settings from our usual dinner for three, plus a highchair. I had moved back into my childhood home.

"Just preparing for dinner." Mum positioned woven placemats within her reach before stretching across the pine dining table—its length now extended at the ends—and slid the remaining mats into place. "Since you missed your birthday and Christmas, we thought you'd like to celebrate."

I furrowed my brows. "But I already said I don't need a party."

She lay a dinner plate on each placemat. "It's not only for you, darling. Christine and the boys struggled with their separation over Christmas, so I wanted some family time while they visit this weekend."

Christine found it hard to be separated? From *her* children? My heartbeat escalated. What about me? Was my pain forgotten? I would never again share Christmas morning with my children. I turned my head and swiped at a tear.

Mum fussed over the table arrangements. "Our guests will be here soon."

I trudged up the stairs and sat rigid on my single bed. The floral doona cover was a relic from my teen years along with the small desk and wheeled chair in the corner of my bedroom. Even the Care Bears lampshade I received for my fifth birthday balanced on the same wooden bedside table almost thirty years later.

I fisted the bedlinen in both hands and punched into the mattress. Tears wet my cheeks. The neon digital clock beside my bed flicked over another digit, and I groaned. Almost five o'clock. With a sigh, I dragged myself into the shower to look presentable for unwanted company tonight.

Thirty minutes later, I opened my bedroom door and caught the shrill giggles of a toddler. Sucking in a breath, I flexed my shoulders. I could do this.

Happy laughter and chitchat amplified each step I trod down the stairs. A simulated smile touched my lips when I entered the lounge room.

"Vic! You look great!" Amber leaned in for a hug before Mike kissed my forehead.

My nephews and Amber and Mike's two children waved from the floor near their Lego fort.

Christine crushed her arms around me. "You do look great, sis."

"Thanks."

Steve and Stacy peppered me with kisses before Stacy thrust Toby into my arms. "Here, I need to pee. Give Auntie Victoria a kiss, Toby."

He pressed a wet kiss to my cheek.

A soft laugh gurgled from my throat. What a gorgeous little boy. He reminded me of a younger Ryan. My smile dimmed, and I handed Toby to Steve with shaky hands.

"Dinnertime!" Mum waved her hands and shooed everyone from the room.

Blair prayed over the meal before conversations flowed about work, family commitments, and the marriage seminar at church. A party for me and my family discussed marriage?

I chewed with slow bites and struggled to consume each mouthful. My appetite had absconded with the usual quiet of the house.

Across the table, Patrick had his arm draped across Christine's shoulders while he spoke to Dad. Christine smiled at Patrick between mouthfuls and leaned into his side.

I forced another forkful of chicken into my mouth.

Amber nudged my arm. "You haven't eaten much."

I shrugged and chewed.

"You want to talk about it?"

"Not really." I excused myself and carried my half-eaten dinner to the kitchen, where I scraped my plate and stacked it into the dishwasher.

"What's wrong?" Christine had followed me.

Great. "Nothing."

She crossed her arms. "I know you, Vicki. You're upset. What's up?"

I gritted my teeth.

"Would you spit it out already?" She arched an eyebrow.

I peered out the kitchen window and glimpsed the ancient swing set my children had loved to use. I ground my molars and turned. Photos of Jessica and Samantha tormented me from the fridge door. I clenched my fists. "Everyone here is happy, talking about marriage seminars, hugging their husbands, and loving their children. No one understands what it's like for me." I brushed tears from my cheeks.

Christine's warm hand touched my arm. "We're so sorry. We miss those babies so much."

I stepped away and crossed my arms. "But you have your children. And your husband. And your house."

She shook her head. "We lost them too, you know."

I hissed a bitter laugh. "Please. You have no idea. I live in our parents' house in my old room ... like a failure!" My lungs choked. "My husband likes to beat the crap out of me, my children are dead, and you think you know how I feel? Really?"

Tears trickled down Christine's face and dripped off her chin.

My shallow breaths induced dizziness, and I grasped the kitchen bench.

"We've all suffered with you," Christine said between sniffs. "It's been painful to experience and watch what happened to you."

I flailed my arms. "Exactly! It happened to me! This is *my* life gone, not yours! I wish you'd flaunt it less in front of me."

Christine's eyes and mouth widened. "Flaunt it! How am I flaunting my life by living and breathing?"

Dad stepped into the kitchen. "What's going on?"

Silence had apparently settled on the house while I yelled at my sister.

I wheezed. "Nothing. I'm going to bed." I pushed past Christine, lurched up the stairs, and slammed my bedroom door. With a heave and a groan, I flopped onto the bed and screamed into my pillow.

CHAPTER SEVEN
The Great Escape

"Victoria?"

I burrowed deeper under the covers of my bed when Mum tapped on the door. Was it too much to ask for a little peace and quiet on a Saturday morning?

Hinges creaked before soft footsteps padded across the carpet. The mattress dipped near my thigh, and a gentle weight rested on the curve of my hip.

"Darling, I know you're awake. Don't you want to come down for breakfast?"

I lay still and breathed slow and deep.

"Dad and Patrick went fishing, but Christine and the boys are downstairs eating. They'd love to see you."

I doubted that, not after the way I had treated Christine last night.

Soft, soothing strokes brushed against my side. Mum had motherhood perfected.

I clamped my eyes shut against the sting of tears. My chance at motherhood was over. I pressed my lips together to contain a whimper.

Mum sighed. The weight near my thigh lifted a few moments before my door squeaked shut.

Wet streaks coursed across my cheek and soaked my pillow. My chest burned, and a moan spilled out, followed by a muffled cry.

I had lashed out at Christine like a hormonal teenager. A hormonal, *envious* teenager upset at her friend for kissing the boy she liked. But Patrick had nothing to do with my reaction. The love and affection he gave his wife was what I craved. His devotion to her, to the boys. To God. Things any decent man could give. Things now vacant from my life.

My hot breaths thickened the air under the covers. How could I make my family understand everything inside me—my desperation and unhappiness, the torture of my mind and my brokenness which seemed incurable—before I destroyed every remaining relationship?

I uncovered my head in the darkened room. The hint of a name glowed in the stars stuck to the ceiling, their light faded to a faint lustre. I ground my teeth, turned to my side, and cursed my sixteen-year-old self and her infatuation with Jude.

A blue light flashed on my phone. Text messages from a disgruntled sister? Pulling myself up with a sigh, I reached for my phone.

Amber: CALL ME IF YOU NEED TO TALK. XX

Stacy: I HOPE YOU SLEPT WELL. YOU UP FOR A TOBY-FREE COFFEE NEXT WEEK?

Christine: I LOVE YOU. :)

Fresh tears ran down my cheeks. Could I stay in Melbourne, knowing my loved ones had my back, and become a whole person again? Their simple messages comforted me, but how many arguments or pangs of envy would I endure before becoming the person I used to be? Or a better version of myself?

I dropped the phone on my bedside table, climbed out of bed, and opened the curtains. The welcome April sunshine warmed my skin.

Clean and dressed, I descended the stairs and greeted Mum with a kiss.

"Christine went outside."

"Thanks, Mum." I stuffed a pancake in my mouth and headed for the sliding door. Cold air hit my face and sent a shiver down my back. I stepped out into the sunlight, spotted Christine on one of the swings and flopped next to her on a rubber seat. "You think we'll break these?"

"Probably."

I pushed off with a laugh and enjoyed the cool breeze on my face, whipping my ponytail behind me. "We're a bit heavier than we were thirty years ago."

Christine snorted. "Just a tad."

A lump lodged in my throat, and I swallowed. "I'm sorry about last night."

"I know."

"It sucks to be me at the moment." I tilted my head back and watched a cloud in the sky.

"I also know you're not into Patrick."

I stared at Christine. "Definitely not into him. That's ... gross."

Christine burst out into loud laughter. "Thanks a lot! He's my husband, yanno."

My cheeks burned. "I didn't mean it like that. It's, well ... he's like a brother."

"I get it. Like Mike and Steve."

I wrinkled my nose. "Yeah, them too. That's ... sick."

Christine laughed again. "I'll have to tell Stacy and Amber the next time I see them."

I sucked in a deep breath, a lightness in my chest sending a smile to my face.

Although forgiveness freed me now, how many days would pass before something or someone triggered my frustration again? I gazed over the backyard, and a flood of memories filled my mind. Could I continue to ride this wave, surrounded by constant reminders of what I had lost?

No. The time to move on had arrived. I owed it not only to my loved ones, but also to myself to heal.

♥ ♥ ♥ ♥ ♥ ♥ ♥

"Seeking an experienced English teacher for Tellarine Secondary College in Tellarine, Victoria. Twenty-five kilometres south-east of Robinvale. Full-time position with usual benefits. Immediate start."

Dad leaned back from the computer monitor and seesawed his shoulders in an effort to stretch. "Seems like the perfect scenario in an area on the map you designated. See?" He leaned forward and clicked the computer mouse onto another tab. The little town of Tellarine appeared on a map. Dad pointed at a larger neighbouring city. "Look, darling, it's ninety minutes from Mildura airport. You have the experience required, and with an immediate start, they must be in a real pickle. Potential leverage for your negotiations."

I scrunched my brow. I had chosen to start my job search south of the New South Wales border, away from all things familiar and haunting. Although the prospect of beginning again had its positives, my parents living far from family distressed me.

Mum leaned into my shoulder on the small couch seat we shared in Dad's office and squeezed my hand. "Darling, your father and I aren't getting any younger. Christine's intimated for years for us to move closer to her. Tellarine would be a five-hour drive to Wagga Wagga. I know your father would be interested in relocating sooner if you moved north." She gave me a conspiratorial wink.

"That's a thought."

The doorbell chimed. Mum leaned forward.

I lay a hand on her lap. "I'll get it." My stomach and heart buzzed with each step. Could I make this big move away from everyone to some little backward town in Woop Woop? If Dad and Mum moved north near Christine, seeing my family would be so much easier. And my parents would not be alone. Perhaps this could work?

The corners of my mouth lifted as I turned the door handle.

"Can I help—"

"Hi, baby."

My pulse rebounded against my throat as my gaze darted to the face behind the screen door. "What do you want, Jude?"

His pleading gaze searched mine through the honeycomb metal protection.

Thank God for security doors.

"I wanted to see you."

I glared at his still handsome face. "You've seen me. Now you can go."

He smiled a perfect grin. "I expected better from you, Victoria."

I glanced at the door handle, tempted to open the door and shove it against his perfect nose. "The feeling's mutual."

Any humour on his face vanished. "Baby, I've said I'm sorry for everything. I ... I want us to start again." He rubbed a hand over his firm chest. "Standing here throws me back decades. I feel like the nervous boy waiting for his girlfriend."

I sighed, drained from the roiling inside my heart. "Jude. Please. Let's not make this any harder. We're—"

"Who's at the door?"

I spun around, wide-eyed.

Dad stepped around the corner and halted. His face morphed from its pleasant smile to a snarling lip and fiery gaze. He stomped to the door and stood between me and it. "What do you want?"

Dad's growling tone sent a shiver through me. I placed a hand on his back. The muscles vibrated, taut and alert. I breathed a prayer of peace.

Jude's jaw tightened, and he shifted on his feet. "I'm here for my wife."

"Not on my watch, boy." Dad straightened to his six-foot-one height, half a head taller than Jude. "You lost that privilege the moment you laid a hand on her, you ..." Dad sucked in a breath. "You won't hurt my baby girl again. Now, get ... off ... my ... property." He spoke through his teeth, his voice low and tone menacing.

My feet rooted to the floor.

Dad reached for the wooden door handle. "If you step foot on my land again, I'll have you arrested for trespassing."

My body shook. I closed my eyes to the click of the entry door.

Dad enveloped me in his strong arms. "You're okay, darling. You're okay." He kissed the top of my head. "I love you."

Thickness clogged my throat. "I love you too, Daddy," I whispered.

He led me back to his office, where Mum leaned forward on the couch. I flicked my gaze to the computer screen, the small country town of Tellarine front and centre.

Mum reached out, and I fell into her embrace.

Jude would never stop, and my healing would never happen here. I needed sound guidance, and I needed it now. I sighed, closed my eyes, and breathed a quiet prayer. The biblical story of Abraham and his faith journey away from all things familiar and loved filled my mind. I opened my eyes with dampened lashes. "Dad, please keep the computer tab open for the school in Tellarine. I'll send through my application once I'm back from Haileybury this afternoon."

My heart lightened with the promise of a new tomorrow. I missed my children so much—a physical ache prodded my heart at times—but I knew they would want me to live with purpose. To step out in faith and take hold of the dreams in my heart. To be bold and courageous.

To do all the things I had encouraged them to do.

Jessica's favourite verse floated into my memory, and her young, yet strong voice spoke to my heart: *And the peace of God, which surpasses all understanding, will guard your heart and thoughts ...*

Unlocking my car in the Haileybury car park, I dialled Mum's phone number and threw my handbag on the passenger seat.

"Hey, darling, you all done?"

"Yes, said my goodbyes and have in my possession a written reference." I lay back against the headrest and clicked the seatbelt into place. "You need anything while I'm out?"

"Hmm, let me see."

I surveyed the nearby buildings with misted eyes and imagined my past students tapping on their laptops, studious and focused on their work. I brushed a finger under my eye and blinked. I would miss this place.

"You still there, darling?" Mum sounded out of breath.

"Yes. You running a marathon?"

She chuckled. "I was in the garden when you called. Okay, we need milk, please. And maybe some of those special chocolate truffle things you like to melt for your indulgent hot chocolate? I think we should indulge this afternoon."

"Sounds perfect. I'll see you soon."

"Okay, love you."

Milk in hand, I scanned the chocolate aisle for my favourite dark chocolate Lindt balls. I grinned when I located them with a discounted price tag. Reaching out to grab the glossy black bag, my shoulder bumped a woman to my right. "Oh, I'm so sorry I—"

"Mrs. Burke!"

I gaped, and blood surged through my veins and thundered in my head.

My former babysitter assessed me with a sorrowful expression. "I'm so—"

"Don't, Alexa." Fire burned a trail down my spine. My jaw hardened, and my nostrils flared. "How dare you look sad after what you did to me? You should be ashamed of your actions."

Alexa's face paled. She stared at me with wide eyes and a slack mouth. A small V formed in her brow. "W-what do you mean?"

I narrowed my eyes and stepped close. "I mean your little romp in the hay with Jude."

The furrow in her brow deepened. "My ... my what?"

I growled. "You heard me. I trusted you, and you betrayed me!"

Her half-filled shopping basket slid into the crook of her elbow when she lifted her hands high like someone surrendering at gunpoint. "Mrs. Burke, I-I don't know what you heard or what M-Mr. Burke said, b-but I didn't do anything with him." Tears pooled in her eyes. "You th-think I slept with him?"

My chest heaved with oxygen deprivation, and my cheeks flamed. I fumbled with the milk container and gazed down.

Alexa steadied the plastic bottle in my hand. "I'm sorry, Mrs. Burke. My heart bled for your children, but please believe me. I never slept with Mr. Burke. I could never do that to you."

I dipped my head and blinked back tears. Jude lied to me? Why be so cruel? I swallowed against rising bile, my cheeks on fire. "I-I apologise, Alexa. I ..."

With a trembling hand, she handed me the packet of chocolate I had failed to grab. "Enjoy your hot chocolate. You deserve it." With tears in her eyes and a small smile, she turned and walked away.

My gaze glued to the floor, I brushed aside a tear and scurried to the checkouts at the end of the aisle, my face and ears burning.

CHAPTER EIGHT
First Impressions

I blew out a sigh and shook off the threatening shroud of loneliness. The distance back to Melbourne multiplied with each kilometre, along with the jitters in my hands. What a contrast to last night's festivities.

I hunched behind the wheel of my blue Mazda 3. The early morning chill had seeped into my little car overflowing with my scant possessions. I glanced in the rear-view mirror and spotted the extra items friends and family had gifted me at an impromptu farewell party Amber threw last night. I appreciated seeing familiar faces on my final night in Melbourne and had handled myself with more grace than when Mum had sprung guests on me three weeks earlier.

I eyed the clouds, reminded of the silver linings in my circumstances. I was alive and embarking on a new journey. A new beginning.

Living five hours from Melbourne had its positives. The absence of Jude being the number one advantage, avoiding Alexa a close second. My cheeks warmed. Milk and Lindt truffles were forever tainted with last week's humiliation. I pushed back the memory.

Tremors travelled down my arms, and a heavy, wet blanket wrapped my heart. Could I start again? Alone? I bit my lower lip and stared at the straight road ahead. Why had I left my sole support network? How had my family allowed me to leave?

I gripped the steering wheel with stiff fingers. My family loved me and had agreed with my decision. If Amber thought I had lost my mind, she would have stopped me. Instead, she had supported me and had even helped me with tonight's Airbnb accommodation booked with a local family. The tightness in my chest eased, and hope snuck out of the confines of the invading darkness. Amber had shared her concerns over the potential isolation of my new life—concerns I also held—but she never stopped me.

I focused on the road and my house-hunting plans for tomorrow before I peered at the dashboard clock. I relaxed my shoulders. An early arrival for my two o'clock appointment with Principal Marsden was still within reach. I wanted time to freshen up before the meeting.

My stomach squirmed, and my nerves needled me. I had already secured the job, and things would go well unless Principal Marsden probed me with personal questions. Then who knew the impression I would leave?

"Victoria Burke?" A tall redhead with a pinched nose stood in the doorway of the principal's office.

I smiled, grabbed my bag, and approached her.

"I'm Sandra Fishbourne, Principal Marsden's assistant."

"Pleased to meet you."

Sandra ushered me inside the room before she stepped back and closed the door.

A stout middle-aged woman in a navy skirt suit and starched white shirt stood next to a large oak desk and clasped my outstretched hand in a firm shake. "Elsbeth Marsden. Wonderful to meet you, Ms. Burke." She glowed with an affectionate smile.

"Thank you, Principal Marsden. I'm excited to be here."

She offered me a cushioned chair in front of her desk and

returned her plump girth to a large executive swivel chair. "After Mrs. Donald's sudden resignation—for personal reasons—I was excited to receive your resume. We have not engaged a teacher on staff with this much experience since Mr. Briggs joined our team a few years ago." She stared at the paperwork on her desk. "You have achieved a great deal during your career and with glowing references too. I had several principals return my calls, saddened by their loss, urging me to offer you a position. I accepted their advice, and I am overjoyed you accepted."

My cheeks heated and I ducked my head. Recognition never fuelled my choice to teach English. I had compromised to stay sane and, now, my job served as one of my few remaining joys. I was surprised to be informed of my impact on peers and superiors.

I refocused on Principal Marsden's kind face. "I'm grateful for the offer and hope the bar isn't set too high after that report." Nervous laughter bubbled in my chest.

Her hearty chuckle stilled my nerves. "Do not concern yourself. All I ask is you give your utmost to our students and provide them the best start in life through education, encouragement and sincerity. We are the sole secondary school within a twenty-kilometre radius, so our responsibility to the community is critical."

I nodded at the gravity of my new role and lifted a thankful prayer in my heart for the opportunity to teach and nurture the youth of Tellarine and beyond.

Principal Marsden shifted in her seat. A thoughtful expression crossed her features. "I do have one question to ask in strict confidence. Regarding your personal situation." She cleared her throat. "When speaking with two referees, they mentioned your husband ... and children. I do not wish to pry, but your application is marked 'Ms.' without mention of family in any of your documentation."

I thought how best to respond, determined not to cry even though my circumstances left me on the brink of tears. I had moved to Tellarine for a new start. My past hurts needed to stay in the past if I were to have any chance of a future here.

Principal Marsden leaned in. Her arms rested on my paperwork. "Ms. Burke. Victoria, dear. Are you able to shed light on these discrepancies?" She shuddered a breath. "I am sure you understand staff and student safety is paramount."

I wobbled a smile and breathed. In. Out. "My husband and I are separated. A divorce should be granted next year." I pulled my shoulders back and clasped my hands. "Staff and students have nothing to fear by my presence."

She squinted and focused on my face.

I pinched the back of my hand and stared at her. I could not mention the children without tears spilling over.

She pursed her lips and I blinked. After a few moments, she nodded. "Very well." Her chair groaned as she stood. "How about a tour?"

I stood and followed Principal Marsden out of her office. We toured the grounds and the four main wings of the school. The vastness of the campus surprised me.

We poked our heads through the doorway of the VCE English classroom, where a class discussed John Donne poems. Principal Marsden lowered her voice and said, "This will be your headquarters, where you will spend the majority of your time."

I examined the room and quelled my nerves.

"I will entrust our Year Eleven and Twelve students into your capable hands, with the possibility of one Year Ten class. Sandra will give you keys and an access pass on Monday."

We continued our conversation along the corridors. My tour concluded in the administration hub of the school when we reached the Staff Lounge.

She ducked her head inside the doorway. "This room is self-explanatory. Staff bathrooms are through to the left, with a kitchenette here to the right. The fridge is a decent size, so feel free to bring food or drinks if you require."

I peeked inside at its neat organisation. Five small tables were positioned around the modest room with seating for twenty people. Several two-seater couches were scattered in the remaining space.

We weaved around partitioned desks, where teachers and administrative staff worked with diligence, through the doors leading back to reception.

Principal Marsden checked her watch. "Our weekly staff meeting occurs at eight o'clock every Monday. Your introduction will be first on the agenda."

Sandra approached. "Mr. Reynolds is waiting."

"Thank you, Sandra, I will be there shortly." Sandra disappeared, and Principal Marsden turned back to me. "I look forward to working with you and having you as part of the great team here." She glanced out the large glass exit doors. "But for now, I suggest you head home before the weather turns. I will see you first thing on Monday. Have a lovely weekend."

We shook hands and headed in opposite directions.

I had accommodations booked with a lady named Diana Jacobsen and her family a few streets away. Whispering a prayer, I walked to the car, thankful for my new job, and relieved I did not have to go home to an empty house yet.

CHAPTER NINE
Raining Petals

The skies opened when I pressed the start button on my car, and rain battered down in a blasting deluge of water and ice. After a painstaking search, I found house number nine and parked out the front under a eucalyptus tree.

"Cute house. Amber would love it." The pelting rain drowned out my words.

A quaint, average-sized weatherboard home occupied a large block behind a simple shrubby garden spattered with tall trees and a hinged metal gate.

Stuffing my handbag inside my overnight bag, I tucked them under my arm and scurried from the car. Icy rain hit my head and ran down my back. I shrieked and dashed to the gate. Freezing water saturated my clothes while I fought with slippery fingers to work the cold metal latch free, which became colder by the second. With a final budge, the gate swung open, and I ran down the concrete path toward shelter.

As I ascended the steep steps, a gust of wind blew me off balance. I clutched the wooden railing with my free hand. Rain and wind plastered loose strands of hair into my eyes and mouth, and an onslaught of white hydrangea flowers slapped my face and torso like confetti. The tiny petals assaulted my mouth and nose. I squealed and pulled myself up the stairs to the safety of the verandah. A sigh rushed from my chilled body when I stepped under the shelter.

Releasing my damp bag from under my arm, I gripped the handles with stiff fingers and loped to the front door. My dishevelled appearance reflected back in the sidelight, and I gawped. I resembled a soaked sewer rat. Petals clung to my skin. My jacket, shirt and pants were drenched and covered in shrapnel from the hydrangea explosion.

With shaking limbs, I dropped my bag, turned from the door and preened with haste.

"Enjoy your afternoon stroll?" an amused, deep voice uttered from behind me. "You might want to check for hidden cats or dogs in your pockets."

Wringing water from my ponytail, I whipped my head up and spun around to glare at Mr. Oh-So-Funny.

The tall form of a chiselled man in his mid-to-late-thirties leaned against the door frame. With dark-brown hair tousled atop his head, he watched me with a wide grin.

My glare abated, and a semi-genuine smile touched my lips. Transfixed by the sparkle in his deep-brown eyes and his angular chin peppered with sexy, dark stubble, I was drawn to his tanned, muscled arms next. They lay crossed against his black polo T-shirt, which covered a broad chest and tapered with perfection into his blue jeans. Heat warmed my cheeks.

"Didn't mean to startle you, but your battle with nature amused me from the lounge window."

My cheeks flamed hot enough to barbeque a steak. I was a wreck of a human being, with a head more messed up than a box of jumbled Lego, yet my brain kept my 'hot guy' radar up and running. How was this possible?

I extended a hand in greeting, but my cold, damp hands were decorated with plant debris, so I dropped my arm to my side. "Glad to have entertained you. I'm Victoria Burke. I hope I have the correct address? You must be—"

"Nicholas Jacobsen. I'll get you a towel." He disappeared inside.

Lost on where to begin, I unbuttoned my jacket and detected dirt on my pants. Brushing my trouser leg, the lacy edge of my white bra peeped through my damp, see-through shirt. I gasped and refastened two jacket buttons.

Footsteps approached. "Would you like a coffee?"

I peered up.

Nicholas's gaze trailed my soaked figure, and an amused smile lifted the corner of his mouth. "Or perhaps a warm second shower?" His eyes sparkled as he held up a towel.

With a thin-lipped smile I snatched the proffered towel and wrapped it around myself. "A shower would be preferable, thanks."

"No worries." He leaned in and clutched my overnight bag. "Follow me."

I slipped off my saturated shoes and followed Nicholas inside. Squelching down the hallway, my wet footprints marked the polished pine floorboards in my wake. I nodded toward the floor behind me. "I'm sorry about the mess."

Nicholas shrugged and turned his head toward me, his lips curved in an easy smile. "No problem. This floor's seen far worse."

I lost myself in his smile.

Before I had gathered my wits, Nicholas leaned through the bathroom doorway and lowered my bag to the tiled floor. He smiled and vanished down the hallway, leaving me to the wonders of hot water and my bewildering thoughts.

I vacated the bathroom twenty minutes later, clean and calm, with my still-damp overnight bag slung over my shoulder. I retraced my steps through the house and followed a low, resonant hum to where Nicholas stood in the kitchen with his back to me, washing dishes.

Four white leather bar stools lined the island bench. I sank onto one with a contented sigh, slipped my bag to the floor, and drank in my host.

Nicholas's broad shoulders rotated as he twisted his upper body and trim waist with each plate stacked to drip dry.

Heat stung my cheeks, and I shook my head abruptly. I had no right to ogle a married man and his magnificent, sculpted back and defined biceps.

"Feeling better?" Suds splashed Nicholas's forearm.

I cleared my throat and my mind of its tempted thoughts and raised my gaze to his head. "Yes, thanks. Need any help?"

"Nope. That's what the drying rack's for." He glanced over his shoulder with a smile. "Want that coffee now?"

I scanned the bench and open cabinetry for a coffee machine and grinder. A Sunbeam espresso machine rested near the kettle. Real coffee.

"Yes, please. A latte would be nice if it's not too much trouble?"

"No trouble at all. It's a nice change from making coffee for one." Nicholas dried his hands and pulled two cups from a shelf above the coffee machine. "My daughter, Diana, is a great barista but doesn't drink coffee."

Diana was his daughter? I had imagined Nicholas married *to* Diana. My cheeks flushed. Regardless of his marital status, I had allowed my mind to wander. Lustful thoughts were off limits.

"Oh. I assumed Diana was your, ah, wife o-or partner." Heat crept up my neck.

Nicholas squinted.

My chest burned, and I wished the floorboards would swallow me whole.

The creases around Nicholas's eyes eased. "Ah. Diana manages our Airbnb ad. She wanted to raise money for a holiday in January, and I said if she did the hard work, I had no issue with it. We've several more bookings in the calendar until we reach our goal."

"Diana sounds like a grounded young lady—"

"I'm glad to hear!" a girl's voice sang out moments before a soaked long-haired brunette of fifteen or sixteen years bounced into the kitchen. She wore the uniform for Tellarine Secondary College. Close to six foot in height, Diana towered over me, yet Nicholas still had a height advantage.

She surveyed me with rich brown eyes similar to her father. "You must be Victoria Burke. I hope Dad's been hospitable?" She glanced down at my overnight bag and arched an eyebrow in her father's direction. "He hasn't shown you to your room yet?" She sighed. "This way." Her heavy school bag jolted against her back on each step.

I followed Diana down the hallway to my transitory refuge.

The average-sized bedroom contained a selection of tasteful furnishings. A queen-size bed covered with a stark-white eiderdown huddled underneath a slate curtained window. White and lilac cushions decorated the bed.

Diana reviewed the room with a soft smile. "I hope you like the artwork Mum painted."

I peered at the paintings. One depicted a field of vibrant purple lavender, another a seaside scene at dusk with violet hues in the clouds reflecting calm waters below. Scrawled in small script in the bottom right corner of each painting were the initials DMJ.

"Your mum likes purple?"

Diana nodded.

A painting above the desk drew my interest, where a little girl played with her doll in a grassy paddock. Wildflowers surrounded the child, her dark hair tied back in pigtails. She wore a lilac pinafore which matched the dress on her doll.

"Is this you?"

Diana regarded the picture with a faraway smile. "Yes. I was four. I remember the day Mum photographed me playing at my grandparents' farm. She painted this for my fifth birthday." Diana fiddled with her school jumper. "Mum died when I was six, so it's a special painting to Daddy and me."

My heart cramped at the thought of a sweet six-year-old girl processing the trauma of losing her mother. Tears welled in my eyes. Memories of my six-year-old son lying in ICU nudged tears down my face. Would it have been better if I had died and Ryan had lived? I swiped a hand across my cheek. "I'm sorry, Diana."

"Thanks." She rubbed her nose. "What brings you to Tellarine?"

"A teaching position."

She raised her eyebrows. "Where?"

I nodded at her uniform with a smile. "Your school."

Her eyes sparkled. "Really? Wow! Are you taking over for Mrs. Donald as VCE English Coordinator?"

"Yes." I tilted my head. "Do you know why she left midyear?"

Diana's smile dimmed. "Her husband and brother-in-law died in a light aircraft crash, so she moved to be with her sister and nieces."

I gasped. "That's awful. Does she have children?"

Diana shook her head. "No. But she's younger than Dad, so I wonder if she'll remarry one day."

I clutched my bare ring finger and bit my lip. "Did your father remarry?"

She blinked. "No. He's never met a woman worthy of my awesomeness." She waggled her eyebrows.

I giggled.

Diana sighed. "I'm not sure if he's given up. He rarely dates. He misses Mum."

We walked back to the kitchen, where I drew comfort from the two kind souls familiar with my pain. If God could help this family through their loss, He would do the same for me. I hoped.

I accepted the mug from Nicholas. "Thanks." Sipping my coffee, I hummed in appreciation. "Coffee's delicious."

Diana bounced on her toes. "Guess what, Dad? Victoria's the replacement VCE English teacher at school!"

Dark chocolate eyes focused on my face. "Is that so? Congratulations, Miss ... Mrs.—"

"*Ms.* Burke."

"Ms. Burke. Cool." Diana opened the pantry door and peeked inside. "Any banana bread left?"

Nicholas retrieved a container from the shelf. "I saved the last slice for you, Princess Diana."

She kissed her father's cheek. "Thanks. I've got lots of homework, so let me know when you need help with dinner."

"Dinner's all sorted for tonight."

"Okay." Diana disappeared down the hallway.

Nicholas sipped his coffee. "So, why'd you choose our humble little town?"

"A sea change."

"You're a bit inland." He smirked.

A light laugh rebounded in my chest. "True. What do you do?"

He rubbed the back of his neck. "I'm an electrician."

"What a shocking job." I stifled a laugh.

He chuckled. "It is some days."

I rubbed along the groove in my ring finger. Months without wearing wedding rings had not stopped the sense of nakedness.

"Were you married?"

My head jolted up. "Pardon?"

"I asked whether you were married." He nodded to my hand. "You keep touching your ring finger. I did the same for a long time after I removed my wedding band."

I stared down at my hand, then up to his face. What could I say? I was reluctant to divulge my painful past to a stranger. I blurted, "I sustained serious injuries in a car accident before Christmas."

What did that even mean? I stared at my mug, my heart hammering.

"Sorry to hear." He lifted his left index finger. "I broke this a few years ago. Everyday life became so much more difficult, but it was only a finger. Are you healed from your injuries?"

He assumed I had broken my finger in the accident. I gulped air and nodded. "Yes, the majority of my injuries. I had to learn to walk again and still have problems with my right leg, but I've been referred to a local physio. I've also found a local women's basketball team to help keep me in shape."

Nicholas grinned over his coffee mug. "Basketball. Let me guess, point guard?"

"Did my lack of height give me away?"

He laughed and placed his mug in the sink. "You *are* a bit of a shorty."

"Thanks!" I burst out in laughter.

He leaned his elbows on the smooth wooden surface of the island bench opposite me. "There's nothing wrong with being short." The deep timbre of his voice caressed my ears. His eyes darkened, and he curled his lips into a grin. "I like short."

A breath caught in my throat, and the hair on my neck and arms stiffened. Goodness gracious, was he flirting with me? Or wishful thinking on my part? We met less than an hour ago!

I pinched my leg, hoping the pain chased my foolish thoughts away. "Thanks for the coffee. I remembered something in the car. I'd better get it before the rain starts up again."

He smirked. "Let me know if you need a hand."

I turned and walked to the front door. Fast. Perhaps the cooler outside air would lower my body temperature from the heat in the kitchen.

CHAPTER TEN
New Beginnings

Mrs. Arby, the elderly owner of a self-contained bungalow I hoped to rent, unlocked the door and showed me inside. "It's not big, but it's got everything you'll need. If you want the furniture to stay, lemme know. Mr. Arby thought a young lady relocating from Melbourne would travel light."

The bungalow was furnished and affordable. What an answer to prayer.

I analysed the small flat and smiled. It guaranteed privacy an apartment I had inspected earlier had failed to offer and fit my budget better than the house on the other side of town.

I bounced from foot to foot. "It looks wonderful. I'll take it!"

"Great." She pointed at two doors opposite the kitchenette. "One's the bathroom, the other's the bedroom. There's a queen-size bed base, but I had to toss the mattress, so I left an airbed in the bedroom to use until you buy a mattress. Drop by my house to sign the documents." Mrs. Arby handed me the key and left.

"Thank You, God, for my new home. You never fail to look after me even when my whole world crumbles." I sniffed and blinked back tears before locking up.

I loped down the driveway to the Arby residence, signed the rental agreement, and returned to the Jacobsens' for lunch. We chatted about Melbourne and things familiar but nothing too personal. Diana's mannerisms reminded me of Jessica and dampened my pleasant mood.

After a polite farewell, I returned to my new home and emptied the contents of my car, cramming my things into the spaces available. The main living area housed a retro three-seater couch striped in lime-and-white calico, with a matching armchair and overstuffed ottoman. A tall pine bookshelf beside the front door now stored my small collection of books, mementos and photo albums of the children. I filled a large pine sideboard with linen, crockery and baking dishes. An aged rectangular wooden table, with four padded chairs, filled the tiny space near the tidy kitchenette consisting of overhead cupboards, a white retro all-in-one oven, grill and stove, a mini fridge and freezer, and a vintage top-loading washing machine. Perfect as extra bench space.

Satisfied with my progress, I snapped several photos and sent a group text to Amber, Christine, and Stacy.

Me: WELCOME TO MY NEW MINIATURE HOME!

Amber: GORGEOUS! IS THIS THE PLACE WE FOUND ONLINE THAT'S 6 SQUARES?

Me: YEP!

Christine: LOVELY! REMINDS ME OF MY HONEYMOON SUITE. HA HA! MEMORIES.

Stacy: CLASSY, CHRISSY. ;) UNPACKING ON A SATURDAY NIGHT, VICKI? PARTY GIRL.

Me: HA! THANKS, LADIES. LOVE YOU XX

After a bite to eat, I crawled into bed and drifted off to sleep cocooned in the warmth of my loved ones.

Sunday morning, I awoke with a start after *that* dream. Lying in bed, I stared at the aged white ceiling, slowing my breaths to alleviate my heart's intense pace. The remnants of my vivid dream faded with each breath. I banished the fog of slick, warm skin and hot, sensual kisses from my mind and murmured a prayer for strength to live above the desires which stirred me. Not the first time I woke in this manner, I grasped hold of the hope to overcome my flesh.

The dreams had begun several years ago when Jude had distanced himself. With fewer "I love you" moments, like little touches to my hand or arm when he spoke, I had despaired. Eye contact disappeared, along with his consuming gaze when we made love. In reality, love had not been made in our bed for years. Jude was always young in my dreams, a mental nudge that the adoration in his eyes had not been a figment of my imagination, and the mutual passion to please was once his top priority.

I scrubbed my face with my hands. Single and deprived of my husband's body, these thoughts had become a significant issue for me, a battle I had to release into God's hands. I offered up my concerns with a silent prayer and whipped my carnal thoughts back into submission. Time to focus on readying for church.

I climbed out of bed into a cool shower before I dressed, then donned my trusty leather boots. They were comfortable and hid my hideous scar.

Tellarine Christian Church was located two streets north from my home. An unhurried stroll on a beautiful autumn morning helped ease the stiffness in my right leg and gave me a quiet moment to think and pray.

I absorbed the delightful scenery around me. Tall liquidambar trees towered overhead with brilliant yellow, orange and scarlet foliage. Birds twittered in the soft breeze. Fallen leaves crunched under my feet. I inhaled the cool, fresh morning and smiled at the quiet beauty of this little town.

His mercies are new every morning.

My growing contentment hummed in a sigh. I turned the corner and walked a short distance before the church appeared on the opposite side of the street.

The small building seemed to have survived eons in time, trapped in the nineteen-seventies with its orange brick veneer, dark-brown trim, and rusty-orange roof. Patches of moss clung like barnacles to the bricks and roof tiles. The shrubs under the tall trees needed a good prune.

A cheery, well-endowed woman in her mid-twenties with long, cascading blonde hair and a bright floral V-neck midi dress shook my hand in welcome at the entrance. The lanyard around her neck revealed her name: Belinda.

"Welcome to Tellarine Christian Church. Enjoy the service," Belinda said with a smile.

"Thanks." I smiled back and entered the foyer.

The interior was dated like the building exterior, with well-trodden beige carpets, oatmeal walls, and mission-brown architraves. The main auditorium accommodated eighty or so seats, and close to half were filled. Congregants chatted, and children raced around a row of seats despite their parents' protests. Ryan had been notorious for pew racing. I gulped and blinked.

A small team of musicians and singers readied themselves on the platform, and my heart twinged when I spotted an acoustic guitar. I pushed aside thoughts of Jude. My first Sunday in Tellarine would not be ruined by anxiety.

From the back of the room, I surveyed the available seats. My throat clogged at the sheer number of families sitting together, and my heart skittered when a group of pre-teen girls giggled nearby. I glimpsed twice at heads with hair like Jessica's and Samantha's. I walked down an aisle where Diana appeared, conversing with friends. She noticed me, and her face lit up.

My steps lightened at the sight of her familiar face. If Diana was at church, would Nicholas be here too? My pulse thundered in my neck.

"Victori–oh, I mean, Ms. Burke! It's wonderful to see you." Diana squeezed my arm. "These are my friends Madison Taylor and Grace Robinson. They attend the school."

I smiled at the young ladies and clasped their hands in greeting. "Madison. Grace. It's a pleasure to meet you. We may cross paths in the coming days."

Madison and Grace exchanged looks with Diana.

"I'm the new VCE English Coordinator."

Grace clapped. "That makes two Christian teachers at our school! We'll be a force to be reckoned with soon, don't you think?"

Diana nodded toward the foyer. "Miss Davies is the Food Technology and Textiles teacher. She's greeting at the door."

I glanced over my shoulder—excited at the prospect of befriending Belinda—when my chest seized and cheeks warmed.

Nicholas's head jerked back and eyes widened before his handsome clean-shaven face smirked. His long gait brought him closer within seconds, his cologne intoxicating. "Good morning, ladies."

"M-morning, Nicholas," I breathed. My face burned.

Madison tittered. "Morning!"

"Hey, Dad."

Grace smiled. "Morning, Mr. Jacobsen." She linked arms with her friends and pulled them away.

A sprite young man with gelled auburn hair launched onto the small stage, microphone in his hand. After a warm welcome, he requested the congregation to take their seats.

Nicholas pointed to a nearby seat. "You're welcome to sit with me."

"Thanks."

The band played as we stood at our chairs.

Nicholas leaned close. "Don't worry, I won't bite." The dissonance between his smile and his serious gaze threw me.

I nodded and focused on the pulpit. My stomach agitated, my nerves at war with my senses. How was it possible the first man I met in Tellarine was not only single and attractive, but also a Christian? My gaze fell to the guitarist on stage, and I inched a step away from Nicholas. I had already learned this lesson the hard way.

CHAPTER ELEVEN

A Whole New World

"Ms. Burke!"

Delighted giggles greeted me after lunch when I entered my classroom on my first day of work. Diana, Madison, and Grace waved like loons from their desks.

I stifled a laugh and winked. "Afternoon, ladies and gentlemen. I'm Ms. Burke, and I'll teach your Year Ten English class for the remainder of the year. How about we take a few minutes so I can get to know you?" I marked the class roll before asking about their future aspirations and interests.

Andrew Daley, a young man with sandy-blond hair, raised his hand with a confident smile. "I want a career in aerospace engineering."

"A noble aspiration. What inspired you to aim for the stars?"

"I've always been fascinated with avionics."

"Very nice, Andrew. Anyone else?"

Diana raised her hand. "I like writing."

I smiled. "So do I."

"I don't." A young man with a set of dark, mischievous eyes peered at me from underneath his mop of dark hair. Keanu Everton.

"Oh shush, Keanu." Diana elbowed his arm with a grin.

I held back a laugh. "That's fine, Keanu. Do your work, and I won't force you to write more than is required."

"Much appreciated." Keanu's dark eyes sparkled.

While the students worked, I wandered the room and observed class dynamics. Anna Beaufort and Gabriella Matthews whispered with Diana, Madison and Grace often. Keanu received assistance from Diana while Andrew finished his work in record time, giving him long minutes to stare at her. I hid a grin and rounded my desk, wondering what Nicholas would do if he knew a cute boy had a crush on his daughter. If I were him, I would—

I grasped the chair back and collapsed into my seat. My three cheeky monkeys would never navigate the choppy waters of adolescence. My chest ached, and I blinked back tears. I would grieve those lost years for the rest of my life.

The subsequent days and weeks were a whirlwind affair. Many nights I collapsed into bed while uttering prayers that my brain would not explode overnight.

Belinda Davies was a God-given lifesaver. She directed me to the correct rooms at work during the day and pointed out the local highlights of the town in the evenings. She also encouraged me in my desire to volunteer at church, and my thankfulness overflowed to have found an all-rounder of a friend.

Belinda leaned on the edge of my desk while I perused a selection of assessments completed by my Year Twelve students earlier in the year.

"Dinner?"

I lifted my head. "Sure. Where?"

"I haven't taken you to Benanu's yet. It's essentially the local pub, but the current owner renovated it two years ago, and now it's pretty schmick." She leaned closer. "The bar has a great selection of drinks, if you're into that sort of thing, with a casual couch area for tapas and a pool table tucked around the back. The dining area offers full table service including booths for privacy, and the food's pretty good"—Belinda wrinkled her nose—"even to your snobbish

Melbourne standards. And the coffee?" She sighed and fluttered her eyelashes. "I think you'll be happy."

I pursed my lips. "Hmm. Okay."

Belinda entered the street address for Benanu's into my phone's GPS, a block south from home. If the pub lived up to her praise, it might become my new hangout.

I stepped across the threshold of Benanu's, and my breath hitched. "Wow."

Belinda nudged me toward a cluster of tables close to the bar.

"This is better than the pubs I've been to in the city." I lounged with my friend on comfortable leather-padded black seats at a small table and scrutinised the large premises. Splashed with white, black, silver and blue, Benanu's neoteric design suited the relaxed atmosphere for casual or intimate dinners, yet the space worked for those interested in a game of pool or a catch-up at the bar. Young families dined around joined tables. A few older couples laughed in groups, and young men flanked the pool table.

Belinda settled back in her chair. "Pretty nice, hey?"

I poured two glasses of water from the bottle on our table. "Sure is. Someone spent decent money on the place."

Belinda snorted. "It was falling apart before the renovations."

A throat cleared next to me, and I turned. "Ms. Burke?"

I cocked my head and beamed. "Keanu! To what do I owe the pleasure?"

Keanu placed a menu in my hand, then Belinda's. "I'm working tables tonight, so I'm your man if ya need anything." He winked, and a grin spread across his face. "Want the specials or my personal recommendations?"

I bit my bottom lip. For a sixteen-year-old, Keanu was tall and imposing, yet personable. His dark, boyish features were attractive. I stared at the menu. "This is my first time here, so perhaps your recommendations?"

"Your virginal visit. I'm glad I'm your first ... server."

Belinda snorted into her water.

My cheeks suffused with heat.

Keanu's grin stretched farther across his face. "The chicken strips are a great 'anytime' snack, same with the nachos and bruschetta." He squinted over my shoulder and pointed at the menu. "I'm a steak man myself, but the rabbit's full of robust flavour, and the lamb's delicious." He stepped back and gazed between Belinda and me. "My brother likes the salmon, and Mum loves the country-style chicken."

I eyed my choices. "I haven't had rabbit in a long time. I'll have that, please."

Keanu nodded with a smile. "Nice. And you, Miss Davies?"

Belinda observed him. "You didn't say what your dad likes."

Keanu shuffled on his feet and shrugged. "Dad spends too much time in the back office running the place. He often grabs whatever's on hand."

I blinked, open-mouthed. "Your family owns Benanu's?"

"Yup." His solemn gaze fell on me. "I'm working to take some of the burden off Dad."

My heart softened. "Your parents must be proud."

He glanced away. "Maybe. But school comes first. I need good grades so Dad can give me more responsibility."

I gave him a warm smile. "Of course. I'll help you as much as I can, okay?"

He nodded.

"You can speak to me any time you need help. I'm sure Diana would be happy to help too."

Keanu's eyes lit up. "Yeah, Jacobsen's awesome. She's always got time to nerd me up."

Belinda and I laughed. She ordered the chicken, and Keanu saluted before he stepped away.

"Great kid," Belinda said. "Terrible at sewing, though."

Twenty minutes later Keanu returned with our meals, and my mouth watered. My rabbit was tender, infused with garlic and rosemary, and paired with scalloped potatoes, asparagus and steamed vegetables.

Belinda laughed at the moans I hummed while I ate.

Keanu delivered two cups of coffee. "On the house, ladies."

"Thanks!" Belinda and I said.

I sipped, closed my eyes, and imagined sitting at my favourite South Yarra café with a warm latte. This coffee was *good*.

Amber and I used to indulge in an occasional Saturday breakfast when the opportunity arose. We would walk from her house to the café and talk about our week, enjoy a quiet moment to ourselves, and drink enough coffee to fuel a missile. I missed my friend and recorded a mental note to message her about my new find.

"Belinda, thank you for introducing me to my new hangout."

Her face lit up with a beautiful smile. "It's my pleasure. You can't imagine how excited I was to discover the new chick at church is also a colleague. I mean, a friend in both spheres of my life? You're an answer to prayer."

I beamed. Belinda's prayer was far from one-sided. She was a gift from above I cherished with all of my heart.

I lingered with closed eyes at my classroom desk after school and massaged my neck with deft fingers. A string of groans vibrated in my throat. My chaotic life had prevented me from performing my usual five-minute lunchtime stretches, and now I paid the price. Two weeks ago, I had added a quick neck and shoulder massage with my leg and back routine to counteract the prolonged sitting. Marking schoolwork had taken its toll.

"Don't quote me, but I'm pretty sure noises like that are illegal in all Victorian classrooms."

I raised my head and stared at the intruder. In the doorway stood the tall, blond, well-built form of Matt Briggs, head of the STEM department. His mischievous blue eyes beamed, and a grin danced on his splendid face.

We had conversed within a group in the Staff Lounge but never in one-on-one conversation. He was a single, attractive guy in his mid-thirties. Any woman would drool over him, and he wielded a smile which could melt my resolve to remain single. Everyone knew magnificent men like him used plain Janes like me.

I peered up at him with a perfunctory smile. "Can I help you?" I wished he would leave. Good-looking men triggered my nerves, but Matt was in another league, like Jude, and this terrified me.

"I wanted to see how you're adjusting to country life. I heard you're from the city."

My smile tightened. "I'm adjusting well. Fresh air and open spaces beat gridlock traffic hands down."

"I spent the first six months forgetting Woolies wasn't around the corner when I remembered to shop."

I straightened in my seat. "You're not a country boy?"

He laughed and shook his head. "Nope. I'm a Melbourne High boy, born and bred. When I arrived two years ago, staff and management thought I was from another planet, wanting to drag the school into the twenty-first century." Matt chuckled, and I arched an eyebrow. "I asked for a 3-D printer. You'd think I asked for tickets to the moon. No one recognised it as a necessary resource until I brought my case forward. Now it's a foundational tool in our curriculum."

I ignored the warmth in my cheeks. "What a remarkable job you've done. The technology here is impressive." I smiled and glanced down to my papers and chided myself for having judged him by appearance.

"Thanks. Speaking of work, I'll leave you to it. I dropped by to see if you know about our monthly after-work drinks and casual dinner? It's this Friday. We have a lot of fun. I hope you can make it."

I gazed up to respond, but Matt was gone. An uncomfortable warmth spread across my chest.

The next morning, I found Belinda in the office-supplies room immersed in coloured sheets of paper.

"What's the staff catch-up all about?"

"You mean drinks and dinner at Benanu's on the last Friday of each month?"

"Yes. Matt Briggs mentioned it yesterday."

Belinda giggled and gathered the coloured papers into a neat pile. "He did, did he? Typical." She shook her head with a big grin. "Matt likes to make sure new staff, typically of the female persuasion, attend these casual events so he can use his charm to woo them and score on the side."

"What!" My cheeks ignited.

"He preys on the young secretaries or fresh-out-of-university teachers, but it seems you made the cut. You're lovely to look at after all, with your envious figure, gorgeous shiny brown hair, and eyes deep as the ocean."

I stared at Belinda, flabbergasted the words "envious", "lovely" and "gorgeous" were used in a sentence to describe me.

Belinda squinted. She appraised me up and down. "Let me guess. You're either a late bloomer who struggled to lift off the veil of unkind words spoken over you as a teenager, or you suffer from a serious case of low self-esteem."

I opened my mouth, but words escaped me.

She cocked her head and tapped her finger against her lips. "Hmm, yes, a destructive past relationship."

My face flushed. How easy was I to read?

Belinda smiled and reached out a hand. "It's a good thing we're friends because I have firsthand experience with both scenarios. The journey from negative self-image to seeing yourself as God's masterpiece is not only possible but life-changing."

Tears welled in my eyes. Amber called a spade a spade, and now my new friend possessed the same uncanny ability.

Belinda embraced me, and once again I thanked God for my

precious friend.

♥ ♥ ♥ ♥ ♥ ♥ ♥

I avoided Matt while milling with co-workers around the bar at Benanu's on Friday evening, waiting for other staff members to arrive. I enjoyed a mocktail while Belinda and Anita Doe, one of the art teachers, stood nearby sipping on their alcoholic beverages.

"What're you drinking?" Matt stood near and eyed my glass.

"Virgin piña colada. Why?"

"Interesting."

I clenched the glass. "What's so interesting about a mocktail?" The coconut and pineapple concoction coated my throat with a cool tingle.

Matt anchored a hand on his hip. "You don't drink alcohol, and you and Belinda are as thick as thieves. You must be a Christian."

"A-plus, Mr. Briggs. Do you spend time with Christian women in order to decrypt them?"

His face clouded, and his voice dropped. "I did."

I lifted my eyebrows. "R-really? When?"

He stared at the wall behind me. "I grew up in the Salvation Army"—his gaze flicked to me—"and learned it wasn't for me at sixteen."

What had happened to turn him away from God and church? I ran a finger along the side of the glass. Or was this an act? A way to persuade me to drop my guard? Would a playboy like him stoop so low? I hoped not.

I bit the inside of my cheek. "Not all Christians are church repellent."

"I know. You and Belinda are pretty cool even if you go to church." His laughter shot a fizz of bubbles in my abdomen.

"I'll take that as a compliment."

Staff wandered into the dining area. "We'd better follow the crowd before people start talking and tarnish the flawless reputation

I expect you possess," Matt said.

I laughed and shook my head. "Hardly flawless, but I've been here three weeks and don't want to earn a reputation yet."

Matt winked. A quirky smile danced on his lips. "Don't worry, your virtue's safe with me."

CHAPTER TWELVE

Turning Up the Heat

"**Why won't you** start, you ancient thing!" I grunted and dragged my palms down my face.

My appetite craved hot apple pie while I scored more School-assessed Coursework on a wintry late June evening. Unfortunately for my palate and my sanity, my oven refused to ignite no matter what I pushed or pulled.

The month of June had snuck up on me, filled with midyear assessments and faux exams. I thrived on the mental challenge of stretching my students in their learning, but my desire to hide paperwork for twenty-four hours—or sleep in—was at an all-time high. Drained by the end of each workday, still I was glad for the exhaustion which allowed an escape from thinking about my babies.

I checked the time and hoped Mr. Arby could help. Rushing out the door, I exhaled when the Arbys' front porch light was still illuminated.

Mr. Arby opened his door with pink cheeks and laboured breaths. "Why, it's the lovely Victoria Burke. Can I help you?"

"I apologise for the late intrusion, but my oven won't heat. Could you investigate the problem for me?"

"I'm terrible with electric gadgets, but I know a brilliant sparky that's certain to help us tonight. He's the best this side of the city!"

My hands trembled. Nicholas was an electrician, but many qualified professionals must work in the area. I wiped a sweaty palm down my pants leg. "O-okay. Thanks, Mr. Arby."

I hurried back to my bungalow to make a dent in the pile of papers before I indulged in dessert. My need for food therapy had reached an unparalleled high.

I had settled into reading the first SAC when someone knocked. I swung the door open.

A man, whose broad shoulders and styled dark hair I would recognise anywhere, slouched on my front step in the middle of boot-removal duties with his back to me.

My jaw dropped, and butterflies danced in my tummy.

When he stood with boots in hand to place at the front door, his eyes brightened.

I closed my gaping mouth and opened the door wider. "You must be the best sparky this side of the city Mr. Arby said to expect."

Nicholas rubbed the back of his neck before he grabbed his toolbox. "I can't say I'm all that, but I'm pretty good at what I do and enjoy the work." He bounded to the oven, and I closed the door.

I returned to the table and neatened my papers. "I'm glad you enjoy it. Not everyone can say the same about their jobs."

"An astute observation, Ms. Burke." Nicholas grinned in my direction while he removed a panel from the oven.

"Why, Mr. Jacobsen, no wonder your offspring is my star pupil when you speak with such eloquence. Were you academically inclined during your formative years?" I still played the role of snob quite well.

With a chuckle Nicholas inspected some wiring. "The academic side of school was a breeze, but dismantling things interested me more than writing essays. I didn't have an English teacher like you to encourage and challenge me like you do for Diana."

"I'm sorry your teachers failed to do their jobs, Nicholas." His name came out like a sigh. I cleared my throat. "I endeavour to give all I can to my students."

Nicholas wiped an oily hand on a cloth. "You sound dedicated to your vocation. But remember there's more to life than work."

Tears pricked my eyes. I had thrown myself into my job, a distraction from the void my children once filled.

Nicholas stood and leaned against the stove. "Okay, here's the good news. It's a simple issue with the element that I've replaced three times in eighteen years. They don't make ovens like this anymore." Nicholas rummaged through his toolbox and retrieved some tools and parts before he kneeled in front of the oven.

I averted my gaze from the delights of his back and threw a wistful glance at my freezer before I sagged onto a chair and read more essays.

Ten minutes later, Nicholas packed up his tools.

I turned in my seat. "All done?"

"Yes, you shouldn't have any issues. I'll turn the oven off in five minutes." He washed his hands at the kitchenette sink.

"Thanks so much. Can you leave it on, please?"

"Sure."

I stood and leaned against the dining chair. "Would you like a cuppa before you hit the road?"

He shuffled on his feet.

"I understand if you need to go home. Your days must be long if you make callouts after eight."

"Mr. Arby's a special customer, so I do what I can to help. Late-night emergency callouts are part and parcel of the job. Thankfully, country folk know what a real emergency is." He rubbed the stubble of his cheeks and chin with his large hand. "A cuppa sounds great, thanks."

I slipped past him, filled the kettle, and turned it on to boil.

Nicholas pulled up a chair at the table behind me. "Is it always this cold inside? Don't you believe in heating?"

A breathy laugh bubbled in my chest. "It's always this cold or worse." I pointed to the thick white blanket draped over the couch back. "That's what the fluffy blanket's for."

He narrowed his eyes and shifted in the chair. "There's no

heater in the house?"

"There's a wall heater in the bedroom, but it barely radiates heat ten centimetres away, let alone out here."

Nicholas launched to his feet, chair legs scraping the floor in his haste, and inspected the heater in question.

I peeked over my shoulder before I pulled a store-bought family-sized pie from the freezer, hid it in the overhead pantry to thaw, then grabbed two mugs from a neighbouring cupboard.

He reappeared and rummaged through his toolbox. "I suspect the element's gone in this one too."

"That explains a lot." I rifled through my tea collection near the kettle. "Would you like tea, hot chocolate or Milo? I don't have a coffee machine, and instant coffee's a sin."

Nicholas laughed, and the husky sound reverberated in the small space. He peeked over my shoulder, and I held in a breath before he reached around me and placed a peppermint tea bag in my hand.

My pulse tripped.

He sauntered back to the bedroom.

I managed to place a few biscuits on a plate without dropping them.

Nicholas returned to his seat at the table. "It's the element. I'll order a replacement part and let Mr. Arby know when I give him my invoice."

I poured hot water over our tea bags and placed tea and biscuits in front of my guest. "Thanks for looking into it, but it isn't necessary. I spend most of my time out here when I'm home. I researched buying a portable column heater, but the blanket's cheaper."

He sipped from his mug and eyed me over the rim. "Hmm. I'll still mention it tomorrow." Nicholas watched me nibble on a biscuit. "You enjoy living here?"

"This place is an absolute godsend. I've enough space for the things I need and furniture to borrow as long as I want. The rent's cheap enough to squirrel away some savings." I sipped my chamomile tea and surveyed the room. "I've only needed to buy a queen bed mattress so far, which is perfect for when my friend stays over."

Nicholas spluttered and coughed on a mouthful of tea.

I rushed to the sink and poured a glass of water.

He accepted the drink, nodding between coughs. His reddened face and watery eyes appeared distressed. "Friend?"

I stared at him, puzzled, and mentally replayed my last words. His question seemed odd until it dawned. My eyes grew wide, and my ears burned.

"Oh!" My face heated, and I once again wished myself out of his presence. "No, that's *not* what I meant! My best friend from Melbourne is visiting during the July school holidays. The bed's much more comfortable than the couch. She thinks it'll be bliss sleeping in a bed without two children and a husband lying on her."

I smiled before memories flashed of my children climbing into bed with me to snuggle on Saturday mornings. My mouth drooped, and my stomach churned with a sudden coldness. I missed them. So much.

Nicholas shifted in his chair. "I, ah. Not that it's any of my business."

I shook my head. "I beg to differ. Doesn't the Bible instruct us to encourage one another in our faith and be accountable to our Christian brothers and sisters? Our actions shouldn't be a stumbling block for others. It's fair you asked the question, given my position and influence with Diana."

I smirked. "That being said, should God publish a memo amending that particular standard, I'll be first in line for those ... blessings."

Nicholas burst out laughing. The deep rumble warmed my chest. His broad shoulders shook on every breath while the lines around his mouth and eyes deepened as his irises sparkled.

A sudden heaviness swept over me and I stared at the table. Did

Nicholas think my comment inappropriate? Did I have a real problem? The stigma of being a Christian woman with apparent purity issues would be harder to deal with than the thoughts and dreams themselves.

Nicholas consumed the last of his tea. "Can't say I'd do any different if He released that memo." The twinkle in his eyes matched his boyish smirk. "And on that note, I'd better go. Thanks again for the tea."

I walked Nicholas to the door before I retrieved my pie from hiding and popped it in to cook. A mouth-watering aroma permeated the house, and I breathed in its comfort, a childhood reminder of my nan's amazing pies. My darling Ryan came to mind, his sweet face filled with remorse when I had scolded him for stealing apple pie two Christmases ago. I had spent hours baking pies for a family Christmas function and had been disappointed in his thievery.

Tears clouded my vision, and a cold chill ran through my body. Now I would give up apple pie for eternity if I could have Ryan here with me.

I blinked and retrieved my warm grey cardigan from the bedroom, glancing at the bed when I pulled the cardigan from my drawers. Oh no. After work I had thrown my black bra on the bed less than a metre from the heater. Nicholas must have noticed it! My face now burned hotter than the faulty bedroom heater.

With a sigh I shuffled back to the kitchen to comfort myself with food.

CHAPTER THIRTEEN
Cyclone Amber

I waved to my basketball teammates and exited the Robinvale Leisure Centre, pumped from the away-game win. My sweat-soaked body appreciated the bracing evening breeze as I jogged to my car.

Tossing my backpack on the passenger seat, I pulled on an old jumper and settled behind the wheel. My body vibrated with excitement. I had missed playing. The drills. The mental strategies. The on-court adrenaline rush. After six weeks on the team, the rust had been blasted off my game, my thirteen-year absence from the sport forgotten.

Thirty minutes later I parked under my carport and dragged myself into the shower. I dressed and reheated some leftovers for dinner before I retrieved my phone from my backpack and settled at the table. Amber had called me.

I dialled her number and updated her on my latest interactions with Nicholas.

"You said *what* to him?" Amber's hysterical laughter echoed on the other end of the phone. She found each situation hilarious. "Eleven days until I see your beautiful face and meet this interesting man of yours. And sleep with you!" Fits of laughter overcame my friend.

"He's not my man. He's just a friend." I wet my lips.

"Hmm. An attractive friend with a heart for God, a steady job, and a daughter who likes you? Seems like the real deal."

I scrubbed a hand over my face. "I can't divorce until next year, and no one here knows about my past." The weight of loss pressed against my lungs and shortened my breath.

"C'mon, Vic, it's only been six months since the accident. No one will hold it against you if you keep it to yourself for a little longer. The time will come when you're ready to share your pain and the memories of your beautiful children."

A sob tore from my lips. "I miss them so much. It hurts." A lump formed in my throat, and tears stung my eyes.

"I miss them too, hun."

I dedicated my spare time thinking of places to take Amber in Tellarine. Now that I worked full-time, volunteered at church each fortnight on Fridays with the senior Meals on Wheels ministry, and assisted Belinda with offering and communion duties most Sunday mornings—not to mention the local women's basketball games on Monday nights—my time was limited.

Before I knew it, Amber flew through my front door and straight into my arms, in time for dinner.

My heart soared and I gushed with conversation like a giddy student. "Ready to eat?"

"I'm famished, so bring it on!"

We drove to the local fish 'n chip shop, collected two steaming bags of fatty goodness and returned to my place for a girl's night on the couch.

Skype, phone calls, and text messages paled in comparison to in-person conversations with Amber. Our evening reminded me of meals at her house, where our children had eaten and carried on at the dining table while we squatted at the kitchen bench to eat and chat. I missed those chaotic days.

Amber gathered and discarded our rubbish then pulled the large oil heater across to the couch. "You must love this."

"You know the evening I embarrassed myself for the hundredth time with Nicholas? The sleeping-with-friends-and-bra episode."

Amber cackled and wiped her eyes from stray tears. "The day he fixed your oven?"

"Two days later I found this on my front step. Brand new in its box."

Amber's big eyes widened. "Are you serious?"

"No note attached. No mention of where it came from." I snorted a laugh. "It couldn't be the Arbys because Mrs. Arby would've claimed ownership of such generosity. It could only be Nicholas."

Amber smiled with a headshake. "We can add generous to his long list of desirable qualities. Are you certain he's not interested in you?"

I creased my forehead. "I'm not sure. I don't want to take his kindness the wrong way. I'm a single woman in his church, and he seems the type of man to look after someone like me in a platonic way." I shrugged. "Maybe he's being the perfect big brother."

Amber rolled her eyes. "Or maybe he's marking his territory to repel the competition."

"I don't think so. Even if he were, I'm not ready for a relationship." Amber was wrong to assume Nicholas's interest. How could he be interested in me when his own daughter had said he still missed his wife? And how could I ever fill those shoes in Diana's life? I was not worthy of her awesomeness, not by a long shot. And I knew long shots with my three-pointers back in action.

Amber lay her cutlery across her empty plate. "You weren't wrong, Vic. Breakfast here's delicious!"

We occupied a small table in Benanu's, stuffed to the brim like those Saturday mornings Mike had watched all five of our children.

I smiled at her satisfied face. "Wait until you taste the coffee. Perfection in a cup."

Amber stared past me and arched an eyebrow. "Speaking of perfection in a cup, who's the man behind you?"

I turned with a chuckle.

Matt stood near the bar in a pair of navy running shorts with a light-blue Nike T-shirt pressed against his damp torso. Earbuds dangled around his neck. He reached out for a takeaway coffee cup and turned to leave when his gaze fell on me. He grinned and sauntered to our table.

"Why, hello, Ms. Burke," his velvety voice purred my name. "Are you going to introduce me to your pretty friend?"

"Amber, this is Matt Briggs, a colleague from work. Matt, this is my happily married friend, Amber. She's visiting from Melbourne."

Amber and Matt shook hands. A waiter approached and cleared our table. Amber ordered two coffees before he carried our empty plates away.

Matt grinned. "So, you're the best friend. Vicki talks about you and Mike often." He winked at Amber, and her eyes widened. "Can you shed light on the mysteries of Victoria Burke? She doesn't share much about herself yet knows more about me than my friends and family combined."

Amber chuckled. "Yes, Vic's a great listener, but not so great when roles are reversed."

I poked out my tongue at her, and she laughed. My past and current lives had collided, and I was unsure if I liked it or not.

"Tell me, ladies, are you free for dinner tonight? I'm catching up with some friends here. The more the merrier."

Amber accepted the invitation, and unease slid into my gut.

Matt grinned at me. "Want to message Belinda and see if she'll come along too?"

"Of course, she'd love to be part of the frivolities."

"Excellent. I'll be here around six. I'll see you both later." And just like that, Matt left me dazed by what we had agreed to.

"Partying with Mr. Briggs tonight?" Keanu lowered two

coffees to our table.

I had not heard him approach, and my head jerked up. "Didn't your parents teach you not to eavesdrop?"

His cheeks coloured. "Sorry, Ms. Burke."

Amber hid a smirk.

I sipped my coffee and sighed. "Delicious."

Amber hummed. "Compliments to the barista."

Keanu smiled. "I'll let her know."

"You working tonight, Keanu?" I asked.

"I'm studying in the office with Jacobsen so I'm on hand if Dad needs me. I'll probably spend the night bashing my head against the desk while Diana laughs." His eyes glimmered. "Enjoy yer day, ladies." He disappeared from view.

Amber chuckled. "Student?"

I nodded.

"So, I met the infamous Matt Briggs, eh? He *is* smoking hot like you described. Tonight should be fun." She glanced at her phone. "We'd better get to the farmer's market and the winery you mentioned so we're back in time to change for dinner. Mike will shower me with kisses when I bring home a few bottles of Shiraz."

I grinned. "You could arrive home empty-handed, dressed in a plastic bag, and that man would shower you with kisses."

A mischievous grin stretched across Amber's face. "I think I'd end up with a whole lot more than kisses if I came home in a skimpy plastic bag."

I squeaked a laugh. "Don't remind me of the things I'm missing."

She grabbed my hand. "Chin up, babe. When the time's right, a wonderful man will sweep you off your feet, desperate for the blessing of you."

I grabbed my bag, prayed Amber was right, and hoped nothing disastrous happened tonight.

A few minutes before six o'clock, Belinda arrived at my place.

I enjoyed introducing my two closest friends and listening to their animated conversation. We travelled in convoy to Benanu's with Belinda's vehicle in the lead.

Matt and his mates were playing a game at the pool table. Belinda chose a nearby booth for us to observe the men in action, their competition fierce. She glanced often in Matt's direction. Had she warmed to his softer side?

Matt plonked himself next to Belinda. "What're you ladies having for dinner? I won, so it's the perfect time for a break. Gives me more time to gloat before I'm thrashed." He laughed and waved off the mock bows from his mates, who disappeared in the direction of the bar.

"Want me to order some sharing plates?" Belinda asked.

Matt winked, and her cheeks reddened. "Great idea, Bee. You up for it, ladies?"

Amber and I nodded, and we ordered our food.

"What about drinks? My treat," I said. Inundated with a drinks list, I headed to the bar and ordered with the bartender.

Possessing the closest bar stool, I scanned the room. A familiar face met my gaze, and Nicholas stepped away from his friends.

"Good evening, Victoria. I trust you're well?" Nicholas's smile warmed my insides faster than a glass of red wine.

"I'm well, thanks. Did you just arrive?" My senses were so attuned to his proximity, I always spotted him in a crowd.

"Yes, catching up with a few school mates. We get together one Friday a month, but Saturday worked better this time."

I recognised a few local businessmen at his table. "Did you all attend the school here?"

Nicholas leaned against the bar with a grin. "We're all products of the local education system. Not bad for a backward country town, hey?"

I giggled and twisted on the stool. "Not bad at all."

The bartender touched my shoulder, and I turned to thank him.

Nicholas raised an eyebrow. "You on a drinking binge? Do I

need to intervene?"

I nudged him with my shoulder. "These are for my friends. They're the noisy ones near the pool table."

His grin faded. "At last glance, a bunch of guys were playing pool."

Discomfort snaked up my spine under his scrutiny. "They're Matt's friends. A colleague. He invited Amber, Belinda and me to dinner."

"I know Matt. He doesn't seem the type of man you'd spend time with."

A blush imbued my cheeks. "He's not a bad guy," I said, my voice quiet. "Aren't we meant to show the love of Christ to the lost?"

Nicholas's dark eyes blazed. "So long as you don't become lost in the process."

Why was he behaving like an over-protective big brother? I sighed. Men. "Trust me, that won't happen."

His shoulders relaxed.

I reached for the drinks tray, but Nicholas grabbed it.

"Allow me."

I strode to my table with Nicholas fast on my heels. Raucous laughter filled the air.

"Fancy Victoria finding you, Nicholas," Belinda said.

Amber's eyes widened along with her smile. "It's nice to put a face to a name. I'm Amber, Victoria's friend from Melbourne."

Nicholas smiled, placed the tray on the table, and shook Amber's hand. "Nice to meet you, Amber."

I resumed my seat next to Amber while my friends chatted. My pulse increased with each word.

Matt smiled up at Nicholas. "Want to join us for dinner?"

"Thanks, but I should rejoin my friends. I might swing by later if you're still around when my group heads home."

My gaze lingered on Nicholas and his sculpted back before I turned to face my friends.

An amused smile travelled Matt's features. "Now it all makes sense." He winked at me. "You're into Nick."

My face blazed.

Amber squeezed my hand with a smile. "He seemed more intent on looking at you than the rest of us."

Food arrived at the table, and I sagged against the backrest. Our conversation morphed into delighted gasps at the flavours of our meal.

After dinner, Matt returned to the pool table, and the ambient noise increased. Amber, Belinda, and I joined the group to cheer on the players. With a little encouragement from the guys, Amber and Belinda joined the game. I had no desire to play.

The night progressed, and alcohol emboldened Matt's friends. Several tried to chat me up, the latest man too free with his heavy hands on my rear end. His advances went unnoticed by Matt, who seemed preoccupied with the game and flirting with Belinda, and Amber, who delighted in trash talking the other players. The stench of alcohol permeating from Mr. Handsy brought Jude's drunken face to mind, and my stomach twisted.

I contemplated an exit strategy while trying to catch my friends' eyes when a shadow fell over my unwanted admirer. His untoward presence was replaced with a scowling, arms crossed, Nicholas.

My legs wobbled, and my chest lightened. I scolded myself for having thought Nicholas's big-brother protectiveness unnecessary. Gratitude flooded my heart.

I leaned in on tiptoe, and Nicholas inclined his head. "Thank you. I was scrambling for a way of escape, including kneeing him in the groin."

Nicholas smirked, his eyes bright. "Knew I should've waited longer."

I punched his toned bicep, and he laughed out loud.

"Okay, I deserved that. Are you okay?"

I faltered on my feet. "Y-yes." I mustered a smile, conscious of the excess body heat dampening my armpits under my jacket. "I'm tempted to hire you as my bodyguard."

An unexplainable expression flashed across his face before transforming to his easygoing smile. "I'd be happy to play bouncer if it meant you were safe from"—he shot a warning glance at a man nearby—"the likes of him."

A shiver ran up my spine at the objectionable nature of the man's stare. I still had to get my head around my singleness. I kept an eye on the rowdy men and stood closer to Nicholas. Any man interested in my plain-Jane package craved one thing. Beer goggles must blind them.

I pressed into Nicholas's arm. "Would you please check if Amber and Belinda are ready to leave? I'd rather stay over here."

Nicholas nodded with a grim smile and walked to the pool table.

Nervous energy danced in my bones.

He reappeared with Amber clutching his arm a minute later. She seemed tipsy. "Your knight in shining armour said you'd like to go home."

I shot her a hard glance before we trekked to the exit.

Passing through the door Nicholas cleared his throat. "Belinda said goodnight, and she'll see you bright and early tomorrow morning."

Amber turned to him, still holding onto his arm. "You know, you're a huge improvement on her ex—"

"Let's get you home, Amber. I think you've indulged in more wine than normal." I avoided Nicholas's gaze and unlocked my car by remote.

After Nicholas opened Amber's door, she released her grip on his arm and climbed into the passenger seat. He ambled to my side of the car.

A warm tingle danced around the pit of my stomach. "Sorry about that. Amber's a wonderful friend."

He rubbed the back of his neck and gazed into my eyes. "That's okay. I'm glad you're fine."

I smiled and placed a tentative hand on his arm. "Thank you.

For tonight."

His gaze zoned in on my hand touching his arm and blazed before lifting to my face.

My cheeks flamed. I retracted my hand, fumbled with my keys, and opened the car door. "Goodnight, Nicholas."

"Goodnight, Victoria." Nicholas stepped back and walked away.

I loitered in the car, confounded by the power of his gaze.

Amber slurred, "He loves you."

I scrunched my brows and evaluated her, nestled into the seat with her eyes closed, and a smile on her lips. She was more than tipsy. She was drunk.

I flopped onto the couch. Alone. Loneliness and grief were terrible friends. I missed life with my children and Jude's warm body at night. Perhaps the single life was not for me. I shuddered at the memory of Mr. Handsy at Benanu's.

Amber had returned to Melbourne, and the next two-and-a-half months dissolved into thin air. The gaping holes in my heart hurt less when I threw myself into my work and sport. I loved playing ball, excited when each game became easier on my leg and rebuilt my self-confidence. My rediscovered flexibility encouraged me and the local physiotherapist I visited every few weeks.

No longer a wife and mother, I pondered who I was and who I wanted to be. By mid-September, I spent Saturday mornings and Wednesday afternoons at Benanu's, journaling my thoughts, feelings and memories.

I almost ran myself ragged during the September school holidays volunteering at the church-run holiday program. Diana, Madison, and Grace also volunteered, and I enjoyed chatting when time permitted. I never tired of their conversation, no matter how adolescent it became. How could something I had lost with my own children annoy me? I missed Jessica and her friends coming home after school, discussing Netflix shows and their insufferable younger siblings.

With the holiday program over, I returned to the darkness of my house. My isolation and grief hit me hard, and I struggled to get out of bed again.

October ushered in VCE exam preparation and an increased workload. I pressed pause on my volunteer roles and even missed a game of basketball.

Now I sat alone on a Saturday night. Sadness had repressed me the moment I woke. I stared at a bookshelf of photos from my past life, unable to focus on work. My quiet country home mocked me. I no longer needed to bribe the children with TV, ask them to play outside, or suggest for the tenth time to play in the other end of the house.

I brushed away tears and reached for a book. Perhaps Emma St Clair could make me laugh. I needed a moment away from the papers and the work. Away from my suffocating life. I needed a lifeline.

The next morning, I chatted with Belinda and Nicholas before church. Nicholas stared at something behind me, and I turned around to identify what had caught his attention.

An instinctual scream burst from my lips, and I wrapped my arms around my cousin. "Stevie! What're you doing here?"

He laughed and returned my hug before stepping back for Stacy and Toby.

I pulled Stacy close.

She hugged me. "When I discovered I had no court appearances tomorrow, we booked BnB accommodation for two nights, and here we are! We don't often do things on the spur of the moment." She pulled back from me and beamed. "We arrived last night."

My heart was lighter, excited. Far too long had passed since I had seen my cousins in the flesh. I turned to Belinda and Nicholas.

"This is my cousin, Steve, his gorgeous wife, Stacy, and their adorable son, Toby."

The group exchanged greetings, and Stacy caught my eye. "So, Nicholas, are you the same gentleman who rescued dear Vicki from broken appliances and undesirable rogues?"

Nicholas grinned in my direction. "The one and only, at your service."

Stacy beamed. "I'm glad gentlemen here watch out for single ladies. In case you haven't worked it out, Victoria Jade Burke is a one-of-a-kind treasure. Not just a pretty face."

Heat spread across my skin. I knelt to talk to Toby, who was wrapped around his mother's legs. I focused on the high-fives my little cousin slapped against my hand, relieved when our pastor invited everyone to sit. Tears welled from seeing Stacy and Steve next to me. God knew what I needed.

I spent the afternoon and evening with my cousins.

At Stacy's insistence, Nicholas joined us for dinner at Gustoso, the local Italian restaurant.

Stacy flashed one of her disarming smiles. "So, Nick, I assume you're not married, or I would've met your wife by now." She speared a green bean. "If you don't mind me asking, what happened to Diana's mother?"

I held my breath. I knew nothing about how his wife had died.

Nicholas's shoulders slumped. "We lost Debbie to a drunk driver when Diana was six."

An explosion detonated in my brain, cutting off all rational thought, blocking my senses. I fought tears, my breaths erratic.

What were the odds? Both of us had suffered the torment of our loved ones snatched away at the hands of drunk drivers?

The haze lifted, and I found myself in the ladies' bathroom with Stacy.

She cupped my face. "I'm sorry. I wouldn't have asked if I knew." Her grey eyes shimmered. "Did you know?"

"No," I whispered. I fell into Stacy's embrace and allowed my tears to flow. "I-I want to go home."

"Of course. Dinner's pretty much finished. Toby will be getting tired, so I'll think up some excuse to satisfy Nicholas." She stepped back from our embrace and exited the bathroom.

Ten minutes later, Stacy assisted me into my bungalow, while Steve stayed in the car with Toby, and set me on my couch ensconced in my blanket. I wrapped my cold, clammy hands around a hot cup of tea. My tears refused to abate.

Stacy cuddled me until Steve came inside with an irritable toddler. They hugged me while Steve prayed, and then the Morgan family kissed me goodbye.

After their departure I cried on and off between prayers and went to bed in a haze of exhaustion.

CHAPTER FOURTEEN
Growing Pains

"Ms. Burke, do you have a moment?"

I had dismissed my Year Ten English class for lunch. My arms laden with essays, I placed the pile of papers onto my desk and turned to face Diana. Keanu hovered in the doorway. "Of course, Diana. How can I help?"

"Do you know how many students are needed for a VCE Literature class?" Her uplifted brows drew together over her deep-brown eyes.

"Oh." Warmth stirred in my chest. An entire year had passed since I taught literature. "No, I don't. What a wonderful idea!"

Diana's shoulders relaxed, and she beamed.

"I assume Keanu's not interested," I whispered.

We glanced at the doorway and giggled.

I grinned. "I'll see what I can find out. Give me a few days." I held back the urge to jump on the spot. "I'm glad I'm not the only person at school interested in literature."

Diana thanked me before she glided out of the classroom with Keanu.

I gathered answers to Diana's query, and a few days later scheduled a lunchtime meeting. I created and displayed A4 fliers in the Year Ten and Eleven English rooms and locker areas. I also mentioned the meeting during my morning classes.

When the lunchtime bell rang, the room filled with the sounds of chatting teenagers. I blew out a breath, counting nine heads in total. Not enough for a timetabled class, but an after-school class was now a real possibility. With a warm smile, I pointed the students toward the front tables.

I leaned back against my desk. "Thank you for giving up the start of lunchtime to find out about next year's VCE Literature classes. I promise to be brief." I surveyed the faces of my potential students. "The school's happy to facilitate the subject if there's a minimum of five students per year level, but in order to have a timetabled class, we need ten."

Diana raised her hand. "What does that mean, Ms. Burke?"

"If five students from Year Eleven or five from Year Twelve commit to the subject, I'll take on the responsibility to teach after school. I expect two longer sessions a week will suffice, perhaps Tuesdays and Thursdays. Talk to your parents and work out whether you can commit to this arrangement. I'll send you and your parents a detailed email later this afternoon to share some information about the subject, my expectations, and my suggested times for class." I stepped closer to the students. "Any questions?"

Anna Beaufort raised her hand.

"Yes, Anna?"

"My brother and I catch the school bus home. Mum doesn't drive, and Dad doesn't get home until dinnertime." The smile on Anna's face faded with each word.

"How far away do you live from school?" I asked.

"Fifteen minutes."

"If your parents sign a release form, I'll drive you home after each class."

Anna's face glowed. "Oh, Ms. Burke! I'm sure Dad and Mum will agree!"

I smiled at each student. "Okay, you're free to go. Enjoy your lunch."

♥ ♥ ♥ ♥ ♥ ♥ ♥

A sea of voices shouted "Boo!" from the sidelines as my final shot swished into the hoop, followed by screams behind the baseline. A whistle momentarily drowned out the hullabaloo in the school gymnasium.

Hands slapped my sweaty back, and I chuckled at the scowls on my young opponents' faces.

The annual Year Twelve-students-versus-teachers basketball match had finished moments earlier, and the teachers were victorious.

"You did it!" Belinda handed me my drink bottle.

I slurped a long sip. "That was fun!" I exchanged the bottle for a towel and rubbed my face and neck. "You should play with us next year."

Her eyes widened. "I don't think so. I played my first year here. Never again."

Someone bumped my shoulder, and I turned. "Yikes, Vicki, you could've told me you're a pro." Matt rubbed a towel across his face before slinging his arm around my neck.

I flashed a toothy grin. "You never asked."

"Seriously, what an amazing game. I think you beat the entire student team on your own." He nodded to Belinda, and we headed toward the change rooms.

I slipped out from under his arm while we walked. "I was born and raised to worship God first and NBA second. I'm still quite passionate about both."

Matt whistled. "Sounds like you had an interesting upbringing. Care to elaborate?"

I darted a glance at him. "Dad travelled in his twenties and ended up in San Francisco along the way. He lived and worked in San Fran for three years, and his love affair with the NBA began when he fell head over heels for Rick Barry and the Golden State Warriors."

A sudden pang hit me square in the chest. I missed my parents, their warm smiles and loving embrace. Two and a half months to go until we were reunited for Christmas.

"Your dad sounds like a cool guy," Matt said.

We stopped in front of the ladies' change room.

Belinda shifted on her feet. "Well, Matt, now you know first pick for next year's team. The students will be prepared for Ms. Burke's ability, so you better strategise and get your edge back."

Matt grinned. "Let's talk about it with the other teachers tonight at Benanu's."

I eyed my sweat-stained tank top and grimaced. "First things first, I need a shower." I grabbed my bag from Belinda, smiled, and shuffled through the door.

♥ ♥ ♥ ♥ ♥ ♥ ♥

I dropped my pen onto the dining table and rotated my neck. Another Monday night post-basketball spent immersed in schoolwork to the sounds of TobyMac's voice. I now dealt with the quiet better than six months ago, but not complete silence. Music filled the void.

Thank You, God, for Your mercies. They are new every morning.

I stood and stretched my legs. My movements were no longer restricted, but when I stood or sat for long periods of time, that familiar ache set in.

Someone tapped at the door, and I stilled. A visitor at eight o'clock? I unlocked and cracked the door open.

Diana stood on my doorstep, her eyes red-rimmed and blotchy. Fresh tears ran down her face.

Adrenaline pumped through my veins in tandem with an overwhelming sensation of dread.

I pulled the door open and wrapped an arm around Diana's back. She heaved a sob, highlighting wet droplets on the front of her top. I brushed stray hairs from her wet face and ushered her to the couch, where she collapsed in a heap.

With prayerful steps, I locked the door, then reclined next to Diana. My abdomen tightened.

She launched into my arms and thudded against my chest. Her long arms wrapped around my torso and hugged me tight, her sobs and sniffs muffled by my shoulder.

I soothed her with a gentle sway and rubbed her back. She appeared so young, so fragile. I missed my children coming to me with their needs. My eyes misted over, and I held Diana close. "Diana, darling. What's wrong? Does your dad know you're here?"

Her sobs morphed into soft hiccups. She wiped her sleeve across her face and eyed me. "No. He h-hates me." She fell back against my chest and heaved a sigh.

I smothered a gasp and stared at the top of her head. How could she believe such a thing? I kissed her crown, and her cascading dark hair brushed my cheek. "Darling, I don't think it's possible for your dad to hold anything in his heart but great love for you. What happened?"

Diana sniffed, and I reached for the tissue box on the coffee table. I pulled out several soft squares and handed her the wad.

She blew her nose. "I broke curfew last night. I-I was out with youth group, and some of them got into a long game of pool at Benanu's. Usually, my group leader takes me home, but she went home sick." She hiccupped. "David MacLeod offered to give me a ride. I've had a crush on him for a while."

David was several years older than Diana. Self-assured, handsome and talented. Often flocked by girls, he played guitar at church, and he reminded me of Jude.

I squeezed her hand. "Go on."

She shivered and wiped her nose. "I've always been nervous around him, not my usual self, if that makes sense."

I hid a smile. Her father did a similar thing to me.

"W-when the game finished, it was ten minutes past curfew. By the time I walked through the front door, I was half an hour late."

I squinted at her. "What happened in the twenty-minute gap?"

She blushed. "David parked outside my house, and we talked a little." She lowered her head. "Th-then he kissed me."

The mother panic button shrieked in my brain.

Diana stared at the floor. The redness in her cheeks deepened before she peeked up. "My first kiss."

A reminiscent smile traced my lips.

"My tummy tingled. It was like a drug." Her blush intensified. "And then h-his hands touched my ribcage, and I freaked out when his fingers skimmed my bra." She hunched and curled her arms in front of her chest.

I pulled her into a tight hug.

She shuddered in my arms.

"What did you do?"

"I bolted from the car and rushed inside, but D-Dad was waiting in the lounge. I-I'm sure he knew what happened because he was quiet, angry. He stared at my face, then my untucked top." A sob racked her chest. "Said I was g-grounded until Christmas, and when he allowed me out next, my curfew would go from eleven to ten o'clock."

The sight of her innocent, blotchy face hurt my heart. I rubbed her back while she sniffled.

"Dad told me at dinner tonight he spoke to David. That David's never coming near me again, and I lost it. Dad humiliated me, and I yelled at him, saying th-things I didn't mean. He yelled back, and I freaked out. Dad never yells at me, Ms. Burke. I ran here as fast as I could." Tears slithered down her cheeks. "He h-hates me." She buried her face in my neck.

I whispered prayers over her, a silent cry for wisdom from above, and pressed another kiss on top of her head. "We need to call your dad. He'll be worried."

She nodded, and I slipped off the couch to grab my phone from the dining table. I dialled Nicholas's mobile number with shaky fingers.

He answered within a ring. "Hello?"

"Nicholas, it's Victoria."

"Oh, hi, Victoria. H-how can I help you?"

I clutched the phone in my hand. "Diana's here."

"Thank You, God," he said under his breath. "I'll be over soon—"

"If you don't mind, I'd like to bring her home ... soon." I slipped into my bedroom. "Diana shared what happened, and I thought I could give her a female perspective on this important topic. And dispel the falsehood her father hates her before she faces him again."

A sob garbled over the line before he whispered, "She said I hated her?"

I blinked back tears. "Yes, but I quashed the thought."

He sighed.

I cleared my throat. "So, is it okay if I chat with her a little longer?"

"Yes, thank you, Victoria." His voice cracked on my name.

"Anything for your beautiful daughter. We'll see you soon."

I returned to Diana on the couch. "When I was sixteen, I crushed on a boy at church. A guitarist like David who was adored by the girls. We dated for a few years, but in the early days I clashed with my parents. They understood the bigger picture, something I couldn't see until my friend revealed her pregnancy. She was seventeen."

Diana's eyes bulged, and her mouth fell open.

I squeezed her hand. "Annaliese was my best friend at church. A good girl like me. She never behaved inappropriately with a boy until she met her kryptonite. It happened in the backseat of a car with a guy she had met at a youth conference and was all over fifteen minutes before her midnight curfew." I lifted Diana's chin with my hand and searched her eyes. "I wouldn't wish that heartache on anyone. Your dad wants to protect you."

Diana wiped her eyes with the back of her hand. "I didn't realise how fast a situation can escalate. And the feelings which come with a kiss?" Her shy smile was almost dreamy. "Wow. No wonder people get married. It must be amazing to live in blissfulness all the time."

An assault of memories pummelled my mind. I pushed them back down. "Now you understand why marriage is God's best. He's not a prude. God designed sex and all the amazing feelings and emotions as a package deal. Knowing your husband promised his all to you for life gives you that security to be intimate." My stomach roiled at my own words. Each of Jude's broken promises punched me in the gut. I suppressed a threatening sob.

Diana leaned against my side. "Can I talk to you about things like this in the future? It's so awkward with Dad."

"Of course, sweetheart. Any time, day or night. I'll give you my mobile number."

Her eyes brightened, the blotchiness in her face waning. "Okay. I left my phone at home."

"No problem." I blew out a breath. "Ready to face the music? I bet your dad's more upset than you." I would have been if I were him.

Diana peeked at my face. "Maybe." She scrunched her brow. "I know I upset him because his voice went all weird, then he was silent for ages before he started yelling again."

Nicholas's voice went all weird? Jude seldom shed a tear or verbalised his emotions. An unexplainable warmth spread through my body.

We reached the Jacobsen house minutes later, and I led Diana inside, her hand clasped in mine. Within moments Nicholas held his daughter in a firm embrace. Wetness clouded my vision.

Nicholas's voice quavered. "I'm sorry, Princess. Forgive me."

Diana hugged her father with renewed vigour. "I forgive you, Daddy." She pulled away and glanced over her shoulder, beaming a smile at me before she turned back. "Ms. Burke helped me understand you're protecting me. I promise to make wiser decisions in the future. Will you forgive me?"

Nicholas stared across at me with tear-filled eyes.

My skin tingled under his gaze.

He turned to his daughter and kissed her forehead. "Of course, I forgive you. I love you, Diana."

"I love you too. I think I'll go to bed." Diana planted a gentle kiss on her father's cheek before she squeezed him in a final hug. She turned and ran into my arms, leaning down to place a similar kiss on my cheek.

Nicholas's watchful gaze weighed on my shoulders.

I dragged my focus away from him.

"Thank you," Diana whispered in my ear. "If he wants details, please tell him. I'm too embarrassed."

"Sure. Goodnight, sweet girl." I turned toward Nicholas as Diana left the room, and my stomach jumped at his steady gaze.

He cleared his throat. "Would you like a cup of tea before you leave?"

I nodded, followed him into the kitchen, and occupied a bar stool.

Diana bounded down the hallway. "Ms. Burke, I almost forgot! You promised me your phone number." Diana's happy countenance had resurfaced.

"Of course." I entered my details in the proffered phone and returned it.

She hummed another farewell before she disappeared.

Nicholas assembled cups. "What would you like to drink?"

"Chamomile, please." Anything to help calm the flutters in my abdomen.

He prepared the tea and placed it in front of me.

"Thanks, Nicholas."

He leaned against the opposite side of the bench, mug in hand. His glassy gaze locked onto my face. "Thank *you*. I let the situation get the better of me and went into protective-father overload."

I sipped the floral bouquet. "And so you should. Diana must've been a sight when she returned home last night. She shared the details of her … encounter."

Fire glinted in his eyes. "I was ropeable. That MacLeod boy has a terrible reputation. When I recognised his car parked outside, I almost retrieved her, but she soon ran inside. My mind flooded with ways I could torture him with the contents of my toolkit."

I hid a smirk behind my cup. "Did you use any tools during your discussion today? I imagine a set of pliers would do quite nicely."

He flashed a grin, his eyes bright and mischievous. "It crossed my mind. I used my height to my advantage, and we talked. I was clear he stay far away from her."

"I'm glad it's sorted."

Nicholas stared at his mug. "He didn't hurt my girl, did he?"

I shook my head. "He kissed sense out of her, a memorable first kiss for her to tell her daughters one day, but no. She bolted when his hands went ... wandering."

A scowl darkened his face, and I giggled against my cup. Angry Nicholas was adorable in a frightening sort of way. He peered at me, and his face relaxed. "What?"

"Remind me never to get on your bad side."

"Duly noted."

I ran a finger around the rim of my cup. "Nicholas?"

"Yes?" His dark eyes zeroed in on me.

"You don't mind I offered to talk with Diana whenever she needs to?"

His face softened, and the corners of his mouth lifted. "Not at all. This situation reminded me Diana doesn't have the benefit of a mother to talk to about"—he waved a hand in the air—"things. I know it's awkward for her to talk to me sometimes."

"You're a wonderful father." A tinge of warmth touched my cheeks, and I took in a deep breath. "I told Diana how I clashed with my parents over a boy. What I didn't tell her was that my godly dad almost punched my boyfriend, so no dad's perfect." Not the only punch Dad ever launched at Jude.

Nicholas let out a low whistle. "Good grief, what were you caught doing?"

My blush flamed. "We were on my parents' couch. I had three buttons undone on my blouse, and you can guess where Dad found Jude's hand."

Nicholas choked on his tea.

A nervous laugh slipped from my lips at his heated face. "Sorry. That's the second drink you've choked on in my company. It isn't intentional, I promise." I dropped my gaze to my almost-empty mug. "If it's any consolation, I didn't do anything inappropriate after that point, so I'm hopeful Diana will make a similar choice."

His large, warm fingers touched my chin and lifted my head.

My lungs stalled.

Nicholas stared into my eyes. "With you encouraging Diana in her academic, spiritual, and social worlds, I've no doubt she'll make many wise decisions. You're a natural, Victoria. Thank you." Nicholas released my chin.

My pulse pounded, and I gulped. Of course, I was a natural. I had mothered three children, not that he knew. I dropped my gaze to my hands. They shook around the mug. I imbibed the last mouthful of tea and deployed a hasty exit to my car.

My hands trembled on the steering wheel, and pain stung the back of my throat. Why was it so hard to talk about my past? I had shared how my ex-husband had groped me as a teenager yet struggled to communicate about the three beautiful gifts from my womb. What sort of mother chose not to brag about her babies? I could counsel Diana and help her reconcile with her father, yet I denied myself the same courtesy to reconcile my past with my current life.

What was wrong with me? I wiped tears from my cheeks on my short journey home.

CHAPTER FIFTEEN
Slip and Fall

I walked into Benanu's for our final staff catch-up of the year. With a furtive glance back at my car, I charged toward the bar and ignored the school papers crying out from the car park. I needed to get away from it all.

I breathed in the festive scents of cinnamon and pine. Small twinkling lights and Christmas decor sparkled against the mirror behind the bar, a noticeable change from my visit on Wednesday afternoon.

Belinda and Matt stood close together near a small Christmas tree next to the bar, their eyes focused on one another.

I recalled the warmth of past conversations with a man I once loved. The possibility of future dialogues with someone special of my own dug deep and burrowed into my heart.

I shook my head to clear my mind and ventured in their direction. In the midst of my distracted thought, I bumped into Nicholas, who held a tray full of drinks.

"Oh my goodness, I'm so sorry!"

His warm smile ignited heat up my neck and onto my face. "No worries, my beautiful Victoria. I'm glad you turned in time." He flashed a wide grin, winked at me, and continued his journey to his table of school mates.

I gaped at his back in the wake of his brazen flirtation. When I turned around, Belinda stared at me, wide-eyed.

"Well, well, Vicki, looks like you've caught the attention of one very eligible bachelor," Matt said.

The heat in my cheeks climbed several degrees. I should have spent the night amongst the familiarity of white paper and red-inked pens.

Matt laughed and rested a hand on my shoulder. "Looks like you need a drink. Why don't you ladies head to our table?"

I grabbed Belinda by the arm and pulled her close. My frazzled brain needed time to sort itself out, so I asked, "What's going on with you and Matt?"

Belinda blushed and shrugged. "I'm not sure, but whatever it is, I'm enjoying it. You don't think the eight-year age gap should be an issue?"

I squeezed her hand. "Not at all." We interlocked our arms and walked toward the dining area. "Matt's a nice guy. Just be cautious with your differing moral views." I avoided glancing in the direction of Nicholas's table even though I wanted to peek.

Belinda chuckled and dug into my ribs with her sharp elbow. "Speaking of nice, older guys, you know he's staring at you, right?"

A nervous laugh exited my lips. "I doubt it, Bee." But the memory of Nicholas's smile, his words and uncharacteristic wink were dangerous and electrifying. He thought I was beautiful?

Belinda nodded at the rowdy table. "He's smitten, Vicki. Either that or he's drunk."

I let out a loud laugh.

Belinda stopped mid-step and cocked her head. "You're right. He couldn't be drunk." She glanced in Nicholas's direction. "Maybe one of his mates slipped him a mickey as a joke. Or the tall blonde over there. I'm sure she's eyeing him off."

A shiver ran down my spine, and I followed her line of sight.

A blonde woman slinked toward Nicholas's table and planted herself amongst the men.

We stood, fixated, until a redhead approached the table.

My stomach churned, and my mouth dried when the blonde

danced her fingertips across Nicholas's muscled shoulders. A sharp jab twisted in my chest when she lowered her mouth to his ear, her full red lips far too close for comfort. I imagined her words of seduction, to entice a man to do whatever she wanted.

Words Jude must have heard often from his secretary.

Queasiness raked my insides. "Bee, we have to do something. This situation doesn't sit right. I-I don't want Diana seeing her dad in any state other than his usual."

"What's up, ladies?" Matt flicked his gaze between us, drinks in hand. "Why aren't you at the tables with everyone else?"

Belinda volleyed her gaze from Matt's face to Nicholas's table. "We suspect those two ladies are making a play for Nick's table and think they've spiked his drink. Got a creative idea to get him out of this situation?" Belinda plucked the drinks from his grasp.

Matt cocked his head. "Anything for the fair Belinda Davies." He grinned at Belinda's blush before he grabbed my hand. "I'll need your help, though, Vicki. You're my draw card."

What was I about to get myself into? "I'm not much of a draw card."

Matt aimed his grin at me. "You underestimate the power of an attractive woman without an agenda. A virtuous woman wins every time."

A pleasant warmth rose inside me. The more time I spent with Matt, the more he surprised me. No wonder Belinda liked him.

He dragged me to Nicholas's table.

We stopped in front of Nicholas and the temptresses. "Evening ladies, we need our mate Nick here." Matt's words were polite, but his rigid shoulders and flexed arms gave away his displeasure. He turned to Nicholas. "Any chance we could pull you away?"

I placed my hand on Nicholas's upper arm.

Tension rippled through his muscles, and he stared up at me. His dilated eyes darkened at my touch, his gaze on my lips.

My skin heated.

His friends seemed to catch every moment of our exchange.

Shouts of encouragement, loud hand slaps on the table, laughter, and various inappropriate comments brought Nicholas to his feet.

I grabbed his hand, to the fanfare of hoots and jeers, and we led Nicholas toward the exit. His unstable steps confirmed he was under the influence of something. Memories of assisting Jude to the car in a similar state sobered me.

Matt helped me straighten Nicholas against the wall near the exit. "It's seven-thirty, mate. Seems a tad early to be sloshed."

Nicholas recoiled in slow motion. His large hand pressed against his chest. "I'm no-t sssloshhhed."

A question I had asked too many times slipped from my lips. "How much did you drink?"

Nicholas flinched.

I regretted the edge to my voice.

He sniffed. "One b-beer."

"Were the beers on tap?" Matt asked.

Nicholas scratched his head and dipped his eyebrows. "Um, on tap. Thossse women fffluttered around Shaun w-when he collected our fffirst rrrr-ound. D'you thinkkk—"

"Yeah, we do. Vicki was concerned by your response when she bumped into you. Bee and Vicki requested I got you away from your table before the hussies pounced."

I could have smacked Matt. Hussies, indeed.

Nicholas searched my face with glassy eyes. "I'm ssssorry I concerned y-you, Vvvicc-toria. W-what did I sssay?"

Someone tapped my shoulder, and I turned around. Keanu leaned close, his forehead creased. "Is everything okay?"

I glanced at Matt. He steadied Nicholas as I pulled Keanu away.

"Is Mr. J hammered?" The disbelief in Keanu's voice soothed me.

"I think he's been drugged." I nodded toward Nicholas's table. "Possibly those women."

Keanu scowled. "I'll let Dad know. You'll be okay with him?" He stared at Nicholas.

I nodded.

"Diana's staying at Anna's tonight."

I blew out a breath. "Thanks, Keanu."

He dipped his head before marching toward the back office.

I turned back to Nicholas. "Let's get you home. Is anyone staying with you this weekend? Boarders? BnB guests?"

His head lolled to the side. "N-no."

I raised a brow at Matt. "Can you help me get him in my car?"

Matt's forehead creased. "You sure? His walking's deteriorating. Will you be able to get him to his front door?"

"Don't worry. I'm more than capable. Trust me."

Matt's eyes narrowed before he nodded.

I blew Belinda a kiss goodbye and assisted Matt with Nicholas's weight.

We proceeded to my Mazda, strapped Nicholas in the passenger seat, and closed the door.

I hugged Matt. "Thanks. Please give my apologies to everyone inside."

"Will do." He re-entered Benanu's, and I marvelled at the friend he had become over the last six months.

I opened the driver's door and assessed the drooping man, whose behaviour I had never expected to mirror another man I had shunned for almost a year.

"Where are your keys?"

"Um." Nicholas patted his chest and jacket pockets like a man performing an airport security search. He squinted while he continued to hunt. All of a sudden, his eyes opened wide, and he grinned. Nicholas dropped his hands to the right front pocket of his Levi's and fumbled about.

I sighed and removed his hands from their hapless work. Slipping my fingers into his jeans pocket, I stifled a gasp. The pocket lining was thin and warm. My pulse raced as my hand inched deeper until I touched warm metal.

His chest rose and fell in shallow bursts.

I enveloped the keys with cautious fingers.

He hissed a harsh breath. The stimulant in his bloodstream may have impaired his balance, but his physical senses were on full alert.

With deep breaths I withdrew the keys from his pocket and glanced up into his eyes. My throat constricted and heart thundered at the hunger on his face. I spun around, fumbled with the keys in the lock, and opened the door. "Come on, you lumbering elephant. Let's get you inside."

His eyes seemed to dance above a tilted smirk.

The tightness in my chest relaxed. Nicholas differed from Jude's moody, tense drunkenness, and I whispered a thankful prayer.

Supporting Nicholas's gargantuan frame, I assisted him into the house and propped him against the entry wall. Stepping away, I retrieved the keys and closed the door. I turned back to the sozzled man and panicked.

Nicholas was slumped against the wall on a downward path to the floor.

With a grunt and a heave, I pushed my body against his and pulled him up. Beads of sweat slid down the back of my neck. Thank God for my workouts.

I had learned the hard way of the physical strength required to lift the dead weight of a drunk man. Memories flooded back of the nights Jude slept on our bedroom floor. I shuddered at the thought of Diana arriving home tomorrow to her father passed out in the entryway.

With my determination renewed, we continued the laborious trek through the house. Exhaustion pressed against my limbs with each step holding and guiding the giant, uncoordinated man. Perhaps turning down Matt's helpful offer was unwise.

We reached Nicholas's open bedroom doorway. The Promised Land. I loosened my grip and switched on the light.

Nicholas slipped and lost his balance.

I cried out and rammed his large form hard against the wooden door with the full length of my body. The bedroom door slammed against the doorstopper with a shuddering clang. I held my weight against his in an effort to keep him vertical and prayed like never before.

Nicholas's woodsy cologne filled my head and set off flutters in my midriff. Butterflies danced to the rhythm of my rapid pulse.

I gazed up at his wide eyes and slack mouth.

His handsome face hovered centimetres from mine, and our rapid breaths mingled in the gap.

My throat clogged, and a soft whimper hummed from my mouth. "Don't fall, Nicholas. Please."

"Issss too late, Vvvvviccctorrria." His darkened eyes seemed to consume me.

My pulse thumped in my throat.

His heart palpitated against my chest, matching my heart, beat for beat, while his gaze dropped to my lips. Nicholas angled his face.

My eyelids closed, and our mouths collided. The softness of his lips sent shivers through my body.

Nicholas was gentle, yet firm, a heady mix of hops and mint. The tenderness of his kiss overwhelmed me, and sensory overload swept through my body and ignited my skin wherever our bodies touched.

My hand glided up his chest and around the back of his neck. I raked my fingers through the hair on his nape and lost myself in the beery sweetness of his mouth. Moans drifted to my ears, with no idea if the sound came from my throat or his. Time stood still while we touched.

Emotional overload short-circuited my brain, and tears clouded my eyes. Never had I experienced such a gentle, yet passionate, moment with Jude. One kiss with Nicholas overshadowed a lifetime with my estranged husband. Tears spilled over.

Nicholas eased the pressure of his lips and released my mouth.

I wiped a tear from my cheek, and his body tensed. My stomach plummeted at the devastation in his eyes.

"I'm ssssorry, Victoria."

My throat choked, words frozen on my tongue. That awful, familiar sense of speech delay iced my vocal cords and squeezed my breaths.

I helped Nicholas cross the room and parked him on the end of the bed before pulling back the doona and sheet.

He swayed as I pulled him upright, and I pressed close. His cologne teased my nose. We shuffled to the head of the bed where he collapsed on the mattress. His shoulders relaxed, and his head nestled in his pillow before his eyelids fluttered shut.

I pulled the doona up to his neck and brushed stray hairs from his face. My hand lingered on his temple, and his eyes opened.

A sad smile veiled his face and highlighted his swollen lips.

My heart lurched, and I retracted my hand. "Sleep. I'll put some water next to your bed and pray you don't feel like rubbish in the morning." I hoped he would forget everything by morning although I never would.

I found a decent-sized bucket in the laundry and poured a tall glass of water in the kitchen. Grabbing a pile of serviettes from the dining room, I crept back down the hallway. With shaky fingers, I arranged the glass and serviettes on Nicholas's bedside table and positioned the laundry bucket on the floor near the bed.

My gaze dropped to the slumbering man. Tears pricked at the memory of his pained expression after our kiss. Had Nicholas thought he overstepped the mark?

I stared at his parted lips and touched my own with my fingers. His kiss had electrified my entire body. Every atom inside me had burst into flames the moment his mouth had melded with mine.

I stepped back on unsteady legs. I was falling for Nicholas.

CHAPTER SIXTEEN
Empathy in Pain

December third. My knees threatened to buckle under me, and I gripped the edge of the desk with a quaking hand. Today was my fourteenth wedding anniversary.

A heavy weight pressed down onto my shoulders, and I sank back in the chair, powerless. The loss of my marriage had torn my heart out at the time of its demise, and a gaping hole remained in my chest almost twelve months later.

I tried to focus on classes, but a heaviness overshadowed and haunted me throughout the day. Was life with Jude better than life alone? Was the devil you knew truly better?

Life had once bordered on bliss. Waking to Jude's beautiful blue eyes full of admiration, transfixed on me from his pillow. I could still picture the shape of his lips when they curled up in tease. The sound of his laughter reverberating in his chest. I missed his smile-inducing laugh.

I ate lunch in the courtyard near the school office and meditated on my thoughts. The creaky wooden bench seat beneath me lay in the shade of a beautiful white crepe myrtle tree, its flowers bold and fragrant. My attention was drawn to the wonder of God's surrounding creation in the midst of the struggle battling within me.

I sighed. Little by little, darkness had replaced our mutual joy. Moments when Jude worked late without communication. My disappointment when a case trumped my birthday celebration.

Witnessing the persona of a perfect gentleman at yet another work-related function while our private world fell apart.

Footsteps tracked along the concrete path. "Thought I'd find you here. It's a nice place to think." Matt settled beside me.

I appraised him with a faint smile before I stared at the little birds in front of me. I embraced the companionable quiet, comforted in sharing the space without the need to say a word. The feathered bodies bounced from flower to flower with beaks extended into the centres of the native bush blooms.

I tried to shake the thoughts of my past and concentrate on my future, but the memory of Nicholas's kiss held no power against his downcast gaze at church. We had not communicated in days, a double blow to my fragile heart.

"I never told you why I rebelled against the church, did I?"

I turned my head toward Matt. "No, you didn't."

He focused on the path at our feet. "I disappointed my family from my earliest recollection and never reached the standards my parents and grandparents set. I wasn't deemed a good Christian soldier and lived with my uncle and his family in Year Ten."

My heart tugged for the lost, teenaged Matt, and I frowned.

"Hey, don't be sad, beautiful." He nudged my shoulder and huffed a laugh. "I was a rude, disrespectful young man—don't get me wrong—but my inability to measure up fuelled my attitude. My parents' last straw was when I got a girl from church pregnant."

A gasp escaped my lips and my eyes bulged before I relaxed my face.

Matt rubbed his chin. "You grew up in the church and might guess the responses we received. They ranged from shock, like yourself, through to pity and sheer anger. My dad reacted with anger, and my uncle took me in when he heard the news."

I shifted on the bench seat and imagined a confused sixteen-year-old Matt in the midst of heartbreak and rebellion. I rested my hand on his arm. "It must've been a confusing, difficult time for you. I'm glad your uncle had the capacity to love you unconditionally."

Matt rested his hand on mine. "So am I."

My breath hitched. "Did your girlfriend keep the baby?"

A small groove appeared between his eyebrows. "Yes, she kept the baby, but our daughter was stillborn." His voice wavered, and he lowered his head.

My heart reeled. I squeezed his arm as my hand trembled. "I'm so sorry. It's devastating to lose a child." Tears welled in my eyes, and I blinked several times.

Matt pressed down on his thighs with outstretched hands and blew out a long breath. "I never saw her, but I've imagined her for twenty years." His blue eyes stared into mine. "It never leaves you."

I wiped tears from my cheek. "No, I'm sure it doesn't."

His gaze returned to the birds flitting in the garden, and we lingered in the peaceable surrounds until the bell rang. Matt turned to me with a smile. "Thanks for listening."

A matching smile lifted my cheeks. "Thanks for your bravery."

Perhaps in twenty years I would be brave enough to share my story.

♥ ♥ ♥ ♥ ♥ ♥ ♥

A soft knock stole my attention from my laptop screen. I lifted my head.

Nicholas stood in the English classroom doorway. "Can we talk?"

I nodded, and he let himself into the room.

His gait was slow, almost awkward. We had not spoken since our shared moment against his bedroom door.

I walked to the student desks and pulled out two chairs.

Nicholas eased down next to me on the other seat and braced his elbows on his knees. He clasped his hands together and heaved a breath. "I want to apologise for Saturday night."

I glanced at the floor. "You don't need to apologise."

"Yes, I do." He straightened in the chair. "My behaviour was unacceptable." He shook his head. "I shouldn't have taken advantage of you."

I snorted a laugh. "You were hardly in your right mind."

His gaze zoned into mine. "I knew what I was doing at that particular moment."

The air in my lungs thickened, and I fought back a cough. My cheeks heated, and I surveyed the floor. "It's okay. I—"

"It's not okay. You cried," he said, his voice hoarse.

I gazed up and shook my head. "It's not like that. Really, it's not."

"Then tell me how it is."

I closed my eyes and fortified myself with a slow, deep breath. When I lifted my eyelids, the depth of caring on his handsome face warmed me. "I've never been kissed like that before."

One side of his mouth twitched up. "I find that hard to believe."

I stared at him. "It's true! Y-you have a potent kiss," I said, soft and breathy, "and my emotions got the better of me."

A wide grin lifted his stubbled cheeks. "So, you cried for a good reason?"

I nodded.

"If that's the case"—his velvety voice sent tingles down my spine—"would you like to go out for coffee?"

I bit my lower lip. So, he *was* interested in me? "I, ah. Um. Well, the thing is—"

"You like my kisses but dislike my company?"

"No!" My voice cracked. "It's not you, it's me." I sighed. "That sounds so cliché."

He tilted his head. "Is this about your ex?"

I choked on a breath. "No! W-what ex?"

Nicholas shrugged. "Your friend Amber mentioned an ex when she visited."

Amber. I could smack her. I waved my hand in the air. "She talks nonsense after too much wine." My cheeks inflamed. Alcohol heightened Amber's honesty.

"So, there's no ex?"

My throat dried. I pasted on a smile and hoped I sounded casual. "Well, you know, there's that guy from high school." That guy I married.

Nicholas laughed, and my stomach swirled with warmth at his deep chuckle. "I see." His chest heaved, and his eyes lost all of their playful mirth. "You lost someone."

I choked on an involuntary cough. "Excuse me?" There was no way on God's green earth Nicholas knew about the children. My cowardice ensured this outcome.

He shrugged. "Your face when I spoke about Debbie with your cousins." He dropped his chin. "It's not possible to empathise so convincingly without firsthand experience."

My hands trembled. "I have things to do so I can get home."

"Yes, of course." He stretched his long legs and stood. "For what it's worth, I understand your hesitancy. It's been over ten years since Deb died. Dating has only appealed to me recently."

I gaped. "You haven't dated in a decade?"

He rubbed a hand over the back of his neck. "Not exactly. I've had my fair share of first dates, but I never found a woman who piqued my interest." His potent gaze zeroed in on mine. "Until now."

"Oh." I bit my bottom lip.

"Have a good evening. Don't work too hard, Victoria." Nicholas disappeared through the doorway with confident strides.

A smile played on my lips.

On my short walk to the church entry, someone called my name from behind me. I slowed my steps before Diana skipped into my arms and embraced me. I smiled at her infectious grin.

She linked our arms, and we strolled into the noisy building together.

I listened for each footstep belonging to Nicholas a few paces behind us.

Now that Nicholas had cleared the air, I hoped we could go back to our easygoing friendship. I craved his conversation, the cheeky gleam in his eye and his quick wit. I had missed his smile last Sunday.

I could imagine a life with the Jacobsens. My pulse walloped in my neck as I imagined being someone important in Nicholas's life. The opportunity to mother Diana in a way I had not been privileged to do in almost a year set my mind in a spin.

Diana tugged on my arm. "You haven't sat with us for weeks, and I'm not letting you get away today. I miss your beautiful singing, Ms. Burke. Plus, Dad hasn't been himself this week. I'm certain you can cure him with your company."

My cheeks burned, and I resisted the urge to cover my face with my hands. I glanced past Diana's shoulder to the smile on Nicholas's face. I averted my gaze to the expectant face of his daughter. "I'd love to sit with you, but first I have a friend to greet. Save me a seat?"

Diana nodded and released my arm.

I brushed against Nicholas when I passed him, and a bolt of awareness shot through me. I clenched my hands and aimed for a pair of blonds seated in their chairs. "Welcome, stranger."

Matt stood with a nervous smile.

I stepped close and pecked his cheek. The medicine worked, and his shoulders eased. I reached across and hugged Belinda. "So excited for you, Bee." Nothing would wipe the smile off her face today.

"Would you like to sit with us?"

"I'd love to, but I promised Diana I'd sit with her."

Matt smirked. "I bet Mr. Jacobsen's glad to have such a thoughtful daughter."

I smiled and squeezed Matt's hand. "Enjoy the service." I headed in the direction of Nicholas's tall frame. My seat was saved between his and Diana's.

Nicholas cleared his throat. "I don't want to assume anything, so I can sit on the other side of Diana if you prefer?"

Butterflies danced in my belly. I glimpsed at his lips, and the memory of his kiss warmed me. "I. Ah."

A smile curved his mouth. "Ah?"

I blushed under the weight of his stare, and his grin widened. "What did you ask?"

He chuckled. "Sit with me?"

I ducked my head in an awkward nod, planted myself beside Nicholas and ignored the lies piled between us.

CHAPTER SEVENTEEN
Family to the Rescue

"You're presenting the awards after the middle school band performance."

I nodded to Sandra. "Okay."

Sandra smiled and dashed off to accost tardy band members.

My hands shook. I was presenting the Highest Distinction in English awards to six students at tonight's Secondary Presentation Night, one from each year level. In the past I had avoided public speaking, but I had to face this particular duty with my head held high and my lunch on the edge of expulsion. I bounced my knee where I perched next to the other presenters.

When the song finished, I stood. My hands stuck to my notes as I strode to the stage. I grasped the lectern with whitened knuckles to steady my legs and survived my speech without a muddle. Thank the good Lord. Loud applause tilted my lips up, and the after-effects of my adrenaline rush gushed to my armpits and beaded on my brow. The evening had unfolded without disaster.

I slipped into my allocated post-presentation seat next to Matt.

"Well done, Vicki. You didn't mispronounce a word or name, although I thought you'd vomit all over the microphone."

My discreet elbow jabbed Matt in the ribs and silenced his laughter. "Thanks for the support," I whispered with narrowed eyes.

"Any time." He winked at me.

I turned my attention back to Principal Marsden, in the middle of her final speech, and allowed myself a quiet moment to rest. I pinched the top of my blouse and flapped the soft fabric. The light breeze it generated helped cool my overheated body and slowed my pulse.

With two days of school remaining, Principal Marsden's words of encouragement flowed from stage and struck a chord with my unsettled sensibilities. Another school year over meant a year since my babies had left me. Despite my distraction with plans and packing for my trip east, reality had finally caught up to me, and my lungs struggled under the heaviness. I choked up and brushed aside a tear.

Matt leaned close to whisper, "Most of your students will return next year. We'll see some of the others at church on Sundays too."

"Thanks."

With the evening of accolades over for another year, I mingled with teachers, students and parents until I tired. Diana called out as I left the auditorium. She approached with her father by her side.

I blew out the twist of emotion on seeing Nicholas and turned to Diana. "And how's my exemplary pupil? Congratulations on your award, Diana. You absolutely deserve it." Diana had guaranteed a painless process in choosing the Year Ten award recipient.

Her face shone. "Thanks, Ms. Burke. What a surprise!"

"It wasn't a surprise to me. I'm looking forward to teaching you in two classes next year." Although disappointed none of next year's Year Twelve students were interested in literature, the Year Eleven English Literature class had enough pupils enrolled for after-school sessions.

"Same!" Diana said. "The other girls and I are excited!"

I turned to Nicholas. "You must be proud. Diana's hard work has paid off."

"She also has a wonderful teacher supporting her."

My cheeks flushed. I smothered a yawn and laughed. "I'd better head home."

"Oh!" Diana clapped. "Before I forget, we're having a small

party on New Year's Eve. We'd love for you to come."

Her request surprised me, and warmth spread through my chest. "That's kind, but I'm driving to Wagga Wagga on Friday night to spend the holidays with my family."

She pouted and then smiled. "I'm sure you'll have a great time."

"Yes, I will. I feel the urge to thrash my nephews in a game of basketball."

Diana and Nicholas laughed.

I cleared my throat with a soft cough. "I'd better go. I'll see you both in the new year. Merry Christmas, Diana." I lifted my gaze. "Nicholas."

"Merry Christmas, Ms. Burke." Diana leaned in for a hug.

I stared up at Nicholas over Diana's shoulder.

His intense eyes stared back.

She released me as Andrew sidled up to her. He nodded to her achievement trophy. "Congratulations."

"Thanks!" They wandered toward a group of teenagers.

I lay a hand on Nicholas's arm. "See you next year."

His lips quirked into his signature grin. "Bye, Victoria."

I hoped he would still be interested in me in four weeks.

"You've got to be kidding me." I blew out a frustrated sigh and stared at the congested freeway clogged with cars, SUVs, utes, and trucks. My car limped down the road. Using my Bluetooth connection, I voice-dialled Christine.

"Hey, sis," she chirped after three rings.

"My Christmas cheer's being suffocated by exhaust fumes."

Christine laughed. "Please drive safely, even if it takes an extra hour to reach us."

"That's easy for you to say."

"Yeah, well, be safe."

I wrinkled my nose and angled an air-conditioning vent toward my face. "Yes, Mum. See you soon."

My expected five-hour journey extended close to six, and I collapsed on Christine's couch a little before midnight. Chamomile tea and a brief chat with my sister drained the last dregs of stress from my weary body before I succumbed to sleep.

I spent Saturday with my three nephews in the backyard playing horsey and jumping and laughing through two games of basketball. I also mock suffered through a long, drawn-out game of Monopoly. It was the most wonderful day I had experienced in over a year.

I had missed the chit-chat of sibling banter, random conversations about Lego movie characters, and why basketballs deflated when the bicycle pump was lost. The witty one-liners from my seven-year-old nephew, James, left me in stitches. Memories resurfaced of the times I had laughed so hard my voice croaked after something funny Samantha would say.

Christine observed me through the day even when she returned from saying goodnight to the boys. She settled herself on the couch with Patrick.

I arched a brow. "Yes, Chrissy? I know you've been analysing me all day, so out with it."

She caressed the greying waves of dark hair at Patrick's temple. He lay on a cushion across her lap, already falling asleep.

"Thinking how blessed my boys are, having such an amazing auntie ... and how much I miss my nieces and nephew."

I stilled. How would I feel if Christine's boys died tonight? My heart would shatter knowing we had played our final game this afternoon. My throat constricted. I had dismissed Christine's grief months ago, and my heart hurt for her. She had suffered too. Tears clouded my vision, and I swiped my fingers under my damp eyes. "I miss them too. It doesn't feel like a year's passed. My memories are still so fresh. I see them most nights as I drift off to sleep."

Patrick's soft snores filled the room.

Christine stroked his hair. "Any updates on the man who has your heart all aflutter?"

"You mean Nicholas?"

Her eyes gleamed. "Yes. Nicholas."

My cheeks scorched. The heated memory of his kiss stirred up a mixture of excitement and terror.

Christine straightened. Her laser gaze bore into me. "What happened? Spill it." The glint in her eyes warned me I risked my well-being if I ignored her request.

"It's ... complicated."

"Of course, it's complicated. You haven't been in this position for close to twenty years! Your divorce is on the horizon but far from complete. At least you're a step closer with twelve months of separation. Have you filed yet?"

Stacy had sent me the documentation a week earlier. "I have the paperwork upstairs to error check and sign."

Christine massaged Patrick's neck. "Good. Jude screwed up big time, and you need to move on. So, what did you do to poor Nicholas?"

"We kissed."

Christine squealed. She covered Patrick's ear with her hand while she giggled. Her eyebrows danced. "So? How was it?"

I closed my eyes with a dreamy sigh and recalled the firm muscle of his torso under my hand. The softness of his mouth against my lips. "Incredible. I've never experienced a kiss like it. Tender, yet passionate. I didn't want the moment to end."

Christine gazed at her still-sleeping husband. Her thumb brushed against his cheek, and her face softened. "I believe I know that feeling."

I inspected the cushion in my lap and twisted the soft threads of the tassels. "Unfortunately, there were ... extenuating circumstances and—"

"Tell me what happened."

My blood pumped faster and warmed my skin. I shared my anger over the whole situation from how his beer had been spiked through to the moment we kissed against his bedroom door.

"I lost myself in his touch. My emotions had the better of me and, well, I cried a few tears, but he noticed. Nicholas apologised immediately, but the pain in his eyes crushed me. It was awkward between us afterwards until he came to the school a few days later to clear the air."

Christine slipped out from under the weight of Patrick and nestled next to me. She enfolded her arms around me. "And that's all that bothers you?"

I sighed. "I'm so drawn to him. I-it frightens me." I snuggled into my sister's warm embrace. "He invited me out, but I couldn't. Not until the divorce is over." I sniffled. "And what about the children?" Tears pooled in my eyes. "How can I think about being happy when—"

"You need to find peace and not feel guilty starting again." She kissed my temple. "Your gorgeous babies would want you to be happy. From what you've told me about Nicholas and his daughter, your kids would've loved them."

"Yes. They would. But he doesn't know about them. He thinks I'm single, carefree, not bogged down with grief and a dead marriage."

"Then tell him." Christine kissed the top of my head. "You'll have to tell him sometime."

"I know. It's so hard to talk about." I slipped out of her arms. "I'm scared he'll think I'm not worth the effort. Who wants a divorcee incapable of keeping her own children safe?"

"Victoria," Christine growled. She lifted my chin with her hand, her gaze fierce. "A drunk driver killed your children. Not you." Her face softened. "Nicholas knows that pain too well, remember? He'll understand."

I nodded. Why was life so complicated? When would things get easier? My stomach pitched knowing I was misleading Nicholas, but what else could I do? Only a few more months to string the poor man along and then I might take that rain check for coffee.

♥ ♥ ♥ ♥ ♥ ♥ ♥

"Happy birthday, darling." Mum wrapped her arms around my torso and drew me close.

Dad smacked a sloppy kiss on my forehead. "Can't believe my baby girl's thirty-five."

I wrinkled my nose. "Thanks for the reminder."

"Amber and Mike are so sweet," Christine said. "Flowers and a large bottle of J'adore Eau de Parfum? I wish I had friends like that."

I lifted the lid off the gift box from my nephews.

"Makes our pile of books look lame."

I whipped my head around and eyeballed Christine. "Don't say that, it's sacrilegious! Books are never lame. What more can I want than books and Mum's strawberry sponge cake?"

"And my delicious barbecue!" Patrick called from the back verandah.

I smiled. "Yes, that too."

And my little butterballs.

My chin quivered, and I wrapped my arms around my nephews. I showered kisses on their silky heads before they could escape my clutches.

Christine handed me a tissue, and I inspected my gift. Hand-drawn pictures of favourite toys, games and sports on crinkled papers filled the box, along with a beautiful poem written by Blair. Their drawings stabbed my heart more than they comforted it. Jessica, Samantha, and Ryan used to give me gifts like this.

Patrick booked a dinner reservation at the local Thai restaurant. Dad and Mum were taking the boys via the park, and Christine and Patrick were still readying themselves in their room when the house phone rang.

"Want me to get it?" I called up the stairs.

"Yes, please!" Christine yelled back.

I dashed into the kitchen and pulled the handset off the wall. "Ellison residence, Victoria speaking."

"Happy birthday, Victoria."

I gasped, and my heart walloped in my chest. Why had I answered the phone?

"What do you want?" My tone was clipped.

Jude's voice lowered. "I wanted to wish you a happy birthday."

I clenched my jaw. "Mission accomplished. Good nigh—"

"Please don't hang up." Desperation choked his voice.

I flexed my fingers around the handset and waited.

"Please, Vicki. I-I haven't heard your beautiful voice in over six months. I took a chance you'd be with Christine for Christmas."

I bit my lip. The anguish in his voice burrowed into my heart.

"I miss you, baby."

My vision blurred under a sheen of unshed tears. "I'm sorry, Jude, but it's over."

"I need to see you. I'm lonesome without you. Without the children." My breath hitched at a low sob on the other end. "No one else understands my despair like you do." He sniffed. "You know my pain, and I know yours. Please. I need to see you."

My head spun, and my heart tore wide open from Jude's brokenness. "I can't. I'm sorry, but I have a new life."

His deep sobs vibrated down the landline and splintered my heart. "I-I've been seeing a therapist. He th-thinks it'll help if you attend a few sessions."

I gawped. "You're seeing a therapist?"

"Yes." Jude blew out a sigh. "I fired Paula."

For his benefit or mine? "That's great, but it doesn't change anything."

"Please," he breathed.

"I don't live in Melbourne."

"Y-you don't live here anymore? Where are you?"

"I can't afford time off work. I'm sorr—"

"Don't hang up yet. Please." He released a noisy breath. "I miss them. It's like someone carved their names on my heart with a knife."

Salty tears dripped down my chin. "I miss them too."

"I miss you the most."

"I can't do this. It's over. You need to stop calling."

He huffed a breath. "But it's your birthday. And almost Christmas. I think of how we decorated the tree as a family. How the children schemed for gift ideas for you."

The stairs creaked. Christine and Patrick stood motionless on the bottom step, their concerned eyes trained on me.

"I'm sorry. Goodbye." I ended the call and stared at the handset clutched in my fingers. "You'll need to check the history and block the number."

Footsteps padded closer.

I placed the handset back in the cordless phone cradle and gazed up. "Jude."

They nodded like I had solved the mysteries of the universe.

CHAPTER EIGHTEEN

Pain and Hope

Christine clung to me. "Promise me we'll talk more this year. Text messages are great, but I love hearing your voice and seeing your gorgeous face. Skype was created for a reason."

I nodded against her silky hair and swallowed the lump in my throat. "I promise."

Time with my family ended sooner than I had hoped and the drive home quicker than my original trip east. I contemplated what I would face when I arrived in Tellarine.

My mind drifted to Nicholas. Could we be happy? Heaviness weighed on my chest. True happiness was rooted in the depth of friendship. And trust. Something I could not offer right now.

After many hours I turned onto the main road into town and pulled into a narrow parking bay at the IGA to restock my kitchen with groceries.

I grabbed a shopping trolley and half-filled it with goodies before I reached the freezer section.

Matt stared into the frozen peas compartment with a hand on his brow.

"If it isn't Mr. Briggs buying vegetables for a change."

He gazed up and grinned. "Hardy har har. How else do you think I fuel this rocking body of mine?"

I giggled.

Matt dropped a packet of organic peas into his basket. He

fidgeted with the basket handle. "Did you just get home? Has Belinda contacted you?"

"I drove into town and haven't been home yet. Bee messaged two nights ago. Why?"

Matt shrugged. "Perhaps she's the better one to tell you." He stepped down the aisle.

I groped his arm. "Tell me what?"

His shoulders drooped. "We broke up yesterday."

The air in my lungs rushed out. Matt and Belinda had seemed like the perfect couple four weeks ago. What had happened? I locked my trolley's wheels and stepped closer. "I thought everything was going well?"

"So did I, but it appears I was wrong."

"What happened?" I squeezed his arm and wrinkled my brow.

He dredged up a groan. "We went out for lunch after church, like we often do with you. We discussed the service and what Pastor Davidson had shared. It impacted me, you know? Bee seemed distracted. I had lots of questions, when all of a sudden she's saying we should take a break." Matt's face contorted and he rubbed his chin.

"Did she explain why?"

He shrugged and focused on at the floor. "Something about my being an immature Christian, how she wasn't comfortable in the teaching role all the time." He lifted his head and searched my eyes. His desperation squeezed my heart. "I thought she enjoyed the discussions. You and I talk about spiritual stuff, and you like our conversations, don't you?"

I smiled a bright smile. "Of course, I do. I look forward to every opportunity to encourage you in your faith."

"I guess I'm too much for her. Everyone's wired differently, I suppose."

I squeezed his arm once again. "Give her some time."

He shook his head. "She was quite clear we end it now. Said to pull up the seedlings of affection or something metaphoric like that.

I'll have to make the best of the situation. I mean, we work together, attend the same church. What else can I do?"

"I'm here if you need to talk."

"Thanks, Vicki." Matt headed to the register.

I continued shopping, deep in thought. I would talk with Belinda tomorrow, on our first day back at work, and find out what had happened.

Belinda hunched on a tall stool at a high wooden bench in the textiles room, surrounded by cotton reels. Her fingers flicked through an array of blues and blacks before she slotted a grey spool into a box. Dark smudges stained the delicate skin under her eyes.

"My darling Bee."

She glanced up, and her eyes misted over.

I enveloped her in my arms.

Belinda sobbed.

"What happened with Matt?" I held her until she regained her composure, then released her and gazed into her puffy, glazed green eyes.

Belinda sighed. "I was scared."

"Scared of what? Did Matt hurt you?"

Belinda shook her head, and relief coursed through my veins. I pulled out another stool from under the table and settled close.

"He asked s-so many questions about my faith, the Bible, and m-my answers were so inadequate. I mean, what if I said something wrong? Or confused him? Turned him off God again? I can't be the reason he stumbles." She sighed. "I'm not confident like you. The pressure without you being here to talk was immense. You're so good with biblical truths and the Christian way of living."

I feigned a smile. If she only knew my messed-up history. "I'm sorry, Bee." I rubbed her back. "I bumped into Matt at the supermarket yesterday. He was gutted."

Tears welled in Belinda's eyes again, and I wrapped my arm around her shoulders. "I've overcome a lot with God's help over the years, but I can't take the fall this time." She sniffed. "Matt's too special to be toyed with. I need time to think, and we both need time to grow."

I stilled. "This time?"

Belinda shuddered. "When I was sixteen, I crushed on a boy at school. I invited him to youth, and he went for months. We became close. His family believed religion was a waste of time, and I wanted to prove them wrong." She lowered her gaze. "But I couldn't. I didn't know enough. In time he stopped going to youth. Avoided me at school. I failed him, and I failed God."

"Surely you don't believe that? You were sixteen. You can't change how people think. Only Jesus can." Coldness flooded my chest. "I should know. I couldn't change my husband."

Her eyes bulged. "You were married?" she whispered.

"Still am. He lied, cheated. Our divorce is being finalised."

She gasped. "I'm sorry, Vicki. I had no idea."

"I don't broadcast my private life." I sighed. "But I trust you and should've told you sooner. I'm sorry."

We both stood and hugged. The magnitude of Belinda's decision overwhelmed me. I kissed her forehead. "For what it's worth, you've grown spiritually in the past ten years. Surrender your fear to God." I stepped back. "I'll keep you both in my prayers."

"Have you lived out here long?" I was driving Anna home after our first literature class.

"All my life. I can't imagine living anywhere else." Anna stared out the passenger window.

Willowy trees swayed in the breeze, shading livestock from the late-afternoon sun. I smiled at the beautiful scenery and lowered my sun visor to block the glare. Each kilometre away from town brought me closer to paradise and a sense of peace.

The new school year had started well, and our first literature lesson went better than I had predicted. All five students had been diligent over the holiday period and read their texts. We recorded major tasks, tests and exam dates in our diaries.

"I think Mum and Dad feel the same way. Dad grew up on the farm." She giggled. "Nan tells me he and Uncle Cole got up to no good."

I laughed, picturing two young boys running wild on a farm. "It sounds like a wonderful way to grow up. I loved the country trips to my grandparents' farm and have many cherished childhood memories of our visits."

Anna pointed out an open gate off the gravel road where a long driveway led to a farmhouse. "This is it. Please be careful of the pothole near the gate. Dad said he'd fix it over the weekend."

A large, dirty-white weatherboard house occupied an idyllic spot on the property, surrounded by an expansive garden. Several tall eucalyptus trees overhung the carport. The farmhouse appeared old and in need of a decent wash or coat of paint although the roof appeared to be brand new.

I pulled up in front of the carport near a bricked path.

Anna smiled and thanked me for the ride home.

"It's my pleasure. I'll see you in English class tomorrow." I waited until Anna entered the house. With a quick turn of the wheel, I headed back down the driveway.

The beautiful scenery stretched out like an artist's canvas. Greens, browns, and rusty reds filled the landscape. I let out a gentle sigh.

I stopped at the end of the driveway and waited for a passing vehicle which approached at high speed. Locals. Gravel sprayed from underneath its tyres against the front grill of my Mazda, and I growled. I checked the road both ways and noticed a sign outside the gate advertising two half-acre lots of land for sale. Butterflies danced in my midriff at the prospect of owning my own piece of land someday. A seed planted in my heart.

♥ ♥ ♥ ♥ ♥ ♥ ♥

I trudged along the dusty school car park and gazed up at the tall, slim eucalyptus trees reaching for the heavens with their spindly limbs in their quest of survival. Atop the trees perched hundreds of white-and-yellow cockatoos. The birds squawked and shrieked at the tops of their lungs and bounced up and down in the wind. I imagined the fun God had when He created these outrageous, noisy birds and partnered them with the limbs of gangly trees planted in quiet surrounds.

"They're beautiful creatures, despite the sound."

I lowered my head and regarded the speaker.

Matt walked toward me, briefcase in hand, and matched my unhurried pace.

"Yes, they are."

He kicked a stone, which whipped up some dust when it hit the dirt. "Will you be at Benanu's tonight for the catch-up?"

"No. I've been called in to cover the other manager's shift at the church kitchen."

"Oh."

His one-syllable response stopped me in my tracks. I glanced at his face. Downcast eyes and pouty lip. He reminded me of Ryan the time I cancelled our trip to the zoo, and my heart squeezed. I touched his hand. "Sorry. I'll see you on Sunday?"

A smile replaced his melancholy features. "Of course. I'm no heathen."

I chuckled, dropped my hand, and walked. "I'm happy to hear. It's been an honour witnessing your transformation and being part of your journey. Truly."

Matt cleared his throat and squeaked out his thanks when we reached my car.

I stopped and pressed the remote release button to open the boot.

His warm hand folded over mine.

I raised my head.

Tears glistened in his eyes. "Thank you, Vicki. For everything." He leaned in close and kissed my forehead. His lips were soft in their gentle caress, and the smell of CK One filled my senses.

"You're welcome."

His gaze dropped to my lips, and my chest tightened before his gaze returned to mine with a smile. "See you on Sunday." He walked away, and I frowned.

What had just happened? Had I imagined that look? Of course I had. Matt was grateful for my support and friendship. Being his friend and Belinda's was still awkward, but they had only broken up three weeks ago.

I dropped my bag in the car, closed the boot, and drove to the bakery to collect our ministry's allotted leftover bread rolls, plus some vegetables from the grocer next door, then drove to the church to see how the team fared. As I ambled through the car park, my heart flooded with love for the little church and town I called home.

CHAPTER NINETEEN
Blueberry Bluff

"Yes! In your face, stinky boys!" primary school-aged girls screamed in high-pitched squeals.

I burst out in laughter. "How about we behave like gracious winners, ladies?"

On the last Saturday in February each year, Tellarine Christian Church held a picnic on the church grounds for the congregation to invite people, meet new faces and share with old friends. Between my church involvement on Sundays, my Meals on Wheels commitment, and frequent interaction with students and parents from the school, I already knew many churchgoers.

This year's picnic fell on a bright, sunny day. After a pleasant afternoon of food, conversation, and fun group games, Matt and I had coached the teams for the primary school-aged girls-versus-boys' basketball match. I had guided the girls' team while Matt had managed the boys. When the game became rowdy and competitive, we attracted a crowd of adults and youth, and when my girls triumphed over Matt's team, I beamed.

"Ms. Burke," piped a voice at my chest, "you should coach my basketball team. Our coach is rubbish."

I chuckled at the serious face of the outspoken ten-year-old girl. Her arms were crossed, and her lips were pressed down. "That sounds like fun, but I'm pretty busy. Perhaps we can do this again after church one day?" I winked at her and raised an eyebrow to

Matt.

A fire lit in his eyes and replaced the grumpy frown lines. "That sounds great. Gives us boys the chance to practice and trounce you girls."

Six weeks had passed since Belinda ended their romantic relationship, and I was glad his cheerfulness had returned. The same could not be said for Belinda.

I laughed. "Not on your life, Mr. Briggs. Admit it. Girls are better than boys."

Matt quirked a cheeky grin. He cocked his head and eyed me from head to toe. "Oh, girls are definitely better."

I caught my breath. What was his game? I turned to my team. "Okay, ladies, let's go get some dessert!"

Juvenile screams pierced the air. The children descended on the food tables, now laden with sweet treats. An image of Ryan filled my vision, and I blinked. His excitement over the desserts would have rivalled all the children present.

I pushed the image aside and followed in hot pursuit, happy to escape Matt's stare.

Madison and Grace intercepted me at the baked goods stand and grabbed my arms. "You've spent enough time ignoring your star pupils, Ms. Burke. Come with us!" Madison said.

I freed an arm and snatched the last blueberry muffin, then allowed the girls to lead me away. Diana and Gabriella waved. I flopped on the woven rug and bit into my muffin, chewing on the crumbly, moist cake.

Matt plonked next to me and nudged my shoulder in a playful manner. "You going to share?"

I shook my head and swallowed the delectable treat before I snatched another large bite. "Noth a chanf." I chewed the slurry in my mouth and gulped with gritted teeth. "You'll have to pry this half from my fingers before I share this exquisite treat."

He cocked an eyebrow. "Is that a challenge?"

"I'd like to see you try." I regretted my response a nanosecond after the idiotic words departed my mouth.

Matt's strong arms welded to my torso and screams of laughter seized my lungs.

"Stop!" I said on a breathless laugh.

"You asked for it." He tried to bully the muffin half from my grasp.

I attempted to escape his grip, but his hands were like metal vices. "Fine then!" I kicked my legs, my feet aimed for his shins, while I tried to wriggle away to the delighted shrieks of our student audience. I managed to free an elbow and jabbed Matt under the ribs before I scrambled to my feet with the muffin half still clutched in my hand.

I sprinted away from the blueberry-muffin lunatic and ran for my life. Laughs and squeals gushed from my lungs while tears ran down my cheeks. I weaved around a table, dodged camping chairs and picnic rugs, and raced toward the church building.

Turning the corner, I ran full pelt through the entry door with Matt close behind. I lost ground as Matt's long legs caught up with me in the church foyer.

He grabbed my waist from behind, flipped me around, and pinned me against a wall. Both breathless from our sprint, we panted through our laughter.

I thrashed my arms in an attempt to escape. Nervous giggles racked my chest.

One by one he claimed control of my arms.

"Hey! That's not fair." I examined his face, and my laughter died in my throat. Heat flooded my body, the simple task of breathing now almost painful.

Matt was more beautiful than Jude. My head spun with a sudden lightness.

The edges of Matt's mouth turned up, and a heated blush stung my cheeks. He scrutinised the muffin, which trembled in my hand, before he focused on my face. "Maybe you should eat the muffin. You have the shakes. Is your blood sugar low?" He leaned in so close I breathed in the delicious scent of man and cologne. "Or is your heart rate too high?"

My lungs seized when his gaze caressed my lips. Twice in three weeks? Not possible. My imagination had gone rogue. How could my body respond like this when I had kept my promise to Belinda and prayed for reconciliation between her and Matt? My eyes pricked with tears.

Matt blinked, hesitated a backward step, and walked outside.

My brain buzzed, and my legs trembled. I sucked in several deep breaths before I trundled into the kitchen, dumped the squished muffin in the bin, and guzzled a cup of cold water.

I returned to my students, where Belinda and Nicholas now chatted with the girls. My stomach churned.

Belinda waved and I glued on a smile.

Madison and Grace tittered. Diana glared at them.

I sat, slid an arm around Belinda, and nodded to Nicholas. My already flushed cheeks redoubled in heat when he stared back with familiar intensity. My elevated heartbeat thundered in my ribcage.

I turned my full attention to Belinda. "You missed some fun. My girls' basketball team creamed the boys!" With a grin I leaned back on my hands.

Belinda turned to me. "I heard you're having fun. Did he get the muffin?"

My elbows buckled and I almost fell backwards. The memory of Matt's sapphire eyes flooded my mind. Heat singed my cheeks, and I chastised myself for my earlier behaviour. What had I been thinking getting lost in the moment?

I peered at Nicholas, and my heart stung at the apparent hurt in his eyes. I ripped my gaze from his dark orbs and regarded Madison and Grace, who sported huge grins.

"Did he, Ms. Burke?" Gabriella leaned forward, her eyes bright and focused on my face.

I cleared my throat. "No. We called a truce." I pulled my phone from my pocket, opened the photo application, and handed it to

Belinda. "The girls snapped some photos of the game."

"These pics are great. Nice action shots." Belinda nudged my shoulder. "That's a hot photo of you." She turned to me, squinted at Nicholas, then at the phone screen. "See?" Belinda lifted the phone.

I smiled at a photo of me in pep talk mode with my young team. My ponytail blew in the wind, and my blue T-shirt complimented my wide eyes. "Not bad."

"Not bad?" Belinda thrust the screen into Nicholas's face. "Please tell me this is more than a 'not bad' look? She's a babe, hey?"

Nicholas smirked, and I blushed, my cheeks now used to their ever-present warmth. "I can't argue with your observation, Belinda."

A generic ringtone blared on my phone, and Belinda whipped the screen back to her face.

I squinted at the number. "I don't recognise the caller. I'd prefer if you did—"

Belinda set the call on speakerphone. "Hello?"

I elbowed her in the ribs.

"Victoria?"

My heartbeat tripled its pace at my husband's deep vocal reverberation.

"Sorry, it's her friend, Belinda. Can I help you?"

Words died in my throat, and I stared at the scene in front of me, desperate to stop the unfolding disaster.

"Belinda. What a nice name. I don't believe we've met?" Jude's words dripped like honey and set a smile on Belinda's lips.

She nudged me, and I sat with my mouth open, unable to process what to do. "Considering I haven't met many of Vicki's friends, it's no surprise. Are you another cute cousin?"

Please let this conversation end.

"Another cute cousin? Are you telling me she's not told you about me?"

Everything around me seemed to spin. Nicholas scowled.

"I'm her hus—"

"It's so nice of you to call," I blurted, my vocal cords no longer frozen, "but I can't speak now." I yanked the phone from Belinda's slack hands. "I hope business is well. All the best."

"Vict—"

I pressed the End Call button, blocked the phone number, and set my phone to silent. Lesson learned.

A deep V wrinkled Belinda's brow. "What was that about?"

"He, ah, breeds huskies. I had a husky in Melbourne, and h-he bred her. Chuckles." My cheeks flared, and I bit the inside of my mouth over the dumbest lie I had ever spouted. I held in a scream.

Nicholas's eyes narrowed. "So, you've been in contact and wanted another pup? In your tiny box-of-a-home?"

"Are you insane?" Belinda said, her voice shrill. "That's tantamount to animal cruelty!"

Every set of eyes homed into my face. Some people were slack-jawed, others had grooves in their foreheads.

My chest burned as though flames licked at my organs and consumed my lungs. "I wanted t-to see, um, when the next few litters might be planned?" I sounded like an idiot. "You know, in case I end up moving … to a bigger place."

I shot to my feet, mumbled my farewells, and hastened toward home. The mountain of cover-ups, little white lies, and deceptions weighed on my conscience.

"Wait up!" Belinda called, breathless, from behind me.

I slowed my steps, and her panting grew louder.

She nodded to her car nearby. "I'll take you home."

Belinda drove us and parked on the street outside the Arbys'. She unbuckled and turned to me. "That was him, wasn't it?"

I nodded.

She grabbed my hand. "I'm sorry, Vicki. Gosh, I feel awful."

I shrugged. "It's okay."

"Why'd you lie? Does your ex breed huskies?"

I huffed a laugh. "Because I'm an idiot. And, no, he's a lawyer."

Belinda's nose scrunched. "Of course, he is. Manipulative smart guy." She pursed her lips. "So, you're not getting a dog?"

I laughed. "No."

"Good. I don't want you going to jail for animal abuse."

I poked my tongue out at her, and she laughed. We hugged, and I ambled up the driveway, my chest easing with each step.

CHAPTER TWENTY

To Purge One's Soul

The following Thursday I jogged out of the Staff Lounge. I had forgotten the brief staff meeting and hoped my literature ladies had waited. When excitable conversation drifted from my English room, I breathed out a sigh.

As I walked into the room and apologised, an odd silence filled the air. The girls' gazes darted between each other.

I assessed their five faces and raised my brow. "Anyone care to tell me what's up?"

Gabriella twiddled her fingers, and the other girls exchanged more looks between themselves.

I narrowed my eyes, hoping my Jedi mind trick would force someone to talk. With a sigh, I headed to my desk.

"Tell her, Gabby," Grace said. "She won't tell your parents." She fixed her gaze on me. "Will you, Ms. Burke?"

I pondered Grace's lips pressed together and Gabriella's drawn features. "So long as no one's been abused or broken the law, I'm not obliged to share private information." I occupied a nearby desk and waited.

Gabriella let out a long sigh. "I've been dating Brandon for six months. My parents know that much, but they don't realise how serious it's getting." Her cheeks flushed.

My stomach clenched. I fastened an I-am-not-here-to-judge-you smile and asked, "How serious?"

Gabriella squirmed in her seat. The redness in her cheeks deepened.

After some hesitation, I bit the bullet. "Are you and Brandon sexually active?" I blushed and focused on Gabriella, not my own discomfort.

"N-no, but Brandon thinks it's time. I'm not ready. What should I do? I like him."

I blew out a sharp breath and squeezed her shoulder. "What have your friends suggested?"

Diana's voice rang out strong and clear. "We think she should wait. Brandon's a nice-enough guy, but no guy's worth the time if he pressures for sex. Dad's been clear about that. He says a real man keeps his pants on until he's put a wedding ring on your finger."

Heat rose up my body. Hearing about family conversations from my students was typical, but the topic and parent in question dragged my mind to another place. A place where the man I longed to kiss stared back at me with chocolate-brown eyes and delicious stubble. "Your dad's wise."

"And super-hot!" Madison said. "You don't mind being my stepdaughter, Di? I could totes be the next Mrs. Jacobsen."

The girls erupted in laughter, and I tried to hide my giggles.

Diana snorted. "Sorry, but you're too late. When I grilled Dad last week about why he wasn't dating, instead of changing the subject like usual, he asked if I'd be okay with him seeing someone. Of *course,* I said yes. He wouldn't even hint at who the mystery lady is." Diana evaluated me, and a breath hitched in my throat. "I think I know, but I'll have to wait and see."

I cleared my throat and reined in the subject at hand. "Gabriella, it's clear your friends love you and want what's best for you. If I may be so bold, I wouldn't give up an irreplaceable gift like my virginity to any guy who pressured me, regardless how I felt about him. You'll thank yourself for being brave and saying no. You're worth the wait." My eyes clouded over.

"Ms. Burke?" Madison asked. "Are you a virgin?"

The question hit me square in the chest. I knew any answer I offered would alter their opinion of me. After last weekend's debacle with Jude's phone call and the ridiculous lies I had spouted, I sent up a brief prayer for courage. "No, but I was on my wedding night."

Five girls stared at my face, mouths agape. Diana's expression, brows drawn together and eyes tearing up, hit me the hardest.

"You're married?" Anna's shrill cry replaced her usual quiet tone.

Too late I realised the classroom door was open. I prayed no one in the hallway had overheard her outburst. "Keep it down, please, and let me explain." I shifted in my seat in a fruitless attempt to calm my jitters. With a low voice I said, "I was married—well, am still technically. Waiting for my divorce to be finalised."

I sucked in a breath. Jude must have called because he had received the papers I finally sent off to Stacy two weeks ago.

I cleared my throat. "I hope you can keep this confidential."

Anna stretched out her fingers and placed them over my fisted hands, which were balled up in my lap. Her expression was that of a woman much older than her sixteen years. "Did your ex-husband hurt you?"

Tears welled in my eyes. "In every way possible." I stood and plucked a tissue from my desk.

When I glanced ahead, Matt stood in the doorway, his face grave. "Ms Burke, a moment of your time, please?"

I wiped my eyes and directed my students to the printed worksheets on my desk before I excused myself. Panic gripped me with each step to the door. How much had he overheard?

Matt closed the door with a stern expression. His eyes were filled with … disappointment?

My gut cramped, and my lunch teetered on the edge of escape.

"Why hasn't an abusive ex-husband come up in conversation?" His face softened.

My gaze dropped to the floor.

"It explains so much, but it hurts. You didn't trust me. Even after I told you about my daughter," he whispered.

The floor became watery under my gaze. "Matt," I breathed. I blinked back tears. "I trust you, but it's hard to talk about. I ..." All my excuses fled my mind.

Matt lifted my chin with a finger, and his gaze captured mine. "You need to start somewhere. We're debriefing over dinner tonight. My shout." He smiled, released my chin, and left me in the hallway. Tight knots still pulled against my tummy, but now Matt knew this skeleton in my cluttered closet, the encumbrance on my chest lifted.

Benanu's was quiet, and I jumped at the chance to sit on the comfy couch near the bar. Keanu delivered a bowl of potato wedges and some spiced chicken tenders Matt had ordered. Keanu was right, they were delicious. Alcohol filled my glass for the first time in years. I needed something with more substance to drink and savoured the cocktail Matt chose for me.

"So, Ms. Burke, tell me about this execrable ex of yours."

I smirked at him.

"You're not the only one with a vocabulary. And you'd probably wrinkle your nose at the profanity I wanted to use." He grinned before he sipped his beer.

"You know me well." I sipped my cold drink. Delicious. The elderflower, mint and ginger liquid tasted little like alcohol, but I knew it would hit my system hard after years of abstinence. I cleared my throat in a nervous cough. "Can you keep this conversation to yourself?"

Matt nodded and I sighed.

"Thanks." I inhaled a deep breath and shared about Jude and the children, the entire story from wonder to woe. I cried within two minutes and Matt within five. Sharing the memories of my marriage and lost babies hurt but was also cathartic.

My strength crumpled, and I leaned against Matt's chest. His strong arms enveloped me in a tight embrace. My eyelids drooped closed. I had another friend in Tellarine who knew my story and still accepted me.

I remained in our embrace. The steady rhythm of his heart, firm and constant, reminded me of the times growing up when I had snuggled with Dad on the couch. My superhero. Whether after an argument with a friend, a disappointment with a crush, or an emotional moment in my teenage life, Dad had always come to my rescue. Safe in his strong arms, I had admired the tenderness in his powerful limbs. Matt had the same innate ability to set my mind and body at ease.

I opened my eyes. My body stiffened, and my heart walloped.

"Yep," Matt said, "Nick's been at the bar for, hmm, seven minutes casting covert glances in your direction. It's been fun to watch."

I straightened and nudged Matt hard on the shoulder.

His laughter reverberated like my arm from the impact.

"You unfeeling brute. When were you going to tell me?"

"Well, I figured he'd get the wrong idea and leave so I'd have you all to myself."

I stared at him, wide-eyed. Was he serious or joking?

"But Nick doesn't give up. So, if you'll excuse me, I'm off." Matt released me and planted a gentle kiss on my forehead before he strode to the bar. He whispered in Nicholas's ear, then slapped him on the back in a genial manner before he left.

I pulled my cardigan close after Matt's warmth abandoned me, like its maker. Reaching across for my drink, I savoured the final drops when Nicholas approached.

"Matt said you could use some company. Need a top up?"

"I'd better not. I've already had two of these delicious cocktails and need to be sober for my students tomorrow." I grinned with a slight alcohol buzz. Warmth pooled in my belly. Placing the empty glass on the coffee table near my knees, I burrowed back into the couch and tucked my legs under me.

Nicholas dropped onto the far side of the couch with a bottle of beer in his hand. His eyes darkened. "He wasn't plying you with alcohol, was he?"

I chuckled, and his expression eased back to its attractive default setting. "I asked for it."

He blinked and furrowed his brow. "I don't think I've seen you drink anything alcoholic before. Figured you weren't interested."

I offered a weak smile. "No beer on tap?"

He shuddered. "Never again."

"Where's Diana tonight? She was a godsend in class this afternoon. You've raised her well."

He drained his beer bottle, placed it next to my empty glass, and lounged back on the couch. Right leg crossed over his left knee. The picture of relaxation. And perfection. Super-hot, like Madison said.

I salivated and gulped with wide eyes. No persuasion was needed for his kisses tonight.

"She's at Madison's."

I stifled a laugh.

"What?"

An impish smile fused to my lips. "Well, you mustn't say I told you"—I winked—"but several sixteen-year-old girls are infatuated with you, and one in particular asked Diana if she could be her stepmum."

After my heavy emotional session with Matt, light and playful banter was a welcome distraction. The cocktails worked for my good.

Nicholas's adorable face flushed to his ears, and he squirmed.

My cackles reached uncontrollable heights, and tears streamed down my face. My mourning had been exchanged for rib-stinging laughter.

Nicholas threw a cushion at my head, and I erupted in more giggles.

Once I calmed down, Nicholas leaned close. His direct gaze sizzled, and my skin tingled. "Jealous?"

My pulse thumped. Electricity crackled between us. I leaned closer. Not even a handbreadth of space remained between our noses.

His pupils dilated, and he pressed his lips together.

"Wouldn't you like to know, Mr. Jacobsen."

His fervid stare seared my soul.

I spied his lips before I stood. A bout of dizziness struck me and I swayed. Was this the effect of alcohol or intoxication of another kind? "And now, I bid thee farewell." I stepped away, but a warm, calloused hand grabbed mine. My heart stuttered, and I turned.

Nicholas stood with a triumphant smirk, and I squinted. "Seems I'm obliged to take you home."

Pooh! I forgot Matt had picked me up to thwart any plans to run and hide. A walk in the evening air would do me good. I extracted my hand from the source of my inner flutters and stepped back. "I appreciate the offer, but I'm capable of walking home alone." I hoped my smile convinced him because I doubted my capacity to do so.

Nicholas shook his head. "Not on my watch. Belinda would have my head if something happened to you."

I sighed. "So be it, Saint Nicholas." I flashed him a cheesy grin and headed to the door. He trailed behind me. Shivers from the cool outside temperature tickled my spine, and I regretted refusing Nicholas's offer to drive me home. My cardigan was warm but not an effective barrier against the elements I now faced. I pulled the knitted garment tight around me and thrust my hands into its pockets with a sideways glimpse at Nicholas. The memory of our flirtation moments ago kept me warm against the chill.

"What did Diana do in class? You alluded to something earlier."

"Oh. Yes. That." I sucked in a breath. "Someone shared about an issue, and Diana took a bold stand and encouraged her friend to make a wise decision." I doubted Nicholas would leave the conversation be.

He stopped. "How so?"

My cheeks warmed and I twisted my hands. "One of the girls shared how her boyfriend's pressuring her for sex. She didn't know what to do." I shuffled my feet. "Diana said no guy's worth the time if he behaves this way and a real man keeps his pants on until he's put a wedding ring on your finger." I walked ahead. Why did I discuss church-taboo issues with this man?

Nicholas's footsteps crunched behind mine. He reached my side seconds later, chuckling. "I'm glad the message is getting through even if my views are seen as old-fashioned. Even in the church."

"Saving that particular treasure for marriage isn't the norm. It saddens me when young Christian men and women think it's an unreasonable goal."

Nicholas focused on the footpath ahead. "Do you subscribe to this way of thinking for older, unmarried Christian men and women?" His tone was thoughtful, serious.

Nicholas's arm brushed against mine with each step and brought everything to life inside me. My desperation to love him in a way only a woman could increased my pulse. I wanted to share the deepest, most intimate part of myself with him.

I snuck a furtive glance his way. "Young people look up to older singles. Although I'm selfish to wish it weren't so, rules don't change because someone's middle-aged." I rubbed my chest. I battled this beast even now.

"True."

"Having said that, wouldn't it be more difficult for widows and divorcees to cope with temptation? I mean, they know what they're missing out on, right?"

He snorted a grunt.

I suppressed a smirk. "Surely it's easier to remain a virgin for thirty years than to be married for a time, taste all of its pleasures, then be left with the fire stoked and too many memories to sabotage one's resolve."

Nicholas shuffled his feet up the long driveway to my bungalow.

I unlocked the door. Looking into his eyes, I was overcome with a deep love for him.

He grasped my hand and placed it on his chest. His heartbeat hammered under my fingertips.

My pulse tripped with the warmth in his gaze.

"I'm so glad we have the same resolve." Slowly, ever so slowly, he leaned down and kissed my cheek, his cologne filling my nostrils.

My heart slammed, and my fingers curled under his hand and gripped his shirt.

His warm lips brushed close to my mouth before he pulled away at a snail's pace.

My lips parted as his breath caressed my neck. I struggled to anchor my head and needed his mouth on mine. So close.

He straightened, and his dreamy smile transformed into a provocative glance.

I caught my breath when he released my trembling hand.

"Goodnight, Victoria." He disappeared into the night, leaving me breathless and wanting so much more.

CHAPTER TWENTY-ONE
Regrets

In the church foyer, Belinda greeted another congregant. She leaned into my shoulder afterward. "Thanks for helping today. I was surprised Nick couldn't do his usual shift."

I flexed my hands. "I hope everything's okay."

Belinda shrugged. "He said he couldn't be here early. Maybe something came up."

"Maybe."

Matt wandered in with a firm handshake and a grin before he entered the auditorium. Churchgoers filed into the foyer, and we greeted them with smiles and welcomes. Praise and worship music echoed through the building, sending latecomers scurrying through the doors.

The flow of people came to a trickle. "Want to get our bags and find a seat?"

"Sure." I stepped into the front office and retrieved Belinda's purple tote bag and my small black handbag.

Diana ran to me when I re-entered the foyer. Her eyes appeared glassy, her brow crinkled and her lips downturned. She wrapped her arms around me. "I'm sorry, Ms. Burke. Truly I am." She stepped back and rushed into the auditorium.

I blinked. Sorry for what?

"We need to talk. Now."

I flinched at the angry request and met Nicholas's fierce scowl.

His jaw was rigid, and the pulse in his neck thumped.

I opened and then closed my mouth. I searched the room and found Belinda, wide-eyed.

She extracted her tote bag from my stiff fingers.

What was happening? I turned to Nicholas. "W-where did you want to talk?"

He scratched a hand over the bristles on his chin. "My place. Let's go."

The world tipped for a moment and I swayed.

He stalked out of the foyer and left me shaking in his wake.

Belinda grabbed my hand. "What's going on?"

I shrugged and shook my head all at once. "I-I don't know. Pray for me."

She squeezed my hand. "I will. Talk later." She glanced at the front door. "You'd better go."

I jogged to the car park.

Nicholas stood next to his ute, arms crossed and foot jiggling.

"Bee picked me up today to help with greeting. Can I ride with you?"

He nodded once before he opened the driver's side door. Chivalry must be dead today.

I opened the passenger door and climbed into the cab. With trembling hands, I locked my seatbelt in place.

I screamed internally the entire car trip. Ominous black clouds hung between us, and I prayed in my head, afraid whispered pleas might upset the beast in the driver's seat.

Nicholas parked in his driveway and killed the engine. He remained motionless with his hands glued to the steering wheel. His chest rose and fell with ragged breaths. At long last he removed the keys from the ignition and stalked to the house.

I unbuckled and exited the vehicle in record time. We were seated in the lounge room moments later.

Nicholas closed his eyes, and his head hung near his chest.

My stomach twisted in sickening knots, and I clenched my

teeth. I clasped my hands in my lap and waited in the excruciating unknown, my legs jittering nonstop.

He opened his eyes. His stormy expression pierced my heart. "I need the truth from you, Victoria. Are you capable of honesty?"

I gasped. "I beg your pardon?"

He narrowed his eyes. "Can you answer me honestly?"

"Of course I can." My chest heated with the sting. "Ask your question."

"Are you married?"

My mouth opened and eyes widened. "I ... I—"

He slammed a hand against the couch arm. "Tell me!"

I flinched and shrank back in the chair. His harsh tone dragged me back to another lounge room in my former life. Tears blinded me, and I shook. "Y-yes."

"For crying out loud, Victoria!"

A sob strangled me. "I'm sorry, but I don't appreciate your tone."

"You lied to me. Repeatedly." His brusque manner gave way to a brokenness which pierced my heart. "Why? Why didn't you tell me?"

Tears coursed down my cheeks. "B-because I was afraid."

"Of what? Me?"

I dragged a hand across my face. "I'm sorry." Streaks of dark brown lined my palm, and I rubbed my hands together. "My life imploded, and I came to Tellarine to start afresh."

"A fresh start doesn't mean you play games with people." He stood and paced the floor. "Do you understand how embarrassed and betrayed I felt overhearing my teenage daughter and her friends discuss your marriage and speculate why you left your husband? For me to walk into a room and be blindsided by this information?" He stilled. "You trusted teenagers with your secret, but not me?"

I shook my head. "It's not like that. They c-cornered me. The truth came out in answering a question."

A sardonic laugh bubbled out of his chest. "They cornered you.

A group of teenage girls. Right. So, you thought it important to tell them the truth, but Nicholas? Why, he's some idiot bloke you can string along? I don't need the truth?"

I straightened in the chair and stuck out my chin. "Everything else we spoke about was truthful. I a-avoided conversation about Jude."

His eyes bulged. "Jude? Are you serious? Your handsy boyfriend? You married him?"

Why did he have such a good memory?

"Does anything truthful come out of your mouth?" he yelled.

I gritted my teeth, stood and planted my feet on the carpet. "Stop it! I refuse to speak to you if you're going to raise your voice and rant like a lunatic."

He shook his head. "I'm the lunatic? What about you and your 'No, Nicholas, it's not a ring mark, my finger was broken' speech or 'No, no, there's no ex in my life' rubbish?" He pointed a finger at my face. "Lies. Plain and simple." His jaw twitched. "No wonder your comment about memories sabotaging one's resolve flowed so naturally. You're living it."

I closed my eyes and filled my lungs with oxygen. My brain strained to channel the storm of words swirling in my mind. I returned my gaze to Nicholas's miffed face. "Firstly, I never denied the ring marks. You came to that conclusion."

"What! I—"

"I'm not finished!" I pressed my lips together and rotated on the balls of my feet. "Yes, I let you believe your assumptions. I'm sorry for hurting you, but you need to understand something." I wiped away fresh tears. "Until you've been married to a narcissistic, sadistic philanderer with a passion for whisky, money and keeping up appearances, you have no right to judge me for the decisions— stupid as they may seem—I've executed to preserve my sanity." My chest heaved with increased gasps for breath. My mind spiralled. "And if you ever yell at me again, or threaten me in any way, be prepared for me to fight back because I'll not be beaten by a man's words or fists again!" I triumphed at his slack jaw and frozen movements.

"I would never, ever hurt you, Victoria. I ... what on earth have you suffered?"

He stepped toward me, and I stuck out my hand, palm facing him. "Don't touch me."

Nicholas halted. "Okay. I apologise. But what about us?"

My head spun from my shallow breaths. "Us? There is no 'us.' We're not a couple, and I'm not willing to partner with a man who yells and slams fists against furniture." I stepped backwards. "I can't be with someone who treats me like a rebellious adolescent when I do something wrong."

I sucked in a deep breath. "I'm a screw-up. Imperfect. I'm waiting on divorce papers for a relationship I've been in since I was sixteen! But I refuse to be judged by you with your perfect parenting and your socially acceptable widow status. *You* won't be plagued with the smear of 'divorcee' over your future relationships. You won't be scrutinised for your choices because your wife died tragically."

I sobbed and shook my head. "But me? I'm stained for life because my husband found me undesirable. Me, the woman who relinquished her dreams to facilitate his. Who paid for his law degree, ironed his shirts, provided dinner every night. Me, the woman scorned because I'm not beautiful like the secretary." My chest vibrated with deep, moaning sobs. I reached for my bag.

Nicholas's shoulders dragged low. His chin wobbled, his face wet with tears. "Victoria. Please—"

I violently shook my head. "What's the point trying if you don't trust me? You'll question every word I say." I shook my head again. "I'm sorry, but I can't be that woman anymore." Yanking my bag over my shoulder, I ignored Nicholas's pleas to stop and raced out the front door.

The moment I ran from Nicholas's house, I thought I would cease to exist. A desire to lie on the side of the road and give up burned brighter than the hope I had held for him. For us.

What was wrong with me? Why was I so stupid? Nicholas was the second man I had run from in the past eighteen months. Men that had captured my heart.

One still held my heart captive.

I stumbled home, tired from crying, and collapsed on the couch. My phone beeped. I removed it from my bag and pulled the blanket over me.

Belinda: ARE YOU OKAY?

My hands shook as I dialled her number.

"I'm sneaking out of church, don't tell anyone," Belinda whispered.

A laugh puffed to the surface of my sorrow.

The sound of high heels clacked through the phone. "Want me to pick up some lunch so you can tell me everything?"

"Yes. Please," I whispered.

"Okay, I'll see you soon."

The next weeks blurred. A dim haze settled in my head and infected my heart. Sobs shuddered in my chest when my Year Eleven English students entered the classroom. I swallowed the lump in my throat and sent angry messages to my brain to get with the program and shut off the waterworks. Enough was enough. I had pushed my hope of love away and now had to live with the consequences.

Fourth period flew by, and before I knew it, the lunch bell rang. I dismissed my students and remained at my desk, listening to chairs scrape and shoes pad across the floor. I sighed and entered my password on my laptop.

"Ms. Burke?"

I gazed up at Diana and her big chocolate eyes stared down at me. "Yes, Diana?"

She shuffled on her feet. Her mouth opened, then closed. Tears pooled in her eyes. "I'm sorry things went bad with Dad." She sniffed.

"Me too." I stood, pulled a tissue from the nearby box, and dabbed her cheeks.

"He's been a complete basket case."

I wrapped an arm around her. "I'm sorry to hear."

"He cries more. Like he used to after Mum died."

My chest burned, and tears welled. "I'm sorry, sweetheart."

"It's all my fault."

I pulled her close and shook my head. "It's not your fault, Diana." I captured her gaze. "Don't blame yourself for my stupidity, okay?"

"Do you love him?"

My lungs seized. "I'm sorry, but that's a personal question I can't answer."

"It's okay. I wanted to tell you he smiles less now, just like you." She slipped out from my arm, collected her books, and walked out.

CHAPTER TWENTY-TWO

Letting Loose

I stared in my bathroom mirror and applied mascara to my eyelashes. An unfamiliar giddiness buzzed through my veins over tonight's Year Twelve formal. Six long weeks had passed since my yelling match with Nicholas, and I needed to stop thinking about him.

My phone rang, and I almost stabbed my eye with the mascara wand. "Hey, Bee!"

Belinda groaned. "I think my lunchtime curry gave me the runs."

"Oh no! Are you okay?" My own stomach tied up in knots.

Another low moan sounded. "Gotta go. Sorry, but you're on your own tonight. Love you."

"Love you too. I'll be praying. Call or message if you need me."

"Mmm, yeah, okay. Bye."

I sighed. Should I even go now? Belinda and I had looked forward to our time together with our pretty dresses and non-teacher personalities.

I prayed for her before I applied my remaining makeup. My not going would make Belinda feel worse. At least I could feel pretty for a few hours and hang out with Matt. After I tied my hair back in a neat ponytail, I slipped into my A-line scoop neck sleeveless black dress. After a battle with the zip enclosure, I caressed the smooth fabric with its ruffled waistline and admired my pleasant shape in the mirror. The dress flowed down my body to a hemline long enough to cover my elongated scar. The last dress Jude bought me.

I blinked back tears, grabbed my bag, and raced out the door. I entered Tellarine Hall ten minutes later when the first students arrived. A few of the young men stared at my cleavage, and one student complimented my dress. I smiled and headed in the direction of the huddled teachers.

Matt stood on the outskirts of the group.

I stepped over to him. "Hey."

"Evening, beautiful." He winked.

My cheeks warmed.

He looped his arm through mine. "Let's get a drink."

We walked to the bar. Matt ordered two ginger beers in champagne flutes. He tapped his glass against mine with bright eyes. "To the future. May it be as wonderful as you."

My breath caught. "Y-yes. To the future."

The cold beverage helped cool my body after Matt's words had shot warmth to my abdomen. He looked exquisite in his tailored black satin lapel tuxedo. James Bond in the flesh.

He reached out and tucked a stray hair behind my ear. "Walk with me to the dining tables?" His fingers lingered near my neck.

My heart ricocheted. "Okay." A shiver rippled through me when his warm hand pressed against my lower back. I thought my dress would combust in a blaze of fire. Why did my body ignite after such an innocent touch? Was this attraction or the lustful thirst of a lonely woman? I peeked at Matt as we walked. His side profile reminded me of Jude. So what if I responded to him? Everyone had attractive friends, and tonight was about having fun. My chest eased, and I smiled.

We spent most of our evening together, talking and laughing. The more we joked, the lighter I became.

Several students badgered us to dance together, and we accepted the challenge. Once I relaxed in Matt's arms and moved in time to the music, my mind stilled and body loosened. When was the last time I had danced? I breathed in the fragrance of his cologne, which had teased my senses all evening.

"You smell wonderful."

Matt winked at me. "Burberry Brit. Glad I haven't lost my touch."

"Hardly." We proceeded back to the bar. "How about you order drinks while I freshen up in the ladies'?"

He nodded, and we went our separate ways.

I walked through a side door and followed the signage into a wide corridor. A cold draft chilled my body, and I shivered. Goosebumps pimpled my skin. I bounded down the corridor, my heels clacking on the hard surface, and found respite in the warm haven of the ladies' bathroom, across from the kitchen.

The ladies' room lobby exuded old Parisian ambience, with thick maroon carpet and gilded mirrors near a two-seater tapestry couch. One doorway led to the toilets and another to a room filled with sinks and mirrors. A fresh vanilla scent permeated the room and pleased my senses. Belinda was missing out.

I washed my hands and studied myself in the mirror. For the first time in years, my appearance pleased me. I looked pretty. The dark splotches under my eyes were hidden underneath makeup, and a real smile reached my eyes and brightened my face. The joy of Matt's company brought a natural rosiness to my cheeks. Never in my wildest imagination had I thought life could be fun again. I dared to dream my future held more joy than my painful past.

With a final check in the full-length mirror near the bathroom exit, I stepped into the cold corridor and tripped on the threshold. A startled cry later, I found myself protected in a set of strong, masculine arms.

"I'm so sorry!" I lifted my gaze and gasped.

Nicholas's deep-brown orbs stared back. Light grey smudges under his eyes marred the perfection of his face.

I pressed against his chest and stilled my fingers from running through his hair. His trademark woody cologne mixed with masculine sweat stirred my insides. A blush rose to my cheeks.

He lowered his arms, and I stood back to balance myself.

"You look lovely, Victoria." His gaze shifted from my face and caressed the length of my dress.

My blush heated.

"I hope my dirty clothes haven't soiled your dress."

My brain whirred into motion. "What brings you out tonight?"

He rubbed the back of his neck. "Problems in the kitchen."

"Ah." I peeked around his shoulder to where tools lay on the metal kitchen counter. "Looks like you've been working hard."

He stepped closer and lowered his voice. "Victoria, I'm so—"

"I thought you'd lost your way, Vicki." Matt stood in the doorway to the dance hall with a strained smile on his face. He strode over and placed a hand on the small of my back.

Nicholas flinched and stepped backwards. With a nod, he returned to the kitchen.

The opportunity to say goodbye was lost. I clutched my cramping abdomen.

"Let's go inside for that drink," Matt said.

"Sure."

We returned to our table while my body shook. I wilted onto a chair and sipped my drink, my brain a frazzled mess after seeing Nicholas. Our first interaction since I stormed from his house over a month ago.

The following day another English period flew by, and the bell rang for lunch. I dismissed the students, grabbed my sandwich, and ambled to the Staff Lounge. I wrestled over last night's events. Why did Nicholas have such a strong effect on me? Why was my life complicated instead of simple and fun, like when I spent time with Matt?

The Staff Lounge bustled with teachers and administrative

staff. Belinda and Anita were seated on a two-seater couch, deep in conversation. Anita was the staff busybody. Her artistic nature appealed to Belinda's creative side, so I tolerated her in small doses for my friend's sake.

I plopped onto the carpet at their feet.

A hand grasped my shoulder. "You're the woman I wanted to see," Anita said.

I glanced up to where she leaned forward in her chair, her eyes seeming to dance. "Yes?"

"Tell me." Her gaze darted around the room, and she lowered her voice. "Is something going on with you and Matt?"

If I had taken a bite from my sandwich, I would have choked. "What makes you ask?"

Belinda shifted. Her eyes lacked their usual sparkle.

"The way you interact. Body language. Meaningful conversations. I heard you two were chummy at last night's formal."

A blush warmed my face. "We're good friends."

She wiggled her eyebrows on her round face. "Are you sure? You spent most of the evening with each other."

My cheeks burned at the memory of our subtle flirtation.

Belinda stared past my shoulder.

"Just friends, Anita."

"But you're open to more?"

I clenched my jaw. When would she stop the inquisition? I stared at my sandwich, no longer hungry.

Belinda pursed her lips and straightened her shoulders. "Matt's a great guy. If he makes you happy—"

"I appreciate it, Bee, but—"

"You deserve happiness." She swallowed. "Maybe that's Matt."

I feigned a smile and returned my sandwich to its container.

Anita stood. "I'm finished, take my seat." She gave Belinda a meaningful look before she turned and walked away.

I occupied the vacated chair and clasped my hands in my lap.

When I faced Belinda—and her cool green eyes and stiff smile—my stomach twisted. "A-are you feeling better?"

She tilted her head. "Better?"

I pinched the back of my hand. "From yesterday's curry attack."

"Oh. Yes."

I nodded. "Good." I crossed and uncrossed my legs.

Belinda picked several crumbs off her skirt.

I bit the inside of my cheek. "So—"

"I haven't prepared for my junior class." The corner of her mouth lifted. "I need to chain everything down before they destroy my equipment."

I smiled and nodded. "I'm glad I teach English."

She stood and disappeared from the room.

My stomach still churned, so I headed back to my classroom. A Scripture came to mind, and with each step I mumbled prayers of blessing over Anita.

CHAPTER TWENTY-THREE
Freedom Directive

"**Grant Michael! Hand** me back my chocolate bunny this instant!"

"But Mum!"

My Easter weekend visit to Wagga Wagga was flying by. This trip was a ray of sunshine in the dismal weather of my life in Tellarine. How had everything become so complicated?

"No buts. Untie my bunny, Mister Cowboy Justice."

My nephew groaned and untied Christine's chocolate bunny from a shoelace noose. I snickered. The bunny had been convicted in the Lego court of law for impersonating a bilby and was sentenced to hang from Grant's shoe perched high on a shelf.

He returned the bunny to his mother, pulled his shoe from the shelf, and ran from the room screaming "Avast, mateys! I have returned!" at the top of his lungs.

Christine shook her head. "Some days ..."

I chuckled at the decapitated bunny crumpled in her hands. Yet another reason I loved visiting my sister and her crazy boys.

Earlier in the day, I had arranged an Easter egg hunt for my nephews and enjoyed their search for hidden chocolate. Memories of similar hunts for my children had flooded my mind. Ryan had been an excellent chocolate-egg hunter. With senses like a bloodhound—or a chocolate hound—he beat his sisters each year. The memory of his victorious smile triggered goosebumps, and his chocolate-smeared cheeks and lips roused my laughter. The knife in my heart twisted with the heavy loss of him and his sisters.

Parking my car under the carport, I trudged up the driveway with overnight bag in hand and checked the letterbox. Plodding to my bungalow, I opened the front door, and tossed the letters onto the coffee table before I stowed my bag in the bedroom.

I flicked through the mail and picked up a letter from Stacy's office, my hands clammy. With shaky fingers I opened the letter. A Divorce Order issued by the Federal Circuit Court of Australia. Dated six days ago.

Tears welled in my eyes. Jude and I were no longer one, our marriage dissolved into nothingness. All that remained was a trail of heartbreak, the loss of my innocence and self-respect, and enough memories to haunt any future relationship I might have. My relationship breakdown with Nicholas proved my brokenness.

A tear spilled down my cheek. Too little, too late. I retrieved my mobile phone. Three missed calls from an unknown number flashed on the screen.

I ignored my unease about the calls, tapped out a quick message to Stacy, snapped a picture of the document, and sighed.

Me: IT IS FINISHED.

Stacy: YOU RECEIVED THE DOCUMENTS FROM OUR OFFICE! PRAISE GOD! CELEBRATORY DRINKS WHEN I SEE YOU NEXT. LOVE YOU. XO

Me: A HUG WILL SUFFICE. I LOVE YOU TO THE MOON AND BACK. XX

Stacy: TO INFINITY AND BEYOND!

I hurried along the narrow concrete path at midday, wine bottle in one hand and a sparkling apple drink in the other. I hoped they were partial to red wine because I had no intention of drinking it.

Anna's mum, Rebecca, had phoned before Easter and invited me for lunch on the final Friday of the holidays. Nervous jitters skittered in my midriff. Other than meals with Nicholas and Diana, I had not entered the home of a Tellarine student and their family. I looked forward to being introduced to the Beauforts.

A fragrant rose garden of reds, pinks, purples, and yellows weaved its way around the side of the house. The heady aroma of roses, the clean smell of eucalyptus, and the perfume of lavender filled the air.

Anna greeted me and seized both bottles before she ushered me to the kitchen, where her mother and grandmother worked. The ladies glanced up when Anna popped the bottles on the bench and picked up a pile of plates. She carried the plates out of the room.

"Welcome, Ms. Burke," Rebecca said. "This is my mother-in-law, Mumma Joan." Rebecca gave me a smile and a warm hug before she returned to her mixing bowl. A pretty yet somewhat weathered lady with plaited mousy-brown hair similar to Anna's, Rebecca appeared closer to forty than I was.

"Please call me Victoria. It's a privilege to have been invited."

Joan pulled me into a firm hug and kissed my cheek before she wrapped her fingers around my forearms. Average in height, her mature age could not hide her beauty or graceful mien. Her luminous dark-brown eyes held remarkable depth, their vibrancy familiar. She must have been a becoming young lady.

She inspected me from head to toe. "Aren't you a pretty lass? Anna's told me so much about you."

A tinge of warmth touched my cheeks. "You're very kind, Mumma Joan."

Joan squeezed my arms before she returned to lunch preparation.

I ambled over to Rebecca, who sliced cabbage into thin, even strips. "Can I help with anything?"

Rebecca's smile was soft and sweet. "No, you're a guest and already do so much for our Anna. Why don't you pop your drink in the fridge? You didn't need to bring anything but thank you."

I found a gap for the sparkling apple drink between a bottle of milk and a slim glass bottle of water in the fridge door.

Anna re-entered the kitchen. "Ms. Burke, would you like to see our library?"

Rebecca laughed. "It's not much of a library, but it's satisfied Anna's cravings over the years." She paused her knife and eyed her daughter. "Anna darling, please pop Ms. Burke's wine into the wine fridge."

Anna grabbed the bottle and directed me to the book collection.

I loped through the dining room and gasped. A wall at least six metres wide contained floor-to-ceiling pine bookshelves. I ran my fingers across the books' spines. My gaze fell on favourite literary authors and a few Christian fiction books.

Anna slipped into the room.

"You have so many of my favourite authors. I've read many of these books, but I often borrow them from a school library. You're blessed." I regarded Anna with her wavy, mousy-brown hair and large hazel eyes.

She smiled with a sigh. "I was home schooled. Mum needed to be home, so I spent the better half of my childhood with a book in my hand." Anna glanced out the window. "Pop and Dad managed the farm together, and Nan and Mum looked after us between work duties. By the time Pop died unexpectedly, most of the livestock had been sold and Dad had an accounting job lined up in town. Mum thought I was old enough to catch the school bus for Year Seven." Her usual cheerful, soft features bordered on melancholy.

"I sure am glad you're in my classes."

She gave me a wonderful smile. "Thanks, Ms. Burke."

Rebecca called everyone to the dining room.

I sat and admired the spread. A huge platter housed a mound of roasted potatoes with green beans and carrots. Joan carved a large beef roast. The gravy and peas lay next to a bowl of coleslaw and a smaller bowl filled with sliced tomatoes and cucumber. I spotted a plate piled high with squares of white bread accompanied with softened butter and a bowl of sugar.

Rebecca introduced me to Anna's dad, Chris, and Anna's younger brother, Mitchell. I recognised the rough-and-tumble middle school footy player from my rostered yard-duty shifts and wondered why I had never noticed the connection. Mitchell bore a freckled, elongated face and mousy-brown hair identical to his sister.

I answered polite questions and redirected my answers into questions of my own. Chris and Rebecca shared subtle looks and gestures. The nuances of their words to one another and love in their eyes pierced my heart. I longed for a relationship like theirs. After a delightful lunch, I was almost disappointed when Anna and Mitchell cleared the table.

I reached for Joan's plate to stack with mine and was given a gentle swat on the hand. "Don't even think about it, young lady. Why don't you browse the bookshelves while Rebecca and I do the dishes?"

I slipped away from the table, pulled *A Light in the Window* from a shelf, and nestled on the padded window seat.

While I was immersed in the first chapters of Julie Lessman's novel, Joan reclined next to me and patted my knee. "That young Patrick character reminds me of my darling Benjamin."

I gazed up.

Her brilliant brown eyes focused on mine. "And here I thought you'd never married, but your face tells a different story."

The book fell into my lap. Was a neon sign lit above my head declaring my divorce?

Joan grasped my hand in her weathered one, and a tear slipped down my cheek. "It's okay, dear."

I sniffed. "How did you know?"

A smile slid to her lips. "I've seen your face in the mirror, and I identified the longing and loss in your eyes when you watched my boy. Chris is a wonderful husband." She narrowed her eyes. "Death or divorce, dear?"

I released a shaky sigh. "Divorce."

Joan enveloped me in her arms.

I melted into her warm embrace. A sob shuddered in my chest for the life I now lived, but my eyes remained dry.

Joan kissed my cheek. "As God is my witness, He'll give you the desires of your heart."

"I hope so."

She squeezed my hand. "Thank the Lord His mercies are new every morning. He promised never to leave us or forsake us."

I closed my eyes and thanked God for sending this sweet woman of faith to encourage and love on me when I needed it.

CHAPTER TWENTY-FOUR
The Proposition

"Matt? I thought you'd gone home?" I had just donned my woollen coat to ward off the mid-June chill awaiting me outdoors.

Matt, his gaze glued to me, stalked through my English room to my desk. He stood so close I could hear him breathe. His eyes were stormy blue, full of fervour.

I faltered on my feet. "Matt?"

He slid his hands around my waist and pulled me against his chest.

I gasped on impact. My heart thudded, and my mouth went dry.

His eyes flickered. A slight grin crept to his face before he lowered his lips to mine and kissed me.

I reached out and touched his jaw, his contours similar to Jude's. I craved being touched. My insides burned with need, but my mind shouted to break away.

Matt pulled back with laboured breaths and glazed, almost groggy eyes. "I've wanted to do that for a long time." His lips were a shade redder than before.

My heart galloped, and I reigned in my ragged gasps. How was a girl meant to respond to something like that? I pushed away, leaned against my desk, and allowed my coat to slide off my shoulders. "I'm not sure we should do that again."

All cheer fled his face. "Why not?"

I gripped the desk behind me. The heat in my body dropped,

and its overwhelming control siphoned away, one breath at a time. The passion of Matt's kiss had sparked a match in the dry expanse of my heart and unrelenting libido. I searched his eyes. "I don't want to do something I'll regret."

His face lit up. "So, you *do* want me."

I laughed and nudged his arm. "How about we explore the idea? Pause the kisses and spend time talking."

Matt extended his right hand. "It's a deal."

My stomach tossed, a step away from a turbulent heave. I moved my attention away from my digestive system and onto Belinda's fingers, where they tapped against the desk.

"What's up?" She crinkled her brow.

I bit my bottom lip. "I, ah, wanted to be the one to tell you—"

"What?" Her fingers stilled.

"Matt and I are seeing each other."

Belinda's eyes widened.

I wrung my hands. Nerves skittered through my body.

"Oh."

My fingers burned on every twist. "I hope this isn't an issue. You'll tell me if it ever is, won't you?"

Belinda pinched her lips together, then said, "I've no claims on him. You don't need to tiptoe around me." She offered a small smile. "I hope he makes you happy."

The vice against my chest eased. "Thank you. It means so much to me." I rubbed a hand across my sternum. "Promise you'll tell me if you ever have concerns."

Belinda smiled, and the warmth of it reached her eyes at last. "Of course. I'm your number one cheerleader."

Matt and I shared long conversations about our childhoods, experiences and vulnerabilities. He loved to listen to stories about my children, and we shared our shattered dreams for our lost babies. My heart soared as I shared my memories of my children with someone else.

My struggles with Jude's abuse and Matt's family issues bonded us closer together.

Word of our relationship spread via the efficient church gossip grapevine. I endured glares from several young women and some terse comments from Belinda.

We hit our first bump in the road after our intentions to travel to Melbourne together during the September school holidays came to light. Belinda's bristled reaction upset me.

"Do you think that's wise?" Her lips pursed and she narrowed her eyes. "I mean, what sort of example does this show the youth? That it's acceptable to holiday away with a boyfriend?"

"It's not like that. I'll stay with Amber, and Matt will stay with a friend."

She planted her hands on her hips. "But that's how it appears. You driving off together for a week of who-knows-what."

I exhaled. "Do you want me to email the entire youth group? Let them know I'm staying pure? I've undoubtedly kissed fewer men than most of the girls in that group."

She huffed a laugh. "I'm saying it looks bad."

I shrugged. "So, I need to drive five-plus hours alone to the exact same location as Matt on the exact same day and repeat it the next week so it looks like we're not travelling together?"

Belinda pulled a face. "I don't know. I just—"

"Just what? What's going on?"

She shook her head. "Nothing. Do what you think's best."

I squeezed her arm. "Thanks. Now, are you up for dinner tonight?"

"No, sorry. I can't."

I pouted. "But we haven't dined together for ages."

She blew out a breath. "Things keep popping up."

I fidgeted my fingers. "Okay. I'd better go. See you tomorrow."

"Yeah, bye." Belinda walked to her car in the school car park.

Doubts niggled my mind with each of my steps to my own vehicle. Was it me, or had Belinda been distant? Her text messages had been shorter, less frequent. She had not asked me to volunteer at church in three weeks. And another dinner refusal? I rubbed my chest against the ache blooming inside.

Belinda's response to our plans paled in comparison to Nicholas's. Nicholas and I had come to a standstill, a ceasefire of sorts. Diana meant too much to me, so I determined to be civil to her father and try to forget the mess of our relationship.

I relaxed at Benanu's alone—my stomach satisfied with my Saturday morning breakfast indulgence—when Nicholas occupied the seat opposite mine. A smile traced my lips. "Nicholas, it's nice to see you."

"Are you going to marry him, Victoria?"

I dropped my smile at his accusatory tone, reclined in my chair, and crossed my arms. "Excuse me?"

"I spoke with Matt last night at Dave Phillip's bachelor party. He told me about your trip to Melbourne."

I squeezed my hands into fists and pressed them against the insides of my elbows.

Nicholas stared at me, his shoulders rigid. The pulse in his neck thumped.

"I'm not sure how our trip to Melbourne relates to marriage?"

His grimace was no match for my glare. "I recall a previous conversation about not being a stumbling block." He shifted in his chair, and his gaze darted around the room. Was he uncomfortable?

"Are you concerned we're giving the wrong impression to immature Christians?" I breathed out and rested my elbows on the table. "We have separate accommodations. Other than the commute to and from Melbourne, we'll spend time in public places. I've got it covered."

His gaze softened.

I quelled my heart to stop the uncontrollable flutters when his gaze held mine. I leaned in on my elbows. "Did Matt say something to concern you?" I cleared my throat. "If he did, I want to know."

He pursed his lips.

"Nicholas, please." Hypothetical scenarios of devastating consequences ran rampant in my mind.

Nicholas rubbed the back of his neck. "Matt had a few drinks with the guys. I heard them boast about their conquests." His pulse jackhammered in his neck. "I was s-surprised when Matt shared about the two of you." He stared at a glass on the table.

What brag-worthy thing had we done? My eyes widened the same moment Nicholas raised his gaze. Our first kiss.

He shook his head and slouched. "So, it's true?"

"If you're referring to the single kiss we shared, then, yes, it's true."

He narrowed his eyes. "The story I heard was more involved."

I straightened against the chair back, my mouth agape. What had Matt said? Heat built in my body like a volcano preparing to erupt. I clenched my fists in my lap. How could Nicholas think so little of me?

I inhaled a deep breath. "What did he say?"

Redness stained Nicholas's cheeks. "Things I assumed you were saving for your next husband."

I flinched. Alexa's shocked face fleeted through my mind. Had she experienced the sting of indignation too? My heart stuttered. I shook my head to dislodge frozen words from my slack mouth. "I, ah." I blinked. "That wasn't me."

Nicholas rubbed his chin and arched an eyebrow.

I zoned onto his dark chocolate eyes. "Want me to tell you all the intimate details of our kiss? So, you know it was far from a scene in an MA-rated film?" Fire blazed in my eyes, and icicles formed around my heart.

His cheeks ruddied and he cringed.

I leaned in, my chest pressed against the table. "We weren't sandwiched hard against each other." My stomach tingled with the memory of Nicholas's touch. "It didn't even come close."

His eyes burned.

I gulped down my glass of water, groped for my bag and stood. "I'll see you around."

Power-walking at lightning-break speed to my house, I ground my teeth at my harboured attraction to Nicholas. It had to stop.

Unlocking the front door, I threw my keys on the couch and dialled Matt's number.

"M'yeah?" Matt croaked.

My jaw clenched. "Enjoy yourself last night?"

He groaned. "Ah, yes."

I paced the room. "That's nice. Care to tell me why you told people we're sleeping together?"

A choking sound vibrated over the phone. "What?"

I clenched my teeth. "You heard me."

A crash clanged in the background followed by a low curse. "W-who said that?"

I pursed my lips and flopped on the couch. "Does it even matter?"

"N-no. I'm sorry, Vicki, I don't know what to say."

I scrubbed my face with my hand. "Matt. You know my past." My voice quavered. "I-I thought I could trust you. I can't be with a man who overindulges in alcohol and spreads lies about me." My vision clouded. "Our Melbourne trip is off."

CHAPTER TWENTY-FIVE
Shock of Impact

Matt knocked on my front door. "Ready to go?"

"I was born ready." I handed him my suitcase.

He chuckled. "You're a dag."

Moments later he stowed my luggage in his car, and we departed for Melbourne. Matt had pursued me with little scrumptious treats and apologies over the last two weeks. I had finally forgiven him and re-established a tentative trust.

The morning sunshine brightened my mood, and our conversation steered into personal territory kilometres down the highway.

Matt shared how he slept in a different stranger's bed several nights a week for years on end in an attempt to show and experience love.

I struggled with the modern concept of casual sex. How could anyone be satisfied without an emotional attachment? I had only ever shared Jude's bed and was crushed when our marriage ended in a series of one-night stands with each other.

"Do you miss the physical side of relationships?" I asked.

Matt stared out the windscreen. "Yes." His brow creased, and a frown tugged the corner of his mouth. "I'll be honest, following your non-contact rules is tough. I willingly gave up sex a while ago but never imagined we wouldn't kiss."

I placed a hand on his arm. "I'm sorry it's been a struggle, but it'll make us stronger as individuals." I emitted a shaky breath. Memories of Jude's drunken kisses battered my mind. He had known which buttons to press to get what he wanted. My cheeks flushed. "Before Jude and I became less intimate months before the accident, there were times I ... let him use my body." I chewed the inside of my cheek. "He was often drunk." I burrowed back, and my chest shuddered.

Matt's warm hand found mine resting on my knee.

"He'd take what he wanted, then roll over and sleep. Many silent tears soaked into my pillow on those nights." I sniffed.

His hand squeezed mine.

"I felt compelled, duty-bound as a good Christian wife to satisfy his needs while my own burned without release."

Matt squinted at me. "I had no idea."

I turned to the passenger window. "My mind clouds when I'm overcome with physical affection." And baited words spoken to guilt my conscience. "It's best you discover my imperfections now."

"You're the closest I've met to perfection." He moved his hand back to the wheel and overtook a slow vehicle. "You've been a true example of Jesus, and I count it an honour to know you." His hand rested on the gear stick, and I covered it with mine. "You've strengthened my resolve."

Tears pricked my eyes. I squeezed Matt's hand, and we rested in companionable silence.

Matt dropped me off at Amber's house in South Yarra.

Mike hugged me. "I hope the trip was uneventful." He disappeared down the hall with my suitcase.

Amber scrunched her eyebrows. "Hopefully not too uneventful."

I slapped her shoulder before pulling her into a tight hug.

The three of us lazed in the sunshine on the back deck and chatted like we had never separated. My heart filled with happiness. I sipped from a glass of cold, sparkling lemon water Mike handed me. "Where are the children?"

Amber winked at Mike. He stretched out next to her and draped an arm across her shoulder. "With the grandparents for the weekend."

I gaped. "The entire weekend? While I'm here?"

Mike chuckled. "Yes. I promise to behave, but I can't vouch for my wife."

"I'm amazed I have a bed in the house and not a mattress on the deck."

Amber lifted her eyebrow. "Stay out late tonight, and you'll be fine. I have plans for my man." She winked. "Let Matt know we'll attend the late church service in the morning. If you want breakfast, I suggest you go out." She turned to Mike with a teasing smile. "You won't be so lucky, Mikey. Breakfast in bed for you, lover boy."

I gazed across the bright floral landscape and smiled. What an example of a real, loving marriage, with mutual give and take, not give and give until your soul bled.

I sucked in a calming breath. "Speaking of children, can I borrow your car?"

Amber and Mike's smiles dimmed. Amber nodded. "Sure. Now?"

"Yes."

Amber retrieved her keys. "We'll see you soon."

In the cemetery several families spoke nearby in hushed voices, my heart saddened by our shared losses.

I stared up at the colourful balloon sculptures and blinked before focusing on the three graves at my feet. Wiping my eyes, I withdrew three items from my handbag. I placed a tube of lip gloss at Jessica's grave, a whoopee cushion at Samantha's, and a matchbox car against Ryan's plaque. My chest clamped, and my vision blurred.

Would sitting here ever get easier?

♥ ♥ ♥ ♥ ♥ ♥ ♥

That evening I inspected my reflection in Amber's bathroom mirror for the tenth time. Queasiness swirled in my middle, and I shifted on my restless legs. Matt would arrive soon to pick me up for dinner with Steve and Stacy. They had listened to plenty about Matt, but when they had visited Tellarine, their attention had been on Nicholas. Stacy had always liked to compare things. Boys, food, cars, movies, you name it, she compared it. I tried to quell the tremor in my hands.

A soft knock vibrated against the bathroom door.

"I'm almost ready." I opened the door and breathed in a delicious waft of Burberry Brit.

A smile illuminated Matt's face. Dressed to impress, he wore a midnight-blue suit with a crisp open-collar white-and-blue-check shirt. His gaze scanned my figure and smouldered.

I wore a simple midi-length pale-pink lace and contrast georgette dress with a delicate silver-encrusted diamanté belt. Once Amber spotted my silver block-heel sandals in my suitcase, she had convinced me to wear her dress.

"Wow, you look amazing."

I turned in a slow circle, conscious of my exposed scar. "You think so?"

Matt stepped close and drew me into his arms. His lips pressed against my hair. "I think so."

I pulled away from his embrace. "Well, I think you win, Mr. Briggs. You make me want to break my own rules."

He laughed, grabbed my hand, and led me down the hallway toward the front door. "Do let me know if you change the rules."

I chuckled. Tonight compelled me to stick to my 'no kissing' resolve now I knew the temptation Matt had become.

Steve and Stacy met us outside Rockpool Bar and Grill with huge grins. Stacy introduced herself to Matt while Steve pulled me into his arms. "Well, I'll be. You're more gorgeous than the last time I saw you."

I clung to him. "It's so good to see you, Stevie. I've missed you." And I missed his hugs.

"Same here, beautiful."

I stepped back from his embrace and introduced the men.

Stacy leaned close. "He's spunky. I can see him as a bad boy. Good thing he reformed."

We walked through the restaurant doorway and my mind flooded with memories.

Jude had invited his senior staff and their partners to dinner in the Private Terrace dining room. I spent the evening primarily alone, mesmerised by the beautiful aspect of Southbank from the floor-to-ceiling windows. Debate over designer clothes and toy boys held no interest for me, nor had conversations tainted with corporate blood lust and sexual conquests.

I tightened my grip on Stacy's arm when we were directed to our table. With a graceful nod I accepted the chair Matt pulled out for me. The tension in my shoulders eased when I focused on my friends.

The food was on an echelon higher than any meal I had consumed in years, and I savoured every morsel. Steve interpreted aloud the moans and sighs which exited my mouth, a childhood habit he had mastered. Tears streamed down Matt's and Stacy's faces at Steve's David Attenborough impression as he expressed the meaning of each hummed note. I ignored him and enjoyed my meal, a skill I had learned and practiced for decades. We waited for dessert, a selection of petit fours I was desperate to try despite my overfilled belly.

Stacy cleared her throat. "I have an announcement." She withdrew an envelope and slid it across the table to me. Her eyes sparkled, and her smile grew. "It's your divorce settlement cheque. I know it's taken months but was worth the time and effort."

I peered at the envelope, then back up at Stacy. Tears stung my eyes.

She smiled. "Open it."

I glanced around the table, my nervous stomach at battle with its Scotch fillet inmate. I picked up the envelope, and my hands shook when I removed the cheque from its confines. "One point two million dollars?" my voice cracked in a whisper.

"Sorry it wasn't more. Extensive fees were allocated to various agents, governing bodies, legal representatives. It's the best I could do, given the circumstances, but I think this will look after you for a few years."

A prodigious smile spanned my face. "Thank you, Stace, and thank You, Jesus!"

Matt pulled me into a warm hug. Dessert arrived, and we ended our evening on a high of sugar and coffee. God had provided like He promised.

Matt and I sauntered hand-in-hand to the undercover multi-level car park after my emotional farewell with my cousins. His hands were smooth, like Jude's.

He pulled me close so our arms touched while we navigated past cars. "I find it ironic I'm dating a rich chick."

"Why?"

"I chased wealthy women in my wanton twenties." He winked. "Now on the straight and narrow, money never factored in. It's still not important." His mouth twisted, and he stared into my eyes. "How about an early breakfast on Monday before we laugh all the way to the bank?"

A playful giggle rose up inside my giddy body. "That sounds like a great idea." A vision of Anna's property popped into my thoughts. "What do you think of my buying land just outside of Tellarine and building a house?"

He unlocked his car and opened my door. "That sounds promising. And hectic."

My chest warmed. I slid into my seat. "Yeah. It was a thought."

Matt leaned against the car. "It's a good thought." He closed my door and I sighed.

♥ ♥ ♥ ♥ ♥ ♥ ♥

Matt and I reclined on a public park bench near Amber's and admired the gardens. I mulled over this morning's service at my old church. Although memories of Jude and the children had stolen my breath at times, my friends had given us both a warm reception.

A toddler squealed in his father's arms, and I swallowed a lump. "Which of your family will I meet on Tuesday?"

Matt rested a tanned arm behind my back.

I leaned into his warmth. How many times had Jude and I cosied up together like this?

His lips lingered on my temple. "We're taking Uncle Brian, Auntie Crystal, my cousin, Pip, and her husband, Troy, out for dinner. My treat."

I warmed at his generosity. "I insist you let moneybags pay, so it's my treat."

A deep laugh echoed in his broad chest, and I chuckled.

"I'm looking forward to meeting your uncle and auntie. Will I meet your parents?"

He shook his head. "I visited Mum yesterday. I don't intend introducing you to her or her husband."

"You mean your father," I whispered.

A cheek muscle flickered, and his jaw clenched. "Uncle Brian's more of a father than that man ever was."

I held his hand. "Matt, you need to forgive your dad. The book of Mark says to forgive so our Father in heaven will forgive us."

I inhaled a deep breath. Jude's face came to mind. "I know how hard forgiveness can be. But by God's grace, it's not only possible, it will free you." I caressed his jaw, which flickered under my palm. "I want you to enjoy all the good life has to offer."

A tear splashed on my hand. I wanted to wrap Matt in my arms and take his pain.

"When I told my parents about Danielle's pregnancy, Dad lost it. I was petrified." His breaths shuddered. "He hit me. Hard."

My breath snagged in my throat.

"Over and over, like someone possessed. Mum tried to stop him, but he wouldn't." A strangled sob wrenched from his lips. "H-he broke my nose, loosened teeth, cracked two ribs, and f-fractured my arm. My chest hurt two months later."

I stared in a daze.

"I had first confided in Pip about the b-baby, then spilled the news to my uncle and auntie. Uncle Brian drove me home and waited in the car. He heard M-Mum's screams and stopped Dad."

Fiery heat rose inside me and spilled over in a torrent of tears. How could someone beat their own son? I held Matt tight against me. He wept like a frightened teenager, and I thought my heart would break.

We cried together on the park bench seat.

Our Melbourne visit ended. After an early breakfast with Mike and Amber before the children awoke, Matt and I joined the trickle of morning traffic and inched our way home.

"Want to swing by your old place?"

My heart floundered. "No."

"You still okay to stop by Craig's?" Matt had mentioned a brief detour to visit a friend.

"Sure."

The idea appealed yesterday, but when I recognised the direction we travelled, a tremor set in my hands.

When we entered the Dandenong Ranges, blood drained from my face, and my brain short-circuited from all rational thought. My tongue froze. Minutes passed, and my breaths laboured. My entire body trembled. Heat, then perspiration flushed over my skin before nausea spiralled in violent waves within my midriff.

I stared out the windscreen and clenched tight fists on my thighs. Pain coursed through my fingertips from my grasp. The road narrowed and twisted around towering trees.

Matt's muffled voice pushed against the fog in my head. "Victoria? You okay?"

The landscape morphed into a misty dream scene. Distant memories I had thought lost forever now flew before my eyes, and I remembered snippets of my apocalyptic drive along this same road.

Childlike giggles. Inspirational music soothing the hurt Jude had inflicted on me.

A huge truck on a collision course, hurtling at us. Weightlessness to a cacophony of glass explosions.

A white airbag and the sudden punch from its impact. Sharp, severe pain.

No movement in my leg. The wet trickle of blood down my neck.

Trapped. No escape. Unmitigated panic, lungs gasping for air. Darkness.

I closed my eyes. Bile rose up the back of my throat, and fresh panic set in. I concentrated on my breathing.

Deep breath in.

Slow breath out.

Another deep breath, another breath released.

In. Out.

You can do this. God is with you. You are not alone. Breathe until the fear passes.

A hand pressed against my arm, and I jolted in my seat. We were parked at an observation point on the side of the mountain.

Matt unbuckled and cupped my cheeks in both of his hands. My view of the windscreen shifted to his face. "Victoria. You're frightening me. What's wrong?"

A flash flood of my tears overflowed onto Matt's fingers. I was not prepared for this place. A place which once nurtured happy childhood memories now symbolised my shattered life. My world had twisted like the grotesque metal of the crushed vehicles which once lay near this peaceful spot. Death in the midst of tranquillity.

My stomach seemed to drop out from inside me and sucked my heart down with it. When would I be free from this torment?

A whisper, soft and gentle, reignited my hope. My prayers joined with the prayers of the man who held my face. God had shown mercy and given me a flesh-and-blood being for support during my re-encounter with this nightmare location.

"I haven't returned here since the accident."

Matt's breath hitched, and his thumb stroked my chin. "You never said where the accident happened. I'm so sorry." He slipped his hands from my face and rested them on my shoulders.

I exhaled. The mounting tension extricated from my limbs.

He drew me close. "If I'd known, I wouldn't have suggested seeing Craig. Please know I'd never intentionally hurt you."

"I know."

We waited until the tide of nausea and tears subsided. His arms were a true refuge, but we needed to continue our journey to make it home by the afternoon. I pulled away with a regretful sigh. "We'd better go."

He nodded, restarted the car, and set us back on the road.

Our visit was short, pleasant. After a brief lunch and fuel stop, we arrived home in time for a quick nap snuggled on Matt's couch. Having survived an emotional rollercoaster week in Melbourne, I indulged in the strength of Matt's arms. I hoped God would not begrudge me one injudicious snooze. Matt's soft snore vibrated next to my head, and I let sleep take me before my mind ventured into dangerous territory.

CHAPTER TWENTY-SIX
Complications Rekindled

Private Number: MY APARTMENT IS EMPTY WITHOUT YOU.
Private Number: HOW CAN YOU EXPECT ME TO FORGET PERFECTION?
Private Number: WHERE ARE YOU? I NEED TO SEE YOU.
Private Number: COME HOME, BABY. LET ME SHOW YOU HOW GOOD LIFE CAN BE.
Private Number: I WANT YOU. DESPERATELY. LET ME LOVE YOU THE WAY YOU CRAVE.
Private Number: I WILL NEVER GIVE YOU UP. NEVER.

Chills coursed through my body. I had blocked the sixth phone number in as many days. Hissing a breath, I steadied my hands on the steering wheel. Life was hard enough without Jude's interference. He had spurned me when he had me, so what stopped him from moving on? I parked the car and pulled up the handbrake.

My hands now shook for a different reason. My literature students had pleaded for an extra class before their end-of-year exam next week. I had only this afternoon available, so Diana had offered her large dining room table.

I walked the path to the verandah and climbed the stairs on shaky legs. Memories flooded my thoughts as I knocked on the front door with a trembling hand. I smoothed my shirt front and bounced on my toes.

The front door swung open, and my breath hitched. Nicholas greeted me with a cordial smile. We had shared brief nods or smiles since our encounter at Benanu's in September. I missed our conversations.

A warm smile laced my lips. "Thanks for making your home available on a Saturday."

"No problem. You know it's every father's dream to hear about the conceited, callous, but swoon-worthy behaviour of Mr. Darcy from his romance-obsessed daughter," he said, deadpan.

I burst into giggles.

His face shone with a brilliant smile.

I uttered a soft prayer of thanks, entered the house and headed toward the sound of noisy teenage girls. Books and papers littered the table. Young ladies chattered away without end. After I refocused conversations about boys and end-of-year plans, I handed over more practice exams.

Once the girls settled into their work, I popped into the kitchen, turned on the kettle, and grabbed a mug. I rifled the pantry for tea bags.

"Need any help?" Nicholas hunkered at the bench.

I ripped a tea bag from its paper package. "I'm fine. I hope you don't mind my making myself at home? The girls are in test mode, so I thought I'd take advantage of the quiet." I glanced up from my tea bag and mug. "Would you like a cuppa?"

Nicholas smiled and shook his head. "No, thanks. Was making sure my kitchen wasn't being ransacked."

I chuckled. "I didn't make that much noise."

He smiled and shifted on the stool.

I cleared my throat. "Matt tells me you and he had a great chat last night at the men's session at church."

Matt and I had breakfasted at Benanu's, where he had shared about the evening and ignited more biblical discussion. God's impact on Matt's heart awed me.

The whites of Nicholas's eyes widened a second. "You must see each other often."

I furrowed my brow. "I believe it's what you do when you're

dating."

His jaw twitched.

"But then again, I could be wrong." I grabbed my mug and glanced up.

Nicholas's intent gaze burned into my skin.

Heat climbed up my neck. With a forced smile I returned to my students. I clenched my fists against the unceasing belly flutters and the way Nicholas sent my body, mind and emotions into a frenzy.

I prayed for peace and slumped into my chair.

"Thanks for promptly fixing the oven and pitching in. You saved me from overwhelming panic. I hope I didn't spoil your evening plans?" I rinsed a huge stainless-steel pot at the church kitchen sink. Resting it on the drying rack, I immersed another large pot into the soapy water.

"No plans this evening." Nicholas inserted a knife into the knife block. "But I would've rearranged my plans to help."

I concentrated on the pot in my hands and scrubbed at the burnt residue on its base. Warmth spread through my chest with each vigorous stroke. I closed my eyes and sighed before I reopened them to work on the pot. "I enjoy this part of the evening. I miss having a proper kitchen and double sink."

Nicholas cleared his throat. "I applaud you for living in that tiny box for so long. Let alone using a kitchen never designed for daily use."

I peered up at him.

He dried a pot with a now-damp tea towel.

"I know this is temporary. One day I'll have my own home again." I thought of my country property dream. "I'm thinking of building on a block of land outside of town." My gaze glued to the stainless-steel interior of the pot.

"Really? Where?"

I rested my hands on the edge of the sink. "I drive Diana's friend Anna home Tuesdays and Thursdays after literature class. She lives on this gorgeous farm, and her dad's selling off land. Last night Anna said he's putting the acre block adjacent to her home on the market next week. I want to submit an offer."

I placed the pot on the drying rack, drained the water from the sink, and leaned back against the benchtop. I looked over at Nicholas.

Something unreadable brewed in his misty eyes.

I reached out by instinct and touched his arm. "Are you okay?"

He stared through me. "That's my land."

What? Cogs turned in my mind. "You're Anna's Uncle Cole?"

"Yeah. Dad's nickname for me."

A laugh bubbled up in my chest. "I-I had no idea. Chris is your brother?" I crinkled my forehead. "But the different surnames?"

Nicholas shared how his mother's first husband, George Beaufort, was killed in a freak accident when Chris was almost a year old. Nicholas's father and Beaufort had been best mates, so old man Jacobsen worked to acquire the love of the widow Beaufort and his adorable son.

"Chris is almost two-and-a-half years older than me. I arrived ten months after my parents married."

I whistled. "My, my, you come from good stock."

He wrinkled his nose. A deep sigh surfaced, and his smile dimmed.

"You must miss your dad. Anna said he passed away a few years ago."

"He'd barely retired from farm work when his heart gave out. Mum struggled after his unexpected death, said it was ten times harder losing Dad than Chris's dad, and from what Dad had told me, Mum was crushed when George died. I guess decades of partnership will do that to a person. Mum lives with my brother."

I examined his downcast face. "I met her a few months ago when I visited for lunch. She's a wonderful woman. A real dynamo."

The memory of her dark-brown eyes came to my mind. "Now I know why her eyes were so familiar!" My airways squeezed, and I drowned in his eyes. The barriers we had fought so hard to keep up tumbled down. My hand burned on Nicholas's arm.

He stepped closer and enclosed my hand with his.

Breathless, I stared at the deep chocolate windows to his soul before I drank in his perfect facial features. The straight nose. Strong jaw. His full lips. I stroked a finger across his stubbled cheek. My skin tingled when his eyelids closed at my touch.

Nicholas was the North Pole and I the South. The magnetic pull drew us back to each other, regardless of circumstances. My pulse thundered in my throat. When I contemplated planting a gentle kiss to his lips, the delivery guys wandered into the kitchen.

I pulled away and turned to greet them, thankful my voice remained unchanged.

"We were ten minutes behind schedule, so you did a marvellous job getting through tonight, Vicki. See you in two weeks?"

"Yes, Michael, see you in two weeks. Thanks again for your service."

The men left, and I pivoted around to Nicholas with a smile. "I'd better mop this floor. I'm meant to be going out for dinner—"

"With Matt."

I nodded, and the softness disappeared from his eyes.

"I'll leave you to it." He straightened with a curt nod. "Goodnight, Ms. Burke."

I grabbed his arm, and he stopped. "I'm sorry, Nicholas."

"Me too." He left without a backward glance, never witnessing my wet cheeks.

I brushed aside my tears, speed cleaned the floor, locked up and raced home.

I arrived at Benanu's still a little unsettled from my encounter with Nicholas.

Matt was bowed over the side of the pool table, mid-stroke. A cheer exploded after he performed his shot. He straightened, and a ginger-haired man nodded in my direction. Matt turned, smiled and relinquished his cue.

I fell into his embrace and welcomed the comfort of his body. "Tough night?"

In more ways than I cared to admit. I nodded.

He turned me around and walked us to a table with his hands on my sides before plonking me in my seat. "What disasters did you overcome tonight?"

I grimaced. Fatigue blanketed my entire body. "Two volunteers called in sick, and the stove died."

Matt touched my hand across the table. "That would've been challenging. All fixed now?"

"I had to call in an electrician."

He narrowed his eyes. "Nick, I presume?"

I shrugged. "He's the only one I know. Nicholas had it working in record time, I was so grateful."

"I bet." Matt smirked into his glass of water. "Nick loves saving a damsel in distress, especially when that damsel's you."

My stomach flipped. An ache pressed in my temple. "Be nice. Jealousy doesn't become you."

"No, but I bet he stayed when he discovered you were down on helpers?"

I bunched my eyebrows together. "Wouldn't you do the same?"

"Maybe. But he's a sucker."

"Leave him alone. He's a good friend."

"To you, maybe, but he's not much into socialising with me." Matt rubbed his chin. "His sole interest in me is my girlfriend."

I perused the menu with narrowed eyes. "Don't be silly." Matt's words, Nicholas's kindness, and our brief moment in the kitchen troubled me. Why did Nicholas still affect me?

We ordered our meals.

"What's happening with Christmas and New Year's? Did you say Christine's in-laws were visiting?"

"They arrive New Year's Eve. I'll visit from Christmas Eve—so I'm home in Tellarine for my birthday—then return New Year's Eve morning. Are you in Melbourne for Christmas?"

Matt shrugged. "Not sure. Belinda mentioned yesterday during lunch break that she's staying in Tellarine for Christmas. A few of the staff want to arrange something at her place. Think I might go."

"Oh. Okay." I forced a smile. "That sounds, ah, great. And New Year's? It'll be my first one here."

Matt sipped his drink. "Hmm. Stuart from church has his boat party, and Tom Daniels has a big bash at his place every year. Belinda's interested in doing something at the local park."

"Hey, have you thought about the block of land? Do you think it's a wise investment for me?"

Matt rubbed my hands with his fingers. "Your heart's set on a country property, so I say take the plunge. It's not like you don't have the money."

I thought of my term deposit. "The thing is, I found out the land isn't only owned by Anna's family."

An odd expression flickered across his face. "What do you mean?"

I thought of Nicholas, and a mild flush rose to my skin. "Nicholas is Anna's uncle. He owns the land too."

His face scrunched up. "Wow. Small world."

"Should this change my views on the land?"

Matt patted my hand. "No. What're you waiting for?"

Our food was delivered to the table. "That settles it. Summer cricket matches on my block!"

He chuckled. "Maybe we can spend New Year's there instead of the park."

A huge grin eclipsed my face. "That's perfect! I need to call Chris. Would you excuse me?"

He eyed the fat potato wedges in front of him. "I can't promise any of these babies will be waiting for you."

I placed a gentle kiss on his cheek and found a quiet spot near the disabled bathroom entry.

Chris sounded surprised by my excitable and flustered gush of words, but by the end of our conversation, his enthusiasm rivalled mine. We arranged to share dinner on Tuesday to look at and, hopefully, sign documents. If everything was in order, I would deliver a bank cheque. Once I handed him the cheque, I would own the land.

I wandered back to my dinner with a dreamy smile.

CHAPTER TWENTY-SEVEN
Extending an Olive Branch

I had spent the second anniversaries of Jessica and Samantha's deaths on my couch surrounded by photos, precious videos saved on my laptop, and many, many tears.

Matt offered to stay with me, but I declined. My parents called, as did Christine and Amber. Love overwhelmed me on one of the darkest days of the year. I contemplated sharing my hidden grief with Belinda but chose not to burden her. Our friendship had improved in recent weeks, but I remained guarded, conscious of how I behaved with Matt when Belinda spent time with us.

"I'm so excited about New Year's Eve on the block," Belinda said after church the Sunday before Christmas.

I still pinched myself when I thought of my property.

"Matt and I have everything organised. He's spoken to the neighbours, and we'll clear the front section of the block while you're at Christine's. All you need to do is drive safely."

A part of me mourned the pink mulla mulla and golden everlasting wildflowers to be razed. "Yes, Mum." I gave Belinda a quick hug.

I enjoyed dinner at Gustoso with a few church friends, work colleagues and basketball teammates for my birthday.

Christmas was a joyful week with my family—minus the ignored phone calls and text messages from Jude. Had he given himself the Christmas gift of a dozen mobile phone numbers to use? Hugs and tears were shed when I left Christine's house.

I stopped by to farewell my parents in the privacy of their new home, now two streets away from my sister.

"So, darling, how're things with Matt? Will we get to meet him?" Mum was never one to hold back.

I settled next to Dad on the aged three-seater in the lounge. "Not an easy feat, Mum. We're busy with work and other commitments."

Dad leaned closer, his steady gaze on me. "Are you sure about your relationship with him?"

My heart rate increased. "Why? Matt and I are happy."

"Yes," Mum said, "but Christine says your friend Belinda dated him last year, and you've shared concerns over Belinda's reactions."

"Of course, Chrissy couldn't keep our conversations to herself," I mumbled under my breath.

Mum handed me a cup of tea. "Christine loves you." She reclined in her armchair. "She's uneasy, thinks you're dating the wrong man."

I stared wide-eyed at Mum. "Matt's a good man. He's grown leaps and bounds in his Christian walk."

"I'm sure he's wonderful, darling, but is he the right man for you?" Mum raised her brow. "What about the other gentleman Amber raved about? Did you make the right decision?"

My pulse spiked. "I'm praying I'll know that answer soon."

Dad smiled. "So are we, baby girl."

I drove home thinking about my family in Wagga Wagga and loved ones in Tellarine. My heart and tears overflowed for each and every person.

Even Nicholas.

Diana and Anna traipsed across the neighbouring field to my land with party preparation underway. I met them at the fence. Diana gave me a hug, followed by Anna.

"Merry Christmas, ladies. How's your week been?"

Anna beamed. "Wonderful! Diana's stayed with us since Christmas. Uncle Cole's away."

My heart stalled. "Is everything okay, Diana?"

"It's all good. Uncle Tim—Mum's brother—lost his home in a bushfire in February. Dad promised to complete all the necessary wiring and installations once the new house was built."

I gasped. "That's awful! I'm so glad your dad could help."

"Well, Dad's not been himself lately, so it'll do him good to spend time with Uncle Tim. They were best friends in school."

A smile slid to my lips. I had not been myself since that hectic Meals on Wheels shift. I closed my eyes and remembered the short stubble of Nicholas's day-old beard. How it scratched my fingertips when I touched his face. His chiselled jawline strong under my hand, the quickened pulse in his throat sending thrills through me. The warmth of his hand over mine, and the sizzle of heat between us. How close I had come to kissing him.

"Ms. Burke?"

My eyelids popped up, and a blush stung my cheeks. How could I forget where I was? "Sorry. You caught me daydreaming. What brings you by?"

Anna grinned. "Mum said we can help tonight! We're in charge of cold drinks."

"We promise not to drink any alcohol," Diana said.

"I'll keep an eye on you to make sure of it." I winked.

I turned to assess where my help was needed next. My friends had mown the weeds, leaving the ground dusty, yet even, underfoot. I missed the wildflowers, but plenty still beautified the back of the block.

Belinda greeted me at the food tables with a smile and a hug. I helped her assemble canapes onto platters. Matt unloaded stacked chairs from a trailer with several volunteers, along with a huge barbeque grill. Some guys from church hammered portable gazebos into the dirt while others set up an audio system.

The New Year's Eve 'Party on the Block' was gearing up to be a delightful evening full of delicious food, great company and loud music.

Matt kissed my cheek. "I'll be over with the church guys." He stepped back from the drinks station, where I monitored Diana and Anna on occasion, and faded into the crowd.

Anna chortled behind her cup. "Look at Miss Doe dance with Mr. Masters."

I glanced up and almost choked. Anita was adhered to the front of the middle-aged science teacher, her face smashed to his as they moved on the dance floor.

I turned to the girls, the image of my colleagues burned into my brain. "Cover your eyes!"

They laughed and sipped their drinks. Diana nodded toward the food tables, now laden with desserts. "Would you like anything, Ms. Burke?"

I stood on tiptoe and ogled the spread. "I stuffed myself with tapas, sausage sizzle and salad, but I noticed Bee's creamy raspberry-and-vanilla trifle earlier. Maybe a tiny scoop please? Oh, and grab her delectable double-chocolate brownies while you can. Thanks, sweetheart."

"No worries. I'll get us something, too, Anna." Diana stepped away.

Anna straightened the unused paper cups. "Tonight's been fun. Miss Davies knows how to organise a party. I counted around sixty people at dinnertime."

I nodded. "Now the sun's set, I think the numbers will drop."

She turned to me. "I'm super excited about your house plans. We'll be neighbours!"

I laughed. "I can't see it happening for a while, but I hope to start planning in the next few months. Maybe." Life was already busy.

Diana returned, burdened with food. "Miss Davies said to light some citronella candles. They're near the eskies."

"On it." I gathered and lit some candles at the drinks station before nabbing two brownies from Diana's food stash. I hid them in my handbag, wrapped in a napkin, for later.

After overindulging on Belinda's trifle, a desire to pray and think burned in my chest. "Why don't you two go hang out with your friends? I'm going to take a walk up the back of the property. If anyone's looking for me, I'll have my mobile."

I shooed them away, grabbed a picnic rug, and retrieved my handbag. Weaving through the crowd, I walked a moonlit path up the incline until the lights and sounds behind me became background noise to the chirps of crickets.

Unfolding the rug, I smoothed it on the ground and rested in the comparative stillness of the evening. I read Scriptures from my Bible phone application before I paused, eyes closed, to meditate on the words I had read.

Two years without my children. A heaviness encroached on my festive mood and replaced my earlier cheer. I missed them so much. Jessica's fourteenth birthday was days away. Another birthday she would never experience.

I whispered a prayer and recalled all God had done for me in the last twelve months. Opening my eyes, I glanced up, astonished by the vastness of the stars. At home with the heavenly bodies above, I rested in God's plan for my future. Several tears slipped down my cheek.

Footsteps crunched on the ground before a deep voice said, "I used to sneak out my bedroom window and lie on the roof on nights like this."

I chuckled. "You must've been a handful growing up, Nicholas."

"Yeah, I suppose so."

I scooted across the rug and patted the now empty space available.

Nicholas reclined with his long legs outstretched and leaned back on his hands.

I flushed at his nearness. "How's your brother-in-law? Did you get everything done?"

"Yes, thanks. It's been a while since I caught up with Tim and Carla." Nicholas cleared his throat and nodded in the direction of the party. "Why're you hiding up here when everyone's having fun down there?"

I sighed. "It's been such a busy year, I wanted to give my final hour to God."

"Would you prefer me to leave?"

"No."

We studied the night sky. Its display of majestic light filled the expanse of the heavens. This beat fireworks any day.

"Diana didn't think you'd be here tonight."

Nicholas cleared his throat. "I didn't, either. I had planned to drive straight home, but Diana messaged and mentioned where she'd be."

"Oh." My heart beat a little faster.

He stared toward the party.

"Did you come here for Belinda's amazing double choc brownies?"

He turned his head toward me. "Pardon?"

I retrieved the two stashed brownies from my bag. "I figured these must be the reason you're here. Want one?"

He laughed, sat up, and accepted the proffered treat. "Thanks."

The brownie was moreish. Pure chocolate overload. I expelled a small moan while I chewed.

Nicholas laughed. "I've heard about your love affair with food."

"It's much safer than the alternative."

Steel sharpened his tone. "He's not pressuring you, is he?"

I snorted. "The complete opposite. Matt's changed. Your friendship would mean so much to him. He didn't grow up in a nurturing home like you and I." I stared up at the stars. "His father beat him severely at sixteen."

Nicholas inhaled a sharp breath. "Why?"

I turned to him. "He got a girl pregnant."

Nicholas shook his head. "How could a father respond to his own son like that?"

I shrugged. "I had broached the subject of reconciliation with his parents, but after Matt unloaded, I needed God's forgiveness for the hateful thoughts I had about his dad."

Nicholas rubbed the nape of his neck before he glanced at his watch. "Less than ten minutes until the new year."

"Already? We'd better go."

Nicholas helped me fold the rug before we headed back to the sounds of music, conversation and laughter.

Matt came into view. He sidled up to me, wrapped an arm around my waist, and kissed my forehead. "Thanks for locating the runaway, Nick."

Nicholas's jaw twitched. "No worries." He cleared his throat. "A few mates are meeting next Saturday for a game of basketball, if you're interested?"

My heart flipped.

Matt gaped before he grinned. "Awesome! What time?"

"Two o'clock on the school's outdoor basketball court."

"Great! Thanks, man."

The noise of excited chatter increased as the end of the hour dawned. With cheers for the final ten-second countdown, Matt pulled me into the crowd, and I waved goodbye to Nicholas.

♥ ♥ ♥ ♥ ♥ ♥ ♥

I stumbled through my front door at three o'clock on New Year's morning. My phone blinked with a message notification. I gritted my teeth and clenched my hands.

Private Number: HAPPY NEW YEAR, VICTORIA. REMEMBER

HOW WE SPENT OUR FIRST NEW YEAR'S TOGETHER?

Jude's message triggered a tsunami of memories. I flopped onto my bed and screamed while my brain delved into the archives and splashed the corresponding images across my mind.

Jude and I had been married less than a month and had spent the public holiday entangled in the cotton sheets of our second-hand queen-sized bed.

My heart thundered in my chest.

Private Number: DON'T YOU MISS US? I MISS YOUR WARM BODY AGAINST MINE.

I hid my face under the pillow. His messages evoked old sensations and renewed my internal struggles.

Another chime. I poked my head out and grabbed the phone.

Private Number: LET ME KISS YOU UNTIL YOU MOAN.

Tears stung my eyes. I turned my phone off, slipped into my summer sleepwear and lay back under the cool sheets.

Jude's messages continued to arrive over the next four days, escalating in their explicit nature. His words tormented me. Each night I awoke in a cold sweat with frenzied thoughts swirling through my mind, barraged by a reoccurring dream.

The dream unfolded in my bedroom in Black Rock. Fiery heat radiated around me before I found myself in the throes of making love to Jude. His face was softer, younger. Happy and attentive in his love, the dream bordered on magical. We stared into each other's eyes, then Nicholas and Matt would appear like apparitions and drag me from the bed. The dream ended in a tug of war, a man on each of my arms, where I stood at the foot of my bed, exposed and confused.

Each night I awoke in the dark to an onslaught of images, a Technicolor invasion in my mind. I would spend the rest of the night in prayer and read Scripture in an attempt to banish the images from my mind, only to drift off to sleep for an hour or two.

After several tormented nights, fatigue took its toll. I wallowed at home while Matt ran a free STEM holiday program for the local youth. Food was an unbearable thought.

Later that week I climbed out of my car, straining under the weight of my body, and knocked on Belinda's front door. The church youth group needed help, and I had jumped at the opportunity to assist Belinda when she asked two weeks earlier.

Belinda opened the door, and her eyes bulged. "You look terrible!"

I followed her inside. "I've been better."

She turned to me with her brow creased and lips downturned. "You should be in bed. Go lie on the couch while I get ready, then I'll take you home."

I shook my head and regretted the movement. My head spun. "No, I'm fine. Maybe a glass of water?"

She narrowed her eyes before she plodded to the kitchen.

I dragged myself to the open-plan lounge and dining room and inhaled sharply.

Nicholas stood on a stepladder near Belinda's dining table, his large back taut and long arms stretched up to manoeuvre wires in a light cavity. His biceps rippled with every movement, the muscles across his back and shoulders visible under his fitted blue polo T-shirt.

How had I missed his parked vehicle on Belinda's street? I swayed and caught my breath again when he bent to retrieve a tool. A flush of heat swept over me when he straightened, and my eyesight dimmed.

The room whirled. Nicholas blurred in and out, an uncanny dance in time to the throb in my temples.

"Enjoying the view, Vicki?" Belinda's voice held a hint of tease.

Nicholas's head whipped around, his face changing from surprise to alarm.

CHAPTER TWENTY-EIGHT

Nurse Nick

"Victoria?" The sound of Belinda's voice woke me.

My eyelids fluttered open. Several seconds passed before I registered where I was and why I lay in her lap.

"She's burning up, Nick. Can you put her on the couch while I find my thermometer?"

Blood rushed through my ears when Nicholas lifted me. He lay me down against the soft cushions and crouched next to me, lines streaking his brow.

My feeble smile siphoned the tension from his shoulders.

His low voice quavered. "You gave us a scare. How're you feeling?"

"A little better."

He rested his hand over mine. His cool palm tingled against my fevered skin.

Belinda knelt next to Nicholas and inserted a digital thermometer under my tongue. Her lips compressed into a tight smile.

The thermometer chimed, and Belinda removed the object from my mouth. Grooves puckered her forehead. "Thirty-eight point nine degrees."

Nicholas focused on the thermometer. "High, but not extreme. We should keep an eye on her."

Belinda nodded. "I need to leave in the next fifteen minutes.

Think you could stick around until I return? Otherwise, I could call Ma—"

"I'll stay."

Belinda kissed my forehead. "It's settled. Nick will stay tonight, and I'll watch you over the weekend." I groaned, and she pointed her index finger at me. "No fighting me on this."

Tears welled in my eyes. "Okay, Bee."

She flashed a triumphant grin and stood. "Nick, there's pumpkin soup in the fridge and bread near the toaster. Sorry it's not a substantial meal, but it should keep you both fed for now." She placed a hand on his shoulder. "Thanks for being such a champ." Belinda left the room.

Nicholas studied me. "I better finish up. Why don't you rest." He strode to the table, climbed the stepladder, and peered over his shoulder with sparkling brown eyes. "Shouldn't you be sleeping? Or is the view that good?"

I snorted a laugh, contented in his tease, and surveyed him from head to toe. "Dream on."

He leaned back and laughed. The sound warmed me more than my fevered body, its cadence music to my ears. Nicholas turned to his work and I closed my eyes.

I drifted into a light sleep. Words swirled in my mind, and I entered a dream world, like Alice down the rabbit hole. A haze undulated to the sound of waves crashing against a cliff face. The gloom dissipated and sky cleared. A tropical scene of sun-kissed palm trees and deep-blue waters stretched across my field of vision. I chilled out on a beach, barefoot, and wriggled my toes in the soft, grainy sand. The heat of the day beat down on me, leaving me hot and parched. Out of nowhere, a cool breeze blew and raised the hairs on my arms. Goosebumps rippled over my skin. The cool air kissed my hairline and caressed my cheeks, a spray of the ocean in the breeze. My name drifted like a mist in the wind. It called again. The words floated in the sky like thin, wispy clouds before the wind flurried.

"Victoria."

I opened my eyes, and Nicholas's wrinkled forehead and pursed lips came into view. He dabbed a cool, damp cloth against my forehead. "You need to keep up your fluids. Drink this."

Nicholas helped me sit upright and placed a glass of water in my fat and clumsy fingers. He caught the glass before I lost my grip and positioned it to my lips.

I sipped and lay back against the hot cushion.

"Have you eaten much today?" he asked with a raised brow.

"No."

He narrowed his eyes. "Did you eat at all?"

I averted my gaze and shook my head.

"No wonder you fainted. I'll get you some soup and toast." Nicholas walked away, returning minutes later with a bowl in one hand and a plate in the other. He planted himself on the floor near me and placed the bowl in my hands. After a quick prayer, he gazed at my face.

"Eat." His firm tone contrasted his warm eyes, something I had not glimpsed in months.

I ladled the orange soup into my mouth and savoured the smooth, creamy texture of butternut pumpkin. A string of soft moans slipped from my lips. Belinda had a delicate skill of bringing out the best in the humblest vegetables.

Impassioned, dark chocolate eyes stared at my face.

I nodded to my bowl. "This soup's good."

"Sounds like it." Nicholas's voice had deepened and my heart palpitated.

"Aren't you going to eat?"

His lips curved into a cheeky grin. "I'm enjoying the show." The sparkle returned to his eyes.

I fluttered my eyelashes and smiled for good measure. With the dexterity of a detention-prone pupil, I scooped soup onto my spoon and positioned it like a catapult, poised and ready to fire. "I suggest you eat before I flick this at you."

His grin widened. "Do you treat all nurses with disrespect?"

His woodsy scent teased my nose, and its sweet, spicy fragrance warmed my chest. Temptation drew my gaze to his lips now close enough to kiss. I inspected my spoon and lowered it to the bowl. "No," I said, almost breathless. I peeked at his face. "But you aren't a qualified nurse, so you don't count." The corner of my mouth lifted.

He chuckled and his breath warmed my face. His gaze fell to my lips, and the warmth in my chest spread. "So, this is the thanks I get for giving up my evening to look after you."

I stared at the curve of his mouth again and fought against its magnetic pull. My instincts screamed, Kiss him! but my mind warned me against the danger.

"Thank you," I breathed. I dropped my gaze and ate.

Nicholas stood and left the room.

I munched on the final bite of cold buttered toast when Nicholas settled at the dining table. He raised an eyebrow. "I figure you can't reach me over here."

"I'm out of soup, anyway." I lay back and closed my eyes, my stomach satisfied.

I dozed in and out until I woke from thirst. Pulling myself up, I sipped my water and discovered I was alone. When I contemplated testing my balance, Nicholas walked into the room with a mug in his hand.

"The kettle didn't wake you, did it?"

"No."

He placed his drink on the dining table. "Want some tea?"

I shook my head, another need springing to mind. "This water's enough, b-but I'd appreciate some prayer, if you don't mind?"

His face glowed and calm eased my heart. "Of course. Anything in particular?"

I inhaled and waited for the right words to form in my mind. "I've had haunting dreams and barely sleep. It's affecting my health and my sanity."

Nicholas resumed his position on the floor at my feet. "Haunting dreams?"

"Yes." I sighed. "A recurring dream where I wake night after night, spend five hours praying and reading Scripture, only to fall asleep for an hour or two."

Nicholas covered my hand with his. His gaze focused on mine, their intensity pinning me to the couch. "Sounds draining and oppressive. Is something provoking the dream?"

How could I avoid answering his question in a respectful way? "Y-yes, but I'd prefer not to go into detail."

Nicholas nodded and squeezed my hand. "Of course. My knowing or not knowing your dreams won't stop God from freeing you from them." He closed his eyes, and I did the same. A few moments later he said, "Father God, thank You for Your precious daughter, Victoria. What a blessing she is." His fingers brushed my knuckles in a rhythmic motion, and his touch stilled my swirling stomach. "We ask for Your peace. Set her free from these troubled dreams and fill her mind with Your Word. Help Victoria to think on things which are true, honourable, just, pure, lovely, and of a good report. Be with her as she sleeps and give her rest and restored health over the coming days."

My eyes misted. Nicholas's prayer was like an anchor to my soul.

He sighed and I peeked an eye open. His lips moved as though in prayer, but no words came out. He ran a hand through his hair and his lips stilled.

I snapped my eyelid shut.

"Father God, You know Victoria's struggles. Give her peace in the midst of the storm. In Jesus' name I pray, amen."

I opened my eyes, and Nicholas's face blurred. I blinked and squeezed his hand before lifting my hand to the dark stubble of his five o'clock shadow.

He closed his eyes and nuzzled his cheek against my fingers.

"Thank you, Nicholas."

His eyes opened, and we smiled at each other.

I dropped my hand and reached for a drink of water. The water quenched my thirst, cool on my lips, like Nicholas's prayer had calmed my soul.

With a weary smile, I moved farther back on the couch, and tucked my feet underneath me. I patted the seat next to me. "Read me some Scriptures, please?"

He stood and pulled a Bible from a nearby bookshelf. The couch sagged when his heavier frame eased onto the cushions.

We read, talked and prayed for another hour. The more time I spent with Nicholas, the heavier my guilt toward Matt weighed against my shoulders.

Nicholas touched my arm. "You okay now?"

I nodded and swivelled my head to look into his deep chocolate eyes and stuttered a breath. Nicholas's direct gaze sent my head and heart into a spin, like he stared right into my soul and discerned the hidden thoughts deep inside of me.

"Why're you with Matt?" His voice was soft, almost inaudible.

His question crushed my heart. I breathed in and exhaled. "He didn't stop pursuing me."

He nodded, stood and walked to the kitchen. My heart could not survive any more what if's. I needed to stay in the here and now.

CHAPTER TWENTY-NINE
Crash and Burn

"A robot would make more noise than the two of you combined."

I had arrived at this year's church picnic and was watching Matt and Nicholas screw in the legs of a large table. An eerie silence permeated their workspace.

They stopped and lifted their faces, one with a twinkle in his eyes, the other with a faraway look on his face.

I greeted Matt with a warm smile and nodded to Nicholas. I had avoided one-on-one conversations with Nicholas since our encounter at Belinda's seven weeks earlier. I struggled to be myself when he was near. Or the 'me' I needed to be.

My day had started with breakfast at Benanu's and two missed calls from, who I assumed was, Jude. I had cut up a basket of fruit, piled food and blankets into my car, and drove to the church early so I could help set up tables under the temporary gazebo canopy.

I approached Matt. "Need any help?"

"I'm ready for a cold drink. What about you, Nick?"

Nicholas wiped the back of his wrist across his forehead. "That'd be nice."

I retrieved two cold soft drink cans from the church kitchen and offered both to Matt.

He accepted one, kissed my forehead, and nodded toward Nicholas. "If you still want to be Nick's friend, you should treat him like one." Matt's eyes seemed distant.

I turned and stepped toward Nicholas, and our gazes locked. Like a moth to a flame, he drew me in. Each step closer quickened my pulse. Heat rose to my cheeks. I handed him the drink, and our hands brushed. A shiver ran up my spine.

His ardent gaze studied me, and I dropped my own to the can he grasped. "Thank you."

I stared back up to his face, and heat stabbed my belly. My boyfriend stood ten metres away, and I melted in the presence of another man. I was gutted. And ashamed. I avoided his gaze. "You're welcome."

Scrambling to the ladies' bathroom, I hid inside a cubicle, overheated and confused. What was wrong with me? Matt was a great man overflowing with redeeming qualities I wished Jude had.

A tumble of thoughts collided in my mind, and I collapsed on the closed toilet lid. Matt and Jude were similar in many ways. Their confidence, body shapes and strong jawlines. Their take-charge mindsets, the feel of their embrace.

I wheezed. My eyes stung with tears. How had I not recognised this sooner? I loved Matt, but not in the way I had once loved Jude. No. I loved him as a friend.

I brushed away tears. Had I used Matt in a do-over of my failed marriage? My stomach somersaulted, and I hung my head between my knees, breathing in and out.

Matt deserved to know.

Disgusted with myself, I hid with my pain for another thirty minutes before I searched for Matt. My chest tightened thinking of him.

He lounged on a rug under a tree in animated conversation with Belinda. Their playful banter contrasted the heavy mess of emotions clawing at my heart.

Belinda leapt to her feet. A blush rose to her cheeks.

I dropped my head. "Just come to say goodbye."

Matt sprang up. "What? You okay?"

I rubbed my tummy. "I'm fine, feeling a little off."

Belinda laid a hand on my arm and squeezed.

"Let me drive you home," Matt said.

"I-I drove. You stay and enjoy the afternoon. We'll talk later." I endured their hugs and left.

During my short journey home, I prayed. My hands shook as I unlocked the front door and turned on my stereo. Worship music blasted through the windows, my brain, and my soul.

On Sunday evening I poured out my heart to Matt about Nicholas. Although Matt deserved to know of my church-bathroom epiphany, I held back all talk of Jude. How would he benefit from this knowledge?

"Do you love him?" Matt's gentle question was free of accusation and flooded my anxious heart with peace.

"I-I don't know. He stokes a fire in me which isn't fair to you."

Matt kissed my forehead and held me tight. "Don't worry about me. I've watched this go on for months and prepared myself. I can't say this leaves me gooey inside, but you're still one of my greatest friends."

"What? B-but Nicholas and I seldom speak to each other."

Matt kissed my nose. "Exactly. You both look like you're using your iron wills to stay away from each other, yet you're conscious of each other. Your body language says it all. I think I knew from the beginning my days were numbered."

I gaped. Awe bubbled in my chest. My stress melted away, and I knew God's perfect orchestration had brought us to this moment.

Matt raised his brow.

I kissed his cheek. "Thank you, Matt."

"Anything for you."

Since the church picnic three weeks ago, Nicholas had avoided me. Confusion and tears were my constant companions. I thought my heart would combust with envy when he settled next to an attractive widow at last week's church service. Hollowed out on the inside, my vulnerable heart bled like the early days after the accident.

Waves of nausea had crashed over me when I awoke this morning and drained my low energy reserves. I spent the day drowning in its wake. The tightness in my chest culminated in bouts of breathlessness, spiking my pulse. Reality bashed me over the head. Once again, I found myself single, shunned by someone I thought cared for me, and mourning for my children.

The dreaded text message tone chimed on my phone. I climbed off the couch and read the message.

"That's it. I've had enough!"

Heat flushed through my body and leaked from the pores of my skin. I stared at the latest message, dialled the phone number with vibrating fingers, and set the handset to speakerphone. My hands curled into fists while I paced the floor.

"Victoria?"

"I've had it, Jude!" I yelled. "I'm sick of your phone calls and messages. You need to stop calling and messaging, or I'll contact the police and a lawyer and throw an intervention order at you!" My chest heaved on every breath.

"Are you okay, baby?"

"No!" I screamed. "And I'm not your baby! Leave me alone! We're divorced!"

I sucked in a harsh breath. Tears filled my eyes, and a lump clogged my throat. I sniffed. "If you call or message me again, my next conversation will be with the police."

"W—"

I ended the call and collapsed on the couch with groaning sobs. Reaching for the tissue box, I wiped my eyes and cranked loud praise and worship music to drown my sorrows.

A thump slammed against the front door.

I groaned. Was my music too loud? I muted the stereo and dragged myself to the door with a ready apology.

Nicholas stood there, toolbox in hand.

Really, God?

I ran a hand through my loose, messy hair. "Nicholas."

He stood ramrod straight with a grim smile on his pinched face. "Victoria. Mr. Arby thought you needed another power point near the dining table."

I flinched. "Oh. Okay. Sure. Come in." I stepped aside and grabbed a duster to wipe the candles on the sideboard.

Nicholas worked without speaking a word.

I stole a glance in his direction and watched his broad shoulders rotate as he bore a small hole in the wall. Thoughts swirled around my brain while anger at the man working in my kitchen built inside of me.

After fifteen minutes, my emotional rollercoaster of a day pushed me over the edge. I walked up beside Nicholas.

He knelt on the floor, focused on the wall.

I lifted my chin and planted my feet wide. With great restraint to speak without accusation, I said, "Have I done something to offend you?"

All he managed was a look and a sigh before he returned to his work.

I clenched my hands, itching for a fight. "You know, I liked you better before the broody, silent routine. I've no idea what I did to you, but it can't compare to the wound you've inflicted on me." Tears slid down my face.

He stood. "I-I'm sorry, Victoria. I—"

"This isn't how friends treat each other." Fire burned inside my chest. I wanted to smack him. "Are we destined to explode instead of talk to each other?" My tears fell unrestrained.

He reached his hand out, but I pushed it away.

"And you still won't talk. Let yourself out when you're done." I stormed to my bedroom, slammed the door, and launched onto the bed. Big, fat, uncontrollable tears saturated my pillow. I cried over my lost marriage, my manipulative ex-husband, my deceased children, and now the man who haunted my dreams.

And I did not care if he overheard.

Not one bit.

The thought of attending church after yesterday's altercation with Nicholas nauseated me, but I had promised to help Belinda and refused to disappoint her. I had to face him sometime, and a public place was my best option.

Nicholas was greeting congregants at the church entrance when I arrived.

I cringed and pleaded with my heart to soften.

I AM WITH YOU.

A blanket of peace enveloped me. I approached Nicholas with more confidence than I possessed.

You can do this.

"Good morning, Nicholas."

His smile reached his eyes, and I shuffled back a step.

I blinked, and we shook hands.

His touch sent a zap of electricity up my arm. "Good morning, Victoria. Thank God His mercies are new every morning, hey?" His smile turned into a cheeky grin, and my heart thumped.

"Amen."

We both grinned, and my shoulders relaxed.

His eyelids flickered before he inhaled a slow, deep breath. "Matt arrived a minute ago."

I squinted. Before I could respond, Belinda waltzed through the entry and embraced me. "Hey, Bee. Nicholas said Matt's inside." I lifted a brow. "I thought you'd have pounced by now." I winked at her, and her cheeks flushed.

"I didn't want to seem opportunistic. Things might change

between you two."

I nudged her arm. "Things won't change, Bee. I'd love to see two of my closest friends back together." I pulled her into a hug.

Belinda's body shook against mine. Was she laughing or crying?

I pulled back to search her face and caught her grin. Unable to see what the big joke was, I turned around.

Nicholas stared with his eyes wide and mouth open.

Belinda held in laughter. She arched an eyebrow. "Didn't you know, Nick?" she half-asked and half-teased. "Come on, Vicki-babe. We better leave before someone pounces on *you*."

Nicholas shifted his weight. A pink hue bloomed up his neck after he missed a visitor's outstretched hand.

I suppressed a laugh. Whatever had gone on in his head, Nicholas seemed to be his usual self. I captured his gaze, winked, and strutted into the auditorium.

CHAPTER THIRTY

All the Time in the World

"It's not too revealing?" I bit my lower lip and appraised my reflection in Belinda's bedroom mirror.

"No, you look classy. Elegant. And so sexy, Nick's going to forget his own name."

I stared at myself in my long, sleeveless berry-red satin evening dress. It had a high back and a flattering cowl neck, which teased at my ample cleavage. The dress glided over my hips and flowed down to my ankles.

Almost a month had passed since my reconciliation with Nicholas. We were navigating back to our easygoing friendship at a slow but steady pace. Tonight's Year Twelve Formal offered the hope of seeing him at the end.

The evening delighted me, filled with time amongst my students. Several precocious young men asked me to dance, the same boys dressed this morning in school uniforms, running through the school corridors late for class.

The most uncomfortable moment of the event was spent warding off attention from several teachers. Married male teachers. The stares at my neckline and brushes to my arms were clear signs my cleavage held more interest than my conversation. I excused myself and hurried in Belinda and Matt's direction.

"I was about to send Matt to rescue you." Belinda's big grin contrasted Matt's scowl.

"You mean you held me back from punching the lot of them."

I squeezed Matt's arm. "I appreciate your concern, but I'm fine."

A slow smile crept across his face. "I told you a long time ago your virtue's safe with me. I'll look out for you until Nick gets his act into gear."

My cheeks heated and he laughed.

He tilted his head toward the entrance. "Speaking of Nick."

I turned toward the large, panelled doors as they banged shut behind Nicholas. Dressed in a white-and-grey chequered business shirt and jeans, he looked inviting.

His gaze scanned the room and stopped on me.

I waved and smoothed the fabric at my waist as he approached our little group.

"Don't forget to breathe," Matt whispered before he shook Nicholas's hand. "Evening, Nick! You've missed a great night."

Nicholas's gaze caressed my figure before he averted his eyes. "Diana's looked forward to it for months."

I imagined Diana in her eagerness to plan. "She looks beautiful tonight and seemed to enjoy herself."

Nicholas smiled.

Principal Marsden tapped Matt on the shoulder. "Sorry to interrupt but I am in desperate need of two volunteers."

Belinda grabbed Matt's hand. "We'll help!"

In an instant, Nicholas and I were alone. I brushed a stray hair from my face and pressed my lips together. I peered up, and he stared back. My heart vaulted. A shaky smile flitted on my lips.

"You look exquisite." His husky voice sent tingles up my spine.

My breath caught. The heat of his words seared my skin.

His smile grew, and my insides quivered when he stepped closer. His cologne teased me; his nearness more intimate than sitting together in church. Could he sense my nervousness?

Nicholas's impassioned gaze bore into me. "Join me for dinner tomorrow night."

My stomach flipped and I nodded with a shy smile. "Th-that sounds wonderful."

He relaxed his shoulders and grinned.

"Where?"

He cocked his head. "Do you have a preference?"

"No."

He pursed his lips. "I'll have a think and get back to you in the morning."

"Great." I blinked and glimpsed around the room. My cheeks flushed. "I see more parents. Want me to find Diana?"

His eyes sparkled. "I spotted her with Grace and Madison."

I nodded, almost at my limit of being the centre of his attention. "Great. Well, I'd better go. I-I look forward to tomorrow night."

Nicholas curled his fingers over mine and kissed my hand with warm, soft lips. His breath feathered my knuckles, and another shiver ran down my spine. "The pleasure's all mine." He released my hand.

"Good night, Mr. Darcy."

"Goodnight, Miss Bennet."

My nerves kicked in. I shook out my arms as I trotted to my front door, fixed a smile to my lips, and opened it.

Nicholas looked oh-so-handsome in a grey suit and open-collared shirt. He beamed. "You're gorgeous. Ready to go?"

I grabbed my purse and locked the door before resting my hand in the crook of his arm. I tried to ignore the firm muscles underneath my fingers.

We were on the main road out of Tellarine minutes later.

"I hope you don't mind the extra travel time, but I thought you'd enjoy this restaurant. I'm a favourite of the owners too."

"A favourite, huh?"

Nicholas surveyed me before he returned his attention to the road. "I helped the Hendersons with several emergencies over the years. When Debbie died, they adopted Diana as another grandchild, and I became the token son amongst their daughters. That's how Diana met Madison."

"Madison's their granddaughter? How lovely."

Sometime later, he navigated down a long driveway and into a gravel car park. Nicholas exited and raced to open the passenger door.

"Aren't you the gentleman?"

Nicholas grinned. "I try to be." His warm hand engulfed mine and shot tingles up my arm. Helping me down from my seat, he escorted me inside the building with our fingers still intertwined. My heart wanted to float away.

The restaurant décor was eclectic, warm and inviting. Reminiscent of a log cabin, dark wood panels and rustic window frames lined the walls, high ceilings and polished floorboards. Behind the front counter, the dining section buzzed with quiet chatter from restaurant patrons.

A petite woman in her early-seventies greeted Nicholas with a hug and infectious smile. She enfolded me in her arms. "You must be Victoria." She pulled back and appraised me. "I'm Jenny Henderson."

"Pleased to meet you, Jenny."

She gazed up at Nicholas. "Let me know when to book your wedding reception, Nicki. Victoria looks like a keeper."

I laughed and Nicholas leaned down and kissed Jenny's cheek.

"No meddling, Jen. I'm a big boy now."

She reached up and patted the side of his face. "I know, but I want more grandbabies. All my girls closed their baby-making factories, so my final hope lies with you."

I smothered nervous laughter behind my hand.

Jenny and Nicholas talked about grandchildren like it was the most natural thing to discuss in my presence.

She grabbed two menus from the counter. "This way."

I fell into step alongside Nicholas as we weaved past occupied tables. Fire engulfed my dress where his hand rested on my lower back.

Jenny seated us, squeezed my shoulder and walked away.

Nicholas rubbed his clean-shaven chin. "So that was Jen."

I smirked. "Does she marry you off on a frequent basis?"

Nicholas chuckled and poured water into our empty glasses. "This was a first. She must like you."

A shy smile claimed my face. "I like her too."

A young man approached our table. I tried to focus on the dinner menu, but my attention was in a constant battle between it and my dinner companion. My body temperature rose every time I peeked at Nicholas. When the waiter stepped away with our meal orders, my words slipped from memory. Had I ordered the beef or chicken?

Our meals arrived twenty minutes later.

"How's your salmon? My chicken's delicious." Yes, I had ordered the chicken.

"My meal's great."

I chewed on some green vegetables.

Nicholas shifted in his seat. "How're the plans with your land going?"

I scrunched my nose. "Not going anywhere. I've been so busy."

He sipped his beer. "If you need help with planning, or a team to build for you, I've plenty of local contacts."

"Thanks. I'll take you up on that offer in the near future."

His expression softened. "I'd be happy to assist with project managing if you wanted. We could come to some kind of arrangement."

"That's a generous offer." I chewed on another bite of chicken and savoured the flavours. "Tell me something I don't know about you."

Nicholas pursed his lips. "I like cars."

I grinned. "Like sportscars? Supercars? Vintage cars?"

He placed his cutlery on his empty plate. "All of the above."

"Is there a dream car?"

His eyes brightened. "A 1986 Ferrari 328."

"Ooh. Colour?" I scrunched my face. "Please don't say yellow."

Nicholas crinkled his nose. "No. Rossa Corsa red."

I wiped my brow with the back of my hand. "Phew. Red's a perfect sportscar colour. Jude's Maserati is bright yellow. So pretentious."

He stiffened his shoulders. "Seems to fit the profile from what you've told me."

A sudden weight pressed against my chest, and I clasped my hands together. Why had I mentioned Jude?

Nicholas cleared his throat. "John eight thirty-six looped in my head when I thought of you today." His gaze held me captive. "Jesus has set you free, so rest in His promise."

Tears burned and I blinked. Jude had not contacted me since I screamed at him on the phone. Was I finally free of him?

"You're never alone, Victoria. Never." Emotion cracked on every word. Nicholas's eyes shimmered.

In an attempt to evade their potency, I dropped my gaze to Nicholas's kissable lips. The memories from his bedroom doorway flooded my mind. I sucked in a sharp breath. Butterflies thrashed against my insides, matching the rate of my quickened heartbeat.

Breathe in. Breathe out.

After paying for the bill, we walked to his vehicle.

He rested his warm hands on my shoulders where I stood near the passenger door. "If you ever need to talk about anything, I'm here for you."

My chest warmed. "Thank you."

The ride home was quiet but not awkward. Nicholas must have come to terms with my divorce. Would he still be accepting of me when he discovered my little secrets named Jessica, Samantha and

Ryan?

We proceeded up the steps to my bungalow.

I touched his arm. "I want to tell you so many things about my past and hopes for the future." I furrowed my brows. "Please be patient with me."

The sweetest smile eclipsed his features. He reached out and held my face. "I have all the time in the world."

CHAPTER THIRTY-ONE

Clean-Up on Aisle Five

With a weary sigh, I carried the shopping basket and gathered the few items left on my shopping list.

Milk.

Oats.

Yoghurt.

Three-and-a-half weeks after my first date with Nicholas, I stumbled along the IGA aisles, my nerves frayed and sanity unravelling. Grief had reared its ugly head. The familiar heaviness had become almost comforting, but not today. Today was similar to the day my girls were buried. The funeral denied my attendance.

Another regret added to the ever-growing pile in my life.

I had pushed down my pain and fulfilled today's work obligations, hiding my anguish. My biggest struggle was concealing my heartache from my perceptive literature ladies as they prepared for Thursday evening's Year Twelve Literature Presentation. Two weeks earlier I had announced the recital as a team-building exercise. Their efforts to remember their passages of text, their growing confidence at each class practice session, and their diligence pleased me. But it had almost pushed me over the edge today.

I sniffed and blinked. Once I was home, I could curl up on the couch under my blanket with a cup of tea and my memories. This thought alone anchored me while I completed my shopping.

I staggered the aisles and willed my mind away from her. Samantha.

Today was May sixteenth. Samantha's twelfth birthday. Two weeks older now than her sister had been when they had died and left me a shell of my former self. My vision blurred when I pulled a milk bottle from the glass-fronted fridge. Wetness trailed down my cheeks in the yogurt section.

I scanned the shelves of cereal for oats. A bright yellow box of Coco Pops caught my attention. Coco Pops had been Samantha's favourite school holiday breakfast treat. She had indulged in big, milky bowlfuls of the chocolate rice puffs. Before she shovelled spoonfuls into her mouth, she would wait for the crispy puffs to soften and leach their chocolatey goodness into the milk.

I stepped to the shelf, pulled by its magnetic force. I stroked the cardboard with my outstretched fingers like I had caressed Samantha's face. My heart broke for the thousandth time, and my chest squeezed to the point of numbness like a tourniquet.

"Ms. Burke?" A fuzzy Diana materialised out of thin air before she disappeared behind a waterfall of tears.

I whimpered under the pressure crushing my chest.

"Ms. Burke? What's wrong?" Her plea disappeared into the din of blood rushing in my ears.

Supportive arms enveloped me, and I collapsed into a sea of sobs, lost in its current with no idea how to stop being pulled under.

Diana held me close and we slid to the floor. Her sweet lavender-and-orange scent embraced me; the fragrance reminiscent of my beloved Jessica.

Muffled words rang out. My pounding head and mournful sobs had overpowered my ability to hear.

Her gentle embrace was soon replaced by strong masculine arms. Their owner lifted me in one deft movement. His even heartbeat and woody cologne silenced my tears.

I wrapped my arms around his neck and lay my head against his shoulder.

His whispers were unintelligible, perhaps a prayer on my behalf.

I offered my own silent prayer.

A sudden gust of wind hit my cheek. I shivered, and his arms tightened around me. His large steps echoed along the asphalt. We reached the twin cab ute, where Nicholas opened the door and balanced me on the front passenger seat, then climbed in from the driver's side.

I stared through the windscreen, conscious of his gaze.

"Victoria." His gentle voice renewed my tears. Nicholas's cool hand covered mine, his thumb stroked the back of my hand. "Victoria, please look at me."

I rotated my neck in slow motion. With swollen eyes I scanned his face.

His countenance mirrored my pain. "I-I want to help. Please. Let me help you." His wet eyes twisted my heart, and I closed my eyes to shut him out.

"I miss them. With all my heart." My whispered words sounded strangled. "I'm still drowning over two years later. The pain's killing me." I stared at him, his expression so broken and beautiful, all in one. "Sometimes I wish I died with them."

His eyes bulged and his shoulders slumped. Nicholas cupped my face in his hands. His tender touch precipitated more of my tears. "Don't talk like that, Victoria. Please." His low tone trembled.

"Without Jesus, I would've driven into a tree long ago." I pulled away from him and turned to the passenger window, too ashamed of the truth, yet lighter for having shared it.

Nicholas expelled an audible breath. I ached for the burden added to his shoulders.

The cloth seat swished and dipped with his shifted weight. He twisted my body to face him and touched my jaw with reverence. A shaky hand wiped tears from my cheeks. The comfort of his nearness was inexpressible. "I know the ache too well. It still grips me at times, a punch of pain taking me by surprise. But I'm still here, and so are you." He stroked my cheek. "I thank God every day for bringing you into my life."

Three fragile words tucked safe inside the confines of my heart rose to the surface and fell from my lips, unstoppable and unintentional even in their raw truth. "I love you."

Diana opened the door with groceries in hand, and Nicholas shot back into his seat. She climbed into the seat behind me and rested her hand on my shoulder.

I stared straight ahead, mute, the entire journey home and avoided Nicholas's gaze when I exited the vehicle. A painful clamp gripped my heart, knowing our relationship was forever changed.

CHAPTER THIRTY-TWO
Head Spin

"I'm open!"

"Push! Take the shot!"

My eardrums vibrated with the cries of unfamiliar voices. My heart pounded. I dribbled the ball and scanned the court. A stout woman with wide eyes and gritted teeth defended me, her height and muscle mass a clear warning against a three-pointer. A familiar blue-and-red uniform blurred to my right, and I wrapped a pass around my opponent straight into my teammate's hands. I tripped on a large foot and righted myself before I face-planted.

"Time out!"

Gathering with my team, I wiped my sweaty forehead with the aged, fluorescent pink-and-purple terry cloth wristband Jessica had given me and listened to the coach. I had been called in to play the Wednesday night game on an unfamiliar team, a pleasant distraction from the turmoil in my head.

Nicholas had left several voicemail and text messages on my phone since my breakdown last night, but I had ignored them all. My mind was a mess, and I needed to find some semblance of normal before I talked to him.

The coach fleshed out our gameplay in a flurry of hand signals and clipboard scribbles. With two minutes left on the clock, the team relied on me to secure our win.

"Show me you want this, ladies!" Coach yelled. My teammates

chorused a string of yeses. The coach turned to me, her smile bright and eyes crinkled at the edges. "If you ever want to switch to Wednesdays, say the word, and I'll make a team slot available."

I nodded, inhaled a deep breath, and returned to my position on the court next to the wall of woman opposing me.

Her eyes glinted. She rolled her neck and cracked her knuckles.

I flexed my hands and stretched on my toes.

She leaned in close, her jaw set and gaze steady, her imposing body rigid. "You're going down, pixie."

I turned away, swallowed a grunt, and fixed my gaze on the ball. My skin prickled with sweat and heat.

A whistle blew, and the room erupted in a clamour. The ball flew through the air, its trajectory in my line of sight.

My arms outstretched, I danced to the right, my feet firm on the polished flooring. Centimetres from my grasp, the ball disappeared behind a fortress of flesh, and the impact burned my left shoulder.

I gasped, and the right side of my body thwacked against hard wood. White stars filled my vision, and pain seared my right temple. My jarred hip stung, and a flash of memories flooded my mind as nerves pinched my right leg. I cried out.

Faces swam in and out of view. My vision blurred with tears, and my chest burned on every breath. Voices murmured above me, muffled by my thudding heartbeat.

"Victoria. Can you hear me?"

I blinked and croaked a yes toward the deep voice.

A dark-haired man squinted at me. "I'm a doctor. May I examine you?"

"O-okay." I shivered on the cold floor during the examination. Someone wrapped their warm hand over mine.

"It looks safe to move her," the doctor said. He turned to me. "Can you sit up?"

Hands grasped my arms. He cradled my head and neck, and I rose to a seated position. The room spun. I breathed through the dizziness.

I pushed with my feet and squeezed my eyes shut with the pain of my sudden movement. Someone rubbed my back, and hushed voices filled my ears. I stood; my body supported by those nearby.

The doctor's lips twitched. "Nice work beating my wife's team."

I wheezed a laugh.

"I've called your emergency contact," Coach said. "Come sit down for a bit." She assisted me to the sidelines and wrapped my jacket around my shoulders.

I had no idea how long I occupied the hard bench. Long enough for people to shift around me and a new game to start.

"Hey, lovely, you okay?"

I blinked at the apparition kneeling in front of me.

Belinda's green eyes shimmered under the bright lights.

I closed my eyes and choked back a sob as she wrapped her arms around me.

A scruffy chin kissed my forehead, the scent of Burberry Brit calming my senses. "Let's get you to the hospital," Matt said. "I'll drive your car while you go with Bee."

My two precious friends aided me to the car park and buckled me into Belinda's passenger seat. Matt placed my bag in the footwell as Belinda climbed into the driver's seat.

He dangled my keys from his fingers. "I'll see you both soon."

The closest emergency department was twenty minutes away. I stared out the window holding my tender head while Belinda drove. My hip ached. I shifted in my seat to relieve some pressure against it.

Halfway to our destination, she cleared her throat. "We got quite the scare when Matt received your coach's call. We didn't know you'd changed to Wednesdays."

Matt received the call? I pursed my lips. I had better update my emergency contact details to Nicholas. I grimaced. Once we sorted out our relationship issues. "I was filling in."

"Oh." Belinda tapped her fingers against the steering wheel.

"Are you okay?"

I turned with caution toward my friend. Pain shot through my skull, and I winced. "I guess."

She glanced at me. Her eyes shone like emeralds in a riverbed. "Nick came over tonight. With Matt." She swallowed, and my chest clamped. "He told us how Diana found you in the supermarket aisle yesterday afternoon. H-how you were hurting over loved ones." Her eyes sheened with tears, and she blinked. "He said he's tried to call you. He's worried about you." She stared through the windscreen. "He's your boyfriend, Vicki. As fresh as your relationship is, you need to let him in. You can't hide stuff like last time. Trust God to work things out between you."

My throat constricted, and my stomach knotted. 'Last time' had been a disaster. We had overcome our issues, but so many months had been wasted. Would God work it out for my good like the Bible promised? And was Nicholas part of that 'good'? The air in my lungs thickened. Losing him a second time was not an option. I had to tell him everything if we were going to last.

"Nicholas was there when Matt received the call. Don't be surprised if he's waiting in emergency for you."

I pressed my hand against the tightness on my sternum.

"Matt said there's more you're not telling me but it's not his story to tell." Several tears trailed Belinda's cheeks. She sniffed and wiped her face. "What's hurting you, Vicki? Please let me help you."

I closed my eyes, and images of my children danced across my vision. I burrowed back against the seat with a prayer on my lips. Tears slipped through their restraints when I lifted my eyelids. "I have three children."

Belinda gasped, and the car swerved. "Do they live with Jude?"

I choked on a sob. "Th-they're dead."

She covered her mouth with her hand, her eyes wide and wet with tears. "I-I don't know what to say." She blinked and focused on the darkened road ahead. "I'm so sorry."

"Yesterday was my daughter's birthday."

"Vicki." Belinda's voice cracked.

I leaned forward and groped for my bag with a moan. My head thumped. "J-Jessica was two weeks shy of twelve when she died. Samantha would've been twelve yesterday." I grappled left-handed with the pocket zipper and paused for a breath. Had my body aged ten years in the last hour? I pulled out my phone and scrolled through my photos with feeble fingers. "Ryan was six. He'd be eight and a half now."

I smiled at their happy faces frozen in time while tears tracked my cheeks.

Belinda inspected the screen and pointed. "She looks so much like you."

I puffed a laugh. "That's Samantha. She was my clown. So crazy." A giggle bubbled in my chest. "When she was five, she announced the names of her future children: Bob, Lily, Ch-Chili a-and," I snorted, "B-Basketball."

Belinda and I burst into laughter.

"She sounds like my niece. Children are funny creatures."

The brief moment of elation fizzled when the familiar ache settled back inside my heart. Blood rushed in my ears, and I dropped my phone in my bag. I rested my palm against my throbbing temple. That polished floor had sucker punched me.

Moments later, Belinda navigated the hospital visitor car park and pulled to a stop. She unbuckled. "I'd love to know more about your children when you're feeling better."

I balled my hand against my thigh.

"You should've seen the worry on Nicholas's face when he spoke about you." Her hand clasped mine. "He's head over heels for you, Vicki. Like you are for him." She squeezed. "Please tell him. He's trustworthy."

I blinked back tears. "I told him I love him."

Belinda's eyes widened before a soft smile formed on her lips. "And?"

"And then I ran away."

She sighed with a smile and a head shake. "Let's get you checked out." Belinda exited the vehicle and helped me to my feet. She threw my bag over her shoulder and wrapped an arm around me.

We crossed the car park at a sloth's pace. My tender hip jolted with every footstep, and I gritted my teeth. The hospital building loomed ahead. I hated hospitals.

Belinda guided me through the sliding glass doors of the emergency department.

I blinked several times, and my eyes adjusted to the brightness of the waiting room. My stomach churned at the familiar smell, and I stumbled.

Belinda's hand on my upper arm tightened and held me upright.

Looking ahead, I sucked in a sharp breath when Matt and Nicholas came into view. They stood close in whispered conversation, a sight I never imagined I would see. Nicholas faced away from the building entry.

I hobbled to the triage desk and tracked Matt's rushed movements toward me.

He grasped my elbow, led me to a nearby seat, and lowered me into the chair before interlacing his fingers with Belinda's. Together they joined the queue of sick and injured people.

I closed my eyes and held my head, thankful to be seated. My skull pulsated. I opened my eyes, lifted my head, and gazed up at the figure lurking nearby. The pain in my head intensified.

Nicholas studied me with his dark eyes. He stepped forward, stopped then stuffed his hands into his jacket pockets. He seemed lost.

Had I stolen his confidence with each ignored message?

I patted the empty seat to my left.

The chair squeaked underneath him. "You okay?" His voice wavered, and my eyes misted. His woody scent engulfed me, blocking out the sterile hospital fumes.

"I don't know." I leaned my head against him, and he pulled me against his side, his arm wrapped around me. I sighed. "I'm sorry."

He kissed my uninjured temple, his breath warm on my forehead. "I know. I ... I need to know we're okay."

Tears slipped down my cheeks. "We're okay."

Nicholas's soft lips became a permanent fixture on the side of my head, and my body stilled. People whispered around us. A baby cried, and a pyjama-clad young boy whined to his mother. A red-headed nurse whisked a man holding a bloodied tea towel against his head from the waiting room.

Nicholas's warmth lulled me into a comfortable state and my eyelids drooped. I leaned further into his embrace, my vision darkening.

"Hey, hey, no sleeping."

I mumbled a complaint. I could sleep like this forever, safe in his strong arms, surrounded by his familiar fragrance.

Nicholas shifted and I straightened. His warm hands covered my cheeks and turned me toward him. "No sleeping." His gaze penetrated mine. "Otherwise, I'll be forced to think of ways to keep you awake." His focus shifted to my lips.

My pulse tripped. "You wouldn't."

He lifted his brow and pressed closer. His magnificent face encroached on my oxygen supply. "Our relationship's still new, so let me give you a hint. You know me quite well as a friend,"—his fingers brushed a stray hair from my forehead—"but this is foreign territory for you." His eyes burned, and I held my breath. "I'll do anything and everything to keep you safe, healthy and happy. If it means keeping you awake,"—his gaze flickered to my lips— "then I'll do whatever it takes."

A thrill went up my spine. "You sure know how to distract a lady from her injuries and keep her on high alert."

He chuckled. "All's fair in love and war."

I gazed into his darkened eyes filled with promise. I could trust those eyes. The heart inside the man. Those lips which would hold my secrets, ears which would listen to every word. I cleared my throat, ready to share everything. "I—"

"Vicki." Belinda's voice caught my attention, and I turned to her and her outstretched hand. "You're up."

I nodded and lumbered to the triage window.

A woman in her mid-forties stared at a computer monitor. "What brings you here today?"

Belinda angled close. "Possible concussion."

The woman typed on the keyboard. "Any medical history we should know about?"

I scrunched my face. "I was in a major accident almost two-and-a-half years ago. Crushed right leg, head injury."

She nodded and tapped the keys. A printer spat out several papers, which she grabbed and handed to a nurse behind her. The nurse disappeared. "Through to the right, please."

We entered a small, partitioned space where the nurse with my papers waited. I wilted onto the chair across from her.

"What brings you here today?" The nurse's accent reminded me of my Malaysian-born high school friend.

"Basketball collision." I pointed to the discomfort in my head. "I fell against my right hip. My head also impacted the floor."

"Headache?"

I squinted. "Yes. A rather painful one."

She inspected my eyes. "Nausea? Vomiting?"

"I feel a little nauseous."

She touched my neck. "Any soreness?"

"No. A doctor checked me on the court."

"Good." She held my wrist with her fingers. "With your history I suggest a CT scan. Best to be safe."

Belinda squeezed my shoulder.

"If the doctors decide you're safe to go home after the scan, you'll need to stay with someone for the next twenty-four hours." The nurse zeroed in on Belinda. "Are you her partner?"

Belinda snorted, and I pressed away a smile. "No, best friend."

The nurse nodded. "Okay, find yourselves a seat in the waiting room."

Belinda helped me stand, and we wandered out to Matt and Nicholas. The men shot to their feet.

Nicholas held my hand. "Everything okay?"

I revelled in the warmth of his fingers. "I need a CT scan."

Matt and Nicholas furrowed their brows.

"It's precautionary," Belinda said, "with Vicki's previous head injury. She'll need to be watched for the next twenty-four hours. Are you going to be around tomorrow morning, Nick?"

"I have a four AM start for a job outside of town, but I'm hoping I'll be home by eight-thirty." Nicholas turned to me. "Can you stay with Belinda tonight? Then I can collect you in the morning."

Belinda shook her head. "No, no, I'll drop Vicki over to your place and ask Diana to stay until you get home. She can find Matt or me to sign her lateness slip if she's late to school. We'll sort it out."

"Good idea. Sounds like we're not needed here anymore, Nick." Matt hugged me. "I'll drop your car at your place." He stood back and faced Nicholas. "Can you follow me and drop me at Bee's so I can get my car?"

"Of course." Nicholas pressed a gentle kiss to my cheek.

Warmth spread across my chest.

"I'll be praying. Call me if you need anything." His lips brushed my ear, his breath tickling my earlobe. "I love you."

My lungs seized. I opened my mouth to speak, but nothing came out.

Nicholas's eyes sparkled. "Let's go, Matt."

I focused on the heart-pounding way his back shifted with each step. What had I done to deserve such a man? And a delicious one too.

"What just happened?" Belinda squinted.

Heat crawled up the back of my neck and flushed my face. "I, ah." I fanned my face. "He, uh."

Belinda touched my shoulders and lowered me into the closest empty chair before occupying the seat beside me. "He what?"

"He said he loved me."

She cracked a huge grin and I laughed. "Praise God! Next time, don't wait for a head injury to sort yourselves out."

I grunted. "He still doesn't know everything."

Belinda scrunched her face. "I don't think the details will change anything. You two are imperfectly perfect together." She rested her shoulder against mine. "I mean, can't you feel how the room crackles with electricity when you're together? The sooner you get married, the better!"

I laughed and then whimpered from pain. I pressed a palm to the side of my head, and my insides roiled. If I remarried, would the problems of my past repeat?

Jude came to the forefront of my mind and my mouth dried. No, the past would stay in the past. Each day away from him brightened my future. "I never told you Jude kept contacting me."

Belinda's mirth disappeared. "It wasn't that one phone call?"

"No. He called me at Chrissy's two Christmases ago and never stopped until the weekend Nicholas found out Matt and I had broken up."

She gawped. "But that was two months ago! Jude was contacting you this whole time?"

"Yes." I sucked in a breath. "He's the reason I fainted at your house."

"What!"

"He bombarded my phone with messages, reminding me of how we spent our first New Year's. How he kissed me, what we did together."

She covered her mouth. "Oh. I thought you said you had troubling dreams?"

"I did." I lowered my head. "Dreams where we were decidedly ... naked."

"Wow." She snickered behind her hand. "They must've been pretty good to keep you awake."

"Belinda!" I nudged her shoulder. "I've an archive of memories I'd rather forget."

"Or replace."

My cheeks warmed and heart ricocheted. "That's not helping, Bee."

She surveyed me with contemplative eyes. "Why didn't you block Jude's number?"

I snorted. "Because I'd block the number and he'd get a new one. There was no mistaking who sent me each and every message."

She pursed her lips. "You should get a new number."

"Amber said the same thing." No longer reliant on my Melbourne contacts, I could email old colleagues and friends and update the people I interacted with every day. My family would keep the new number away from Jude.

"Great minds think alike!" Belinda winked.

"Victoria Burke?" A young doctor stood near a set of interior hospital doors.

I raised my hand. Belinda carried my bag, and we crossed the threshold together.

CHAPTER THIRTY-THREE
To Come Full Circle

"Vicki."

I opened my eyes and blinked up at Belinda's tired face. After my CT scan and several hours of observation, we had arrived home at two o'clock in the morning. The doctor had given me strict instructions not to return to work until Monday, so Belinda had contacted Principal Marsden and my team leader while I dozed in emergency.

Light shone underneath the closed curtain in her spare bedroom. Sitting up to take pain medication during the night had exacerbated my dizziness, but the throbbing had eased.

She yawned. "How're you feeling?"

"Better," I croaked.

Belinda rubbed her eyes. "Thanks for the parenting practice. This wakeup's for painkillers and to get you out of bed."

I grinned. "A newborn doesn't always stick to a four-hour routine like my medication."

Her eyes widened. "I'm not sure I'm ready for motherhood."

I slid up and rested my back against the bedhead. "You'll be a wonderful mother one day. I bet Matt will be on board with that plan."

Her laughter bubbled into the quiet room. "Not for a while. I'm enjoying getting to know him. I've told him I want to take things slow."

"Why?"

Belinda eased herself on the edge of the bed. "We need this time." She handed me two paracetamol capsules. "You and Nick don't. Anyway, isn't he forty next month? Matt's a few years younger and happy to wait."

Nicholas. I clutched the water glass from next to the bed and popped the painkillers. I hoped beyond hope we were married or close to married by the time May came around again. I would marry him tomorrow if I could. I creased my brow. Perhaps not tomorrow. My family and Melbourne loved ones would need a few weeks' notice.

I sipped another mouthful and my cheeks heated. Why was I planning a wedding? I needed a fiancé first! I shook my head and regarded Belinda's thoughtful face.

"Do you want more children?" she asked.

My jaw slackened. "I …" Did I want more children? Warmth pooled in my abdomen. A tiny face with a set of dark brown eyes, sweet chubby cheeks and a gummy smile filled my vision. If Diana were a benchmark, any child of Nicholas's would be beautiful. Could I love another son or daughter along with my babies? Was it possible to be a mother to more than Diana? To have another chance at raising a child?

Tears pooled in my eyes. "I do."

Belinda covered my hand with hers. "Nick's a blessed guy."

"I'm the blessed one."

She stood. "Time to get dressed so I can get to work on time."

"Thanks, Bee."

"Nick's already home, so it'll be a drop and run." She closed the door behind her.

I swung my legs over the edge of the bed and stilled. My right thigh ached, and my head swam. I closed my eyes and inhaled a deep breath. This pain would pass like the last time.

I dressed in the spare tracksuit I carried in my basketball bag, popped my phone in my hoodie pocket and carried my things to the front door.

My sneakers waited in the entryway where I had left them hours earlier. I sighed. The floor was a long way down today. I grimaced and lowered myself onto the tiles, slipped into my shoes and laced them. After a steadying breath, I gathered enough energy to make the journey off the floor.

"Need help?" Belinda stepped from behind me and extended a hand.

Reaching up, I grabbed onto her fingers and grunted as she hoisted me.

She handed me a paper bag. "Your meds and instructions."

I followed Belinda out the door and buckled myself in the passenger seat of her vehicle.

Belinda settled in the driver's seat. "What's the plan for tonight's literature presentation?"

My mouth dropped open, and my pulse thundered. "Oh no."

She glanced at me. "You forgot, didn't you?"

I groaned. "It's been a crazy few days." I rubbed my forehead and sighed. "I can't cancel, not after the influx of interest. I changed the venue to the school theatre because more than fifty people were on the attendee list." My chest cramped.

Belinda touched my arm before reversing the car down her driveway. "It's okay. Matt and I will look after it."

My eyes dampened. "But …"

"But what?"

"I don't want to miss out," I whispered.

She touched my shoulder with a gentle hand. "You can postpone if you like?"

I shook my head and squeezed my eyes against the pain. *No sudden movements, Victoria!* I steadied my breaths. "There's no other time in the school calendar or my schedule. It was a fight to have this recital as it was." I stared out the windscreen while we drove through the neighbourhood. "It has to be tonight."

"Then leave it to me. Do you have a rundown or schedule

written somewhere?"

I squinted. "Check my desk. I printed a few copies for the girls on Tuesday."

We pulled up outside the Jacobsen residence, and my stomach lurched. Belinda helped me out of the car—my bag on her back—and escorted me up the stairs to Nicholas's front door. She knocked against the aged wood.

The door creaked open, and my breath dissolved at the sight of the tall, glorious man standing in front of me.

Nicholas beamed a huge smile. "Hey."

"Hey, lovebirds, gotta go." Belinda thrust my bag into Nicholas's hands. "Has Diana left already?"

He clutched the bag. "Yeah."

"Okay, see you both later." She pressed a kiss to my forehead, then disappeared.

Nicholas stepped back and I trundled inside. He closed the door, and we trod to the kitchen. The quiet of the house flared my nerves. Who cared about a mild concussion when a serious conversation loomed in the air?

Nicholas placed my bag on a bar stool and switched the kettle on. His penetrating dark eyes sent warmth swirling in my chest. "Cup of tea?"

Shivers danced down my spine at the sound of his deep, velvety voice. I nodded. If honesty was on the agenda for the day, my desire was not only for tea.

He pulled out a chamomile tea bag and I nodded again. His handsome face lit up with a resplendent smile. "Go rest on the couch and I'll bring your drink in."

I shuffled to the lounge room, gathered several cushions and stacked them at one end of the couch. I sprawled out and leaned back—my legs extending half the length of the furniture—and adjusted the padding at my lower back. My eyelids drooped.

A snore pierced the quiet. I coughed and opened my eyes. Still alone in the room, I flushed over the noise Nicholas may have overheard. I snorted and convulsed in a string of supressed giggles. I wanted to marry the man. He was bound to witness my snores and snorts sometime in the future.

Footsteps approached. Nicholas entered the room with a mug in each hand. He handed one to me and I breathed in the delicious aroma.

"So good. Thanks."

He lifted my feet, slid under them, and rested my legs across his thighs. He furrowed his brow. "That okay? Doesn't hurt your leg?"

I shook my head and his brow smoothed. Goodness gracious, had Nicholas turned up the heater? The telltale warmth of an imminent armpit drenching increased my breathing. I needed to calm down before I embarrassed myself further.

Nicholas smiled. "You look better than you did last night."

I gulped a mouthful of tea. "I feel better. Just tired."

"Belinda kept me updated during the night. I appreciated reading her messages when I woke up at quarter past three."

I had forgotten he had an early start. I rested my mug on my thigh. "You must be tired too. How much sleep did you get?"

He pursed his lips. "Five hours?" He grinned at me. "I figured you'd nap this afternoon, so I'd be able to catch some shut-eye too."

"Sneaky."

The familiar, faint sounds of youth at the school three streets away comforted me. A ute droned past the house, drowning out the crowing birds.

I glanced across at Nicholas while we sipped from our mugs. His large, calloused hands held his cup against his lips, eyes staring at the window ahead. Sweet Lord above, he was a beautiful man. His dark eyelashes fluttered and I smirked behind my mug. The hair on his darkened chin had grown a tad since last night.

I drank the last of my tea and handed him my empty cup.

He placed both mugs on the coffee table and rested his hands on my ankles. "Is this a good time to talk?"

My pulse raced. Nicholas's spiced-wood cologne teased my nostrils, begging me to move closer and inhale his scent. I gazed at his expectant face and nodded.

He peered at the coffee table before he returned his gaze to me. Fire burned in his dark orbs, a fire I had seen reflected in Jude's eyes once upon a time. "I know our exclusive relationship is weeks old, but I feel like I've known you forever." A gorgeous dimple peeked from underneath his irresistible stubble. "I love you." His thumb stroked the edge of my ankle socks and touched a sliver of my skin, sending my heart into overdrive. "Nothing you do or say will change that."

I swallowed a fevered breath. "You know Jude and I were married for thirteen years."

His body tensed and he nodded.

My throat clogged and my eyes burned with tears. "We had three children together."

A hiss of air exited Nicholas's mouth.

Tears trailed my cheeks. "They were ... are my greatest accomplishments to date." Gut-wrenching sobs racked my body.

Nicholas pulled me onto his lap, my balled hands against the drums beating in his chest. The warmth of his body matched the increased heat under my skin. His large hand stroked my back while I cried into his neck. *Thank You, God, for this wonderful man.*

My tears drenched the collar of his polo shirt. Each breath passed my lips with a strength I knew was not mine alone. The rhythm in Nicholas's chest soothed me and my sobs lessened.

I pushed against his arm, inclined and reached my phone in my pocket. Opening the photo gallery, I found a photo of Jessica, Samantha and Ryan taken in the backyard of our Black Rock home. They stood in front of the lemon tree on Ryan's first day of Prep. I leaned against Nicholas's chest and ran my thumb along each of their sweet faces. "These are my babies. Jessica was almost twelve, Samantha nine and a half, and cheeky Ryan was six."

"They're beautiful," he said, his voice choked. "Y-you must

miss everything about them."

I nodded and stole several deep breaths. "It was Samantha's twelfth birthday on Tuesday." *The night I declared my love for you.* I shuddered with a sob. "The children would've loved you and Diana." I twisted around to face Nicholas.

His damp eyes and what they communicated warmed me deep inside.

I was drawn to the soft curve of his mouth. Those full lips.

His eyes flashed and I brushed my pointer finger along his mouth. Soft and kissable.

The memory of our first kiss heated my belly and I shifted on his lap. "Do you honestly remember the night we kissed?" I placed a hand on his chest and revelled in the thunderous claps of his heart.

Nicholas's gaze drilled into mine. "I do."

I wrapped my arms around his neck and searched his eyes. They were darker than before, almost ebony in colour to match the intensity of his gaze. I licked my lips, my head hazy and abdomen tightening. The tension between us vibrated. "I've daydreamed about your kiss since that night."

He drew me close, wrapped his strong arms around me, and joined his mouth to mine. His lips were soft and warm like I remembered. This time mint tingled my mouth.

I returned the kiss, my brain abuzz with thoughts and emotions desperate to escape their fetters of iron.

His hands moved and burned my lower back, hot enough to brand me as his. A deep ache grabbed me hard and fast, and I wanted to indulge without restraint in the bliss of Nicholas Jacobsen. Our desire dangled us over the edge of a perilous precipice.

We withdrew from the kiss, our gazes never parting.

"I love you, Nicholas."

A broad smile engulfed his face and intensified his laugh lines. "I love you too. I love your smile and the way your ponytail skips when you walk. I love your heart for God, your love for the church, and that prayer's your first response to any situation. I'm amazed by your heart for your students and your capacity to love in the midst of all your grief and loss." He wiped a few more tears off my cheek. A whimsical smile spread across his lips. "I love how Diana gushes about you and feels safe to share her personal struggles with you. It blesses me the way you encourage and guide her. You never undermine my decisions, even when I've been ridiculous or stupid."

I slid a hand to his chest and caressed the side of his face with my other hand.

Nicholas closed his eyes, inhaled a deep breath, and opened them again. Their fire burned bright and sparked the tinder which smouldered inside of me. "I know this'll make me sound like a pubescent teenage boy, but I want you so much." He dusted the pad of his thumb down my cheekbone and across my lips.

I drew in a sharp breath.

His thumb continued on its downward trajectory, his eyes tracking the movement as it slid over my chin and down my throat.

Blood pounded in my heart and rushed between my ears, reminding me of my mild headache. I bit my lower lip and our gazes locked.

He retracted his hand from my collarbone and rested it against my back. "I wondered if I'd ever be interested in another woman again." He winked. "And two years ago a gorgeous, sopping, hot mess of a woman landed on my doorstep, covered in flower petals." He closed his eyes and grinned. "I can still picture you, drenched and flushed." His eyelids lifted. "I almost fell over when I noticed your lace bra all but holding you together. You do recall I sped off for a towel, yeah?"

I stared at him, wide-eyed. "You saw that?"

He chuckled and the creases around his eyes deepened on each breath. "I regretted having offered you the use of my bathroom. I was in desperate need of an ice-cold shower after we met."

Loud laughter erupted from my lungs.

Nicholas's eyes shone. "I'm not sure you understand the power you possess. We've only skimmed over your marriage breakdown, but I suspect you were never empowered in your relationship. God sees who you are and I want to know that woman more. You're a force to be reckoned with and I'm at your mercy."

I held a hand over my mouth and blinked. His ability to speak to my heart overwhelmed me. Jude never spoke with such conviction. Deep happiness filled the void my ex-husband had left behind. Nicholas was a man after God's own heart, and my innermost being soared knowing my future was secure in his love and in the incomparable love of my heavenly Father.

I touched the light stubble on his cheek. A smile crossed my face and I studied his darkened eyes.

"Marry me." He pressed his forehead against mine. "I've loved you since you brought Diana home after our disagreement."

I gasped. "The David incident?"

He scowled. "Yes."

"B-but that was over a year ago!"

He laughed. "And?"

"Nothing. I … needed more time to work it out."

He grinned, his dark eyes capturing my gaze. "When did you work it out?"

I dropped my gaze and stared at the buttons on his shirt. "I knew I was falling for you after we kissed, but only admitted it to myself of late."

Nicholas lifted my chin and met my gaze. His eyes softened. "You still haven't answered my question."

I leaned forward and brushed my lips against his. "Of course, I'll marry you. I was thinking only this morning I'd marry you in a heartbeat."

He laughed.

My heart lightened at the expression etched on his face. "But let's hurry up about it. I don't believe in long engagements, and two and a half years between drinks is long enough for me."

"It's been an eleven-year drought for me, so I welcome your haste."

I flashed my cheekiest grin. "Then it's settled." I wrapped my arms around his neck. "How's a winter wedding sound? School holidays begin in six weeks."

His breath fanned my cheek. "Sounds perfect to me."

CHAPTER THIRTY-FOUR
Worlds Collide

I woke from my catnap on the couch to the sound of quiet conversation. Nicholas lounged on the opposite couch with an arm draped along the back of the seat, his gaze fixed on Diana. My breath hitched at the perfect structure of his profile. And that jawline. Oh my. My heartbeat increased. Had I imagined our engagement, or had that hot specimen of a man determined to spend the rest of his life with me? My face warmed at the implications of such an arrangement. An image of his bedroom flicked to my mind, and I groped for the couch seat beside me.

Diana's soft giggles filled my ears. She lazed on the couch facing Nicholas, cross-legged, with bright eyes and a beaming smile. Would this sweet, selfless Amazon-like beauty be pleased about my marrying her father? Would she embrace the idea of a new mother like I did a new daughter?

I stifled a yawn. Was the literature recital already over? "What's the time?"

Nicholas and Diana turned with wide eyes before smiles eclipsed their faces. Nicholas glimpsed his watch. "Just before six. We arrived home fifteen minutes ago."

I sat up and smoothed my hair. "How'd it go?"

Diana sprang from her seat and kneeled at my feet. She touched my knee, and I clasped her hand in mine. She creased her brow. "The recital was a success, but that's not important. Are *you* okay?"

I nodded and smiled at the lack of discomfort. "I'm feeling good."

She pursed her lips. "Are you sure? You look tired."

I cupped her face in my hands. "Tired, yes, but my head feels clear." I glanced over Diana's head and caught Nicholas's ravenous stare. My cheeks flamed. I sucked in a breath, and he smirked.

Nicholas stood and stalked toward me, his gaze never leaving my face. He settled on the same couch as me to my left, and my heart pounded. His cologne engulfed me. "Princess," he said to Diana, "Victoria and I need to talk to you about something."

I scooted to the other end of the couch and winced when my thigh pressed against the arm. I patted the gap I had created on the seat.

Diana filled the space between Nicholas and me. She leaned back against the couch—giving me an unobstructed view of my big-hearted fiancé—and raised a brow, her gaze flicking back and forth. "What's up?"

Nicholas chuckled. "Nothing's wrong. We have some news to share."

I linked my hand with hers.

Diana relaxed her shoulders.

Nicholas leaned forward and winked at me. "We're getting married."

Diana yelped and I laughed. She jumped up and danced on the spot. "You're marrying Ms. Burke?"

Nicholas joined my laughter with his own soft chuckles. "Yes. July eighth."

Diana gaped. "As in"—she stared up with a squint—"seven weeks from now? After my eighteenth?"

I chuckled, my chest light. "We want to be home on the third for your birthday." I beamed. "Maybe it's a good time to call me Victoria when you're not at school."

Impossible as it seemed, her eyes widened further. "Wait till I tell Madison!"

I burst out in laughter, my chest heaving on every breath. "Won't she be disappointed!"

Nicholas crinkled his brow. "Huh?"

Diana shook her head. "Isn't it obvious after all these years Madison thinks you're"—she wrinkled her nose and exhaled a noisy breath through her nostrils—"super-hot? She wants to be my mum!"

I snorted behind my hand.

Nicholas's gaze darted from Diana's face to mine. "I-I thought you were both joking!"

"Let's not worry about that for now." I shuddered a breath. "I need to share some things with you, Diana, but they can wait until later."

I turned to Nicholas. "Are Bee and Matt coming over as we discussed?"

He nodded and rubbed his hands together. "Our plan's in motion."

Diana squinted. "What plan?"

"To surprise them with our news," I said. "Bee thinks she's coming over to take me home for the night."

"I thought you don't need supervision anymore?"

I shrugged. "You know what she's like."

Diana giggled. "True." She leaned down and hugged me. "I'm so happy, Ms. Bur—ah, Victoria."

I kissed her cheek. "So am I."

She stood back, then launched into her father's lap. "Nice work, Daddy."

His deep chuckle vibrated through the air. "Thanks, Princess. Think you can help with setting the table for dinner?"

"Sure." Diana skipped out of the room.

Nicholas slid along the couch until his thigh pressed against mine. His body heat seeped into my pant leg, and my breaths laboured. His lips twitched before the tip of his tongue peeked out the corner of his mouth and swiped along his lips.

My throat dried. How would I survive seven more weeks of this torture?

His gaze flickered to my mouth and his pupils dilated. "You're so beautiful. I can't believe you're mine."

I drowned in his molasses eyes and breathed in his scent.

He lowered his mouth to mine and I mewled. His lips vibrated against mine before a deep chuckle sounded. "That's the sound you make when you eat."

My face burned and I glanced away. "Sorry, I—"

"Don't apologise." He smirked. "It's nice to know I rank high on your pleasure scale."

I coughed and spluttered and he helped me straighten in the seat. "You've no idea."

Someone knocked at the door.

Nicholas rose to his feet. "To be continued, tempting fiancée of mine."

"No continuing for seven weeks or I'll combust."

His eyes gleamed, and he leaned closer. "I'd like to see that."

I swatted him away. "Go answer the door."

He pressed a kiss to my cheek before he walked away.

I closed my eyes and uttered a prayer for strength. Who knew a beast resided inside the man of my dreams, hungry for release? I had become so used to Jude's indifference over the years that Nicholas's heated gaze seared my insides. Was this a sign of a scorching future together? I fanned my face with my hands and opened my eyes.

Belinda bounded toward me. "You're looking better!" She arched a brow. "Although you're rather red in the face." She scowled. "You weren't doing something strenuous, were you?"

I pressed my lips together and suppressed a smile. "I wouldn't dare."

"Good." She enfolded her arms around me. "Your girls performed well."

I sighed, the corners of my mouth downturned. "I wish I could've been there."

"Matt recorded it all, including my awkward emceeing."

I snorted a laugh. "I'm looking forward to it."

Diana, Nicholas and Matt entered the room. "How's the patient?" Matt asked.

"Improved. Headache's gone," I said.

He plopped on the couch next to Belinda. "Great to hear."

Nicholas cleared his throat. "Victoria and I have some news."

Diana squeaked from her perched position on the armchair.

Belinda and Matt stared at me.

"Are you okay? Tell me what's going on," Belinda said.

I peered up. "Nicholas?"

"How about a demonstration." He towered over me, then dropped to one knee.

My eyebrows shot up.

Matt and Belinda gasped. Diana giggled.

Nicholas turned to our guests. "I didn't get to do this part earlier." He smiled at me and withdrew a box from his jeans pocket.

"Nicholas." I covered my gaping mouth with my right hand.

"I was prepared earlier but remembered the ring in my bedroom after you'd accepted. So"—he opened the box and exposed a beautiful princess-cut diamond on a platinum band—"Victoria Jade Burke, would you marry me on Saturday July eighth at two in the afternoon at Tellarine Christian Church?" His eyes dazzled.

I laughed out loud and Diana's giggles echoed across the room. "That's rather specific. Did you already book Pastor Davidson?"

He rubbed along his bristled jawline with his empty hand. The scratching sound resonated. "Couldn't sleep when you napped, so it's all organised as we'd discussed."

Belinda croaked. "A-are you two—"

"Yes." I beamed at Nicholas before turning to Belinda. "And yes. We're getting married!"

Belinda swung her arms around me and cried. Matt blew me a kiss before slapping Nicholas on the back.

I stuck my left hand out from behind Belinda and wiggled my naked ring finger.

Nicholas slipped cold metal against my skin, followed by his warm, soft lips.

I sighed into Belinda's hair.

She pulled back, her fingers wiping streaks of mascara from her wet cheeks. "I'm so happy for you." Her eyes widened. "Was your face red earlier because you two were canoodling?"

Diana squeaked and Matt snickered.

My cheeks heated. I glanced at Nicholas.

His face split into a wide grin. "A lady never kisses and tells, Belinda."

"Ugh, that's my cue to leave." Diana scuttled out of the room.

Belinda cackled. "You so were." She turned to Matt. "I think Vicki should move in with me so we can watch her. I don't trust Nick."

Laughter filled the room. I stared at the sparkling stone on my finger, and my heart surged.

After dinner I lay on the couch with my feet resting in Nicholas's lap. My new favourite lounging position. I typed a group text message to Amber, Christine and Stacy. Belinda had messaged them—along with my parents—the night before, while I was in hospital, with another update this morning.

Me: THANKS FOR YOUR PRAYERS. I'M DOING WELL. MY HEADACHE'S GONE AND I'M FEELING MORE MYSELF. JUST TIRED. BELINDA SENDS HER LOVE.

My hands shook and I clutched the phone tighter.

Me: I'M HOPING YOU'RE ALL FREE TO VIDEO CHAT TOMORROW NIGHT? IT'LL BE EASIER TO UPDATE YOU IN REAL TIME ALL TOGETHER. GUYS TOO. CHRISTINE, WOULD YOU PLEASE ASK PATRICK TO SET THAT UP? YOU CAN MESSAGE THE LINK IN OUR GROUP CHAT.

Me: OH, AND THINK YOU CAN HAVE DAD AND MUM OVER FOR IT?

I closed my eyes. My phone beeped several times in a row.

Amber: VIDEO CALL? WHAT'S WRONG? ARE YOU OKAY?

Christine: YOU BETTER BE OKAY, WOMAN.

Christine: PATRICK'S OUT AFTER EIGHT, SO ANYTIME FROM 7PM WORKS. HE SAYS HE'LL DO IT SOON. WILL INVITE THE PARENTALS FOR DINNER.

Stacy: STEVE'S ON NIGHTSHIFT. HE'LL WAKE FROM HIS NAP AT 19:30.

I straightened, slid next to Nicholas's warm body and showed him the messages.

He grinned. "You better calm Amber before she drives up from Melbourne."

I snickered and worked my fingers into a frenzy.

Me: AS I SAID, I'M FINE. HAVEN'T SEEN YOUR GORGEOUS FACES FOR A WHILE. AND HAVE A REQUEST FOR THE JULY SCHOOL HOLIDAYS.
7:30PM WORKS HERE.

Nicholas leaned against my shoulder. "You think that's going to satisfy her? She's going to keep bombarding you with questions."

"It's worth a try."

Amber: A REQUEST? TO VISIT? OR TO VISIT US?

Christine: MUM AND DAD ARE A GO FOR DINNER TOMORROW. YEAH, 7:30PM'S GOOD.

Stacy: 19:30. PERFECT. AND AMBER? CALM YOUR FARM.

Stacy: UNLESS YOU'RE PREGNANT, VICKI, THEN STEVE WILL SKIP HIS SHIFT AND MOVE YOU BACK HERE.

Christine: STOP STRESSING, AMBER, AND WAIT FOR TOMORROW NIGHT. ;)

Christine: OH, YOU BETTER NOT BE PREGNANT, SIS!

Amber: CAN YOU IMAGINE HOW PERFECT THEIR BABY WOULD BE? OH MY GOODNESS, YOUR NICHOLAS IS A FREAKING STUD MUFFIN. YOU NEED TO TIE THAT MAN DOWN.

Nicholas choked on a laugh beside me.

I giggled at the banter. I loved my family.

Stacy: HE IS RATHER HANDSOME. I RECALL HE HAS BEAUTIFUL LONG EYELASHES.

Nicholas's cheeks coloured and I snorted behind my hand.

Christine: Yeah, well, I haven't officially met the towering giant of man my sister's desperately in love with, so this conversation ends until I witness those long lashes and stud muffin exterior for myself.

"Looks like you have more members in your fan club, Mr. Jacobsen." I batted my lashes and kissed his rough cheek.

He dug his fingers into my waist and I cried out with laughter. "Watch it, my love."

My chest heaved. "Okay, okay. You win, my sexy stud muffin."

He grinned and flashed his brilliant white teeth. "That's more like it."

I wanted to pinch myself. I was set to be the happiest woman alive.

"I'd better take you home. Did you want me to visit you tomorrow night?"

I rubbed the side of my chin. "I'll come to you. I want to tell Diana about the children."

His eyes softened. "Come over around five and I'll cook dinner."

"I'm not used to having a man in my life who cooks, cleans and likes to be around me."

Nicholas wrapped his arms around my shoulders and pulled me against his chest. "There's lots of things we'll have to get used to, but I know we can do this together." He kissed the top of my head. "I love looking after you, and if that means slaving away in the kitchen"—his Adam's apple bobbed against my head—"or anywhere else in the house you want me once we're married, it'll be my pleasure."

Goosebumps danced up my arms. "Thank you, Nicholas."

"Are you feeling better, Ms. Burke?" Anna's voice warbled

over the speakerphone.

"Is your head okay?" Madison asked.

"I sure hope you are. You're my favourite teacher," Grace said.

I smiled at their tender concern. "I'm fine, girls. I'll be back at school on Monday. The doctor had to make sure I'd rest." I repositioned in my bed and leaned closer to my phone. "I'm sorry about missing your recital last night. I watched the recording, and you all did superbly."

Grace giggled. "We had fun although it was sad performing without you."

Diana's clear voice sounded over the phone line. "I told you she's okay. You're over for dinner tonight, yes?"

"Yes, Diana."

"We're glad you're better," Gabriella said. "Sorry to ditch, but I have to go to the library before recess ends."

We farewelled Gabriella, and I contemplated ending the call when Anna screamed, "I can't believe you're going to be my aunt!"

A hearty laugh gushed from my lips. "Believe it, girl." I grinned at the phone. "Did Uncle Cole visit last night?" Nicholas had mentioned he might visit his mum and brother after he dropped me home.

"He sure did! I think you broke his face, though."

"What do you mean?"

Anna tittered. "I think there's a permanent smile on his face. Dad joked how he couldn't switch it off, to which Mum and Nan scolded him for his cheek."

I pressed my hands to my own aching cheeks. "I'm glad to hear it's a good broken."

"It's true," Diana said. "Dad's so happy. So am I."

Grace and Madison sang their congratulations.

"Thanks for calling me, girls. I think I might rest a little more."

After several goodbyes, the call ended. I snuggled into my blankets, warm from the love and acceptance of my literature ladies. I inhaled a deep breath and closed my eyes. Tonight would be an emotional drain, and I needed all the strength I could gather.

Crumpled tissues and a large photo album covered my lap where I perched on Nicholas's couch next to Diana. Her lithe body leaned against my left side, her arms wound around my middle. Soft sobs hiccupped from her mouth, and I brushed away several tears from my cheek.

I turned another page. A light laugh puffed from the surface of my aching heart. "This was the Christmas Samantha refused to smile."

Diana glanced at me. "Really?"

I pressed a tissue against my nose. "Jude bought the children Christmas gifts when he was overseas for work. He came home with a Beanie Boo penguin for Samantha—"

"The one tiny Ryan's holding?" Diana asked.

I chuckled. "She was so upset he had her new toy in all the Christmas photos."

Diana giggled. "But he looks so adorable holding it."

"He was thirteen months old and had started walking a few weeks earlier. He thought himself adorable." I ran a finger across the shiny, clear plastic covering the photos. "And Ryan was the cutest."

"But Samantha disagreed," Diana said between giggles.

I sniffed and nodded. "I can't imagine any four-and-a-half-year-old would be happy with their baby brother stealing the spotlight *and* their new toy." A laugh puffed from my lungs. "Look at her deadpan face in every photo." My chest heaved with bubbles of laughter. "Such a headstrong child."

We perused the precious photos until Nicholas called us for dinner.

Diana closed the book. "Thanks for sharing this with me, Victoria. It was wonderful meeting my future stepsiblings."

Tears pricked the corners of my eyes, and I kissed Diana's temple. "Jessica would've followed you like a shadow."

Diana stood and extended an arm to help me rise from the couch. "I'd have loved a shadow. Maybe I'll get to love a newborn sibling one day."

I ducked my head to hide the flush in my cheeks. "Your dad and I haven't discussed that topic in detail yet."

She nudged my shoulder, and I met her gaze. "Trust me, he wants in on another baby." She wrinkled her nose. "Or maybe the practice before the baby."

I sputtered a screechy laugh. "Diana!" My cheeks combusted in a ball of heat and my lungs constricted with burning breaths.

"Gross thought for me, but he's keen. Trust me." She grinned and waltzed to the kitchen.

I fluffed my hair in the reflection of my laptop monitor which balanced on Nicholas's coffee table. My pulse thumped in my neck and my dry throat tickled. I wiggled into a more comfortable upright position on the couch before I clicked a button to join the video chat session.

"Take a deep breath, Victoria." Nicholas kissed my forehead and propped himself on a nearby armchair, off camera.

I pulled my shoulders back and forced a smile.

The screen came alive with multiple squares filled with familiar faces. "We're a bit like the Brady Bunch!" Amber said.

Christine laughed. "But funnier. And less dorky."

"You're married to a nerd, cuz." Steve's face was sleepy and adorable.

Christine poked out her tongue. "Nerds aren't dorks. Get your facts straight."

Patrick pulled Christine close with a laugh. "Call me what you want, Steve, just not late for dinner."

"See? Dorky." Steve yanked Stacy against his side.

A laugh snorted from my throat and I relaxed in my seat. I eyed Nicholas. His smile eased the tightness in my chest.

Mum stooped close to her webcam. Her nose almost filled the entire frame she shared with Patrick, Christine and Dad. "How're you feeling, darling? You look pretty good from here, but I did forget my glasses." She leaned back, and I caught the tail end of Christine's eyeroll.

I smirked. "Thanks, Mum. Feeling pretty good considering the mild concussion and large bruise on my right thigh."

Several onscreen faces screwed up and my parents stared back with creased brows.

Amber pouted. "Your right side again? That's unfortunate."

"Tell me about it." I shuddered. "When I fell on the basketball court and my head felt woozy, memories of my stay in hospital flooded back." I shook my head and crinkled my nose. "Not good."

"That's sucky," Amber said.

Dad cleared his throat, and everyone stopped talking. "You're looking good, baby girl. What did you want to talk about?"

I indicated with a quaking hand for Nicholas to join me. "Well—"

"It's the stud muffin!" Amber, Stacy and Christine said in unison.

I choked on a laugh and leaned into Nicholas where his soft breaths ruffled the hair near my ear. I covered my grin with my hand when Patrick, Mike and Steve glared at their respective wives.

"Lovely to meet you, Nicholas," Mum said.

Nicholas cleared his throat. "And you, Mr. and Mrs. Morgan—"

"Please call us Pete and Jacki, darling." Mum beamed. "You're a handsome one, aren't you? Kind-hearted, too, from the stories I've heard."

Nicholas's ears tinged pink at the edges. "Thanks, ah, Jacki."

I covered his left hand with my right and intertwined our

fingers. "Nicholas and I would like to invite you all to Tellarine during the July school holidays and hope you can all get time off work."

Steve yawned. "When?"

I side-eyed Nicholas, and we grinned at each other before I lifted my left hand and displayed my engagement ring. "Saturday, July eight."

The computer audio exploded in a chorus of squeals and shrieks.

"You're getting married?"

"That's wonderful news!"

"Oh, my goodness! Vicki!"

"Congratulations!"

"She's marrying the stud muffin!"

Nicholas and I laughed as my family spewed out their surprise and excitement. Mum hugged Christine in a fit of tears.

"How did he propose?" Stacy asked.

My cheeks hurt from my wide grin. "Well, the first time it happened as part of a serious conversation we were having, and the second time—"

Amber's eyes bulged. "What! You turned him down? Are you crazy?"

Nicholas chortled. "She didn't turn me down, Amber."

"Why twice, son?" Dad creased his bushy brows.

My chest swirled with warmth at the affectionate tone of Dad's voice. I squeezed Nicholas's hand.

He squeezed back. "Well, sir, when I asked the first time, I completely forgot the ring locked away in a room down the hall, so the second time I proposed on bent knee with the engagement ring I had bought"—he rubbed the back of his neck—"a while ago."

I gasped and turned to Nicholas. "When did you buy this ring?"

He pressed his lips in a thin line and avoided my gaze. "Over a year ago."

"What!" I gaped at my fiancé. How could he have bought a ring so long ago? And kept it through our estranged friendship?

"I knew he was the one, Vicki." Christine's soft voice broke the silence and I turned to my laptop. "I never met Nicholas in person, but every time I prayed for you, and when you spoke about him ..." She sighed.

I glanced at Nicholas and breathed in his reassuring scent. His beaming expression stirred my heart and I palmed his stubbled cheek.

He kissed my hand against his cheek.

Steve cleared his throat. "So, July eighth?" He disappeared from the screen and returned seconds later. "Let's see." He inspected his phone, and Stacy glanced down at her own. "Perfect weekend, cuz. I start another round of overnights on the tenth."

I clapped. "What about you, Patrick? Amber and Mike?" One by one all of my loved ones confirmed their availability, and my chest relaxed.

Nicholas kissed my forehead and slipped his arm around me. "Diana and I will stay with my brother, so my house will be here for however many want to stay."

Amber raised her hand. "How many beds, Nick?"

Nicholas pursed his lips. "There's my king-size bed—"

"Ooh," Stacy and Christine chorused.

"A queen-size bed in the spare room. Diana has a king single and a trundle, and there's a queen-size air mattress around here somewhere."

"Sounds good," Amber said. "Maybe the ladies can work out the logistics."

"I've already booked our BnB," Stacy snuggled into Steve's side.

I burst out laughing. "What? Already?"

"Yes! I love that place. We'll stay for Steve's days off. Arrive Thursday, leave after church on Sunday."

"Wonderful," Mum said. "I'll chat with you next week about our visit, okay, Victoria?"

"Sure, Mum."

Patrick piped in. "Sorry to break up the party, but I've gotta go. Congrats again, guys, and we'll see you whenever Chrissy says." He pecked Christine's lips and disappeared from the screen.

"Oh!" Christine leaned forward. "We haven't met Diana yet. Is she around?"

Nicholas removed his arm from my shoulders. "I'll get her."

Moments later, I introduced my almost stepdaughter to my adoring family. They gushed over her good manners and her academic accolades I had shared in the last few years.

"How do you feel about your dad remarrying?" Stacy asked.

Diana's eyes lit up. "I think it's awesome. I couldn't have picked a better wife."

I pulled her into a tight embrace and kissed her temple. "See? Best seventeen-year-old on the planet!"

"Almost eighteen," Diana said.

I grinned and glanced up at Nicholas, where he gazed at his daughter and me. My heart skipped a beat.

CHAPTER THIRTY-FIVE
Ghosts

"Excellent work, Mr. Daley." I stood beside Andrew's classroom desk and returned his English assignment. "You're well on your way to reaching the wonders of outer space with this great work."

Pink bloomed across his pale features. "Thanks, Ms. Burke." He snatched a glimpse of Diana before gazing up at me. "Too bad I won't reach all my goals."

I pressed my lips together and sucked in a smile. "Let me know if you need any school-related assistance."

He nodded, flicked another glance at Diana, and resumed his work.

I sighed. Poor kid. Two years later and Andrew still held a torch for her.

I proceeded to hand out the remaining papers with verbal encouragement for my Year Twelve pupils. My chest warmed with each student's effort. A-plus or D-minus, all I wanted was fulfilled potential. Not one of my students disappointed me.

"Ms. Burke?" Diana's voice travelled across the quiet room.

I turned and approached her desk. "Yes?"

She shrank in her seat and whispered, "Can I get a lift home tonight? My bag's going to be heavy."

I knit my brows together. "Sure." I lowered my voice. "Is everything okay?"

She crumpled her nose. "Don't want everyone thinking I get special treatment."

I stifled a laugh. "Meet you at the library?"

She nodded, glanced around the room, and picked up her pen.

I returned to my desk with light steps and upturned lips.

"You ready?"

Diana piled her books into her backpack and slipped from the library cubicle. We exited the large doorway toward the staff car park.

I clenched the handle of my work bag—lighter than its usual burdensome weight— and relaxed my shoulders. Another long day complete. I stretched my neck and rotated my head from side to side. Two weeks had passed since my fall on the court, and apart from a slight yellow blemish on my right thigh, my body was back to normal.

Diana fished in her waterproof jacket pocket and extended a muesli bar toward me. "Want one? Dad gives me extras for my friends."

Warmth oozed through my chest and down my arms. What a man. "I'm a little peckish. Thanks." I thrust my bag over my shoulder, clasped the bar and unwrapped it. I chewed and swallowed the familiar flavours. "I haven't eaten this since …" My stomach hardened, and I halted my steps.

Since the children.

Oats and chocolate chips caught in my throat, and I spluttered. My chest burned.

Diana whacked my back. "You okay?" She unzipped her school bag and thrust a metal drink bottle in my face. "Here."

I flipped the lid and guzzled a mouthful of water. The food particles dislodged and plunged down my throat. I capped the top and returned her water bottle. "Much appreciated." I coughed against my throaty rasp and eyed the remaining muesli bar in my hands. "Might have the rest later." If my stomach and mind permitted.

We continued to the car. The skies had darkened and the temperature had plummeted. A physical manifestation of my own bleak outlook. We dropped our bags in the boot and drove to the Jacobsens'. Thoughts of my children stayed with me the entire trip, and my breaths shortened.

"How're the wedding plans?"

Right. Back to the present. I parked outside the house and unbuckled. "Getting there. Bee's helping a lot."

Diana opened the passenger door. "I'm happy to help if you need it."

I nodded and popped the boot.

Fat water droplets fell from the thick clouds above. We grabbed our bags and rushed to the verandah. Diana unlocked the front door, hung her jacket on the coat rack, and disappeared down the hallway.

I ambled to the kitchen, dropped my bag next to the island bench, and filled the kettle.

"Here, let me do that." Diana swished along the floorboards in her white school socks and retrieved the kettle. She set it to boil and turned. "By the way, I forgot to tell you how lovely you look today." Her teeth glistened inside her bright grin. "Blue suits you."

My head spun and I groped for the bench. The memory of Jessica's same words to me rang in my ears.

Diana gripped my arm and escorted me to a bar stool. "You okay?"

I sank onto the seat, my body heavy. Tears pooled in the corners of my eyes. I blinked. "Sorry. I …"

She bunched her brows together.

"It's been a long day."

She pursed her lips, nodded and returned to the now-boiled kettle. "Chamomile?"

"Please." I watched Diana prepare the drinks. Would Jessica have been this thoughtful at seventeen? My heart cramped. I had hoped so.

Diana placed my mug on the bench in front of me. She slid a plate of shortbread fingers between us.

I selected a biscuit and indulged a bite. Buttery goodness could fix any problem.

"These were Mum's favourites." Diana glanced at the plate. "It's nice you like them too."

A crumb caught in my throat and I washed it down with hot tea. "Clever lady."

"Yeah, she was. Industrious too. Mum painted the entire house when I was a toddler. My first memory of her is sitting on the dining room floor with my Duplo blocks while she sewed curtains." She tilted her head toward the lounge room. "Those lavender ones. I remember running my fingers across the stiff fabric when it draped over the table onto the floor."

I nibbled the shortbread. My children missed out on similar experiences because I never sewed. Had I deprived them of the joy of seeing something created and fashioned with love like Diana had with her mother? And I had with my mum?

"She chose most of the furniture in the house." Diana stared at her mug. "Dad hasn't changed anything since."

"Oh." My insides churned. How was I meant to step into this home and claim my place? Would Debbie's shadow follow me everywhere I went? Pressure gripped my chest. I eyed my drink and wheezed a breath.

"Mum baked the best chocolate chip cookies." Her eyes sparkled.

I pressed my palm to my turbulent stomach.

Diana's wistful gaze swept across the kitchen. "She'd labour over that stove for hours, humming and chopping, stirring and tasting. Dad loved walking into the house, breathing in the delicious aroma of dinner each night." She sipped her drink. "She was the best mum. Dad spent years getting the knack of cooking. He's pretty good at it now."

I squeezed my thighs against the leather seat. The best mum. I blinked against tears. Something I had failed to be, or my children would still be alive. Would Diana spend the rest of her time under this roof comparing me to a ghost?

And would Nicholas expect similar perfection from me? A woman to manage his home, cook his meals and keep things in order? My mind clouded. How could I work full time, mark all my student papers, and be the perfect wife and mother? Impossible. I had tried this once before and failed. I massaged my temple.

"Victoria?"

I gazed up at Diana and sipped my tea.

She pressed her lips together. Her expression softened. "I hope I haven't upset you by talking about Mum."

I forced a bright smile. "Of course not. Your mum's an important part of your life." I tightened my grip on the mug handle. "She's irreplaceable."

Her gaze penetrated me. "You're an important part of my life too. Please don't—"

The front door creaked open. I pushed my mug aside and swivelled on the seat, sucking in several breaths.

Nicholas stepped inside, his shirt and pants covered in grime.

I occupied the perfect seat with a view.

His dirt-streaked face beamed. "What a wonderful surprise." He turned and braced his hands against the door frame, his long arms taut. He heeled his boots off onto the verandah, his back rippling with each movement.

My heart skittered. No wonder Debbie was Wonder Woman in the flesh. She once had this delectable man step into her home each night.

Nicholas closed the door and entered the kitchen.

"Did you fight in a mud pit?" Diana wrinkled her nose. "Of course, you'd take on a dirty job the week I'm on laundry duty."

Nicholas's deep chuckle untangled my coiled abdomen. "Wasn't intentional, Princess." He leaned close to me, his hip against the bench. "Any chance you're staying for dinner?"

My throat constricted. Did he want me to accustom myself with the kitchen and prepare dinner too? "I-I have some papers to mark."

He squinted. "You okay?"

"Sure." I avoided his gaze.

"I've got homework …" Diana pushed back from the bench and disappeared.

"Victoria?"

I tilted my head up until my neck stretched to its limit.

He scanned my face. His gaze dropped to my neck. Seconds later his large hands circled my waist and hoisted me onto the island benchtop.

I squeaked. "Nicholas!"

He grinned. A dimple peeked out. He stepped between my knees, his hands still heating my sides. "Your neck looked awkward. Better?"

My heart stalled, and my breaths thickened. I wiped my thumb across a mud streak along his jaw. "Why're you so dirty?"

He arched a brow. "Is that what you think of me?"

I snorted a laugh. "Stop it. I mean this"—I rubbed the grit from my thumb with my forefinger—"dirt. Did you have an outside job today?"

"Had to dig a trench to supply electricity to a granny flat. I prefer this to crawling around the roof in the heat of summer." He lowered his head. "Can you cope with a little mud?"

Heat rushed through my lungs and pooled in my belly. "I think so," I whispered.

He leaned closer, and an earthen scent edged with spice tickled my nostrils. His warm breath fluttered against my cheek before he slanted his lips over mine.

I closed my eyes, fisted a handful of his soiled shirt and sighed into his mouth. I parted my lips and basked in the minty tingle.

His fingers dug into my waist. A vibration tremored in his chest and his heart palpitated against my fingers.

Thoughts assailed me. How would I measure up to Debbie, wife and mother extraordinaire? What expectations would I need to fulfil or compromise for this marriage to work? I opened my eyes and pulled away with laboured breaths.

Nicholas panted, his eyes dark and glassy.

Was being love drunk a real health condition? I licked my lips. "You should shower." I sucked in a stabilising breath. "I can make dinner if you like?"

He tilted his head. "Why? I know it's a chore for you and I like cooking." His mouth curled up. "How about you set up your work here on the bench so I can feast my eyes on you while I prepare dinner?"

My face warmed. "I … you don't want me to cook?"

His direct gaze spiked my pulse. "Only if you want to." He kissed my forehead.

I relaxed my shoulders.

Nicholas chuckled. "What, you think I need my woman tied to the kitchen, holding the fort?"

I dropped my gaze.

He lifted my chin with warm fingers. "Victoria. I'm not him."

I nodded and my eyes burned with tears. "You'd better shower."

He flashed his teeth. "Too bad you can't join me—"

I hissed his name and shooed him from the kitchen.

"Thanks for dinner." I leaned against my car door and glanced up.

Nicholas circled his thumb over the back of my hand. "Anytime." His touch sparked tingles under my skin. "Are you free for dinner tomorrow night? I'd like to discuss our new house."

Our new house. So, he was happy to move? My chest lightened. "That's a great idea. But I've no clue what to do."

"Leave the logistics to me." His eyes shone under the moonlight. "You tell me what you do and don't like, and I'll work out a plan. Okay?"

I disengaged my hand and kicked my toe against the asphalted road. "Do I need to take into account all your furniture?"

He narrowed his eyes. "Why? I assumed you'd want to buy everything new?"

I opened my mouth and closed it. He was willing to leave everything behind? "What will you do with this place?"

He shrugged. "Not sure. I wanted to discuss it with you when we worked on the build. I thought we could turn it into an investment property, or ask Diana whether she wanted it in the future." He rubbed a hand across the back of his neck. "I know she's a little sentimental about it."

"And you're not?"

He bent and brushed his lips across mine.

Another flurry of tingles travelled down my body.

"I want to start fresh with my new wife in her grand new house." He winked and straightened.

My breaths eased and I broke out in a wide grin. My second marriage would differ from my first.

"So, dinner tomorrow night?"

I wrapped my hand around his nape. Heat from his neck suffused in my fingers. "It's a date." I pulled his face to mine. Fire surged through my veins and I pressed closer to his warmth. My lips caressed his. I loved this man with everything I possessed.

Nicholas withdrew from our kiss and stepped back. His chest laboured. "I think Belinda was wrong to distrust me when you're the bad influence."

Giggles burst from my lungs and I laughed. "There's more where that came from." I opened the driver's door and settled in the seat. "But I promise to behave for now."

We said goodbye and I drove home, my hope for our future strengthened. I parked under my carport, emptied the letterbox, and deposited mail and my work bag on the dining table. Five more weeks and this little box would no longer be my home.

I ambled to my bedroom and exchanged my heels for slippers.

A memory flashed and I sank to the bed. Ryan. In my arms, ensconced in my plush king-sized doona. His cheeky smile and sparkling blue eyes. Laughter. I snorted as I recalled the time I had been rewarding him for sleeping in his own bed. He had asked to watch TV and I said no.

"But why not, Mah-mee?" His gorgeous nose had scrunched in tandem with his eyebrows.

"Because you slept in my bed last night, remember?"

He sighed and patted my hand. "Accidents happen."

I had smothered the giggles desperate to rise from inside me. The following day we repeated the conversation, but this time I barked with laughter.

"It was a glitch." Yes, my then five-year-old son had uttered those exact words.

I squeaked a laugh and returned to the living area. Sweet memories. I switched on the kettle and browsed through the letters. An envelope bore the DonateLife Victoria logo, and my heart stopped.

The room around me clouded and white walls invaded my mind. ICU machinery beeped. I breathed in a faint whiff of disinfectant and stumbled back against the kitchen cupboards. My lungs strained for oxygen and I closed my eyes. I landed hard on my bottom. Sobs wrenched inside my hollow chest. I wrapped my arms around my knees and leaned my head against the cupboard.

Wetness trickled into my shirt collar. I missed Ryan so much. And my big girls. I sniffed and whimpered, the weight on my shoulders crushing me.

The kettle shrilled above my head.

Deep breath in.

Slow breath out.

In. Out.

I murmured prayers. The hospital sounds and smells dissipated with every word I whispered.

I raised my eyelids. Blurry wooden chair legs. Striped lime-

and-white farther away. I prayed and breathed. The fog cleared and I voiced my thanks to God.

I stood and steeped my tea, arms braced against the benchtop. My body eased. I grasped the mug and letter and crumpled onto the couch.

Why had DonateLife written to me? Was it another fundraiser campaign? Other than an anonymous thank you letter from one of Ryan's organ recipients a few weeks after his death, I had received infrequent correspondence from the organisation.

I stared at the envelope. My heart thudded. I ripped along the seam with unsteady fingers and unfolded a letter. Air evaporated from my lungs.

Dear donor family,

I've stared at this blank page for weeks and feel bad it's taken me 2 ½ years to write. I wanted to send my (literal) heartfelt thanks soon after my heart surgery, but how could I thank a grieving family for the gift of life?

All I can do is just say it: thank you. Thank you for giving me a new life and sparing my family the pain you've suffered.

Most people tell me how lucky I am to be alive, to make the most of the days I have. To be thankful my parents didn't lose me. And don't get me wrong, I'm thankful. Very thankful. But I know you're living on the other side of the coin. Your little boy gave me his heart, a heart which beats inside me each and every day, but his days ended the day mine began. I'm sorry you lost your son. I feel guilty I benefitted from his death. But Mum says I could've died within months, so I like to think of the blessing this heart's been to me.

I turned 17 last week, although I still wear the same school dress from year 7. I'm in Year 11 working hard on my VCE. I want to get a high score for medicine. I've been in and out of hospitals since I was 12 and received grave health reports over the years. I lived in the hospital most of Year 8, and had come to terms with my short lifespan at the age of 14. Then this gift was given to me, and now I want to commit the rest of my life (a life you facilitated) to help others.

I will be eternally grateful to you all.

Yours most sincerely,

Your little boy's heart recipient.

Tears slipped down my face. A life I had facilitated. My heart swelled. I had spared another mother from my own pain and enabled a young lady to chase her dreams and help others. I re-read the letter, my eyes awash with tears, and burrowed into the warmth of the couch.

CHAPTER THIRTY-SIX
Cataclysm

"That's a brilliant idea, Bee!" I typed our plans for Nicholas's birthday into a file on my phone and smiled at my friend. Although planning my wedding was fun, I enjoyed scheming next week's fortieth birthday bash more.

Belinda leaned against the black padded seat and I peered over her shoulder as Keanu approached our table. "Would you ladies like more tea?"

I glanced at the dregs in the bottom of my cup. "No, thank you, Keanu."

Belinda shook her head and Keanu nodded. "By the way, Ms. Burke, Dad said he'd be thrilled to cater your wedding afternoon tea."

A wide smile spread across my face. "That's wonderful news! Nicholas will be pleased."

"How about you and I work it out"—Belinda said to Keanu—"since Ms. Burke has a lot on her mind."

My eyes misted. I reached across the table and clasped Belinda's hand. "Thanks, Bee." I turned to Keanu. "Please factor in your attendance to the wedding while you plan all the logistics."

His eyes bulged and a soft pink hue bloomed on his cheeks. "M-me?"

I furrowed my brow. "You're a good friend of Diana's and her father's getting married. You've been a great student and always look after me each Wednesday and Saturday when you're on shift here." A grin tugged at my mouth. "You never forget your first ... server."

Keanu's cheeks reddened and he ducked his head, but I caught the smile plastered to his face. "If that's all, I'd better check on the other customers." He lifted his head, stepped back and levelled a wink at me.

Belinda laughed at Keanu's retreating frame. "You provoked a blush from Keanu Everton! Well done, Vicki. Well done."

I giggled and glanced at the clock on the wall. "I promised Nicholas I'd be over for dinner soon." I grinned. "I can't leave the gourmet chef waiting."

Belinda chuckled behind her glass of water. "I wish Matt was more interested in cooking, but he tries. I enjoy teaching him although he's not my greatest pupil."

"I recall his rather ... basic attempts." I bit my lip. The time Matt and I had dated was still a sensitive topic for my friend.

Belinda's cheeks infused with colour. "Thanks for letting me crash your Wednesday private time. Does Keanu call this 'Ms. Burke's booth'? Or did I imagine it when he pointed you out?"

I leaned forward. "He said he wanted to make a plaque, the silly boy." I eyed the ring on my finger. My chest fluttered with dancing butterflies. Less than a month and I would be Mrs. Jacobsen. I pressed my hands against my swirling stomach.

"I'd better go," Belinda said. We stood and embraced. "Matt's making spaghetti. Pray we survive the carb overload."

"Enjoy." I slid back into my seat and sipped my water.

Belinda's footsteps faded down the walkway.

I tapped a final note into the birthday file. My phone rang in my hands, and I beamed at the name lighting up the screen. "Hey, handsome."

"My beautiful Victoria."

My heart skipped a beat. I closed my eyes and thought about the man who possessed my heart. "Need something?"

"You." His voice purred over the phone line. "Will you be over soon?"

"I was about to leave."

"Good. I'll see you soon. Love you."

"Love you too." I ended the call and paused. I could spend one more minute working. I opened my private emails on my phone where several friends and family members had RSVPed for Nicholas's birthday and the wedding. I leaned my head against the padded backrest, my face upturned, and relaxed my shoulders.

"Hi, Victoria."

My throat constricted at the sound of Jude's voice. The fine hairs on the back of my arms and neck stood to attention. I stiffened, balled my hands into fists, and shifted my gaze.

His eyes shone like polished sapphires and his mouth crested with what seemed a genuine smile of warmth. His pleased expression cast me back eighteen years.

I opened my mouth to speak, but the sole sound to squeak out was my sharp exhale. My heart hammered. Sweat coated my palms and I wiped them against my tensed thighs.

Jude lowered his sculpted body onto the booth seat across from me and stole a slow sip from my glass of water. His gaze never left mine.

A shudder ran through me and I turned away. Sharp, stabbing pain knifed my chest, and dizziness buzzed inside my head. With a quick, silent prayer, I asked God to keep me safe.

Resting the glass on the table, Jude reached across and seized my right hand.

I flinched at his touch. The smoothness of his skin was foreign. I missed Nicholas's calluses.

My mind screamed to stand and run, but my legs refused to budge. I squeezed my thighs together. My stomach heaved and acrid bile dominated my tastebuds. I gagged and panted for air. The vision of a white, blood-stained T-shirt filled my memory. I slipped my hand from his grip.

"Baby, you look amazing." Jude's gaze lingered on my face before it dipped to my décolletage. His eyes darkened. He stared at my curves and my skin flushed.

Why was Jude here? Our divorce was final, our connection severed.

His gaze lifted to my face. "I'm so glad I found you. Forgive me for surprising you like this, but I was excited to see you."

My heart pounded, and my head spun with heated words, fists actioned in anger, and the devastation of my lost children. Tears clouded my vision.

He cocked his head. "You don't have to be afraid of me. I've changed, baby. I love you and I'm here to take you home."

Home? I blinked, and my mind broke free of its obstruction. Jude intended to uproot me from my life here. Away from my students and colleagues. My teammates. Away from my church family. From Matt and Belinda. Diana.

Away from Nicholas.

I shook my head, my eyes wide. My wedding was less than a month away! Heat clawed through my veins. I belonged in Tellarine with my future husband.

The screams inside me rose to unnerving shrieks and I regained the power of speech. "I'm not leaving with you." I sounded calm, in control. My pounding heart and clammy hands disagreed.

Jude assessed me like a bird of prey, his full lips pressed together, his eyes narrowed. He pierced me with a flinty glare. The suppressed rage had been there all along.

Another silent prayer fired inside me. I slid a few centimetres across the seat in the direction of freedom, but Jude grabbed my wrist. I winced from his tight grip.

A ringtone blared from my phone. Jude stood, his face calm, and inspected the screen. "Who's Nicholas?"

I flashed the ring on my left hand and his jaw clenched. "He's my fiancé."

Jude swore under his breath. "I knew I should've found you

sooner." He narrowed his eyes. "Does he know you warmed my bed first?"

Dryness irritated my throat. "He knows we're divorced."

He unleashed a harsh bark of laughter, leaned over me, and twisted my wrist. "And do you perform for him like you did for me?"

I bit back a cry. "You're the only man I've slept with, Jude. Not that it's any of your business—"

"It most certainly is my business," he hissed. "You're my wife."

"I'm not your wife." Tears wet my cheeks. "W-why are you here?"

His fingers tightened around my wrist, and I groaned. "You left me. Then you had our house sold." He wheezed through his teeth. "Two months ago, the board voted me out, and I lost my job." His face reddened with each spoken word.

I leaned back. "I'm sorry to hear that, Jude, but—"

Nicholas's ringtone continued to scream from my phone.

Jude's chest heaved. He mumbled a curse and snatched the phone.

"Hey! That's—'

"Shut up." Jude's jaw flickered. "You can have it back if you behave." He switched off my phone and pocketed it.

Sweat pooled under my arms.

Jude gestured for me to stand. He pulled a twenty dollar note from his wallet and threw it on the table. "My car's outside. If you make a scene, I'll be disappointed, and we don't want that."

The pain in my wrist worsened and I held in a scream. A cold sensation prickled the back of my neck. His threat was far from idle but getting into his car was not an option. I needed time to think.

Light my way, Jesus. And soften Jude's heart.

Jude yanked me hard against his chest before he turned toward the exit. His cologne suffocated me. The bathroom sign on the wall glowed brighter than usual.

"I need to pee," I said.

He glanced at the sign.

"Please. I'd hate to have an accident in your car."

Jude shuddered. "No thank you." He pulled me toward the stairs and faltered. "I'm not letting you out of my sight."

I racked my brain and an answer sprang to mind. "The family toilet is down this corridor next to the disabled one."

His stare bore into my face. "Okay." His grip tightened, burning my skin.

I prayed with each step, attuned to my surroundings and what I should do next.

Jude opened the family bathroom door, shoved me inside, and snibbed the lock. He crossed his arms and nodded to the toilet.

I gulped. The small white room contained a white loo next to a child-sized one, a collapsible change table station, and a vanity with a mirror. I trembled to the adult-sized toilet, placed my bag on the floor, and stood facing Jude. Thank God I had worn a dress today. The thought of unbuttoning or unzipping trousers in his presence chilled me.

His eyes blazed when I lifted the back of my dress and slipped down my knickers.

I stared at the floor, sat and prayed. My hands shook against my thighs amongst the folds of material I clasped in a rigid grip. My foot twitched. I willed my bladder to overcome its stage fright and clenched my stomach muscles to hold in a scream.

I sighed when the telltale tinkle on porcelain echoed in the room. I extracted a few sheets of toilet paper and discreetly completed the task.

Smoothing down my dress, I flushed the toilet and darted to the sink. I pumped soap with unsteady hands. The sudsy mixture dripped off my fingers onto the vanity top. My second attempt was successful and I scrubbed and washed my hands. I reached for the paper towel and my breath snagged.

Jude's hand slipped around my waist. His other hand pulled the paper from the dispenser and gave it to me.

My stomach roiled on the edge of release. The tremors in my hands vibrated up my arms as I dried my fingers and blinked back moisture.

His hand stilled mine. He threw the paper in the bin and turned me to face the mirror. "Look at me."

My chin quivered. His reflection stared at me.

Jude pulled me against his chest and I gasped. Every hard contour of his body pressed against my back. "This is us, Vicki. You and me."

My knees weakened and I pushed down on my toes.

He inclined his head and pressed his lips to my ear. "You and me, baby."

I squeezed my eyes shut. "You and me" no longer existed. Nicholas and I did. My heart walloped and more sweat beaded under my arms. I had to be strong. I needed to fight.

"Open your eyes and look at me." His tone was sharp.

I obeyed.

He clamped his hands on my hips. His fingers dug into my curves and I bit back a sob. "Remember the times we made love in this exact position?" His gaze in the mirror dropped to the hem of my dress. He inched the fabric higher, bunching my dress at my waist, and bile burned the back of my throat.

My pulse ricocheted, and my eyes stung.

Help me, Jesus.

Goosebumps pricked my thighs as a cold draft glided over my exposed skin. My black lace underwear came into view and Jude's chest vibrated behind me. Why had I opted for lace instead of my usual cotton this morning?

"So beautiful." Jude's lips grazed my neck.

My stomach twisted and I swallowed bile. What had prompted me to think going to the bathroom was a good idea?

His warm hand skimmed my abdomen and the familiar feel of his skin on mine jolted a breath in my chest. "When you carry my baby this time around, I'll do things right."

A garbled wail leaked from my lips. My mind nosedived into a tailspin. The gravity of my current reality pounded with every wrenching breath I heaved.

His velvet voice deepened. "I haven't touched a drop of alcohol in eighteen months, baby."

My head swam and my teeth chattered. I gagged on a mouthful of saliva and bile and spluttered a cough. The constant pungent tang burned my throat and aggravated my churning stomach. I wanted to purge all of Jude—my memories, my feelings, his touch—and get back to my cosy life in my cosy little box.

"Hands on the sink."

My heart constricted, and my ashen face and damp eyes reflected from the mirror. "Jude. P-please."

One of his hands slid away, and the distinct zip of metal teeth forced me to grab the sink before my legs collapsed.

No! "J-Jude." Blood rushed in my ears. Words tumbled from my lips. "Do you want our r-reunion to be in a p-public toilet?"

His roaming hand stilled on my hip.

"Don't you w-want a nicer m-memory?" I swallowed the burn at the back of my throat.

His gaze pierced mine in the mirror. "Beg for it."

Vibrations shook every part of my body and tears filled my vision. "Please, Jude. Let's go somewhere m-more private. Free from i-interruptions." My voice cracked. "Please."

A wicked smile stretched across his face. "That's my girl." He swivelled my shoulders until my front was flush with his and I shivered. "You always know how to please me." He lowered his face to mine and kissed my mouth, bruising my lips.

My leg muscles tightened to match my shoulders and chest.

"Grab your bag." He charged to the door with fly zipper in hand.

I fumbled to the toilet and clutched my bag. Darting through the open doorway, I sucked in a stabilising breath and breathed out another prayer.

My gaze darted around the restaurant in search of help as we walked hand-in-hand. The pain in my chest built with each footfall. Where had everyone gone? Had Benanu's closed while we were in the bathroom? My fingers ached in Jude's restrictive grip. Where was Keanu's muscle when I needed him?

We walked out the exit in the direction of Jude's Maserati, parked next to my Mazda. I huffed, not surprised he had kept up the appearance of success with his pretentious car. My arm throbbed from the yanking and squeezing Jude inflicted, my hand still locked in his firm grip. I surveyed my surroundings, and my heart dropped. I had entered a ghost town.

I kept pace with Jude's triumphant stride. Each footstep ushered a faith-filled prayer from my lips. Hope built in my heart. God would rescue me. I slowed my breaths and focused on my plan of action. When Jude turned a fraction away, I would twist my body as I pulled free from his grasp and run. I would unleash my fiercest screams with each quick step toward Benanu's.

Time slowed. My breathless lungs suffocated me, and my heart floundered. We approached the middle of the car park. My legs wobbled and eyes burned. I plodded to the soundtrack of crunching gravel and whooshing blood. My armpits drenched the bodice of my dress.

Jude turned toward his car.

Now or never. I pulled hard in the opposite direction of my captor, using all of the strength I had accrued in the last two years, and screamed with everything I could muster. "Help me! Please! Someone help!"

In my haste I tripped over my foot and fell onto the hard surface of the road. I cried out in pain. Layers of skin ripped from my knees and the palms of my hands. Wetness dampened my cheeks. *God, help me!*

Fingers dug into my waist and yanked me from the ground.

My back slammed against a solid chest.

Jude spat a string of expletives. His arm coiled around my

middle and I whimpered. He wrapped my ponytail around his free hand and jerked hard.

I squealed.

He twisted my head to face him and bared his teeth. His chest heaved. "You'll pay for this tonight."

I thrashed my arms and kicked my legs. Pain needled my scalp and tears burned my eyes.

Jude dragged me closer to his car.

I fought against the outside threat and the internal struggle against fear and nausea. I choked back bile and screamed, "Help me! Help me!"

Jude's eyes bulged and burned. "Shut up before I shut you up!"

I screamed louder, praying someone would overhear the commotion.

His arm tightened around my waist and constricted with painful intent. The headlights of the Maserati flashed, and I jabbed my elbows into whatever flesh I could hit. He spun us around, and a car door creaked. He twisted me in his arms and shoved me inside the vehicle.

I fell onto my back against the leather passenger seat.

Jude hovered over me, his eyes wild and chest rising and falling in rapid gasps. He dug into my thighs when I tried to knee him in the face and I cried out. He pushed his body against mine, trapping my arms.

I continued to thrash and wriggle, anything to keep him from closing the door. Another scream tore from my mouth, loud enough to drown out the pounding in my head.

He pulled his arm back, fist ready to slam into my face.

Adrenaline surged through my veins. I pushed against his weight with brute force and widened my legs. Wrapping them around his waist, I grunted and squeezed against Jude's sides and clamped hard. Moisture dripped into my eyes.

He growled and tried to pry my naked legs from his waist. His fingers pinched hard against my inner thighs like torture weapons.

"Argh!" I compressed my legs, Jude's gasps and foul language fuelling my resolve, and rocked my body forward. My vision blurred. I twisted my shoulder and freed my arm. Grabbing the car seat, I pulled myself up and butted my head into Jude's face. Stars burst in front of my eyes.

He screamed, his nose bloodied. His fingers eased their painful pursuit long enough for me to jam my shoulder in his neck. "You b—"

I headbutted his chin, sickened by the loud crunch. Fire burned along my skull.

He fell backwards into the car park, and I gasped a scream.

I landed half on Jude and the cold, rough road. I scrambled away. The ground shifted, the sea of cars blurring into a tapestry of colours, and I scraped my hands and knees along the asphalt.

My head spun and my ears pounded. Then pandemonium erupted. A car horn beeped near my head. People shouted. Screams polluted the peaceful country air before the ghastly scent of vomit brutalised my nostrils.

Hands grasped my shoulders and I bucked hard against the restraints. "Victoria! Stop! It's me, Belinda."

I gazed up into Belinda's emerald eyes and all the fight inside of me died. I wiped my wet chin and collapsed into her arms in a sobbing mess.

"You're okay." Belinda's soft words caressed the top of my head. I breathed in her floral perfume, an improvement on the vileness in my mouth. "He can't get you anymore. Look."

I lifted my head and blinked. My vision cleared and I gasped.

Belinda chuckled. "You're not seeing things."

Jude lay prostrate on the asphalt with one cheek pressed against the ground, his arms locked behind him in my fiancé's tight grip. Nicholas kneeled beside Jude, his biceps taut. The fierceness of Nicholas's expression seemed to hold Jude in place.

I closed my eyes and fell back into Belinda's arms. Tears rolled down my cheeks, and chills coursed through my limbs.

Belinda rocked me back and forth, rubbing her hands along my arms. Footsteps approached. "Can you get the blanket from my car? Thanks, babe."

"W-was that Matt?"

She squeezed me against her warm chest. "Yes. Matt burned dinner, so we drove to get some fish 'n chips. I spotted your car when we drove by." Belinda rubbed my back in soothing circles. "I knew you were about to leave Benanu's when I left, so I called Nick to check if you'd left your car behind." Her voice cracked. "He freaked when I mentioned there was a yellow sportscar parked next to it."

I shuddered a heavy breath and winced from the pain in my head.

"Matt alerted the police while Nick stayed with your ex."

"Victoria!" Jude yelled across the car park and I lifted my head. He stood between two police officers, his face bloodied and his arms behind his back. "Don't do this! I love you!"

I buried my face on Belinda's shoulder and the shivers increased. A heavy blanket fell across my body and I sighed at the sudden warmth. My body shook and my teeth chattered.

"Victoria?"

My heart thundered at the sound of Nicholas's voice. My tears unloaded once more.

Nicholas swept me off the ground and into his arms. "Shh, it's okay. I'm here. You're okay." His crooning voice loosened the deep barbs in my chest. "The police have arrested him, and the ambulance is on its way." His warmth and scent enveloped me.

I peered over his shoulder. A police officer slammed a police vehicle door. My chin quivered. "H-he tried t-to ... he allllmost ..."

"Shh. It's okay."

"Y-you cccaught h-him." I tried to control my chattering teeth, but it was difficult to stop.

He rubbed a hand across my back. "And I'd do it again in a heartbeat." His voice trembled. "I'm so proud of you." Nicholas kissed my forehead and I winced.

I stared up into his eyes. "Sssorry. I might have another c-concussion. I headbutted h-him."

His chest vibrated against my body and his eyes shined with tears. "You're so brave. Your quick thinking and boldness drew attention to you." He blinked and kissed my nose. "My brave, clever fiancée."

The soft wail of an ambulance pierced the air. I fell back against Nicholas and watched the strobe lights on the police vehicle disappear down the road. My breaths stuttered, and eyelids drooped. *Thank You, God, for giving me Your strength to fight.*

To survive another day.

CHAPTER THIRTY-SEVEN
Aftermath

"Can we leave now, officer? Victoria's exhausted." Nicholas held my hand—my palms covered in gauze—where we huddled in the waiting room at the police station.

I had overcome the initial shock of my altercation with Jude and spent two nights in hospital. The same doctor who had treated me for my mild concussion less than a month earlier was on shift when I arrived and demanded I be admitted to stay at least a day for observation. Nicholas appreciated the doctor's vigilance on my behalf, and my faithful fiancé stayed by my bedside the entire time.

Several officers visited my hospital room and questioned me about the incident with my ex-husband. After my discharge from the hospital this morning, Nicholas drove me to the police station, where I was reunited with my mobile phone, completed a police report, filed charges, and petitioned for an intervention order.

I rested my head against the wall behind my seat, a stolen moment of respite from the mild pain in my temples. Outside the nearby floor-to-ceiling window shone a rare, beautiful June day. Mid-afternoon sunshine streamed through the glass and touched my bandaged knees. My eyelids fluttered closed. The warmth of the sun could not stop the chill of relived memories still fresh in my mind.

Nicholas's thumb rubbed a soothing circle across the back of my hand and I relaxed my shoulders. Did he realise how much I appreciated his support? I breathed a grateful prayer, added to the string of prayers I had uttered in the past forty-eight hours.

The police officer rifled through papers and said, "Everything's in order, so you're both free to go." I opened my eyes. He nodded at me. "If you need anything else, ma'am, please let us know."

I forced a smile to my lips. "Thank you, officer."

Nicholas shook the police officer's hand, then escorted me to the ute.

My steps were slow and heavy, a suitable match to my sore body.

"I've spoken with Diana and she also feels it's best if you come home with me."

I swayed on my feet, and Nicholas steadied me with his hands around my waist. "I don't know, Nicholas."

"I understand your hesitancy to stay at my house now that we're engaged, but you're not staying home alone while you're this weak." He grasped my elbow, and we continued our slow journey to his car. "Diana volunteered as a chaperone."

I shuffled along the hard surface and stopped at the passenger door.

Nicholas's cheeks lifted in an adorable smile. "Diana's jumping off the rafters, desperate to help. Anna, Madison and Grace are at home preparing dinner." He assisted me into the seat.

My backside hurt and the bruised skin of my inner thighs screamed for attention. I had winced at the distinct finger imprints all around my thighs when I showered this morning. Similar markings wrapped my upper arms and wrist. "I love those girls and I feel awful we've missed so many classes over the last month."

Nicholas kissed my cheek, one of the rare uninjured places on my body. "I think they're planning to visit after school when possible to study and ask questions." He rounded the car and slipped into his seat.

I rested against the seat back and breathed in the familiar surroundings. My heartbeat slowed. The normalcy of my life had disintegrated on Jude's brief visit. Calm and privacy had been exchanged for a bright, bustling hospital room. And the noisy, uninspired police station had exhausted me. Tension unfurled in my chest and I relaxed my shoulders.

Nicholas turned to me. He arched a brow above those dark eyes I loved to gaze at.

I smiled and he winked before facing the windscreen. The first wink he sent my way at Benanu's sprang to mind. My heart skittered. I appraised his stubbled jaw, thankful my heart still appreciated the finer things in life. My pulse spiked when he removed his jumper, leaving his hair in disarray. Messy hair conjured thoughts best left dormant for a few more weeks.

Nicholas rolled back his shirt sleeves and bared his veined, tanned forearms.

Be merciful, God. I sucked in a lungful of oxygen. When every limb and muscle hurt in varying degrees, a chest flutter and near-faint from eyeing one's marvellous fiancé was a welcome change.

I licked my lips and schooled my features. "The girls can camp out in my room if they want. I don't mind the company."

A deep chuckle siphoned from his chest. "Then I better make sure I limit my workload during school hours so I can spend time with you."

"I'd like that. I might spend a lot of time in bed, though."

He glanced from the road with a raised brow. "Is that an invitation?"

I hacked a cough and rasped, "No!"

The vehicle slowed at a roundabout. "I'm kidding, Victoria. I can wait three weeks."

I rested against the seat and closed my eyes. "How about I lie under the covers, and you sit on top of the covers next to me?"

He chuckled. "Yes, Ms. Burke. Any other rules I must obey?"

I tapped a finger against my pursed lips, which triggered an ache in my arm. "Limited kisses. Lots of conversation and cuddles. Popcorn and movies." I peeled my eyes open. "But no sex talk. This isn't our first rodeo requiring awkward conversations about the subject."

He shot me a look. "I'm guessing you experienced something like that with … him?"

My face flushed. "Let's say I still feel the embarrassment of our first clueless conversation with the local pharmacist."

He snorted a laugh. "Got it. No sex talk cos we're seasoned experts."

I leapt forward in my seat. Pain prickled throughout my body, and I winced. "Nicholas!" I shook my head with a suppressed smile.

His laughter filled the cabin of his ute. He pulled into his driveway, unbuckled and swivelled toward me. His dark eyes blazed.

Giddiness buzzed in my aching torso.

He leaned forward and my heartbeat increased. "Mind if I kiss you now? Not sure I want to in front of my fan club inside." He smirked and inclined his head closer.

I laughed. "Talk about too big for your britches."

His breath heated my face. "You'll know soon enough." He swallowed my gasp with a kiss and I melted against his touch. His lips lingered before he pulled away.

"Who are you, Nicholas Jacobsen, and what have I gotten myself into?"

He cupped my jaw and grinned. "You love me and our banter. I'm preparing you for what's to come. When I unleash the real me, sweetheart, you'll never turn back."

I giggled at the gleam in his eye. "I'm looking forward to it."

He unbuckled my seatbelt and kissed my temple. "Full throttle."

I kissed his jaw. "Full throttle in three weeks."

CHAPTER THIRTY-EIGHT

Keepsakes, New Vows and Promises

A loud knock rattled the front door. I dropped my half-eaten toast and almost bumped my coffee mug. I squeezed my eyes shut and murmured a prayer. Last night's impromptu girl's night out with my basketball friends had gone later than expected, although I had a blast. Thank the good Lord for makeup. My under-eye discolouration would attest to its vanishing powers soon.

I checked the microwave clock and furrowed my brows. Had I heard the wrong time, or were the ladies already here to help me prepare for the wedding? I brushed toast crumbs from my dressing gown, pushed off the dining chair, and bustled toward my early guests.

I opened the door. A large black box lay on the front step covered in beautiful red-and-silver ornamentations. Underneath a flounce of bows peeked a pristine white envelope bearing my name. Shivers spread through my middle and my heart raced.

I scanned the immediate vicinity. Where was the gift giver?

Bending down, I cradled the exquisite package, elbowed the door closed, and trundled back to the table. The calligraphy of dark letters infused an old-time glamour to my name. Had Queen Victoria ever seen her name written with such beautiful penmanship? A huge grin stretched across my face. I broke the envelope seal and removed a card covered in red, silver and gold hearts.

"Oh, Nicholas." Tears pricked the back of my eyes and I

blinked against the burn. I read the words with a hand on my chest and a sigh on my lips.

My beautiful Victoria,

Words can't describe how much you mean to me. I thank God each and every day He brought you to Tellarine. Life is richer with you by my side.

Know that the vows we'll exchange later today mean the world to me. I promise to be the best husband I can be because you deserve only the best.

Thank you for loving me.

Nicholas.

I dabbed the corners of my eyes with my sleeve. My heart overflowed with Nicholas's sweet, heartfelt words.

Loosening the ribbon around the box, I opened the lid and gasped. Below several soft sheets of silver tissue paper lay a set of drafted architectural plans with the street address of my property inscribed in the lower right corner. A handwritten sticky note attached to the floor plan read, *Something new on your wedding day.* I grasped the thick paper with shaky hands, unfolded it and investigated the two-storey floor plan with misty eyes.

The lower level contained a spacious kitchen with an island bench, open-plan dining and lounge rooms, and a large family room opening up to an outside deck area. I smiled at the butler's pantry adjacent to the laundry with space enough to hang and dry clothing. The guest room with ensuite shared a wall with a powder room near a large study sufficient for two desks. A three-car garage and an adjoining workshop completed the ground floor.

The top level comprised a parents' retreat with a fireplace, commodious walk-in-robes and an expansive ensuite suitable for a five-star hotel. I grinned at the spa bath and forced my imagination away from how that particular feature would be used. Three more bedrooms—two with a shared ensuite—and a full-sized bathroom with separate toilet filled the remaining second-level floorspace. I squinted at the notes near the large open area around the staircase.

Built-in desks. A homework area would always come in handy for Diana. Or any future children. My chest warmed and wetness coursed my cheeks. Nicholas had listened to all the things I wanted and designed a home ideal for our family. I snatched a napkin and patted my eyes. "Thank you, Jesus, for such a sweet man."

Sniffing, I refolded the papers and placed them on the table. More items lay in the open box. A small, oblong velvet box with a small ribbon and card caught my eye. I flipped the card open, and I scrunched my brows. *This is a mix of old and new, but pretend it fills the old category.* I pursed my lips and pulled the ribbon free. "What have you been up to, Mr. Jacobsen?"

The velvet box snapped open and I burst out in laughter. A silver locket decorated with embossed roses rested on a bed of white hydrangea petals.

"You cheeky man." I giggled and picked up the cold metal. A slender chain twisted in delicate loops. Elegant yet simple. Perfect. I slid my thumbnail along the edge of the pendant until a soft click met my ears. Separating the two halves, I choked back a sob. Inside the locket beamed three beautiful faces. My hands shook and I sank onto a dining chair. "My babies." I clutched the necklace to my chest and allowed my longing and love for them to burst from inside my heart.

My mobile phone buzzed next to my uneaten toast. I wiped my eyes, shuddered a breath, and reached for the handset with my free hand.

Nicholas: I LOVE YOU.

I dialled his number.

"Victoria." His voice sounded deeper than usual.

I wiped away a tear. "What're you trying to do? Solidify your perfection so I go through with our vows?"

Nicholas's chuckles warmed me.

I sniffed. "I've opened two of your gifts and I'm already a complete mess."

"Which ones?"

"Your amazing house plans a-and the locket." My voice croaked.

"You like them?"

"So much."

"I'm glad. I'd contemplated leaving the box on your table while you slept last night but—"

"That'd be a misuse of my spare key."

He laughed and the light tone soothed my tears. "It was more the temptation of you sleeping a room away. I might've stood in your doorway like a stalker and if you'd woken up—"

"I'd have screamed." I laughed.

His voice trembled. "You've had enough scares to last a lifetime."

I fingered the locket and stared at Jessica, Samantha and Ryan's images. "Thank you for this beautiful necklace. It's gorgeous."

Nicholas cleared his throat and I imagined him rubbing the back of his neck. "I wanted you to have them close to your heart today."

Could this man be any more precious? I smiled, my cheeks stretching against semi-dried tears. "Thank you. I'll see you at two o'clock."

"That you will." His voice deepened, and I licked my bottom lip. "Then you'll be stuck with me for life."

My breath hitched. "Sounds like paradise."

A noise vibrated on the line. Was that a low growl? "I love you."

"I love you too." I ended the call, placed the locket against its bed of petals and returned to the large gift box. A final package lay at the bottom of the box, tied up in what appeared to be a man's handkerchief. The inscribed note read, *I'll need the handkerchief when I blubber like a baby later today (something borrowed), but feel free to use what's blue inside however you choose. Belinda helped with this one. Prewashed too.*

I pressed my lips together and ran my fingers along the thin cotton wrapping. What had those two gotten up to? I untied the bow and parted the material. "Oh." Pale-blue satin and lace filled my vision. My mouth dried and my skin sizzled. With a breathless murmur, I lifted the fragile garments and enjoyed the silken touch between my fingers. Belinda had admonished me for not buying new underwear for my wedding day, but even after we trawled the local stores and wedding dress shops, nothing had spoken to me. Or had been comfortable. I held back a grin, shrugged and shuffled to my bedroom.

Moments later, I stepped into the bathroom and admired my new lingerie in the mirror. Wowzers. A fabulous fit. I glimpsed at my reflected face. Wide eyes, flushed cheeks. I knew this expression would stay with me the rest of the day. And this evening. The heat intensified in my face and I palmed my cheeks. Was Nicholas nervous like me? He had been chaste much longer than I had. Would we experience awkward moments of intimacy while we reacquainted ourselves? Or would my nerves dissipate with each kiss we shared?

I dropped my hands to my sides and eyed my body. Scars, stretchmarks and cellulite. How would Nicholas respond to my physical flaws? Would he squint and wrinkle his nose like Jude had in the final months of our marriage? I pressed a hand to my stomach and hurried from the room.

"Splendid father-daughter photo." The photographer smiled from behind her camera and nodded toward the church foyer. "See you inside."

I beamed. "Thanks for all your help today."

"Anytime." Her boots crunched against the gravel with each receding step.

"You ready, baby girl?" Dad radiated with a so-proud-of-my-daughter smile.

A tingling warmth spread through my limbs. I clutched my

pale-pink-and-white bouquet between clammy fingers and inhaled the fragrances of rose and gardenia. "I'm ready."

Christine stepped through the open church doorway in a flowing light-purple dress. The sheer lavender sleeves complemented the sash around her posy of white gardenias. Nicholas and I had agreed to limit our wedding party to siblings only. With a small guest list, a huge group of bridesmaids and groomsmen seemed illogical.

"I'm so jealous, Vicki. This dress is gorgeous." Christine straightened the hem of my off-white lace-and-satin wedding gown. The dress ended several centimetres from the ground exposing my chilled toes. "I love the pearl button detail down your spine." She centred the pendant around my neck. Her hazel eyes shimmered. "And the delicate lace sleeves." She sighed. "So gorgeous. You think Patrick will renew our wedding vows so I can buy another dress?"

I pressed my lips together to stop a giggle.

Dad chortled. "You can always try, pumpkin. How about we get your sister married first?"

Christine nodded and wrapped her arms around me. She leaned close and whispered, "Go get him," before she pressed a kiss to my cheek and returned to the church building.

Dad stepped close and engulfed me inside his strong arms.

Several sobs burst from my chest.

"You're okay."

I breathed in his cologne and closed my eyes. This moment with my dad brought back a surge of memories. I could be sixteen or thirty-six, and my father remained unchanged in his love and support. "Thank you, Daddy, for everything you've done for me. I've always felt safe with you." I pulled away and stared into his eyes. "That means … so much to me." Images of Jude pressed against the ground outside Benanu's flittered through my mind, and I cringed. I breathed a thankful prayer and returned my gaze to Dad's. "You're always the same and I love you."

We embraced. "I love you too and so does Nicholas." Dad kissed my temple and lowered my semi-transparent veil over my face. "Come on." He tucked my arm with his and led me through the foyer.

Instrumental music increased in volume with each step I trod. The auditorium doors appeared and I sucked in a calming breath.

"You'll be fine."

I nodded.

"Don't forget to smile."

I cast him a glance and grinned.

Our musical cue resonated in the air and I leaned into Dad's side to steady myself. This was it. The moment I joined my life to Nicholas's.

The room blurred under my watery gaze and I blinked. A sea of smiling faces watched me with each footfall. Anna, Grace and Madison leaned into the aisle with arms extended and thumbs raised.

I shook my head and chuckled.

Diana and Gabriella smiled while Keanu pulled the rogue aisle-leaners back into their places. Toby waved from Steve's arms and Stacy beamed alongside them. Belinda blew me a kiss from where she stood with Matt, wrapped in his arms.

My cheeks hurt from the smile splitting my face.

Farther down the aisle Patrick and the boys grinned alongside Amber, Mike and their children. Mumma Joan, next to Rebecca Beaufort, caught my gaze as I slipped by, her hands clasped with Rebecca's, both with tears in their eyes.

I inhaled a deep breath, and my heart swooned when Mum smiled at me and then directed her soft, steady gaze toward Dad. Her lips parted. Dad winked at her and Mum's lifted cheekbones coloured.

Christine blew me a kiss from her position near the pulpit. Her eye makeup withstood the tears trailing her cheeks. Chris Beaufort acknowledged me with a nod in his fine-looking suit, but the best man paled in comparison to the groom.

Everything slipped away the moment my gaze fell on Nicholas, all else forgotten in the presence of the man holding my heart. The most important man in my world stood tall in his charcoal suit at the end of the aisle.

My mouth dried when I eyed his handsome features. Immaculate hair, strong jawline, kissable lips. My chest tightened when I deciphered three words uttered from his mouth. I clutched Dad's arm and swallowed the lump in my throat.

Christine clasped my bouquet and squeezed my hand before returning to her position. Dad whispered, "Love you," before he joined my hands to my groom's.

Nicholas's warm fingers caressed the backs of my hands and his soft smile triggered my tears.

My heart pounded and I blinked away wetness. If I had not trusted God with my recent difficulties with Nicholas and Jude, I may not have stood here now.

Pastor Davidson smiled and ministered a word about marriage, love and commitment. I faced Nicholas, transfixed by his eyes and our commitment to each other. Life together. Two now becoming one. The pastor's words muffled and blurred. My sense of time obscured. With tight throats and watery eyes, we muddled through our vows.

"You may kiss the bride."

My stomach seesawed. My gaze darted from the platinum wedding band on my finger to the gold band affixed to Nicholas's. Had I slept through the last part of the ceremony?

Nicholas lifted my veil with a sly grin. He lowered his head and I leaned up on my toes. We met in the middle with a slow, gentle kiss. He pulled away and drew me to his side.

Gazing up into my new husband's face, my throat clogged, and my chest swirled with warmth. "I love you, Nicholas."

A beaming smile stretched across his face. "And I love you, Mrs. Jacobsen."

CHAPTER THIRTY-NINE
New Mercies

The early morning sunshine filtered through the windscreen and I stretched my neck toward its warming rays. Three satisfying pops eased the tension in my neck and shoulders and echoed through the cabin of my little Mazda. I glanced at the dashboard clock. Three hours down, two-plus to go.

I stifled a yawn. Early morning wakeups were Nicholas's forte, not mine. He had been the epitome of the ideal husband this morning, waking me at five o'clock with a tender kiss and breakfast in bed.

Tall trees and greenery whipped past my window as my thoughts whirled, a juxtaposition of euphoria and melancholy. Bittersweet memories fusing with new experiences. Threads of my past weaving into a new tapestry.

With my gaze focused on the road, I switched on the stereo and adjusted the volume with a few steering wheel button clicks. A prayer of thanksgiving rose inside my heart and whispered out in time to the soft melody emitted from the speakers.

Had it been twelve months since I travelled this exact road to Melbourne with Matt? So much had happened since my last trip to the city. My eyes misted. Gratitude spilled from my mouth, and a smile slipped to my lips. God had brought me through so many ups and downs since then.

Jude's face came to mind and I drew in a sharp breath. The pain of his attempted abduction months earlier eased a little each day. I had wrestled with my fears for weeks and had suffered flashbacks up until a month ago. Pastor Davidson had preached about forgiving deep hurts and had encouraged the congregation to pray for those that harmed us whenever they entered our thoughts. Each prayer I uttered softened my heart and helped me along the journey of forgiveness. Now I hoped in earnest for Jude's three-year prison sentence to facilitate his rehabilitation. I shuddered a breath and prayed a blessing over my ex-husband.

The worship music halted for an incoming phone call. I answered through the hands-free system on the second ring. "Yes, Mr. Magnificent?"

"How's my beautiful wife faring?" Nicholas's deep voice rippled through the sound system.

Goosebumps scattered across my arms, and I shivered. "Better now you've called." I sighed and rotated my shoulders. "I could do with a double-shot latte right about now—"

"Do you need to pull over and rest?" Concern tinged his voice.

I smiled and blinked. "I'm okay. I promise."

"Please don't push yourself, my love." A soft grunt muttered over the line. "How did you talk me into letting you travel to Melbourne alone? Diana would've loved the time with you."

I repressed a sigh. "Diana has study to focus on. I'll call you once I get to Amber's."

"I miss you." The softness in his voice melted my heart.

I gripped the wheel tighter. "I miss you too. We can video call once I'm in bed tonight."

Nicholas laughed. "On your first night at Amber's? I'll be sleeping for five hours before you go to bed."

"We won't stay up late with Stacy almost six months pregnant. She's been struggling to sleep. Plus, Steve won't allow it." I shifted in my seat and giggled. "Stacy's been told she turns into a pumpkin at midnight so needs to be home by then."

He chuckled. "I didn't know you'd arranged to see Stacy

tonight too. How efficient of you." The phone line crackled. "How about I call when I go to bed?"

Warmth percolated through my body and I bit back a grin. "Just keep it G-rated, or they'll know you're saying husbandly things I should only hear in private."

His deep laugh reverberated through the speakers. "I wouldn't dare quote *The Song of Solomon* over the phone." His cheeky tone incited more laughter. "I'll be good. I promise."

I grabbed a dark chocolate Lindt ball from the cup holder. The wrapper crinkled with each one-handed twist. With a squeak of success, I popped the chocolate in my mouth. Delicious. And finally, guilt-free.

"Into your chocolate stash already?" Nicholas's amused voice cut through the moans escaping my mouth.

"Hmm-mmm. Yush," I said between chews. The smooth chocolate slipped down the back of my throat and I sighed. "I needed that. My first one."

"You did well to hold out this long. Okay, I'll leave you to it. Call me if you need anything. And pray I'll survive this week of separation."

I had been ambitious to think a week in Melbourne would be an easy feat. "I missed you when I entered the highway ten minutes from home." My throat tightened. "I love you, Nicholas."

"I love you too, Victoria. Talk soon."

"Bye," I whispered.

Worship music filled the airwaves, and I pressed my hand to my abdomen. I could do this. All of it.

Tears clouded my vision and I blinked. With my ears attuned to the music and my heart listening to the words ministering God's goodness, I navigated the roads to Melbourne with peace. Content in the path I walked, thankfulness flowed from within for His daily new mercies.

Dew dampened my knees and I brushed aside a tear trailing my cheek. "Diana found a joke book she thought you'd like, Samantha." I withdrew the book from my handbag and opened to the tagged page. "Sh-she said you'd like this one." I cleared my throat and dislodged the lump restricting my vocal cords. "Okay. Let's see." I squinted at the highlighted joke. "What kind of bees make milk?" I snorted a giggle when I perused the answer. "Any guesses? Your big sister picked a good one." Puffs of air scudded from my chest and I covered my mouth with my hand. I owed Diana a huge hug for the unexpected laugh. "No guesses? You'll love this one. You too, Ryan." I wiped a finger under my wet eyelashes. "The kind of bees which make milk are … boo-bees!"

I snickered and rocked back on my feet with a furtive glance for other visitors nearby. Closing the book, I sealed it into a plastic Ziplock bag and placed it on Samantha's grave. "I wish I could listen to you all laugh again. I miss your contagious giggles." I turned to Jessica's inscription. "Well, maybe not you, sweetheart. Unless your sense of humour's changed." A wistful smile tugged at the corners of my mouth and I raised my head. Sunshine stroked my face. I closed my eyes and drank in its warmth. *Thank You, God, for Your love.*

My eyelids drifted open, and I stared up at the colourful balloon sculptures surrounding the children's section of the cemetery. How could something so simple remind me of the joy my children once overflowed with? My lips upturned for a brief moment. I lowered my head with a prayer on each breath.

Flying a new Iron Man figurine over Ryan's plaque, I stilled my hand. "Diana picked a good joke for today because I have some news." I placed the toy down and sank on the grass, cross-legged. Happiness bubbled up, and I smiled. "Daddy Nicholas and I are going to have a baby." I pressed a hand against my barely there nine-and-a-half-week pregnancy paunch. "You're going to be a big brother, Ryan." Tears heated the backs of my eyes and trickled down my face. "I-I know you didn't want any more siblings, Samantha, but you'd love Diana and hope you'll accept this baby." A memory uploaded in my mind and tilted my lips up. "You didn't want a baby brother, but you loved Ryan. You'll love this baby too."

My chin quivered. Joy and sadness tugged my heart in tandem.

A throat cleared above me and I turned my head. A man with salt-and-pepper hair extended a white tissue between his tanned fingers. "I thought you could use this."

I tugged the tissue from his hand and wiped my eyes. "Thank you. I remembered their gifts but forgot to replenish the tissues in my handbag."

He nodded toward my children's graves. "Your children?"

"Yes."

He pointed to a grave several metres away with a large bouquet of bright-coloured flowers nestled on top. "My daughter."

I shuddered a breath. "Beautiful flowers."

He smiled. "Marcy loved anything bright." His lips pursed together. "We were blessed with our children, and no matter the number of days we had together, they'll always be an important and cherished part of our lives. Never forgotten." A deep V imprinted between the man's eyebrows. His dark eyes stared down at me. "Your children would be proud of you."

A watery smile trembled on my lips. "Thank you."

The man nodded and walked away.

My body trembled and I turned back to the children's plots. I blotted my face with the sodden tissue which now struggled to contain another tear. "I love you, Jessica, Samantha and Ryan. Thank you for each day we spent together while you lived, and all the days I've held you in my heart. You're all so precious. You will never be forgotten, I promise. While breath remains in my body, I'll think of you daily and tell this little one all about you."

A sudden warmth engulfed my chest and my breaths eased. Sweet peace from above travelled the length of my body and my limbs relaxed. "Thank You, God, for everything. I'm a testament of

Your mercy and grace."

YOU ARE MY MASTERPIECE.

I strangled a sob. The whispered words echoed Belinda's long-forgotten comment to me. I could now recognise I was His masterpiece and believed it.

I wiped my wet cheeks, blew a kiss to each of my children and stood. "Goodbye, my darlings. I'll see you again soon. Next time, Daddy Nicholas and Diana will visit. And next year we'll bring your new baby sister or brother."

With a final kiss released in the wind, I returned to the car and drove to Amber's. After a quick check-in with Nicholas, I knocked on the door and stepped into my friend's arms.

"Marriage looks good on you the second time around." Amber winked. "I can tell he's looking after you."

My cheeks warmed. "I'm so happy."

She walked me inside the house, and we reclined on the couch. "You're glowing." Amber clutched my hand. "It's beautiful to see."

"Thanks."

Her eyes shimmered. "Did you go see the children?"

"Yes."

Amber wrapped her arms around me and kissed my temple. "Cup of tea?"

I nodded.

She stood and walked away.

I stretched my neck and relaxed against the couch. My tired limbs loosened. The clock on the wall chimed twelve o'clock. What a long day.

I examined the room. New family photographs adorned the walls near older photos. Updated school pictures filled the space on a side table. I rubbed a hand across my belly. Although my three Burke children's ages stagnated in time, this little one would require an annual school photo.

Tightness diffused through my chest. Pressure weighed on my ribcage and I heaved a breath. I dug my fingers into the couch cushions and closed my eyes. I muttered quiet prayers before erupting into prayers of gratitude, and the vice of self-reproach released its grip and siphoned from my heart. A long breath eased from my lungs.

The echo of footsteps thudded over the adjacent tiled room before Amber padded across the lounge room carpet. "Here you go."

I accepted the outstretched mug and she settled on the couch beside me.

A ringtone pierced the quiet and Amber dug into her jeans pocket. "It's Stacy." She swiped the screen. "Hey, you okay?" Amber's brows dipped. "Oh really? I'm sorry to hear."

I mouthed, "What?"

Amber mimed either someone choking on their tongue or experiencing a serious bout of vomiting, and I screwed up my nose. "No, you stay home and rest. Contracting gastro doesn't appeal." She raised a brow, and I shook my head. Gastro on top of my post wake-up nausea? No thanks.

I pointed to the phone. "Can you put her on speaker?"

Amber nodded and pressed a button on her handset. "Vicki can hear you now."

Stacy croaked over the line. "Sorry, cuz."

"Don't apologise. Do you know how you caught it?"

She huffed a breath. "Childcare. Toby's constantly catching bugs. Steve suggested I go on maternity leave a month earlier than planned. We're saving his leave until the baby's born."

Amber pursed her lips. "Makes sense. If I didn't work, I'd look after the little guy."

Stacy sighed. "I'm considering an au pair or live-in nanny once I return to work next year."

Amber and I laughed. "What I would've done for that," Amber said.

I cleared my throat. "Speaking of babies, I—"

"You're pregnant?" Amber's eyes bulged and Stacy screamed over the phone.

My face broke out in a beaming grin.

I covered my ears as the screams continued, laughing at the faces Amber pulled before she wrapped her arms around me.

"Stupid gastro!" Stacy said. "Congrats, Vicki. Was this … planned?"

Amber gawped. "Honeymoon baby?"

I shrieked a laugh. "Close enough. We figured if it happened, great, but we weren't trying to get pregnant in our first month of marriage."

Amber and Stacy's laughs filled the lounge room and my heart swelled at the happy sound. "So, when's baby due? Are you far behind me?" Stacy asked.

I rested my palm on my stomach. "Baby's due the end of April."

Amber pulled me close for another hug. "I'm so excited." Her smile softened. "Is that why you went to the cemetery first? To tell the children?"

I grabbed a tight hold of her hand. What a blessing God had given me in my perceptive friend. "I know it sounds weird, but I wanted their blessing."

Stacy sighed over the phone. "And did you get it?"

I pressed Amber's hand. "I rested on the damp grass and felt so much love and peace after I shared my news." I sighed and wiped a tear from underneath my eye. "Now everything's settled with my old life, I've had a real sense of peace and joy. Even in those moments when I miss the children. The longing is there, but the emptiness has … vanished."

Amber wiped her palm across her eyes. "I'm so glad, Vicki. Mike and I have been praying for you for years."

"Pretend I'm hugging you," Stacy said in a choked voice, "cos I'd love to right about now."

I sniffled, my heart full. "I love you guys so much."

"We love you too," Amber and Stacy said.

I leaned my head against Amber's shoulder and released a

satisfied sigh. My punctured heart was healing in the light of love.

AUTHOR'S NOTE

Thank you, beautiful reader, for taking a chance on me and reading Victoria's story. The first inklings of her tale formed in 2018, but the true depth of her highs and lows was birthed in 2020 during our extended lockdown in Melbourne, Australia. While my community endured months indoors under curfew, restrictions and border closures, I learned more about writing and editing—aided by the ever-patient Jeanette Cameron—and now you hold those umpteen hours of effort in your hands. Isn't that amazing? I think so.

I'm an avid reader with virtual and physical bookshelves filled with many wonderful authors. But as a born and bred Aussie, so many stories I've read occur in the Northern Hemisphere. I thought it might be nice to share a series based in my home State, even if Tellarine is fictional, and hope you agree.

Being in the Southern Hemisphere, our seasons are different, but you may have also noticed the differences in our school year. The Australian school year follows the calendar year and begins in late January/early February, toward the end of summer, and ends in December, just before the summer Christmas season. We split the year into four terms, with two-week holidays around Easter time, wintertime (late June to early July) and springtime (late September to early October). And until I started reading fiction as a teen, I thought everyone around the world followed the same school year. It's funny what you don't know… until you do.

Thanks once again for your support. I hope you stick around for the rest of this series. Diana's been whispering some rather interesting things to me…

ABOUT THE AUTHOR

Sheridan Lee is an Australian writer with a penchant for true-to-life characters who triumph over adversity.

When she isn't singing along to her favourite Christian artists or watching Hollywood actors named Chris in superhero and Star Trek movies, Sheridan is reading or writing—with at least one of her five daughters lounging on her—and wishing the dirty laundry would clean itself.

Learn more about Sheridan and her books at www.sheridanlee.com.

SUBSCRIBE to Sheridan's newsletter (and receive The Tellarine Series prequel chapter as a gift): www.sheridanlee.com/subscribe

SHERIDAN'S BOOKS:

The Tellarine Series

Punctured Heart

Wounded Soul

Fractured Mind

Broken Spirit *(releasing 2023)*